... the *Romantic Times* Career Achievement Award for Urban Fantasy and has been nominated in the Best Contemporary Paranormal category of the *Romantic Times* Reviewers' Choice Awards. She's a dessert and function cook by trade, and lives in Melbourne, Australia.

Visit Keri Arthur online:

www.keriarthur.com
www.facebook.com/AuthorKeriArthur
@kezarthur

Praise for Keri Arthur:

'Keri Arthur's imagination and energy infuse everything she writes with zest'
Charlaine Harris, bestselling author of the Southern Vampire Mysteries

'Keri Arthur is one of the best supernatural romance writers in the world'
Harriet Klausner

'This series is phenomenal! It keeps you spellbound and mesmerized on every page. Absolutely perfect!'
FreshFiction.com

Keri Arthur skillfully mixes her suspenseful plot with heady romance ... smart, sexy, and well-conceived'
#1 *New York Times* bestselling author Kim Harrison

D0784215

By Keri Arthur

Keri Arthur

ASHES
REBORN

A Souls of Fire novel

piatkus

PIATKUS

First published in the US in 2017 by Berkley,
an imprint of Penguin Random House LLC
First published in Great Britain in 2017 by Piatkus

13 5 7 9 10 8 6 4 2

A CIP catalogue record for this book
is available from the British Library.

ISBN 978-0-349-41101-9

Printed and bound by CPI (UK) Ltd, Croydon, CR0 4YY

Papers used by Piatkus are from well-managed forests
and other responsible sources.

Piatkus
An imprint of
Little, Brown Book Group
Carmelite House
50 Victoria Embankment
London EC4Y 0DZ

An Hachette UK Company
www.hachette.co.uk

www.littlebrown.co.uk

This book is dedicated to my lovely daughter, Kasey.

Proud of you, kid.

ACKNOWLEDGMENTS

Many thanks to my awesome editor, Danielle Perez, for the help and advice over the years. It's been a pleasure working with you

I'd also like to thank my crit buddies and best friends—Robyn, Chris, Mel, Carolyn, and Freya—for being there when I've needed them.

CHAPTER 1

I raised my face to the sky and drew in the heat of the day. It ran through me like a river, a caress filled with warmth and sympathy, as if the sun were aware of my reason for being in this clearing out in the middle of nowhere.

And maybe it was. It had witnessed me performing this ceremony far too many times in the past.

I closed my eyes and ignored the tears trickling down my cheeks. Rory's death was once again my fault. If he hadn't been in Brooklyn with me, he'd still be alive.

And if he hadn't been there, that inner voice whispered, *not only would it be you who was dead, but possibly Jackson and Sam as well.*

I hated that inner voice, if only because all too often it was right.

Rory had died saving our asses, and I knew he wouldn't be angry about that. He'd always had something of a hero complex, and had often said that if he had to go before his allotted one hundred years were up, he'd rather do it saving someone he loved.

And he and I *did* love each other; hell, I couldn't physically survive without him, nor he without me. But we weren't *in* love, thanks to the curse that haunted all phoenixes—a curse that was said to have come from a witch after a phoenix lover had left her with little more than the ashes of broken promises and dreams.

But it was a curse we could have ultimately lived with, if not for the fact that it came with one other kick in the teeth—that no matter whom we *did* fall in love with each lifetime, the relationship would end in ashes, just as the witch's had.

As far as I was aware, no phoenix had ever found a way to break the curse. I certainly wouldn't—not in this lifetime, at any rate. Sam might have gotten as far as talking to me of late, but I doubted it would ever progress beyond that. Not given what he saw as my complete betrayal of his trust—even if he now understood the reasons for it.

I drew in a deep breath and released it slowly, letting it wash the lingering wisps of regret and hurt from my mind. I needed to concentrate. The sun had almost reached its zenith, and *that* meant it was time to begin.

I stripped and placed my clothes on the loose white tunic I'd brought here for Rory, and then kicked off my shoes. The slight breeze teased my skin, its touch chasing goose bumps across my body despite the sunshine.

Within me, energy stirred, energy that was a part of me and yet separate. Rory's soul, impatient for his rebirth. When phoenixes died—as Rory had in Brooklyn—their flesh became ashes that had to be called, and then retained, within the heat of a mate's body. If for some reason that process didn't happen, then there was no rebirth. And that, in turn, was a death sentence for the remaining partner, as phoenixes could only ever rise from their ashes through a spell performed by the mate.

And there was also a time restriction on rebirth. It had to be done within five days of death, or the life and the fire of those ashes would die, and the spirit and energy would be returned to the earth mother, never to be reborn.

It had been three days since Rory had passed. I was pushing it, time-wise—hence his impatience and, perhaps, a little fear. But I'd had no choice—the weather in Melbourne had been so bad, a fire would have struggled to remain alight And while, as a phoenix, I could have kept the flames burning, I couldn't afford to waste energy when I had no idea how much I'd need for the ceremony. Because no matter how long I'd been doing this, no rebirth was ever exactly the same.

I brushed stray strands of red-gold hair out of my eyes as I moved into the center of the clearing and toward the square stack of wood I'd already piled there. The dry grass was harsh and scratchy underfoot, and the scent of eucalyptus teased my nostrils.

It was a perfect day for resurrection.

I reached down to the inner fires and called them to my fingers. As flames began to dance and shimmer across their tips, I stopped on the west side of the bonfire and raised my hands to the sky. Sparks plumed upward, glittering like red-gold diamonds against the blue of the sky.

"By dragon's light," I intoned softly in a language so old only the gods or another phoenix would understand, "and the mother's might, I beseech thee to protect all that surrounds me and the one I call from me."

As the words of the spell rolled across the silence, the air began to shimmer and spark with the colors of all creation. It was the heat of the day and the power of the mother, of the earth itself, rising to answer the call of protection.

"Banish all that would do us wrong," I continued. "Send them away, send them astray, never to pass this way. So mote it be."

The sparks I'd sent skyward began to fall gently down, but they never reached the ground, caught instead in the gentle hands of the shimmering light.

I moved to the north section and repeated the spell. The shimmering net of sparks extended, and the hum of its power began to vibrate through my body. I echoed the process on the two remaining sides until the net had joined and my entire body pulsated to the tune of the power that now surrounded me.

I faced the bonfire and again raised my face to the sky, watching for the precise moment the sun reached the pinnacle of its arc. Heat, energy, and sparks ran around me, through me, a force wanting to be used, *needing* to be used.

Now, that inner voice said.

I called to my flames, then stepped into the center of the bonfire. As flesh gave way to spirit and I became nothing but a being of fire, the wood around me burst into flame. I held out my hands and raised the fire to greater heights, until it burned with a white-hot heat.

It felt like home.

Felt like rebirth.

"I beseech the dragon that gives life, and the mother that nurtures us all, to release the soul that resides within."

The words were lost in the roar of the flames, but they were not unheard. The ground began to tremble, as if the earth itself were preparing for birth.

"Let the ashes of life be renewed; give him hope and bless him with love, and let him stand beside me once more. By the grace of the mother, and the will of the dragon, so mote it be."

As the last word was said, power tore up my legs and through the rest of my body, the sheer force of it momentarily stretching my spirit to the upper limits of survivability. Specks of luminescent ash began to peel away from these overstretched strands, gently at first but rapidly increasing, until it became a storm of light and ash. As the heat of the flames, the force of the earth, and the brightness of the day reached a crescendo of power, the motes began to condense and find form, alternating between our three forms—fire, firebird, and flesh—until what the earth and the day held in their grip was the spirit I'd spent aeons with.

Rory.

I thanked the earth mother and the dragon in the sky for their generosity and the gift of life, and then reversed the spell, this time moving from south to west. The wall of energy and sparks shimmered briefly, then began to dissipate, the energy returning to the mother and the fiery sparks drifting skyward as they burned out and disappeared. Nothing was left but the bonfire and the fiery outline of the adult male curled up in a fetal position in the middle of it.

Weariness washed through me, and I all but fell to the ground. I sucked in several deep breaths to clear my head, then crossed my legs for the long wait ahead.

Rory might now be reborn, but physically he was extremely weak. That was part of the reason I'd piled the bonfire so high—he would need the flames to fuel his body. He wouldn't wake—wouldn't even gain flesh—until the ashes in his soul had refueled enough on the heat of the fire to enable full functionality. And even then it would be days before he'd be back to his old self and fully mobile.

The afternoon passed slowly. I boosted the fire a couple of times and kept the heat at a white-hot level. It was close to four in the afternoon when his spirit form began to jerk and tremble, a sure sign that his inner fires had fully awoken. An hour later, he began to keen—a high-pitched sound so filled with pain that tears stung my eyes. Rebirth was never pleasant, but the pain was so much greater when we died before our time. I had no idea why, but figured it was the mother's way of making us a little more careful about how we lived and, ultimately, how we died.

Dusk had begun to seep across the skies in fiery fingers of red and gold by the time his spirit gave way to flesh. By then the bonfire was little more than softly glowing coals, but they didn't burn him. Which wasn't to say that we, as spirits of fire, *couldn't* be harmed by our element. The scars down my spine were evidence enough of that. But they'd come from a situation in which I'd been unable to either control or feed on fire; I'd been rescuing a child, in full view of a crowd of people. Vampires and werewolves might be out and proud—and had generally been accepted into human society far better than most of us had ever expected—but because there were still enough people who deemed them a threat to civilization, in need of erasing, the rest of us thought it better to remain in the shadows.

Who knew how society would react if people ever realized just how many of us were living among them?

Even though Rory was unconscious, the process of feeding during rebirth was automatic; the coals continued to fuel him, until the light within them was completely drained and nothing remained but cold ashes.

Only then did he stir.

Only then did he open his eyes and look at me.

"Emberly." His voice was little more than a harsh whisper, but it was a sound so sweet it brought tears to my eyes. Because it meant everything had gone right; he was back, and whole, and life for the two of us could go on as it always had.

I smiled. "Welcome once again to the land of the living."

"Not sure this can *ever* be called living. Not when every fucking piece of me is aching like shit."

"*That* is the price you pay for getting yourself shot."

He grunted and rolled onto his back. Ash plumed skyward, then rained back down, covering his flesh in a coat of fine gray. "Did you get the bastard who did it?"

"That depends."

He raised a pale, red-gold eyebrow. "Meaning?"

"That I sent every ounce of flame I could muster, and every bit of energy I could demand from the mother, into the building the shot had come from. It exploded into pieces so small, they were little more than dust, so I undoubtedly got the shooter."

"But it's the bastard who ordered the kill we want."

"Exactly." I uncrossed my legs and pushed upright.

Just for an instant, the clearing spun around me, a warning that Rory wasn't the only weak one right now. "And I thought you might like a piece of *that* particular action."

"You thought right." He looked around. "Where are we?"

"Trawool. Or just outside of it, anyway."

He blinked. "Where the fuck is that?"

I smiled and held out my hands. "It's about fourteen kilometers out of Seymour and just over an hour from Melbourne. Ready?"

His fingers gripped mine and, after a deep breath, he nodded. I hauled him upright; ash flew around the two of us, catching in my throat and making me cough. He hissed, and his fingers tightened briefly on mine as he gathered his balance.

"It never gets any easier," he muttered.

"No."

I held on to him and waited. After several more minutes, he nodded. I released one hand but shifted the other to his elbow. Just because he thought he was stable didn't mean he actually was.

"I wasn't able to drive the car into the clearing— there're too many trees," I said. "But it's parked as close as I could get."

"I'll make it." He took a determined step forward, paused unsteadily for a moment, and then took another. He very much resembled a toddler taking his first steps, and, in many ways, it was an apt image. The two of us might have spent more years alive than either of us cared to remember, but each rebirth came with the cost of major muscle groups remembering how to function again. Sometimes it was almost instant—as had happened this time when it came to speech and arm movement—and other times it could take days. Hell, the last time I'd been reborn, it had taken close to two weeks for full function to return to my legs.

When we finally reached the edge of the small clearing, I quickly redressed, then picked up the soft tunic, shaking the dirt and leaves from it before helping him into it. Right now, his skin was so new that it was also ultrasensitive. Anything too tight or scratchy would rub him raw.

It was only half a dozen steps from there to the rental car, but by the time he'd climbed into the back of the station wagon, he was shaking and bathed in sweat.

Once he'd made himself comfortable on the thin mattress, I slammed the back door closed, then climbed into the driver's seat and started the car up. "There're protein bars and a couple of energy drinks in the backpack."

He dragged the pack closer and opened it up. "Whatever did we do before modern food manufacturing?"

"Snacked on beef jerky and drank unrefined cows' milk boosted with raw eggs."

"Which is probably the reason I hate both with a passion today." He tore open the protein bar and began munching on it. "Except, of course, when said milk is combined with either brandy or rum in the form of eggnog. How many days have I missed?"

I checked the mirror for oncoming cars, even though encountering any was unlikely on such an off-the-beaten track, then did a U-turn and headed down to the main road.

"Three. I had to wait for a hot enough day to perform the ceremony."

He snorted softly. "If Melbourne can be relied on for anything, it's weather that does *not* do what you want."

"Yeah." There were other reasons, of course, such as the Paranormal Investigations Team—a specialist squad of humans and supernaturals who worked outside the regular police force to solve crimes that involved paranormals—wanting a full and detailed debriefing before they'd let Jackson and me go. Then there was the problem of ensuring we weren't being followed—one we solved by Jackson and me temporarily going our separate ways. He returned to the offices of Hellfire Investigations—the PI agency we jointly owned and ran—while I followed the example of so many of our enemies of late, using the stormwater system to get out of Melbourne unseen.

"What happened in Brooklyn after I was shot?" Rory said.

"Nothing. We just ran." Or rather, left as quickly as any of us were able, given we were all more than a little broken and bloody by that time.

"And you haven't heard from either Sam or Jackson since?"

"I talked to Jackson yesterday. I'm meeting him in Seymour tonight if he can get away without being followed." I had no idea what Sam might be doing. He hadn't exactly been communicative since I'd stepped back into his life. He might be one of PIT's top investigators, he might be chasing the same damn things we were, but he'd generally dealt with me only when and where necessary.

"Is that wise?" Concern edged Rory's voice.

"Probably not, but it's not as if we have another option. There are still too many things we need to do."

And far too many people we'd endanger if we *did* stop or disappear. Hell, my vanishing for three days was enough of a risk. I was just hoping Rinaldo—the vampire who was blackmailing us for any and all information on the Crimson Death virus, or red cloak virus, as it was more commonly known—would put our recent lack of action down to injury recovery.

Of course, both he and everyone else currently tailing us also wouldn't have minded our finding the missing scientists who'd been working on a cure for the virus. Unfortunately, they'd been purposefully infected, brought under the control of the red cloak hive "queen," and, right now, were who knows where, working on god knows what.

What we *did* know was that the infected generally fell into two categories—those who became crazy pseudo vampires leashed by the will of the "queen," and the ones who, while they also gained vampirelike abilities, kept all mental facilities even though they were still bound to the hive and its leader. No one really understood why the virus affected some more than others, although the powers that be suspected it very much depended on which lot infected you. The scientists were apparently in this category—no surprise given the hive queen had wanted them working on the cure as much as the rest of us.

Of course, there was a third category, involving people like Sam who, though infected, had no attachment to the hive and did not fall under the will of its leader.

"What about Rinaldo?" Rory asked.

"Jackson's been making the required nightly call." I shrugged. "Hopefully, it'll keep him off our backs."

"If he's as old as you suspect, then it probably won't," Rory said. The more he talked, the scratchier his voice became. "Those bastards see things in rather simple terms—that is, things they want, people they can use to get those things, and people who are in their way."

We were currently sitting in that middle group with Rinaldo. I did *not* want to step into the latter group.

I glanced at the rearview mirror and saw Rory was struggling to keep his eyes open. "Don't fight it; your body needs the rest."

"You can't carry me in, and the last thing we need is you breaking your back and having us both immobile."

I grinned. "Your ass may be heavy, but I've carried it before and I can do so again. Stop being an idiot, and let your body do what it needs to."

He didn't reply, and, in a matter of seconds, he was asleep. I hit the main road and headed toward the small cabin I'd rented for the next week. It was a pretty but basic building, the interior little more than one large wood-clad room that held a bed, a kitchenette, and a sofa, with a bathroom tucked into one corner. But it was the open fire dominating the main room that had drawn me there. Rory needed both flame *and* food to continue his rehabilitation toward full mobility, which was why I'd not only lit the fire before I'd left but had also set up a bed right in front of it. No matter how long he slept, his body would automatically feed on the flames.

The moon was casting its silver light across the shadows by the time I pulled into the long driveway that led down to the half dozen cabins dotted along the banks of the Goulburn River. Ours was the very last one, situated around a slight bend in the river and out of the direct line of sight of the other five.

I reversed up to the front steps, then climbed out and unlocked the front door. A wave of heat hit me, and I closed my eyes, briefly drawing it into my body to ease a little of the tiredness. But this heat was not mine to enjoy.

I severed the connection and returned to the car, opened the rear door, then dragged the mattress—and Rory—closer. He muttered something unintelligible and half sat up, making my job a little easier. I swung his arm around my shoulder, then hauled him upright, being careful not to crack his head on the top of the wagon's door.

He waved his free hand about randomly and said in a rather grand tone, "Onward and upward, my dear!"

I grinned, shifted my grip to his waist, and half carried, half guided him up the steps. His breath was little more than a wheeze by the time we made it inside, and we all but staggered over to the fire. I stripped him out of his tunic, then helped him down onto the mattress. I didn't bother covering him, simply because having his entire body exposed to the flames would hasten the refeeding process.

"Thanks." His eyes briefly fluttered open. "What time are you meeting Jackson?"

I threw some more logs on the fire, then glanced at the clock on the wall. "In twenty minutes."

He grunted. "Bring back some coffee. And fries. And a big burger. Or two."

Amusement ran through me. "Like *that's* a surprise request."

I generally hungered for chocolate and green tea after my rebirths, but Rory had always preferred the fattier foods—a preference that had become much easier to fulfill when fast foods had come into being. Although cheese, eggs, and milk were theoretically healthier, fries and burgers seemed to fuel him faster.

"How long are you planning to be away?" he mumbled.

"Not long." Particularly as he was still in such a fragile state. "But shit does happen."

Especially since I'd saved Sam's life and subsequently become involved in the quest to stop his brother's mad scheme to spread the red cloak virus. Not only was Luke one of the few infected who'd retained his sanity, but he also happened to be the "queen bee" of the red cloak hive and had intended to create an army with which he could rule the world. And while we'd managed to bring Luke down in the Brooklyn madness that had taken Rory's life, I had no idea how much of his army remained or whether he'd had a second in command who could take over. He'd certainly had a witch on his payroll—one who'd been powerful enough to not only create a spell able to contain a phoenix's fire, but also to call *and* control three hellhounds. That I'd survived the encounter had been due to luck more than determination and skill on my part.

"Shit does," Rory said. "And hopefully, the next truckload will happen all over the bastard who ordered me killed."

I chuckled softly and touched his arm. His skin still held an edge of coolness, which meant there was a way to go before he was up to full strength, despite appearances. "I won't be long."

He grunted. I waited until his breathing indicated he'd slipped into a deep sleep, then grabbed my coat and headed out. It didn't take me all that long to reach Seymour. Although there were plenty of good-quality restaurants in the town, Jackson and I had decided to meet at McDonald's, not only because it was easier but because I'd have to stop by there anyway to grab Rory's food.

Once I'd parked, I climbed out and looked around. There weren't many cars here; most customers were content to simply use the drive-through, if the long line was anything to go by. None of them seemed to be paying any attention to me, but that didn't necessarily mean there wasn't anyone out there watching my movements. The feeling wasn't caused by paranoia so much as past experience, given the number of people who'd been following us of late.

I couldn't see Jackson anywhere, so I headed inside. Aside from the couple eating at one of the corner tables, the only other people here were the staff.

My phone—an untraceable one we'd gotten from a friend of Rory's who was heavily involved in the black market trade—beeped as I ordered a green tea, several burgers, and a bag of fries. I pulled the phone out of my pocket and glanced at the screen.

Be there in a few minutes, the message said. Order me an espresso. A large one.

Though there was no name on the text, it could only have come from Jackson as, aside from Rory, no one else had this number. Jackson's phone had come from PIT, and though they claimed it was also untraceable, they meant to everyone but themselves.

And *that* was something of a problem. I trusted Sam, and I trusted his boss—the rather formidable Chief Inspector Henrietta Richmond—but that was about it. I was pretty sure PIT had at least one mole, and it didn't matter whether that person belonged to the sindicati—the vampire equivalent of the Mafia—or was one of Rinaldo's men; the last thing I needed was either group getting our current location or our new phone number. Not when Rory was in such a weak state, anyway.

I ordered Jackson's coffee, then moved across to a table that overlooked the parking lot. I demolished my food in record time, needing to fuel my flesh as much as I'd need to refuel my spirit with flame sometime in the next twenty-four hours. As I started in on the fries, an old van drove into the parking area and stopped on the opposite side of the lot to my car. It was Jackson; of that I had no doubt. A few seconds later, he climbed out of the van, a lean, auburn-haired man who oozed heat and sexuality. Even from this distance, separated as we were by glass, I could feel it. It was a teasing but fiery river that ran delightfully across my senses, and it was something I'd never felt before. Not like this, anyway. Which maybe meant it was yet another side effect of allowing him to draw in my flames—to merge his spirit with mine—in an effort to burn the red cloak virus from his system. And we weren't even sure if we'd achieved *that*.

PIT had recently taken blood samples, but it could be days—even weeks—before we knew the test results. I seriously doubted it would take that long, though, as there was currently no known cure for the red cloak virus. If my flames *had* burned it from Jackson's system, it meant the virus was at least susceptible to heat.

Not that it'd help humanity all that much. Few races were capable of withstanding the high temperatures Jackson had.

I watched him walk toward the main door. If there was one thing literature and movies had gotten wrong when it came to the fae, it was their stature. They were neither small nor winged, and the only ones that were ethereal in any way were the air fae.

He made his way through the tables with a lightness and grace that belied said stature, his easy and de-lighted grin creasing the corners of his emerald eyes.

"Ah, Emberly." His voice was little more than a mur-mur, but one that echoed deep within me. Another side effect of our merging was the ability to hear each other's thoughts. Not all the time, and certainly not without some effort, but it was still there. And still developing, if that echo was any indication. "You have no idea how much I've missed you."

"Let's be honest here." The amusement that ran through me bubbled over into my voice. "You're an over-sexed fire fae who hasn't had much of the intimate stuff of late. You missed my body more than you missed me."

"You wound me to the core with such a comment." He rather dramatically slapped a hand against his chest, but the effect was somewhat spoiled by the laughter dancing in his eyes.

I rose. "Yeah, I can see the tears."

"They are raining inside, trust me." He caught my hand and tugged me closer. "Life in the office has been seriously boring these last three days without you."

He wrapped his arms around me and held me tight. Not only was he delightfully muscular, but deliciously warm as well. Fire fae tended to run hotter than most humanoids, and although their core temperature was nowhere near as high as ours, they did make very compatible lovers.

But Jackson was also a perfect lover in one other respect: Fire fae didn't do commitment, and Jackson was never going to want anything more than a good time from me—which was just as well, considering Sam was this lifetime's heartbreaker.

"You spent years in that office flying solo," I said, voice dry. "I've only been there a few weeks."

"But in those few weeks, I have become so accustomed to your presence, I cannot imagine life without it." His face grew suddenly serious. "And now, if you don't mind, I desperately need to do something that I've been dreaming about for these last few days."

And with that, he kissed me.

It was a long, slow, and extremely sensual exploration, and one that had my pulse racing and inner fires flaring. I controlled the latter, but only just—and *that* was instant cause for alarm. Control was something I'd learned from a very young age. That it threatened to break my restraints here—with this man—was something that hadn't happened in the past and certainly shouldn't be happening now.

I abruptly pulled away. His skin was almost translucent with heat, and alarm washed through me. The lack of control wasn't mine, but rather *his*, somehow seeping through the link between us.

Jackson, I said, trying to put as much urgency as I could through our silent connection. *Control it.*

He blinked, then awareness of what was happening hit,

and he cursed softly. The fiery color of his skin immediately dimmed, but I could still feel the heat burning deep within him. While fire fae generally couldn't produce their own flame—they could only control fire that already existed, even if it was little more than a spark—Jackson had gained that ability when our spirits had merged.

But it was an ability he was still struggling with.

He cursed again and thrust a hand through his short hair. "Damn, I've spent the last few days practicing fire control, but it looks as if the results aren't quite what I expected."

I touched his arm lightly. "It takes a phoenix years to gain full control. You can't expect similar results in a matter of days."

He snorted. "I'm a fire fae. That should give me some sort of an advantage."

"It will. But remember, while you're able to control fire, it wasn't an intimate part of your being until after we merged." I squeezed his arm and sat back down. "You're not used to having to control flames twenty-four/seven. Up until now, you've only had to exert control when fire was already present."

He grunted and sat down opposite me. "It's still fucking annoying. Especially if I now have to think about every little thing I do lest I set something on fire. Or someone."

"Control *will* happen. But in the meantime, I can teach you how to leash it in more intimate moments."

He took a sip of his coffee, then snagged a fry. "That sounds promising. Can we start now?"

I laughed. "Jackson, we're in the middle of McDonald's."

"And I have a van parked outside."

"I don't think either the staff or the patrons would appreciate our doing the horizontal tango out in their parking lot."

"Sadly true." He paused, and that wicked gleam reappeared. "There might, however, be room enough to do a vertical tango."

I threw a fry at him. "We haven't the time."

"It's been more than three days since my last loving. Trust me, it won't take long."

"It's a sad day when a fire fae admits to so little control."

"Woman, you have no idea just how much control I'm exerting right now." He snagged the fry from the table and munched on it. "How's Rory doing?"

"He was reborn without incident and is currently recharging in front of a roaring fire."

Jackson grunted. "How long will it take him to get back to normal?"

I raised an eyebrow. "Meaning, how long do I have to remain with him?"

He smiled. "Yes."

"It depends. Once he's fully refueled, he'll at least be capable of looking after himself even if he's still physically weak. But right now, I can only leave him for small periods of time."

"Small periods are better than nothing."

I frowned. "Why?"

"You know that itchy feeling you get? The one that says we're about to hit a truckload of trouble?"

"I get dreams, not itchy feelings."

"Same, same, just a little more detailed."

I smiled. There was a *vast* difference between getting prophetic dreams that *always* came true and simply feeling the approach of something ominous—and he knew it. "What is this premonition telling you?"

He hesitated. "Just that something bad is happening."

"Happening? As in, right now?"

He nodded, his expression serious. "I don't know what, I don't know where, but whatever it is, it's bad."

"Until we get a little more detail, it's hard to do anything about it."

"Yeah." He rubbed a hand across his jaw. "Why don't we grab Rory's food and get back— just in case he's the reason for the bad sensations."

"No one knows where he is, so I doubt it."

Even so, I finished off my tea and quickly rose. The drive-through queue had tapered off by that time, so it didn't take long to get Rory's burgers as well as a couple extra for the two of us. I might have already eaten, but my stomach was still demanding more. It was just as well my metabolic rate ran far hotter than a human's; otherwise, I'd have been the size of a house.

As we headed out, I added, "It might be worthwhile to leave the van—and your phone—here. I don't want to risk anyone tracing us to the cabin."

He nodded and jogged off to the van. I climbed into my car and drove over to pick him up, then swung back onto the road that would take us to Trawool and the cabin.

Jackson was silent the entire trip, but I could feel the tension in him. Whatever he was picking up, it was growing in intensity. I parked in front of the door again, then grabbed the bags of food and hurried up the steps.

The heat once again surged over me as I opened the door and stepped inside. Rory was not only unharmed but also awake.

"That was quick," he said. Though he sounded brighter, I could still feel the tiredness—the weakness—in him. Refueling was not happening at any great speed, which was frustrating. Not that there was anything he could do about it—it was just the way things were playing out with this rebirth.

"That's because I'm well aware how grouchy you get when you don't get fed in a reasonable time frame."

A smile tugged his lips. "Says the woman who once threatened to cinder me if I didn't present chocolate immediately."

"A statement any reasonable woman would understand." I squatted down beside him, then unwrapped one of the burgers and handed it to him.

"Jackson didn't appear?" He took a bite, then closed his eyes, his expression one of utter bliss.

"Jackson did," Jackson said as he stepped into the room and closed the door. "Fuck, is it hot in here, or is it just me?"

"It's hot." I continued on to the small kitchen table, depositing the rest of the food on it before shrugging off my coat. "And I won't object if you strip off."

"I will," Rory muttered. "Keep your pants on, mate."

Jackson chuckled even as he stripped off his jacket, then began rolling up his sleeves. "Never fear, I have no intentions of giving you an inferiority complex when you're still so new to the world."

Rory snorted. "Dream on."

Jackson pulled the chair away from the table and sat

down, but his grin quickly faded as my phone rang. "Who's got that number?"

Tension ran through me, especially after his recent comment about something feeling off. "No one but you and Rory." I pulled the phone out of my pocket and glanced at the screen. The number was a familiar one. "It's okay. It's a rerouted call from the office."

Jackson's relief was palpable—and said plenty about the tension still riding him. "It's probably one of our other clients, wondering why in the hell we've failed to give them progress reports in recent weeks."

"Probably." I hit the CALL ANSWER button, then placed it on speaker so he could hear it.

For several seconds, the only sound coming from the phone was whisper-soft breathing.

"Crank call," Jackson muttered. "Hang up."

"I wouldn't advise that," a pleasant and unfortunately familiar voice said, "because that might have dire consequences."

Sparks danced across my fingers, and it was all I could do to control them and *not* melt the phone. And this time it had nothing to do with Jackson and everything to do with anger. And if I was being honest, more than a little fear.

"What do you want, Rinaldo?"

"You know what I want," he replied, his tone urbane and ultrapolite. "And you have not been holding up your end of our bargain."

"I've been calling you every fucking night," Jackson growled.

"Yes, but your reports have been scant when it comes to information."

"Hard to give what we haven't got," I bit back.

"If that were true—and it isn't—then perhaps I might be inclined to forgive."

"Oh, for fuck's sake—"

"I told you what would happen if you failed to play by my rules, so you *will* now pay the promised price." Rinaldo paused, and I could almost envision his cold smile. "Or rather, your precious friends now will."

CHAPTER 2

Jackson's face went white. But Rinaldo wasn't quite finished with us yet.

"Be at the Carlton Gardens tonight at three," he said. "That gives you enough time to view the damage you've done first. Oh, and if you contact PIT, there will be further consequences."

The call ended, and Jackson immediately snatched the phone from my hands. He punched in some numbers, and after a few seconds the phone began to ring.

And ring.

Fuck.

I hoped with all my heart that it didn't mean Shona was hurt or dead. She was one of Jackson's lovers and the security specialist who, via the simple act of allowing us into an apartment to search for the missing research notes, had ended up with Rinaldo's death sentence hanging over her head. I hoped it was simply a case of either her being unable to hear the phone or of the phone itself being out of range or dead.

Please, god, don't let her be the dead one.

I raked a hand through my hair and met Jackson's flat stare. Though there was very little in the way of emotion to be seen, the heat of his fury and fear washed through me like lava. "You should go—"

"You should *both* go," Rory interrupted. "It could well be a trap of some kind. You need to protect each other's backs."

"But you're not strong—"

"I'll be okay," he cut in again. "I have the fire and the burgers to fuel me, and then I'll sleep. And you don't have to be here to watch me do that."

"I know, but—"

"Stop arguing and just go."

"Fine." I thrust up. "Jackson, I gather you know where Shona lives?"

His face was grim. "Yes. And if he's hurt her . . ."

If he had, there wasn't a whole lot we could do. Not immediately, anyway. I doubted he'd personally turn up for the meeting later; he'd have to know how angry we'd be, and how dangerous *that* could be.

I walked over to Rory and bent down to drop a kiss on his cheek. "I'll be back by sunrise."

He nodded. "Kick some butt for me."

Jackson was already out the door. I picked up my coat and followed. "We should grab your phone on the way through—"

"We can't afford to waste the time it'd take—"

"What we *can't* afford," I cut in, "is risking anyone getting Rory's current location via the GPS on my phone. Which means I can't ring PIT."

I jumped into the car, started it up, then flattened the accelerator. Dust and stones sprayed out from the rear tires as the car launched forward.

"Why the fuck would we want to ring them?" he snapped. "Especially after Rinaldo's warning?"

"Because Shona wasn't the only one whose life was

threatened the night we raided Rosen's apartment."
Rosen had owned and run Rosen Pharmaceuticals, one
of two private labs hired by the government to help
find a cure for the virus. He'd been murdered by one
section of the sindicati, but, unfortunately for the rest
of us, he'd been infected by the virus, and had subsequently risen and come under Luke's control. Whether
he was still around and sane now that Luke was dead,
I had no idea. PIT was leading the cleanup of the remaining infected and really didn't believe in sharing
that sort of information. I swung the car onto the main
road. "The security guard's life was also dependent on
our good behavior, remember? We can't be in two
places at once, so, like it or not, PIT has to be informed."

Jackson swore and scrubbed a hand across his eyes.
"I'd forgotten about the guard."

"He doesn't deserve to die just because Rinaldo thinks
we're not holding up our end of the deal."

"Which we aren't, given we haven't handed him all the
notes we found."

"But how does Rinaldo know that?" Frustration bit
through my voice. "Especially since we haven't told
anyone—including PIT—about either the USB we found
in the locker or the suitcase notes we photographed but
didn't give anyone."

"He's an exceptionally strong telepath—"

"Which means fuck all when neither of us can be
read," I said.

"De Luca's get were there when we found the suitcase
of notes, remember."

His get—vampires who'd undergone the blood ceremony with De Luca, and who subsequently owed

allegiance to his lair on turning—might have been, but I doubted they'd paid too much attention to *our* reasons for being there. Not when their sole intention had been to kill us in retribution for De Luca's death—a death we *weren't* responsible for, as much as I might have wanted to be. That honor belonged to Frank Parella, a sindicati general and De Luca's factional opposite.

And while some of his vampires might have been present when we'd found the research notes at Denny Rosen Junior's place, they'd been arrested and carted away by the time we opened the case and discovered just how important its contents might be. While some of the notes *had* been virus related, for the most part they'd dealt with a rather startling discovery—James Wilson, who'd been working for Rosen Senior's pharmaceutical company and who was one of the two scientists leading the charge to find a cure for the virus, had isolated the gene he believed responsible for vampirism and thought it might be possible to reverse the process.

If that was true, it was a discovery that could be worth billions to whoever held the information. And while neither of us had any intention of holding it to ransom, we also had no intention of letting it get into the wrong hands—such as those of the sindicati or Rinaldo.

"Yes," I said, somewhat impatiently, "but we *did* hand over the unrelated notes from the case."

"We handed those over to whoever got to our office first, whether that was Rinaldo or Parella," Jackson all but growled. "Maybe Parella got there first, and that's what has pissed Rinaldo off."

"Maybe." We'd certainly taken a risk by making that play, but we'd done it in the hope that either Parella and his vampires, or even the werewolves—whom we'd also notified—might catch Rinaldo in the act of retrieving the notes and take the bastard down for us.

I guess we should have known he wouldn't be caught so easily.

Jackson scrubbed a hand across his eyes. "I'm sorry, I shouldn't be biting your head off when we both agreed it was our best option."

"Well, not exactly." I gave him a somewhat grim look. "I was the one who gave that ultimatum to Rinaldo. You agreed to it only after the fact."

And if my impulsive action *had* caused Shona's death, I would carry the guilt of it throughout this lifetime. But if there was one thing I'd learned over my lives, it was that good people sometimes paid the ultimate price, even if they were not directly involved in whatever fight or war was being waged.

Which didn't excuse what I'd done or ease the guilt in any way.

We reached Seymour in record time, and, after Jackson had retrieved the phone from his old van, he made the call to PIT. Neither of us knew the security guard's last name, let alone where he lived, so the only chance he really had of survival was for PIT to access his firm's employment records for those details and then get there first. Had we had that information, I suppose we could have called the cops rather than PIT, and technically *wouldn't* have breached Rinaldo's warning. But would he care about technicalities? Somehow, I doubted it. Besides, I wasn't about to send ordinary cops up against his men, not after they'd revealed themselves to be rather trigger-happy the one time we'd confronted them.

"Why didn't you tell them Shona had also been threatened?" I asked once Jackson had hung up.

"Because she's my responsibility, not theirs."

And vengeance would also be his, his expression suggested, if the worst-case scenario eventuated.

I sent the car hurtling down the freeway, but even though I egged every ounce of speed I could from the engine, it still took more than thirty minutes to get to Craigieburn. The instinctive part of me that dreamed of death was screaming we were going to be late. I just had to hope this was one of those few times that part of me was wrong.

Shona lived in one of the newer estates in the area, which meant that—at this time of night—there wasn't much activity, especially as there didn't appear to be many other occupied houses in the immediate area.

"It's number twenty-four, down at the end on the right." Jackson's voice remained flat and empty. But I could still feel the emotion he wasn't showing—he was a volcano on the very edge of eruption. "She moved here only a few months ago. If she'd stayed in her rental in Carlton—"

"More people might be dead." Because if Rinaldo *was* intent on a kill, being in a more heavily populated area certainly wouldn't have stopped him.

But Jackson knew that as much as I did.

I switched off the engine and headlights, and allowed the car to coast down the slight incline. Shona's house was opposite a rather wild-looking park and in between two streetlights—very handy for vampires intent on no good. The house was one of those ultra-modern, dark brick and concrete constructions that seemed so popular of late. A Mazda sat in the driveway, and light peeked through the blinds shuttering one of the large front windows. At first glance, nothing seemed out of place. It certainly wasn't the battlefield I'd been expecting.

Maybe we *had* gotten here in time.

Maybe Rinaldo had gone after the less obvious target.

And maybe tomorrow the fae would gain wings and start flying just as they did in fairy tales.

I pulled on the hand brake to stop the car, avoiding the giveaway flash of red that would have come from the taillights had I used the main brake. If there were vampires here, it'd be a wasted effort, as they'd hear our heartbeats the minute we got close to the house, but it was always better to be safe than sorry. Especially when we had no idea exactly who—or what—we were going up against.

I climbed out and walked around to the passenger side of the vehicle. The night was eerily quiet. Nothing moved, and there was little in the way of sounds. Even the rumble of traffic from the freeway, which was usually audible from quite a distance on still nights like this, seemed muted.

Can you sense anything?

No. Jackson paused. *It's situations like this that make me wish I were an earth or air fae. You got any weapons stashed in the car?*

No. I hadn't exactly intended to get into a firefight when I'd hired the damn thing, not when I had Rory to look after. *How would either be an advantage right now?*

Earth fae can sense the presence of others by their weight on the earth, and air fae can hear the whispers of breath on the wind. He paused. Sweat beaded his forehead, but I wasn't entirely sure it was caused by the effort of com-

municating silently. Mind speech might remain difficult between us, but I suspected the sweat had more to
do with the fury and fear that burned inside of him.
Shall we split?

I hesitated. It made sense to split up, but I was reluctant to do so, if only because he'd need me close if those
inner fires got the better of his currently tenuous control.

I'm okay, he said, obviously sensing my concern. *It
won't get away from me.*

Not until he had someone to unleash on, at any rate.
But I kept that comment to myself and motioned to the
right. *I'll tackle that side.*

He nodded and moved toward the car that sat still
and empty in the driveway. I scanned the front windows as I went right, but there wasn't much to see other
than the sliver of light lining either side of that one
window. The other two also had blinds down, so if
someone *was* inside, they'd have as little hope of seeing
me as I did them.

Car is locked, but the hood is warm, Jackson said. *She
hasn't been home long.*

Meaning if the vamps *had* attacked Shona, they'd
been here, waiting for her.

I grabbed the top of the fence that divided the front
yard from the back and pulled myself up, pausing at the
top to scan the nearby area. No shadows, no dogs, and
no sense of the werewolves who *should* have been here.

Fire briefly flickered across my fingertips, tiny sparks
that spun into the darkness and quickly disappeared. I
flexed my hands as I dropped to the ground, trying to
ease the tension. This time, it was all mine, not an over-
flow from Jackson. I walked to the first of three win-

dows situated along this side of the house and, my back pressed against bricks still warm from the day's sunshine, carefully peered inside. The room beyond was filled with boxes, some of them emptied, some of them still sealed with packing tape. There was no evidence of anything out of place or, indeed, any sort of fighting.

Maybe Rinaldo had been bluffing. Maybe he only intended to make us *fear* the possibility of death. But even as that thought crossed my mind, I dismissed it. Everything we'd learned about the man—and that was little enough—suggested he wasn't a vampire who pulled his punches.

Besides, if everything *was* okay, why hadn't the werewolves appeared, asking us what the hell was going on? Baker—the alpha wolf of the city pack—had given them orders to protect Shona against any sort of attack, and that should have meant they'd at least question us.

I continued on, repeating the process with the next two windows. One was a study with a computer sitting on a small desk, and the other an empty room. I ducked past the last window and moved to the end of the building. The small yard beyond was empty and silent. I risked a quick look around the corner—and saw a small paved area, a large sliding door, and, closer to me, a laundry door.

Anything? I asked Jackson.

No. We need to go in.

Yes, we did. It was the only way we were going to discover what was going on. *I'll take the laundry door.*

Wait for my mark, he said.

I edged around the corner. Once I'd reached the door frame, I tested the handle. It turned. And there was a smear of what looked like blood along one edge of the door.

Fuck.

I closed my eyes and took a deep breath, steeling myself for what was to come.

Right, Jackson said. *Go.*

I thrust open the door and went inside—only to be thrust backward as a shadow hit me so hard, we went tumbling out the door in a tangled mess of arms and legs. My back struck the paving, and my breath left in a wheezing rush of pain, but despite the stars flinging themselves across my vision, I had enough sense to throw up an arm. The teeth that were aimed at my neck ripped open my arm instead. Pain and anger rolled through me, and I flamed, instantly cindering the shadowed bastard on top of me. As his ashes rained around me, I scrambled upright and, in full flame form, arrowed for the back door.

Bullets tore into my fiery form but caused no harm. I flung a lance of fire into the laundry, swirling it around the open space but keeping it away from the walls and appliances. Someone screamed, the sound high-pitched and filled with pain, the tone feminine rather than male. She was in the corner, and though she was still partially hidden by shadows, her clothes were on fire. I extinguished her clothing but kept her leashed so she couldn't go anywhere, and then moved on.

The sounds of flesh smacking flesh echoed through the otherwise still house. I followed the noise into the living area and saw Jackson battling two more vampires. Though his fists were aflame, he was using flesh rather than fire against both of them.

Beyond them, the back of her head resting in a pool of blood, was Shona.

I clenched my hands, battling the urge to do what Jackson had not, and instead wrapped both vampires in flame, containing them without burning. As I became flesh again, Jackson landed two final blows, shattering the mouth of one vampire and breaking the nose of the other. They both dropped like stones to the floor and didn't move.

Nor did Jackson. He simply stood there, sucking in air, his entire body taut with tension and flames licking up his arms.

And while he was so very close to losing control and burning the house down around us, the fact that he hadn't was a good sign.

"Imagine the fire is water and that you are a pump with a very empty inner well to fill." Pain from both exertion and the wound on my forearm stabbed through me as I spoke. I glanced down. The heat of my flames had sealed the wound enough that blood was oozing out rather than pulsing, but it still hurt like blazes. I took a deep breath that did little to ease the deeper ache in my head, and continued. "Imagine your fire flowing like water into the well rather than letting it play across your body, then place a cap on it."

As directions went, they were overly simplified, but sometimes such imagery was the only way to teach control, especially when dealing with those very new to their fire—which Jackson was, despite his being a fire fae.

He didn't reply, didn't even look at me, but after several moments, the flames retreated, until all that remained was the glow of heat across his fingertips.

He took another deep breath; then his gaze stabbed to mine, the green depths icy and furious. "Where the *fuck* are the werewolves?"

"I don't know." I moved past him and squatted beside Shona. Even though there wasn't a chance in hell of her being alive given the state of her throat, I still felt her wrist for a pulse. Sometimes hope was rewarded against the greatest of odds, but this wasn't one of those times. There was no life left in her, and her skin was already losing its heat.

I closed my eyes and did my best to stifle the wash of anger and guilt. I'd made my choices, chosen my path, and there was no way I could go back on that now.

And if I was honest, I'd probably make the very same decision if I *did* have the chance of doing it all again. If our plan had worked, if either the sindicati or the werewolves had taken care of Rinaldo as he'd retrieved the suitcase notes from our office, then not only would Shona, the guard, and even Rory have been that little bit safer, but one fewer player would have been after the missing research notes.

It *had* been worth the risk. It just hadn't played out the way we'd hoped.

I pushed upright. "We have to call PIT in on this. We have no choice now."

"Agreed." Jackson's gaze suddenly narrowed. "You're injured."

"It's only a scratch."

He snorted. "That so-called scratch is five inches long—I'm gathering he caught you by surprise?"

"To his cost, yes. But I've contained the second vamp in the laundry."

"Then let's go question her."

"PIT will undoubtedly lock us out of the investigation once they get here," I said, leading the way, "so that's a damn good idea."

The vamp snarled as we entered, revealing bloody canines. Obviously, she was the one who'd taken Shona's life. Anger surged through me. I thrust it away, knelt down, wrapped my fingers around her neck, and then shoved her against the wall hard enough to dent the plaster. And she was damn lucky that was all I did. "Who sent you here?"

She swore, though the sound was somewhat strangled because the force of my grip was restricting her windpipe.

"Answer the question," I growled, "because right now, all that stands between you and incineration is the possibility of information."

She snorted. "Even a fire witch isn't capable of that."

"You have *no* idea what I'm capable of." And it was interesting she called me a fire witch rather than a phoenix. Whoever sent them here either didn't know the truth, or simply didn't care to inform them. "Last chance—who sent you here?"

"No one."

"And *that* is one rather large lie." Jackson crossed his arms as he leaned against the door frame. His expression was contemplative despite the waves of heat and anger rolling off him. "We could just burn her. Start with her toes, then maybe take out a leg. That might loosen her tongue a little."

"You wouldn't fucking dare," the woman snapped.

"We're under the protection of—" She cut the rest of the sentence off and clamped her lips shut.

"A little demonstration of our capabilities is definitely in order," Jackson said. *And it's one,* he added silently, *that you'd better do. My control isn't good enough right now, and while burning her might ease the rage a little, it wouldn't be overly useful.*

I glanced at the woman's left leg and unleashed some fire. Flames shimmered down her jeans and danced across the tips of her shoes. As the smell of burning leather touched the air, the woman began to struggle, fighting my hold even as she flung her leg about in an attempt to smother the flames. Jackson moved past me and planted a rather large boot on her legs, stilling the movements.

"The woman inside—the woman you fed on and then killed—was my lover," he growled. "So believe me when I say I'm barely resisting the urge to cinder you inch by tiny inch right now."

The vampire's gaze rose to his. For several seconds she didn't say anything, but electricity buzzed around my senses. I smiled, though it held little in the way of amusement. She was trying to read him—maybe even trying to control him—and that meant she was older than she actually looked. Despite what humans generally thought, not all vampires were telepathic, and even for those who *were*, precise control was something they gained over centuries rather than decades. Of course, they also had to be very specific about what they wanted, and they certainly didn't have carte blanche access to the mind.

Except, perhaps, for outliers like Rinaldo.

And even *he* couldn't access or control either Jackson

or me, because we were both immune to psychic invasion of any description.

Thank *god*.

I sent a flare of heat to my fingertips and lightly burned her throat. She hissed, and her gaze jumped back to mine. "Talk or find yourself in need of prosthetic limbs."

"Or not," Jackson said. "Personally, I'd prefer the latter. Especially since two of your three companions remain alive; maybe one of them will value their limbs more than you and will give us what we need."

"If I *do* talk," she growled, "will you let us go?"

Jackson snorted. "We'll let you live. We might even let you keep your limbs. But that's it."

Her gaze darted between the two of us, and whatever she saw must have convinced her that was as good a deal as she was ever likely to get. "Fine. What do you want to know?"

"Who sent you here?"

"Rinaldo."

No surprise there, given his phone call. "So are you one of his get, or do you simply work for him?"

She hesitated. "Neither. But he's offered us his immediate protection and promised to approach the council on our behalf if we do as he asked."

"But why would you need him to—" I broke the question off as realization dawned. "You're one of De Luca's get."

"Yes," she spat. "And it's thanks to you that we're currently in a very tenuous situation when it comes to the council and the other dens."

"Tenuous" was putting it somewhat lightly. No master

vampire ever wanted the spawn of another in his or her lair, and that generally meant vampires who lost the protection of their creator were little more than fodder for the rest of the vampire community.

Not that the community generally had much of a chance to play or feed on a rudderless den—the elders usually took swift action to end their lives. While the vampire council as a whole had little fear of humans—who for many elders were nothing more than a food source—they *did* fear the reaction of the rest of us. So they never allowed their numbers to get too out of control, and they kept a tight leash on who could and couldn't start new dens.

"If you think Rinaldo will keep his word, you are more gullible than you look," Jackson said.

She cast him a look that simmered with anger. "He's our one hope of survival now that the council has issued an edict of den eradication. Rinaldo is all that stands between us and destruction."

"Then I'd be prepared to meet your maker in hell," Jackson said. "I doubt Rinaldo is sure enough of his position here in Melbourne to risk going up against the council."

"And *that* is where you'd be wrong," she said. "De Luca's den was a large one. Add that to Rinaldo's, and he has a sizable army at his back. Even the council will think twice."

Rinaldo with an army at his back was *not* something I wanted to think about. "What can you tell us about your new master, then?"

She shrugged. "Not a lot. He offered us the deal, and we took it."

"So you don't actually know where he or his den is currently situated?"

"No." She paused. "We had to prove our worth here before he'd offer us anything more."

"What were you supposed to do after you'd killed Shona?" I asked.

Jackson twitched at the question, and his foot pressed that bit heavier on the woman's leg. She lunged forward, catching me by surprise and getting within inches of Jackson's leg before I thrust her back.

The flames that were dancing across her smoldering boots suddenly flared white, eating down into the leather and then into her toes. She screamed; the flames instantly retreated.

Jackson's doing, not mine.

"Next time, I will cinder those toes rather than merely burning them." Once again, his voice was deceptively mild. "Now, answer the damn question."

Sweat dribbled down the side of her face. "We were supposed to meet him in the Carlton Gardens."

Part of a welcoming committee, perhaps? I said, glancing up at Jackson. The niggly ache in my head flared a little brighter, but I wasn't about to risk her passing any comment of mine on to Rinaldo. I had no idea if she was a strong enough telepath to communicate with him from this distance, but better safe than sorry.

Probably. But if he wants those notes, he needs us alive, so I don't really see the point.

Maybe he just wants to hit home his message that we obey him or else. He seems the type. I returned my attention to the woman. "Is that it?"

She nodded. "He's not the most communicative person, but then, most of the older ones aren't."

That was probably the most truthful thing she'd said all night.

"As I've told some of your den mates already, we didn't murder De Luca." I peeled a sliver of fire away from the rope corralling her torso and wrapped it around her neck. "Frank Parella took that honor."

Her eyes narrowed. "He wouldn't dare."

"Everyone keeps saying that." I released my grip on her and thrust upright. Her neck was burned and blistering, and I hoped it was as painful as hell. "It's almost as if the sindicati generals *haven't* spent centuries murdering their counterparts. Oh, and if you move, those ropes will burn you."

She obviously didn't believe me, because she threw herself sideways, teeth bared as she tried to slash open my leg. I didn't move; I didn't have to. My fiery leash immediately tightened around her throat and chest, and in an instant, she was gasping for breath.

"I did warn you," I said, and walked away.

Only when I was back in the living room did I loosen the leash enough for her to breathe.

Jackson moved past me and squatted beside Shona. After gently closing her eyes, he leaned forward and kissed her forehead.

"May your next journey in this world be filled with love, happiness, and a long life," he said softly. "And as you move on, rest assured that your death in *this* lifetime will be avenged. That I promise you."

I didn't say anything, but I had everything crossed that it was a promise we could keep. "We have to call

PIT. But we also need to find out what happened to the werewolves. Baker wouldn't have gone back on his word; I'm sure of that."

Jackson thrust to his feet. "Depends if he got a better offer."

"Who from? He'd already refused Rinaldo's offer of a partnership, and it's hardly likely the sindicati or the rats would pay him to back away from our deal given they want information about Rinaldo just as much as everyone else."

Especially after Rinaldo had raided several of the rat shifters' main underground gambling operations here in Melbourne.

"Good point. I'll go outside and see if I can find the wolves. You ring PIT." He tossed me his phone, then turned and headed outside.

I opened the contacts list and pressed the chief inspector's number. It was a direct line, and, as far as I knew, we were the only ones outside the organization who had it. Hopefully, that meant it was secure.

The phone rang several times; then a somewhat plummy and decidedly unfeminine voice said, "Chief Inspector Henrietta Richmond speaking."

"Inspector, Emberly Pearson here."

"Indeed," she said. "What can I do for you?"

"Jackson made a call about a security guard in need of protection—"

"And he's been checked and is secure," she cut in. "We have temporarily relocated him."

I closed my eyes. At least I hadn't gotten *two* innocent people killed. But a rather unkind part of me wished the situation had been reversed—that it was

Shona who was alive rather than the guard. Because of Jackson, because he'd cared for her—at least as much as any fae was capable of caring.

"That's good news," I said, "but I'm afraid he wasn't the only possible victim. And we weren't in time to save the second one."

"What?" The inspector's voice was cold. "Why didn't Jackson give us this information when he made the initial call?"

"Because the woman in question was his lover," I said.

"That is no excuse."

Maybe it wasn't, but our decision to come here ourselves was nevertheless one I stood by. I rubbed a hand across my eyes. The ache in my head was getting worse. I needed rest and I needed fire, and I wasn't likely to come by either anytime soon. "We have the murderers in custody. They're from De Luca's get, and the whole den is currently working under the orders of Rinaldo."

"And once again that bastard's name crops up," she said. "Are you aware he sent us a goddamn note the day after the events in Brooklyn?"

"No." I frowned. "Why would he do that? And what did the note say?"

"Who knows why he did it—maybe he simply likes tugging the panther's tail." She laughed, a humorless sound filled with frustration. "And the note simply said, 'The king is dead. Long live the queens.' It was signed with a rather ornate R."

My frown deepened. "What does he mean, 'queens'? Or is it simply a spelling mistake?"

"I very much suspect every move Rinaldo makes

involves very, *very* careful planning—even when it comes to something as simple as a taunting note."

"And you're sure it's from him?"

"As sure as I can be. The only people who are fully aware of what really happened in Brooklyn were my senior advisers and you."

"And you trust your senior staff?" I asked.

"With my life." It was coldly said. Obviously, it didn't pay to question the loyalty of her people. "Give me the address, and I'll send a team over."

I did so, then added, "We have a meet with Rinaldo tonight."

"Do you want backup?"

Fuck yes, I wanted to say, because while I might be a fire spirit, I was neither stupid nor entirely immortal. I *could* die in this lifetime, which would be damn dangerous when Rory wasn't yet up to full strength and might struggle to call my ashes to him.

But Rinaldo's warning kept the words locked inside. "No. Besides, isn't PIT stretched to its limits at the moment?"

"Yes, especially after the mess you made of Brooklyn." There was no hint of censure in her voice. While she might not have given official approval for our actions there, she'd certainly been well aware of our plans and had made no move to stop us. "Which reminds me, I need you and Jackson to meet me there later today. Several fires continue to burn out of control, and we need you to go in there to see what the hell is going on."

I frowned. "After three days of uncontrolled burning, I can't imagine there'd be much of the place left. And why don't you just water bomb the entire area?"

"Believe me, we've tried, but there's a magical barrier of some kind protecting that particular section. The water just sluices off it."

"So what makes you think I'll be able to do anything?"

"Intuition."

"I have no knowledge of magic, Inspector."

"Perhaps, but you have very intimate knowledge of fire. You can go places the rest of us cannot."

"You'd still be better off calling in a witch." They'd at least be able to circumvent the spell, even if they couldn't entirely unravel it.

"We've tried that." Frustration edged her matter-of-fact tone. "But the spell's source is situated within Brooklyn. So again, we can do nothing more until you get in there and uncover what is going on."

I blew out a breath. We really didn't need additional work on top of everything else, but it wasn't like we actually had a choice. I had no doubt the inspector would force us there at gunpoint if necessary. "What time do you want us there?"

"What time is your meeting with Rinaldo's people?"

"Three."

"It would be preferable if we could access the place at dawn. The cloaks are less likely to be active at that hour, but it will still be dark enough that we should be able to avoid overt interest from the public."

Not to mention the press. Though I'd kept away from both the TV and newspapers over the last few days, I could imagine they'd had a field day speculating what had happened in Brooklyn. Especially since PIT wouldn't have told anyone but senior government officials the truth.

But meeting the inspector at dawn meant leaving Rory unprotected for an even longer period, and I wasn't willing to do that. I needed to check that he was safe, that he was refueling his spirit on the flames and his flesh on the food. And nothing, not the red cloaks or Brooklyn or even revenge, was more important to me than he was.

"I'm sorry, Inspector, but I can't."

She was silent for a moment, then said, "Why not?"

"Because of what I am, and because there are certain matters—certain responsibilities—I cannot escape."

"Which tells me nothing."

"It tells you more than you know." And it was all I was willing to say. I had no idea just how much PIT knew about either Rory or me, or even phoenixes in general, but from the bits and pieces Sam had mentioned, it was obviously more than most. But I was betting what they *didn't* know still far outweighed what they did, and I wanted to keep it that way.

Especially when I was pretty convinced there was a mole somewhere in their organization.

I'd initially thought it had been Rochelle—Sam's lover, and a PIT operative who, like him, had been infected by the Crimson Death virus. And while Sam had never been under the control of the hive or his brother, Rochelle's position had been a little more tenuous. She had, in fact, killed herself rather than be forced to turn on both Sam and PIT. And for a dark fae, that was a pretty desperate action.

But Rinaldo had also intimated that he had a line into PIT. Whether that was true, I had no idea, but right now, with Rory so weak, I was taking no chances.

"I'm sorry, Inspector, but I have no choice."

"It would seem that I don't, either, short of dragging your ass there personally." She paused, and a hint of amusement crept into her voice as she added, "And after that rather impressive demonstration in Brooklyn, I suspect that might not be possible. Or even wise."

Surprise ran through me. I'd been expecting a threat rather than a backing down. "You could be right."

"Meet me tomorrow evening, then—nine should do. The peak-hour traffic will be gone by then, and the area will be quiet."

"Fine. But send the fire brigade away. I don't need any more witnesses than necessary."

"Nor do we," she said heavily. "The crew will be at your location in twenty minutes."

"Thanks." I hesitated. "Have you got Jackson's blood results back yet?"

"I chased it up with the lab yesterday. I'm assured they'll have them to me within the next day or so."

Meaning we'd soon know if the virus had been burned from his system.

"Thanks," I repeated, and hung up.

I bent down and checked the two vamps Jackson had knocked out for signs of awareness, but both were still unconscious. I tightened their leashes anyway, then headed out the now-broken front door. The night remained quiet, and the moon was hidden behind a bank of clouds. What few stars could be seen were unusually muted. It was almost as if they'd dimmed their brightness in respect for the death in the room behind me.

I couldn't see Jackson anywhere, and if he was moving about, then he was doing so quietly. *You found anything?*

Pain slithered through my head even as I asked that question—a sharp warning that using our connection was indeed taking a toll. Nevertheless, it was stronger—more reliable—than it had been a few days ago, and that meant it was still gaining strength. It made me wonder just how far it would go—would we, perhaps, be able to do more than merely mind talk? Would we perhaps be able to sense the other's presence, no matter where that person was? Rory and I certainly had that capability, though it was one we rarely needed or used.

Jackson didn't reply, but after a few minutes, he appeared from the house next door. "Sorry for not responding, but all the mental talking is giving me one hell of a headache."

"Did you find the wolves?"

"Yeah." He scrubbed a hand across his chin, the sound like rough sandpaper. "Baker isn't going to be happy."

"They're dead?"

"Not just dead, but absolutely torn apart. I found a dart near one of the bodies. The poor bastards didn't have a chance."

I thrust a hand through my hair. "How the fuck did Rinaldo know about the werewolf guards?" Because he had to have, if his men had come here prepared with darts.

"Baker either has a spy in his midst, or his office is bugged."

"I can't imagine it'd be a spy. He's dealt with vampires for years; he'd be well aware of their tricks."

By the same token, I couldn't imagine he'd be naive enough to believe no one would bother bugging him.

Not when it seemed to be a very common practice here in Melbourne. The lab I'd worked for—as well as many other private organizations that had governmental links—was regularly swept of bugging devices.

"We need to ring him." Even as I said it, I pulled the phone out and did it. The minute he answered, I said, "It's Emberly Pearson, and I'm afraid I have some bad news for you."

He was silent for a moment, and then said, "My men are dead, aren't they?"

"Yes. And they were darted before they were killed. Someone knew they were watching Shona and came prepared."

"Who did you tell?" His voice was flat, angry, but whether the anger was directed toward us or was because of the loss of his men, I couldn't say.

"No one. Not even PIT knew."

"Suggesting I have a leak in my own organization. I'd feared that."

"Rinaldo seems to have a finger on the pulse of all the major players in this city," I said. "But he's an extremely strong telepath, so it might simply be a matter of reading the mind of someone close to you."

"Just as telepathic wolves are a rare find, it's also rare for wolves to be telepathically invaded. We are somewhat immune." He was silent for a second, and then said, "I'll check, however. Thank you for the call, and please remember to pass on *any* information you get on this bastard."

He hung up. I blew out a breath. "Rinaldo is dead meat if Baker ever gets his hands on him."

"That can be applied to us, PIT, the rats, and whomever else Rinaldo might have crossed." Jackson caught my hand, tugged me close, and kissed me. It was as much about grief as an affirmation of life. After a few moments, he added, "What did PIT say when you called?"

"A crew will be here shortly."

"Good, because we need to get moving if we're to meet Rinaldo on time."

I hesitated. "I don't really think—"

"Do *not* try to stop me from coming along." His expression was hard. Determined. "Because you know that's not going to happen."

"But he won't be at the meeting. He won't risk it."

"I don't care. I've already lost Shona. I'm sure as hell not going to risk losing you."

I smiled and brushed my fingers down his cheek. "I have one advantage over Shona, remember."

"The point remains." He took a deep breath and glanced over his shoulder as the sound of a siren began to invade the night's stillness. "We should tie our captives up more conventionally. Just because your ex and Richmond knows we're fire capable doesn't mean the rest of them need to."

"Does Shona keep rope or wire anywhere?"

"No, but I saw some packing tape in one of the open boxes. I'll grab that."

He did so. We taped all three up and, given the woman's proclivity for biting people, shoved several additional layers over her mouth.

PIT arrived a few minutes later. I didn't know either of the operatives, and they certainly didn't say much. Once they'd checked our IDs—both our driver's licenses and the associate badges PIT had handed us just before the Brooklyn battle—we were allowed to go.

Jackson immediately left the house, but I hesitated. "Watch the female vampire. She has a nasty habit of using her teeth."

The taller of the two women flashed me a grin. "I doubt she can even open her mouth with the amount of tape you've wound over it, but she's *most* welcome to try."

Considering the anticipatory edge to *that* comment, if my former captive had any sense, she'd be a model of good behavior. But I had a vague suspicion she wouldn't.

"Oh, and before I forget," she added, "the inspector said you might need some weapons—you'll find them in the trunk of our car. Help yourself to whatever you want."

I nodded and headed out. There was a veritable arsenal in the trunk of the car, and not just guns, but silver knives, good old-fashioned stakes, and several vials of what I presumed was holy water. I grabbed a small backpack and shoved in half a dozen semiautomatics, ammunition, two knives, and some of the holy water. The inspector might not have literally meant "help myself," but I wasn't about to forgo the chance to be fully armed. Not when every other bastard after us seemed to be fully kitted up.

Jackson had jumped into the driver's seat, so I tossed him the keys and placed the backpack on the backseat.

"What's that?" He started the car up and drove off.

"A mini armory, courtesy of the inspector."

"You know, I'm actually starting to like that woman."

I snorted. "I'll like her more if she actually keeps her word and lets us walk away once this is over. Until then, I'm reserving judgment."

"Well, at least we now have more of a chance of walking away from tonight."

"Not to mention something to fall back on if the witch is present and our fire fails."

It didn't take us all that long to get into the city. At this hour of night, the traffic was light, even when we'd pulled off City Link and made our way down Flemington Road to Victoria Street.

Jackson slowed the car as we neared the gardens. "Did Rinaldo say where we were supposed to meet him?"

"No, but the old fountain is the most logical place. People have been meeting there for years."

"I'm not entirely sure Rinaldo applies logic the same way as the rest of us." Jackson pulled into one of the empty parking spots and killed the engine.

"That's to be expected, given he's a very old vampire. He doesn't see the world the same way you and I do."

Jackson's grin flashed, and though it was a somewhat pale imitation of its usual self, I was nevertheless glad to see it. "I'm not sure that sentence applies, as you're vastly older than I am and fae in general think very differently to most."

A smile touched my lips. "You could be right. After all, you're not only a fae but also a male. And it's a well-known fact just what occupies a male's thoughts every seven seconds."

"*That* claim has repeatedly been proven false." He leaned forward and crossed his arms over the steering wheel, his gaze on the park. "Though in my case, it is quite possibly true. I can't see any movement beyond the two possums arguing at the base of that elm."

"If there *are* vampires there, we wouldn't see them

anyway." My gaze swept the shadows gathered around the trunks of the century-old elm trees. The moon might have finally escaped the cloud cover, but much of its silvery light wasn't getting through the thick canopy of greenery. It was the sort of cover vampires intent on no good just adored. "How do you want to play this?"

"Straight." He reached for the backpack. "If Rinaldo *has* arranged a vampire-greeting party, we're better off protecting each other's backs."

I glanced at the time. Ten to three. "I guess there's no point in delaying the inevitable. Let's get this over with."

I accepted one of the guns and some ammo, then climbed out. As I strapped on the weapon, Jackson slammed his door shut. The sound echoed across the stillness, and the two possums scurried up separate trees.

Jackson paused beside me. "Ready?"

"No, but it's not like we have a choice."

I shoved my hands into my pockets, my gaze moving past the bollards that separated the street from the wide path that led directly to the old French fountain. It was a warm beacon of light at the very end of a long arch of tree branches and shadows. No one appeared to be waiting for us, but the stillness now ran with tension, and not all of it was coming from the two of us.

Someone—or something—was definitely out there.

"Let's get this show on the road," Jackson murmured, and strode purposefully toward the fountain.

I hastily caught up with him, my gaze sweeping the surrounding area and looking for some sign of movement. But there was absolutely nothing to indicate there was anything or anyone out of place in the park.

Nothing except that gathering wave of tension.

Our footsteps echoed across the night, Jackson's—for all his size—far softer than mine. Heat burned across my fingertips, and I clenched my hands tighter, not wanting the glimmer to show through the layers of the coat's pockets.

We were about halfway down when energy began to crawl across my skin, its touch foul and dark.

Can you feel that? Pain lanced through my brain as I said it, but it was a warning I ignored. I had no idea what would happen if I kept pushing this developing talent of ours, but right now I had no other option. I couldn't voice the question out loud—I had no desire to inform whoever might be waiting out there that I could feel the caress of their spell.

He glanced at me, a frown creasing his forehead and a glimmer of pain gathering in the brightness of his eyes. *Feel what?*

Magic, I said. *It has the same feel as the stuff that was used in Brooklyn.*

I have no sense of it, but we did theorize that Luke's witch might be a Rinaldo plant.

I'd certainly theorized that, but I hadn't realized he'd caught those thoughts. *If it is, then we should be protected.*

We'd be protected, theoretically, because of the spell blockers we'd gotten from Grace Harkwell, the witch who'd asked us to find her missing friends. While said blockers resembled simple, multicolored string necklaces, they'd been designed to counteract any spell created to either restrict our fire or stop my access to the earth mother. It had certainly worked brilliantly in Brooklyn; I just had to hope it did so here.

But *this* spell had a stronger feel than that one. The

witch had obviously amped things up in an effort to negate a possible repeat of the Brooklyn events.

Even if that is *the case, it shouldn't affect me*, Jackson said. *I'm not a phoenix.*

No, but your fire is phoenix sourced, so that may not necessarily be true.

He grunted and continued on. The closer we got to the fountain, the stronger the spell became, until it felt like I was walking through a wall of razor blades that tore at my skin and sliced through my brain. Then warmth flared around my neck and the sensation fled. Grace's charm, once again coming to my aid.

I continued to keep a tight leash on my flames, not allowing even the slightest flicker to escape. I'd done exactly the same thing in Brooklyn, so the witch might well be aware of the ploy, especially since he'd ramped up the strength of his magic. I wasn't about to give him any indication that once again it wasn't working.

I returned my attention to the gorgeous old fountain ahead, and awareness surged. Someone was there. I could feel them, even if I couldn't see them.

As we drew closer, the musical splash of water began to break the silence, but not the tension gathering within me. I clenched my fists tighter, fighting not only my desire to become fire, but the beating pulse of Jackson's heat as well. And yet, there was no sign of fire. Not even a spark. He was containing it, but now the question was, for how long?

"Stop," a gruff, decidedly male voice said.

It was coming from the fountain, from the presence I could feel but not see.

And it wasn't Rinaldo.

More fucking magic, Jackson said as we both stopped. *But I guess it's confirmation that Rinaldo has a witch working for him.*

And that's something I really don't *want confirmed.* Out loud, I said, "Reveal yourself, witch. Or would you prefer I call you Frederick?"

"You can call me whatever you like, but using my name is always preferable." Amusement edged the gravelly tone. "As to revealing myself—why would I give you that sort of advantage since you know nothing more than my first name?"

"Actually," I said, "we've also seen your face, when you were running for the helicopter." I paused. "Which we subsequently blew up. How the hell did you escape?"

"Luck and good planning, my dear—both of which I think you need more of." The amusement was deeper now. "But that is neither here nor there. I'm here to deliver a message."

"We've already got Rinaldo's message," Jackson growled. "We don't need another."

"Ah, but I'm afraid he begs to differ. It would appear you have learned nothing, as you went against orders and called in PIT."

"We could hardly do anything else," I said, "given we're PIT operatives."

Surprise rippled across the night. "Are you now?"

"Yes, and we have the goddamn badges to prove it." Flames shot out from Jackson's hands as he spoke, reaching with eager fingers for our unseen foe. They hit the barrier the witch was using to conceal himself, and flared across its surface, briefly revealing a thin, shadowed form inside a domelike structure before fading away.

"Interesting," Frederick said. "As is the fact your flames are not contained."

Jackson's grin flashed, though it held little in the way of humor. "No, they're not. But then, I'm a fire fae. A spell designed to contain Emberly will do little to me."

"I didn't think fire fae were capable of creating fire."

"Then you do not know as much as you thought."

"Evidently." His gaze came to me, something I felt rather than saw. "I'm gathering, then, that my magic has had a similar lack of effect on you?"

"Why don't you drop that shield and find out?"

He laughed. "Thanks, but no. I've seen what you're capable of; I have no wish to feel it."

"You're presuming that little bubble of yours will actually stop me. That could be a big mistake."

"It stopped you in Brooklyn when it was protecting Luke—at least until he foolishly stepped on metal—and that spell had half the strength of this. But by all means, test away."

I didn't, if only because he wanted me to.

"However," he continued, "all that is an aside, and it does not change the purpose of this meeting."

"Why are you delivering the message?" I said. "Why isn't your boss here?"

"Who says he isn't?"

I resisted the urge to look around me. "Because while Rinaldo may be many things, stupid isn't one of them. He wouldn't risk appearing when you cannot absolutely guarantee your magic will restrain my flames."

"True, especially since he can be present without being here physically."

"What is it with witches speaking in goddamn riddles?" Jackson growled. "Tell us what he wants, and then get the fuck on with whatever else is planned."

"He wants De Luca's notes when you find them, and he wants the satchel notes you found—"

"He could have already had those," I cut in. "He just needed to get to our office before the sindicati."

"Yes, except *that* was nothing more than a trap. As you said, he is not stupid." The amusement was stronger this time. "You have twenty-four hours to provide those notes."

"Or what?" Jackson said.

"Or," the witch said blithely, "we will unleash red plague hell on this city."

CHAPTER 3

Jackson snorted. "I do so love dramatic statements, especially when the person behind them can't back them up."

"Which is a reasonable enough presumption, given you are not in possession of all the pertinent facts." Once again, Frederick's voice was annoyingly smug.

I had to clench my fists against the desire to batter his shield with flame. "How about getting to the point if you actually have one? We've got other things we need to be doing."

"That is indeed true," Frederick said, and then added in a flat tone, "We control the cloaks. If you don't do as we want, they'll swarm into this city and infect as many people as possible."

"Luke was the only one who could control the cloaks," Jackson said, "and he's dead."

"Luke is certainly *dead*," the witch replied, "but the rest of that sentence doesn't really apply. Luke, I'm afraid, was always destined to burn bright and die fast. He was neither a good strategist nor planner."

With that, I had to agree. "None of which negates the fact that if the infected didn't swarm when he died, they're unlikely to do it now."

"A statement that reveals just how little you truly

understand about the virus." Though I still couldn't see him, it wasn't hard to imagine the smug, satisfied smile tugging his lips. It was evident enough in his voice. "Not all of those infected were of the insane variety."

"Which still doesn't alter the fact Luke was the only one who could control *any* of them."

"You forget there are various levels of infection. Those with the scythe marking on their cheeks would certainly have been either wiped out or reduced to mindless, inoperable flesh. But we're talking about those who retained full brain function yet remained bound to the word of the hive." He paused. "But not, of course, the ones who are infected but not connected, such as the PIT operatives."

"And how would you know PIT has infected operatives?" Jackson asked.

"Come now, don't pretend naïveté. I was Luke's trusted servant for many, *many* months. I'm well aware of his connection to his brother and the other fae."

It was a statement that made me frown. Luke had, by nature, been suspicious of *everyone*. He wouldn't have trusted such a powerful witch unless he truly believed that power was his to command—and there was only one way he'd *ever* believe that.

"You're one of the infected, aren't you?" And the fact that *this* witch would go *that* far to achieve Rinaldo's orders was chilling.

Jackson glanced at me sharply, but the only reaction from our unseen opponent was a sharpening of amusement.

"Yes, I am," Frederick replied. "And because of that,

I provide Rinaldo with the required connection to those who are like me."

Meaning this witch was like Sam—infected but not bound to the hive? But if that *was* the case, how could he be the conduit through which Rinaldo could control the cloaks? As far as I was aware, Sam had no such connection. Though, in truth, it wasn't like he'd tell me if he had. Hell, for all I knew, such a connection was the reason *why* he'd been so good at hunting down the scythe-marked cloaks.

And as much as I wanted to tell Rinaldo to prove his claim, we really couldn't risk it. There were enough infected in this city already, and we didn't even know the full extent of the spread. We dared not risk it by going any further—a fact Rinaldo was no doubt banking on.

"Let's presume you're telling the truth," Jackson said. "Why drag us out here? Why couldn't your boss have said all this when we were talking to him earlier?"

"Because he needed you to witness the results of disobedience. If he makes a threat, he will follow through."

As he spoke, there was a shift in the tension surrounding us. Something was happening out there in the shadows that hugged the century-old trees. Jackson must have felt it, too, because his inner fires flared brighter, and flames were now flickering across his torso and hands. It was tempting to reach out and help him, to dampen his heat and, at the same time, refuel my own, but I resisted. There was really only one way he would find true control, and that was through practice.

"A message we've got," I said, my voice sharp. "So what else does he want?"

Because it was hardly likely he'd dragged us into the city merely to emphasize his desire for the satchel notes.

"What he needs," Frederick said, "is for you to go into Brooklyn and retrieve some information left there."

"What sort of information?" Jackson asked.

"Research matter, of course."

If there *was* research in Brooklyn, it could have only one source—the two missing scientists. And I really, *really*, hoped that Rinaldo wasn't now in control of the pair of them. "Even if we can retrieve the material, what good will it do you? I'm betting neither you nor Rinaldo will be able to understand it."

"We have no need to when we control the two men who have been working on finding a cure—or at least a vaccine—for this virus from the beginning."

So much for hope. And while I had no idea why Luke had wanted Baltimore and Wilson, given he'd been intent on infecting the world rather than providing a cure, when it came to Rinaldo . . . I shivered. His intentions were undoubtedly very similar, but he was a far bigger threat than Luke would ever have been. Rinaldo was a calm, cool killer—the type who acted only after plenty of planning and forethought. Luke had a habit of lashing out when angry, and that, in many ways, had led to his downfall. We would not have that sort of break with Rinaldo.

"If you have the scientists, you don't need anything else," Jackson said, then silently added, *And I don't believe the bastard has them. I think it's a bluff.*

Possibly, but it's not a bluff we can call, I said. *If he has got them, how did he get them out of Brooklyn? The army and PIT were monitoring all the exits, both before and after the dry moat was created around it.*

Meaning maybe the research matter he wants isn't the notes, but the scientists themselves.

I doubt it. Even if they are there, Rinaldo knows PIT is monitoring our movements. He wouldn't risk the scientists being taken from us.

"If we wish to start at the beginning yet again," Frederick was saying, "that would of course be true. But we don't, and until both the satchel notes and the notes De Luca hid are found, we require what was left in Brooklyn."

"So order the damn cloaks in to get them," I said.

"We would if we could, but things are not that simple. Besides, you forget that PIT has the entire area cordoned off."

"As have you," I said. "Or is that fiery, magic-enhanced wall that covers part of Brooklyn not yours?"

"That dome was created to keep the information secure until retrieval arrangements could be made."

There was an odd edge to his voice that had me frowning. "You could have used a shield to hide your presence and walked in, so why didn't you?"

"Because it didn't suit us to."

Which meant there was something else going on—something he wasn't about to tell us. Air brushed past my neck, its touch cold and filled with threat. I briefly studied the shadows clinging to the trunks of the old trees, but I still couldn't see anything.

I flexed my fingers. It was tempting, so damn tempting, to send a river of fire through those shadows and reveal whatever might be hiding there. It was even more tempting to smite Frederick's shield with both flame *and* the mother's energy, but a full assault on his barrier would not only drain me, but leave me vulnerable to whatever—whoever—was waiting out there in the darkness.

Something he was probably hoping for.

"I get why you're using us to get into Brooklyn," I said, "but since you've spent a great deal of time boasting what great strategists you and Rinaldo are, why haven't you already got a line on the location of De Luca's notes?"

"Because he was canny, and because Rinaldo couldn't read him."

Meaning Rinaldo *wasn't* all-powerful; he still had his restrictions, and that at least meant we had some hope of beating the bastard.

"The notes we left at our office weren't De Luca's," I said.

"No, but they're a good start," the witch said. "You have twenty-four hours to get into Brooklyn and get the research matter left there. We also wish to receive the satchel notes within that time frame. If you don't succeed . . ."

He didn't finish, but then, he didn't need to. "Fine," I ground out. "When and where do we meet again?"

"Your office will do. Call first—and *don't* inform anyone else."

He'd barely finished speaking when something sharp hit my neck. I swept a hand up and pulled something thin and metallic from my skin even as Jackson jerked violently, then said, "A dart? What the fuck?"

"I believe you're already familiar with the N41A drug,"

Frederick continued blithely. His voice was farther away. The bastard was leaving us. "It will achieve what my spell failed to. Don't follow me, don't use fire on me, and both of you stay where you are until I've left the area."

Jackson tried to take a step, and failed. He swore and raised a hand, but his fire did little more than splutter across his fingertips. It certainly *didn't* chase after Frederick, as he'd no doubt intended. N41A was the fast-acting drug used by PIT to restrict those with talents such as telekinesis and pyrokinesis. Sam had used it on us both when he'd dragged us down to PIT's headquarters for questioning. And it had certainly worked—up to a point, anyway. It *did* restrict my flames, but only because I'd been so low in energy that I hadn't dared risk returning to my natural fire form. Though I'd never actually witnessed an occurrence, I'd certainly heard enough tales of phoenixes' lives being snuffed out simply because they'd risked such a shift.

That *wasn't* the case now. I might be bone tired, but that wasn't exhaustion. I flamed, becoming spirit rather than flesh, and instantly burned the drug from my system.

Jackson had grabbed the gun from his belt and was now firing in Frederick's direction. The bullets pinged off the dome, protecting him in much the same manner as the flames had earlier.

Jackson cursed and shoved the gun back into its holster. "Go get the bastard for me. I'll head back to the—" He broke the sentence off and frowned.

I instantly regained human form. "What?"

He hesitated, then waved a hand. "It's probably nothing. Go, before the bastard gets away."

I shifted back to spirit form and raced after Frederick, moving so fast, flames trailed behind me like a comet's tail. But the night around me was gaining form and coming to life.

That presence I'd felt—the presence that had felt so wrong—was red cloaks. They surged out of the shadows, a howling mass of putrid, rotting flesh and hair. Some of them came at me—dove *through* me—and ran on, not seeming to care, their skin and hair and clothes on fire.

They weren't after me. They were after Frederick.

There was a squeak of surprise from up ahead; then magic surged. An instant later, a howling wind hit us. It battered my flames, forcing me to slow, and sent the cloaks tumbling. Bits of flesh and blood and god knows what else went flying, and I realized then that they didn't just smell rotten, they *were* rotting.

The wind got stronger, slowing me even further, until it felt like I was battering up against a solid but invisible wall. I swore and gave up the fight. I couldn't feel Frederick's presence anyway, even if the force of his magic continued to whip us. That he could do so from such a distance and on the run only emphasized his strength.

The cloaks were having no more luck against the wind than I was, but they nevertheless kept trying. Maybe they had no other option. Maybe Luke's very last order had been one aimed at his so-called trusted lieutenant—and if that *was* the case, then maybe Rinaldo's boast of controlling the cloaks was little more than hot air.

I called to the mother again. Her energy surged through me as sweetly as a kiss, then fanned outward, seeming to know what I wanted. As fingers of multicol-

ored flame wrapped around each of the cloaks and incinerated them, a weaker source of fire washed across
my senses.

I spun around. Jackson was running, at least a dozen
cloaks on his tail. I swore again and sent the mother's
fire racing forward even as I followed her. As the cinders of the cloaks began to rain across the ground,
Jackson spun around and pointed to the Nicholson
Street side of the Royal Exhibition Building. "There're
other people in the park," he said, shouting against the
howling wind. "They're also under attack."

I altered direction and raced past the old fountain.
The wind abruptly fell silent, and screams filled the
void. As I neared the corner, I shifted back to human
form. No matter how much I wanted to help whoever
was being attacked, I wasn't about to out myself. Far
too many people already knew about my existence—
any more, and we'd have to leave. I wasn't ready to say
good-bye to Melbourne just yet.

Around the corner, I discovered chaos.

There were a dozen red cloaks and five humans—
three men and two women. Two of the men and one of
the women were already down, their clothes torn and
bodies bloodied. Several red cloaks knelt beside each of
them, but they weren't feeding. They were dragging
their claws deep into their skin, cutting them open. Infecting them.

A shudder that was part fury, part horror, went
through me, and fire exploded from my body—fire that
was both mine *and* the mother's. Flaming arrows that
burned with all the colors of creation hit each of the
cloaks, and as their ashes rained across the pavement,

the remaining woman dropped to her knees and started crying. Her companion knelt beside her and placed an arm around her shoulders, but his gaze sought mine.

"I don't know how you did that," he said, his voice hoarse with pain, "but thank you."

There were scratches on his face and arms, and bites down his legs. The woman he was comforting bore similar wounds. But they were both far better off than the three motionless figures beyond them, one of whom was little more than raw, bloody meat.

I shuddered again and dragged my attention back to the kneeling couple. "I'm afraid the danger isn't over yet—there're more vampires in the park."

As if to emphasize my words, the sounds of snarling, of flesh smacking flesh, broke the sharp silence. Concern shot through me; Jackson, more than anyone, knew the danger of engaging in hand-to-hand battle with the cloaks, so why the hell was he doing so? The urge to go help him surged, but I resisted. I had to ensure these people were safe first.

The man's gaze jumped past me, his expression a mix of pain, fear, and determination. "Then we'd better run—"

"No," I cut in. PIT would be less than impressed if I allowed freshly infected people to go wandering off. "They've got the park ringed. You both need to shelter in the doorway over there."

"But if they hit us there, we'll be trapped," the man said, eyeing the huge archway dubiously.

"No, because I'll block it off with a wall of fire they won't get through."

The fear in his expression grew stronger, and this time it was aimed at me. "What are you?"

"Fire witch," I said shortly. "Now go. And no matter what happens, don't move from that doorway until I come to get you."

He hesitated, his gaze briefly sweeping me. Then he nodded. "We won't."

As the two of them rose and staggered over to the doorway, I quickly checked the other three. One was dead, but the other two were still alive. For how much longer was anyone's guess, because there was an awful lot of blood on the ground surrounding them . . .

I dragged my gaze away. The couple had reached the arched doorway, so I called to the mother again and raised the promised barrier. Pain immediately lanced through my brain, and for several seconds, the world faded in and out of existence. It was a very clear warning I was being drained to the point of exhaustion.

But until we were safe, until the cloaks were dealt with, I had no other option but to continue.

I bolted back to help Jackson. As I rounded the corner, I saw him, unhurt and standing. He was holding a silver knife in each hand that gleamed with an almost unearthly fire, and there were three bodies at his feet. Six others prowled around him rather than attacking en masse, which didn't really make sense given they still had the weight of numbers on their side . . . The thought trailed off as my gaze rested on the scythe-free face of one of his opponents.

I'd seen him before.

These men weren't cloaks. They were vampires.

But not any old vampires; these nine were from De

Luca's den, and they had sworn to kill us in revenge for their maker's death. Obviously, our statement that we couldn't actually claim that scalp hadn't yet sunk into their thick skulls.

One of them spotted me and roared an order to attack. I unleashed more of the mother's fire, and pain hit so hard that I stumbled and fell, sliding for several feet on hands and knees, skinning both before I came to a halt. I didn't move; I couldn't move. I just sucked in air, my whole body shaking with the force of it, fighting the cold lethargy assailing me, fighting the pain and the need to give in, to let go. To heed the siren call of the mother's energy and become one with her.

True death lay that way, and it was one from which there would be no coming back.

Maybe one day I'd be so tired and worn by this world and the constant lifetimes of heartbreak that I would answer that call and fade away, but I wasn't anywhere near that point just yet.

Besides, I needed to get back to Rory. Needed to be there for him.

A scuff of movement caught my attention, and I looked up. There was sweat in my eyes, and my vision was swimming in and out of focus, but the figure that approached was familiar enough—Jackson, not the vampires. Not the cloaks. Which was just as well; I had very little fire left and certainly couldn't have even held a damn gun right then, let alone used it.

He dropped down beside me, and it was all I could do not to reach out, to grab all the fire that had been leashed within him by the drug, and draw it into my body.

"But that's exactly what you need to do," he said,

placing one hand over mine. "You're close to the edge of fading. Hell, you *are* fading. You need fire, Em, and right now, I'm your only source."

I didn't move; didn't take. But his fingers were molten against the ice of mine, and they felt so damn good . . .

I licked my dry lips and somehow said, "I could kill you."

"I'll stop you before it ever gets that far."

No, he wouldn't. He couldn't. Not if I got lost in the rapture of feeding, and that was a distinct possibility when I was so close to the edge.

"We can't. Not here. Too dangerous."

"The cloaks are gone, the vampires are either unconscious or dead, and there's no one else around other than the people you saved. You have to do this, Em. Trust me. Please."

There was a hint of desperation in his voice, and that, more than anything, smashed through my reluctance. I had to be closer to fading than I realized if he was *that* worried.

"Fine." I entwined my fingers in his—an action that left my whole body shaking. I was close, so damn close. I clenched his fingers tighter, feeling the pulse of his heat and life against my skin, so warm and tempting. I took a shuddery breath and somehow said, "But if I start draining too much from you, hit me."

"I would never—"

I raised my gaze to his. "It'll break my concentration if I slip into a feeding rapture, and it might be your only chance of survival."

He absorbed the information with barely a flicker of emotion. "Fine. Now feed."

I closed my eyes, drew in another shuddery breath, then opened the floodgates and sucked in his fire. It was a molten river, rich with life and caring, and it washed through every part of me, chasing the ice from my veins and the weakness from my limbs. And oh, it felt good—so, *so* good—that rapture loomed altogether too fast. But as I reached the point of no return, something within me said, *Enough.* With a grunt of effort, I loosened my grip on his hand and thrust myself away from him. For several minutes, I didn't move. I simply lay on the ground, staring up at the night sky as I gulped in air and fought the need to reach out and finish what I'd started.

"That," Jackson said, his voice soft and edged with an oddly husky note, "was totally *not* what I'd been expecting."

I looked at him. His eyes burned with desire, and he was practically radiating lust.

I blinked, caught between surprise and amusement. "You got off on *that*?"

"My god, you have no idea how much." He shook his head, disbelief evident. "It felt as if I were communing with my element, drawing in a sense of strength and belonging. It felt *amazing*."

Meaning it was just as well I'd maintained enough control to break the connection, because he might not have. But his words also had alarm bells ringing. Grace—the witch who'd given us the necklaces that had protected us against Frederick's magic—had said that Jackson's fate was now tied up with mine. I'd thought she meant it was our partnership and this case that tied our destinies together, but maybe not. Maybe she'd meant that by allowing him to merge with my spirit form, I'd become as essential to his existence as communing with his element.

And that, if true, was a consequence I wasn't sure either of us was prepared for.

"Maybe not," Jackson said, "but as you're inclined to remind me, it's a better option than being dead. Besides, it means I now have a whole new and very exciting means of enjoying your lusciousness."

I laughed. "Trust you to put a sexual spin on it."

"Something I can hardly help given that's how the experience panned out for me." He pushed upright, walked over, and offered me a hand. "Feel free to ask for a feed anytime you feel the need."

I clasped his hand and allowed him to haul me upright. "You might have gotten your rocks off, but it really *is* a dangerous thing for me to do. I have killed people that way in the past."

I might have done so under attack, as a last-ditch effort to save myself, but that was beside the point. I'd drained life from people before, and I'd undoubtedly do it again, especially if my reserves got too low and the rapture too great to ignore.

"It was fierce enough this time—I know, because I felt it." He brushed a sweaty strand of hair from my eyes, his touch gentle. "But you didn't. Maybe this connection between us means you can't. Maybe in sharing your life force you really *have* made me something more than a dark fae, but something less than a phoenix."

"That's a whole lot of maybes." And far too many to contemplate now—not when there was still so much to do, and people to save. I stepped away from his touch. "We need to call PIT and get some of their medics here."

"The inspector is not going to be happy to learn the cloaks remain a threat." He pulled his phone out of his pocket. "Especially if Rinaldo really *is* in control of them."

"I don't think he is. Or, at least, he wasn't in charge of this lot. They were chasing *after* Frederick, and Rinaldo certainly wouldn't have ordered that. I think the attack on us was an afterthought."

Jackson snorted. "If that's true, how the hell did they get out of Brooklyn? We destroyed all their exit points, remember."

"Brooklyn might have been Luke's main base, but he had at least one pocket of cloaks stashed in a sewer junction under the city, remember." A fact we'd become aware of when we were hunting for Grace's missing coven friends. We'd not only found them far too late to save their lives, but had almost fallen afoul of the trap Luke and his not-so-tame witch had waiting for us there. "And if he'd had one such bolt-hole, what's to say there aren't more?"

"The fact that he would have had to find an inconspicuous way of feeding them." Jackson brought up the inspector's number, then hit the CALL button. "There were a hell of a lot of bones and bodies in that sewer tunnel, remember. He couldn't feed multiple locations without someone realizing the neighborhood was missing not only all of its animal life, but many of its homeless, too."

I didn't reply as he began speaking to the inspector. Instead, I turned and made my way back to the people

I'd saved. The wall of fire I'd created would have disappeared the minute my strength failed, but the couple I'd rescued was still there, crouched down in the shadows of the large old doors. Relief crossed both their faces when they saw me. The man rose, one hand tucked under his companion's elbow to help her up. "It is done? Are we safe?"

I nodded. "We've called in medics. They'll be here in—" I hesitated and glanced at Jackson. Though he wasn't looking at me, he nevertheless held up a hand, fingers spread. "Five minutes."

Which was damn fast. But maybe the inspector had ordered units on standby, just in case we needed help. And she'd undoubtedly want to contain this situation as fast as possible.

"Are our friends . . . ?" The woman's voice trailed off.

I glanced over at them. That pool of blood was even bigger than before, but at least one of them still appeared to be breathing.

"I'm a doctor," the man said. "I might be able to help them."

I hesitated, and then nodded. In truth, there was nothing he could do to save them now, even if he did manage to keep them alive. The cloaks that had infected them were the mad kind, and that meant that, whether they lived or died, the three would become one of them. Death of the victim didn't stop the progress of the virus, because the virus had been born out of experiments to uncover what made vampires all but immortal. They might not have uncovered *that*, but they'd obviously come close enough since the Crimson

Death virus turned its victims in much the same manner as sharing the blood of a master vampire made mortals turn into vampires upon death.

But that was news PIT could break to them.

I stood beside the woman, comforting her as best I could as the doctor did his utmost to save his remaining companion.

PIT operatives appeared a few minutes later. One of them—a tall, slightly chubby-looking man with dark hair—approached me, and recognition stirred. He'd been one of the two men the inspector had sent to collect Jackson's blood sample.

"Brad Harvey," he said, saving me the embarrassment of not remembering his name. "Nice to see you again, Ms. Pearson. Shame it couldn't be under better circumstances."

"Yes." I hesitated. "Has the inspector told you what happened?"

His gaze swept the young woman I was half supporting. "She did indeed. The threat has been neutralized?"

"For the moment."

His gaze sharpened abruptly. "Meaning?"

"Simply that this situation may be a taste of what is to come."

He relaxed a little. "Let's worry about that when it happens. Now, young lady," he added, returning his attention to the other woman, "why don't you come with me? We've a medical unit approaching right now."

As he spoke, the wail of approaching sirens cut across the night. He took the woman's arm and led her gently—but firmly—away.

Another agent approached. "The inspector asked me to remind you about the meeting this evening."

I nodded. "Are we free to go?"

"Yes—as soon as you make your report. A verbal one will do—I'll relay the information back to base, where it'll be written up."

Which was an interesting way to do things, but at least it saved us the hassle of paperwork. I gave him a quick summary of everything that had happened, including both the attack and our meeting with Frederick. Rinaldo might not be pleased, but PIT needed to know the scientists might not only be out of Brooklyn, but in his hands. Once I finished, the agent nodded and said, "Thanks. You can go now."

I stepped away, then hesitated and half turned around. "What's going to happen to these people now?"

I knew what would happen, but I guess part of me was hoping I was wrong, that PIT would simply hold them somewhere in the hope that a cure could be found.

The agent shrugged. "It depends on what happens when they go through the change."

"And if they're not the sane ones?"

"Then we do what must be done." His soft voice held little in the way of emotion, but I guess that was to be expected since he'd probably dealt with this sort of situation many times over. "When you are fighting a war, there will always be civilian casualties. It can't be helped, no matter what we might otherwise wish."

It wasn't a war yet, I wanted to say, but the truth was, we were certainly on the brink of one. Because if this virus got out of control, then it would be as much a battle for supremacy and survival as any of the world wars.

I nodded and walked away. Jackson was standing guard over two of De Luca's get. Both had been stripped, gagged, and roughly bound with their own clothes. They were also furious, if their attempts to get free and their muffled curses were anything to go by. Jackson stepped back as one jackknifed toward him; then he calmly placed a boot on the side of the vampire's head and held him still.

"Where are the others?" I asked, looking around.

"You cindered five, and the remaining three have been hauled off by PIT. They're coming back for these two."

As he spoke, two men appeared out of the shadows. They gave Jackson a nod of thanks, hauled the vampires upright, and marched them out of the gardens.

"And we," Jackson said, tucking my arm through his, "can now go."

"Good, because I seriously need to sleep right now."

"You're not the only one," he replied heavily.

It was a silent drive home. We stopped briefly at McDonald's in Seymour to move the van and drop off the phone PIT had given us, then continued on. Dawn was beginning to unfurl pink and gold fingers across the night sky by the time we reached the cabin. I bounded up the steps with more energy than I really had and quickly unlocked the door. Rory didn't look up or greet me, but only because he was still fast asleep by the fire. But he must have been awake sometime during the night, because there were protein bar wrappers scattered around him.

The relief that hit me was so fierce that my knees threatened to give way. Jackson stopped behind me and lightly touched my elbow, providing support. "You're letting all the heat out, you know. And while I happen to think that wouldn't be a bad thing given this place feels like a sauna, I'm thinking it's deliberate."

"You're right—it is." I forced my tired legs into action and walked over to Rory. He must have felt my presence, because he muttered something and reached for me. I caught his hand and let his fingers wrap around mine. I felt the urgency to connect, to renew, jump from his flesh to mine.

"How is he?" Jackson headed for the bathroom, stripping off as he did.

"On the road to recovery." And already feeling much stronger. "You can take the bed if you'd like. I'll lie here next to Rory and the fire."

"I'll grab a shower first." He hesitated, a grin flashing. "And I'd better make it a very cold one, since the prospect of loving is very far away on the horizon for me right now."

Meaning, I suspected, he'd sensed Rory's need for me. It made me again wonder just what exactly I'd done when we'd briefly become one.

Once he'd stepped inside the bathroom and closed the door, I quickly stripped off and lay down beside Rory. He stirred slightly and wrapped an arm around me, pressing me closer still, so that my breasts were squashed against his chest and his body was firm and hot against mine. Desire stirred, but it was a languid thing. This was more about reaffirming *us* than anything else.

"Need," he murmured. "Flame."

I called to my fire but kept it under a tight leash of control. While we had a fully fireproofed room in our apartment for moments such as this, the cabin was all wood. If I wasn't very careful, the whole place would ignite.

Rory threw his head back, a gasp of enjoyment escaping his lips. Then he, too, became flame, and the threads of our beings began to dance around each other, gently at first but growing ever more urgent, until there was no him, no me, just one being with two separate souls. But this first joining after a rebirth wasn't about desire, even if that would always be present. It was a reconnection of both fire *and* flesh, and it was the flesh we now had to seek.

As we both shifted shape, his hand followed the line of my waist and hip, then gently caught my thigh and tugged it over his.

"May the gods be witness to our joining," he murmured, and thrust inside me.

"And may fate be kind to us both," I continued, as ever struggling to ignore the glory of his thrust and the need to move, to take the completion my body was beginning to crave. The ritual had to be completed before enjoyment could be had. "And allow us to continue our journey through the decades together."

"As one," he finished, his thrusts increasing in tempo.

"As one," I echoed, and fell into bliss.

The sound of a door slamming shut had me jerking awake. I twisted around, my heart beating somewhere in the middle of my throat and flames shimmering across my fingertips.

"Sorry," Jackson said, his wide grin suggesting he

wasn't at all. "I needed pizza, and you need to get your lazy but rather delightful ass up and ready."

"Ready?" I stretched to ease some of the kinks out of my body. Sleeping on the floor was all well and good for youngsters, but I'd grown used to comfort.

"Soft is what you are," Rory murmured. "And did someone mention pizza?"

"That would be me," Jackson said. "Do you want it served, or are you feeling strong enough to join us at the table?"

"I'll attempt the latter." He paused and lightly slapped my rump. "If a certain redhead would move her lovely but lazy ass."

I snorted, rolled to my feet, and walked over to my bag. "I'm going to have a shower. I'll leave you two to catch up—but leave me some pizza, or there will be hell to pay."

"Bossy, isn't she?" Jackson commented.

"If you didn't realize that by the time you invited her to become a partner in your business, you've only yourself to blame," Rory commented.

I closed the door on their banter and stepped under the shower, letting it run for a very long time over my skin in an effort to wash away all the terror, fury, and helplessness of the last few days.

By the time I'd finished and had gotten dressed, a good half hour had passed.

"I was beginning to think you'd fallen down the plughole," Jackson commented.

"Part of me wished I could." I glanced at Rory. He was looking a whole lot stronger, even if tiredness was still evident in the way he was holding himself. "Did Jackson update you on last night's events?"

"He did. I can't say I'm all that happy about the two of you venturing into Brooklyn alone."

"We won't be alone," Jackson said before I could. "You can bet PIT operatives will be along for the ride."

He rose and walked across to the microwave, hitting the REHEAT button before moving across to the kettle. A few minutes later, he placed a plate of pizza and a large mug of green tea in front of me and then sat back down.

"I think I love you." I picked up the nearest slice of pizza and bit into it. And almost groaned in delight. Damn, it was *good*.

"Which would be a shameful waste of your emotions," Jackson said, amusement dancing about his lips.

I waved a hand. "Consider yourself appreciated, then."

"I'd appreciate your appreciation in a more . . . tactile form," he replied, his amusement growing.

"Please," Rory said, "flirt on your own time. We have a serious discussion happening here, remember?"

I wrinkled my nose at him and picked up another slice of pizza. "Considering we have no idea what the cloaks might be doing in Brooklyn, do you really think PIT will risk sending people in with us?"

Especially when they were already stretched to the breaking point?

"I don't think the inspector will have any other option," Jackson said. "The government will want answers after the events there, and they'll probably force military expertise on her."

"But PIT, not the military, has governance over matters that deal with nonhumans."

"Yes, but we're dealing with a virus that has the potential to become a plague if not contained," Jackson said. "The government will undoubtedly want to ensure it doesn't move beyond Brooklyn."

"And yet by sending in the military, they're risking the exact opposite."

"You'd have to presume they'll be given orders to shoot the shit out of anything that moves."

If that was the case, then it was just as well most of the criminal element as well as the homeless who had once called that place home had abandoned it long ago—or those who weren't already infected had, anyway.

"The inspector didn't mention the military when I spoke to her."

"Why would she?" Jackson asked. "We're only associates."

"I know but—" I paused and shrugged. The reality was they could call in whomever they liked, and there wasn't a damn thing we could do about it—even if we did think it was the stupidest idea ever.

Rory yawned hugely, then waved a hand in apology. "Sorry, it's not the company . . . although the circular conversation is getting a little tiresome."

I flicked the crusty edge of pizza at him. He batted it sideways, and it hit Jackson bang on the nose. "Charming." He picked up the offending bit of crust and put it on his plate. "We'll have to move soon if we want to arrive on time."

My amusement faded as my gaze went to Rory. "Do you need anything before we leave?"

"Other than sleep, and for you to return safely? No."

"And why am I not included in that wish for a safe return?" Jackson's offended expression was somewhat offset by the amusement in his eyes.

Rory leaned across the table and patted his hand comfortingly. "When you become essential to my existence, you will."

"That may yet be a possibility, you know." Jackson rose and glanced my way. "I'll meet you out in the car."

He grabbed his coat and headed out. Rory raised his eyebrows. "What did he mean by that?"

"Long story, but it seems you were right when you said that in merging spirits, I might have made him more one of us than a dark fae." I hesitated and half shrugged. "It's very possible that his life force is somehow linked to mine. And if that's the case, then he's also linked to you."

"Just as well I like the bastard, then." He touched my cheek lightly. "Don't worry about it. And be careful out there."

"And you be careful here." I rose, dropped a kiss on the top of his head, and followed Jackson outside.

It took us close to eighty minutes to get to Brooklyn. Two police officers waved us down as we approached the one remaining road in and out of the area. We showed them our PIT IDs, and after they'd spoken to someone via their com units, we were allowed to continue. Half a dozen black vehicles, which seemed to be the color of choice for PIT, lined one side of the blocked and guarded entrance. Jackson parked beside the last in the line, and we both climbed out.

A gray-suited woman with amber-flecked brown hair and a hawklike nose walked over to us. "The inspector is waiting for you. Please, follow me."

I flexed my hands in an effort to release some of the tension, but it didn't really help. Every time I'd entered

Brooklyn, something had gone drastically wrong. I couldn't help the feeling that this time would be no different.

The difference this time, Jackson said, *is that Luke is dead.*

That might be true, but it doesn't mean the danger has lessened any.

If Rinaldo and Frederick are in charge of at least some of the cloaks, Jackson continued, *they'd surely restrain any attack on us. They haven't yet got what they want, remember.*

I guess it all depends on whether Rinaldo believes we need another lesson in obedience.

True. Jackson's mental tones were grim. *He does seem the type.*

That type being psychopathic?

He certainly fits the classic model of a psychopath.

He did. But he was also an old vampire and, as vampires aged, they tended to lose their more "human" emotions. Which basically meant we were dealing with one twisted and very dangerous individual.

Lucky us.

The inspector was talking on the phone as we arrived, so the gray-suited woman motioned us to wait and then walked away.

My gaze drifted past the inspector to a man standing several yards to her right, and something within me stilled.

Because that man was Sam.

CHAPTER 4

"What are you doing here?"

The question came out before I could stop it. An all-too-brief smile touched his mouth and creased the corners of his vivid blue eyes, and my stupid heart did its usual little dance.

"It's nice to see you again, too." His voice was cool rather than cold; reserved, but not unwelcoming. Both of which were a definite improvement from how he'd talked to me when I'd first stepped back into his life.

"No, I mean—" I stopped briefly, my gaze sweeping his length. The moon's pale gleam lent his short, close-cropped black hair a bluish shine, and somehow emphasized the leanness of his athletic frame. There was little evidence of the wounds that had almost taken his life—although given he was fully clothed and wearing a bulletproof vest, that was hardly surprising. "The last time I saw you, your chest had been ripped open by the skin runes."

"The knife you used to kill them didn't exactly help, either, even if it *did* save my life." There was the faintest hint of amusement in his expression, but this faded as his gaze moved past me, and he added, "Miller."

"Turner," Jackson replied, in the same remote tone.

That the two men didn't like each other would have

been obvious to even the densest person, but it stemmed more from one being a cop and the other a PI than from any hatred on a personal level. Although Sam's riding roughshod over our investigations—to the extent that he'd drugged us to force obedience—certainly *hadn't* helped matters.

The inspector ended her phone call and turned toward us. She was a tall, stout woman with thick black glasses and a stern, unforgiving expression. She was also a shifter of some kind, possibly a panther, if the luxurious gleam of her dark hair and the almost feline way she moved were anything to go by. I belatedly realized that this would explain her rather glib comment earlier about Rinaldo tugging the panther's tail.

"I'm afraid the situation in Brooklyn has become somewhat more . . . difficult," she said.

I crossed my arms and tried to ignore the chill that ran down my spine. "In what way?"

"Military specialists have been called in."

Her expression gave little away, but it was pretty obvious she was less than happy about this development—and that she was complying with it only because she had very little choice in the matter.

"What kind of specialists?" Jackson asked.

"Ones used to dealing with paranormal threats on a scale such as this. Sam, however, is still in charge of the main operation, as he knows Brooklyn better than most."

That was because he'd spent well over a year hunting in the place, killing as many of the cloaks as he could while endeavoring to find Luke. But in the end, it had been Sam who'd been hunted down and captured, and neither of us had been able to fulfill our vows to kill his brother. That honor had gone to whoever had been behind the long-range rifle that had blown his head apart.

And, for the first time, it made me wonder what information he might have given us. Was it just the location of the scientists the shooter had been trying to keep secret, or was there more?

"Knowing the area probably won't help him get into the protected zone." Thankfully, the tension and fear stirring inside me weren't evident in my voice. "In fact, it's possible even *I* won't be able to get in."

Which was an unlikely event, considering Rinaldo wanted us to retrieve whatever research materials might have been left behind.

"We're aware of that," the inspector said. "We still have to try."

I like the use of the royal "we" in that sentence. Jackson's mental tone was wry. *It's not like the inspector is actually going in herself.*

I think she would if she thought she'd be of any use. The inspector might be a desk jockey now, but I suspected she'd been a very active—and successful—field agent in her younger years. She just had that air about her. "Is the military fully aware of what we might be confronted with in there?"

"Yes." Her tone was clipped. "They know a dangerous virus is being contained within the area and that we are seeking two missing scientists."

Which was the truth as far as it went, but not the entire story. But I could certainly understand the inspector—and the government itself—withholding information. News of an uncontrolled virus outbreak would cause problems aplenty if it became mainstream news, but if anyone *ever* got wind of just how bad this particular virus was, there'd be widespread panic.

"What about the cloaks?" Jackson said.

"Any that appear will be shot on sight. The military have been kitted out in full Kevlar gear, as will you two." She frowned. "We've been monitoring the entire area for the last three days, though, and there has been absolutely no movement—either aboveground or below. It makes me wonder if the cloaks are still there."

"All their exits were destroyed," Jackson said. "Where else could they be?"

"That is a question you will undoubtedly be able to answer once you get in and discover what, exactly, is going on behind that shield of magic and fire."

I, for one, would be happy *not* to get an answer. I was really over being attacked by all and sundry. "What have you told the military about us?"

A slight smile touched her lips. "That you're a powerful fire witch, Jackson is a fire fae, and you're both consultants for PIT."

It was a plausible enough story—especially given the number of people who seemed to believe that was exactly what I was—and it was one that would offer me some protection from questions should I need to either call the mother or use fire.

"The military are currently sweeping the fire-free sections of Brooklyn; they have orders to erase any cloaks they happen upon," she continued. "Your task is, as I've already said, to uncover what is going on in that no-go zone."

"Dead easy." Jackson's tone was dry. "So why are we still standing here?"

Amusement lurked around the corners of the inspector's mouth. She made a motion with her hand and, in a matter of minutes, we were wearing Kevlar vests and were fully kitted up with weapons, com units, and cameras.

"I know none of you actually need any of this, but it would raise awkward questions if you and the military were not similarly kitted out."

"Has the military struck any problems or been attacked yet?"

"No. The place is as silent as a grave."

All sorts of warnings went off in my mind. Every time I'd gone into Brooklyn, I'd been attacked. And while Rinaldo might now claim to rule them all, something within me doubted it—especially given the demonstration in the gardens.

"Meaning," Sam said, "we need to get in there before the hornets' nest *is* stirred up."

He spun and led the way across the remaining access road. Silence immediately closed in around us, and the acrid scent of smoke and decay began to fill every breath. Underneath those foul scents ran the biting edge of magic.

But there *was* something else here, something that had the hairs along the back of my neck rising. It was the sense of expectation. I really *didn't* want to discover who or what it was coming from.

I increased my pace and moved up beside Sam. "This might well be a trap."

He glanced at me briefly, his expression giving little away. "I don't think there's any 'might' about it."

"I doubt it's the cloaks waiting for us," Jackson said. "Regular fire *does* kill them, even if it takes a little longer. Surely not even *they* are stupid enough to stand immobile while their flesh burns."

"It probably depends on what—if any—orders Luke gave them before he died." There was just the slightest edge to Sam's tone, one that spoke of sorrow and regret. He might have wanted Luke dead, but, in the end, they'd been brothers, and some part of him still mourned the loss. "And remember, the cloaks with the scythe don't appear to be capable of autonomous thought, so if there *were* no orders, they might well be immobilized."

"Given what happened in the Carlton Gardens—" Jackson paused. "You were advised of that, weren't you?"

A slight smile touched Sam's lips. "I'm still lead investigator, so yes, I was."

"Just why *are* you still lead investigator?" I asked. "You should by all rights still be in the hospital. Those runes did a hell of a lot of damage."

His gaze came to mine. Something dark and dangerous flared in his eyes, but it was anger and frustration—maybe even regret—that stung the air. "Had I still been human, I undoubtedly would be."

Meaning the virus had gifted him with fast healing. I guess that, at least, was something good to have come from the infection, even if it was outweighed by all the bad.

I pulled my gaze away from his and skimmed the lonely street. The buildings seemed more decayed than ever before. Wind keened through shattered windows and rattled loose roof sheeting and broken doors, but nothing else stirred in this place. Nothing other than the ever-present plastic bags that pirouetted down the street, anyway. The only real difference this time to all the other times I'd walked into this place was the soot that fell like black snow all around us, and the orange glow of the fire that was somehow contained within one area. That area might be protected by Frederick's magic, but why, if there were items within the barrier that Rinaldo wanted, would they contain rather than erase the inferno? It made no sense.

The closer we got to that area, the more unpleasant the sting of magic became, though it didn't in any way feel threatening. I guess that was no surprise given Rinaldo wanted us in there to retrieve shit for him.

We passed the intersection where our final battle with Luke had begun. Blood still stained the road—blood that had not come only from Luke but from Sam, the cloaks, and even me—but little remained of the buildings that had lined the intersection. What Jackson and I hadn't blown to smithereens, fire had apparently finished.

But those fires were long gone. There wasn't even any heat left in the few bits of blackened, burned wood that remained.

The night began to take on a deeper orange glow, but there were no plumes of smoke rising to blot out the stars, and the air was filled with not only the stink of death and decay, but also magic. It felt like thousands of tiny gnats were tearing at my skin, and it was a goddamn wonder blood wasn't being drawn.

We turned down another street. At the far end was an almost sheer wall of concrete and metal, and recognition stirred. I'd been here before. My gaze darted to the side street on the right just before the barrier—that was where I'd first confronted Luke. Though he'd been protected from my flames by a barrier of magic, it hadn't saved him from bullets. Rory's shot, however, had only winged him. The bastard had fled into a nearby building, which I'd subsequently brought down on top of him, but he'd escaped that, too. At least Death had eventually caught up with him; now we just had to pray she caught up with Rinaldo and his witch.

I'm thinking Rinaldo is far cannier than Luke ever was.

Undoubtedly. But he will make a mistake eventually.

Then let's hope we're around to both see and capitalize on it.

A smile touched my lips but faded quickly as we walked into the side street and stopped. The fire was now a sheer wall of dancing, orange-yellow flames that rose high above us, and yet the heat that rolled across my skin held none of the fierceness it should have. In fact, the only thing that seared was the closeness of the magic that was somehow containing it.

I rubbed my arms and eyed the street warily. It wasn't very long, and was dominated by the huge pile of rubble that had once been a building. My gaze swept across the destruction, and I wondered again how the hell Luke had survived. He really shouldn't have—though I guess in the end the "how" didn't matter; he was dead, and we were now battling the people who'd stepped into his place.

The fire I couldn't really feel ran across the top of that huge mound of brick, metal, and god knows what else. If we wanted to progress into the fire zone, we'd have to climb up it . . . The thought stalled as my gaze went to the building that ran the length of the street on the opposite side of all the rubble. It was a three-story brick building that had obviously once been a warehouse of some kind. Though the far end of it disappeared into the fire zone, the bricks nearest the barrier weren't holding any heat, and neither the wall nor the roof showed any signs of recent damage, suggesting there was a chance the section we *couldn't* see was also whole. There were two roller-door entrances in the visible portion that were blocked by bricks and metal, and all the windows were protected by heavy-duty mesh. While we had neither the time nor the manpower to remove the debris, the mesh had little chance of standing up to the heat of a phoenix.

Rinaldo might want us to take the obvious entrance, but maybe it'd be better to take a different route. Neither he nor his witch wanted to go into this place, and that suggested there was something wrong here— something they had no control over.

"According to the witches we consulted," Sam said, "there's a break in the fire at the highest point of the building rubble. They believe it's an entrance of some kind."

"And, naturally, it's an *invisible* entrance." Jackson's tone was a mix of amusement and frustration. "Because almost nothing in this goddamn investigation has gone according to plan or been easy."

Sam snorted. "And you've only been investigating it for a couple of weeks. Imagine how we feel."

"I'm thinking 'pissed off' would be putting it mildly."

"Yeah." Sam's gaze came to me. "Can you sense the break?"

"No." I hesitated and waved a hand toward the

warehouse. "What did the witches say about that building?"

He frowned. "Nothing that I'm aware of—why?"

"Because we're very obviously meant to climb that pile of shit ahead, and I'm thinking we should do the exact opposite."

Jackson frowned. "I doubt they'd leave such an obvious means of entry unprotected."

"True, but it's still a better option than climbing a debris mound that may or may not be stable." Sam motioned toward the nearest window. "Care to flex a flame muscle or two, Em?"

A smile touched my lips. "It would be my pleasure."

I did, and all too quickly the mesh was little more than molten gray liquid oozing down the grimy bricks. Sam unclipped the small flashlight from his belt and walked over. The powerful beam parted the shadows that dominated the building's interior, revealing the broken remnants of walls and a sea of hanging wiring and lights.

"There's no life in the immediate vicinity," he said.

"But plenty of the dead if that smell is anything to go by," Jackson muttered. "I wonder if this was one of the feeding areas for the red cloaks."

"Feeding areas?" Sam's question was somewhat remote. His attention was still on the building's interior.

"Luke was using animals of various kinds to feed his army—a fact we discovered when we tried to rescue the three witches he'd kidnapped," Jackson said. "And it strikes me as odd that there was no outcry, given the number of animals that must have gone missing over the past year or so."

"Vampires can go a fair amount of time before the

need for blood becomes all consuming," I said. "If it's the same for the cloaks, then the disappearances could have been spread out."

"It *is* the same for the infected." Sam's voice was clipped. "And people *did* notice. We just managed to keep it out of the mainstream press."

"PIT seems to be doing a lot of that lately. And yes," Jackson added, "I know you have no real choice."

I sidestepped the puddle of metal and stopped beside the two men. My arm brushed Sam's, and awareness surged again; this time it was an all-too-brief flicker that contained far more heat than the flames that towered above us. Rather surprisingly, he made no attempt to pull away. Maybe almost dying for a second time had mellowed him somewhat.

And maybe tomorrow vampires would fly.

I peered into the gloom. Beyond the wall remnants and the gently swinging fittings and wires, there was little else to see but rubbish. There certainly weren't any bones or bodies. If the building *was* another of Luke's feeding areas, then it was happening in another portion of the structure. I doubted it, though. The smell might be potent, but it still wasn't strong enough for the source to be anywhere close.

"I can't sense any additional magic," I said, "but given the strength of the main spell, I might not. Are you familiar with the building's layout?"

"I've been here once or twice." Sam handed me the flashlight, then grabbed the windowsill and very quickly hauled himself up and into the building. Dust bloomed as he landed, a choking cloud of black that briefly snatched him from sight. "Em, you're next."

I handed him the flashlight, then stepped into Jackson's cupped hands. In very little time, I was standing next to Sam. Jackson joined us a heartbeat later.

"This way."

Sam moved forward cautiously. We walked through a series of smashed rooms and rubbish, heading toward what once must have been a wall dividing section of the warehouse from the other. There were two doorways—one into the shell of an office, the other into a hallway. Not even the flashlight's bright beam could penetrate the darkness that held that place captive.

Magic, my inner voice whispered, even if I couldn't actually sense it.

Two metal doors that had once divided the two areas lay on the concrete; one of them so badly twisted, it looked more like a crinkled bit of foil. The other was blackened and covered in rubbish.

Sam skirted them both and stepped into the gloom. I half expected him to disappear, but nothing happened. There was little in the way of sound, and the only thing moving besides the three of us was a stirring breeze. Which was weird when we were so close to the fire zone. Considering the height and strength of those flames, we should have at least heard their roar.

Though there was no immediate threat, Sam unclipped his weapon in readiness. Heat instantly touched the air, a brief but bright flash of orange that lit the darkness.

That flash came from Jackson rather than the nearby wall of fire.

He took a deep, steadying breath and gave me a tight smile. *I'm okay.*

I know. And a flash of light was infinitely better than a burst of flames. He might not yet have full control, but he was improving a whole lot faster than most young phoenixes ever did.

We walked on, our footsteps stirring up a cloud of dust and soot that choked every breath. The flashlight still wasn't having much luck against the almost impregnable darkness, but Sam nevertheless seemed to know where he was going.

"We should be about level with the beginnings of that debris wall," he said. "Feel anything different, Em?"

"No. Nothing different to what I would have outside, anyway." Which was decidedly weird, given they had to be aware that this warehouse was a direct route into the fire zone. Why protect a rubble-filled road with magic and fire, and not the warehouse? Or was it simply a matter of our not having reached whatever defenses had been set up here yet?

"Let me know if it changes or gets worse as we step under the fire wall," Sam said.

"That's presuming what we're seeing *is* actually a fire," Jackson said. "It's always possible it's nothing more than an illusion."

Sam glanced back at us, blue eyes bright in the shadows. "What makes you think that?"

"The fact that I'm a fire fae and feeling no fire." He glanced at me. "What about you?"

"There *is* a fire ahead, but it's nowhere near as strong as it should be."

He grunted. "Meaning it's being enhanced to look worse than it is."

"I guess we'll find out why soon enough." Sam returned his attention to the corridor. "We should be near the magical demarcation zone."

As he spoke, the shadows closed in around us, becoming thicker—heavier. The flashlight's gleam became little more than a glimmer, and I couldn't see Sam's back even though he was close enough to reach out and touch. The magic burned so fiercely across my skin now that my entire body shuddered under its force and sweat trickled down my spine. Had I been this close to a real fire, I could have sucked in the force of the flames and used the energy to fight the sensations. But while there definitely *was* fire somewhere in the zoned-off area up ahead, the rearing wall of flame that dominated this section of Brooklyn was little more than a subterfuge.

Jackson lightly touched my spine, and heat leapt from his flesh to mine. I resisted the temptation to draw it even deeper, to fuel my nerves and my strength with his fire, and stepped away from his touch. *You need to keep your heat to yourself, especially since we have no idea what we're about to walk into.*

I'm barely keeping a lid on the inner flames, he said. *Sharing is helping me as much as—* The sentence was abruptly cut off. "Turner, stop."

"Why?" Sam's voice was curt, but more from tension than anything else.

"There's movement up ahead."

"I'm not sensing any kind of heartbeat," Sam said. "So whatever it is, it isn't human."

"That's not exactly a comforting thought," I said. "Not given that the witch has already used hellhounds against us."

Sam glanced at me, something I felt rather than saw. "Hellhounds actually exist?"

"Most mythical creatures do, even if humans have enhanced the reality of them over the centuries. In this case, hounds are actually spirits who live deep within the earth."

Sam grunted and raised his flashlight; the beam did little more than flare uselessly against the wall of black. "Em? You want to try?"

I called flames to my fingers and shaped them into a ball before throwing it upward. It had no immediate impact on the gloom that surrounded us, so I increased the strength of the fiery sphere, until it glowed white-hot. Still nothing.

"This darkness is definitely sourced from magic," Jackson said, "and it leaves me wondering what, exactly, is being concealed."

"Can you still sense movement?"

Jackson hesitated. "Yes. Just."

"Then let's try my other party trick," I said, and called to the mother. She answered instantly, rushing through me in a wave of power that briefly made my skin glow white-hot, then rolled outward in a wave. Whatever the spell was, it had no counter to the mother's power. The heavy blanket peeled away from her touch, and the source of Jackson's movement was revealed.

It was rats. Hundreds and hundreds of rats.

CHAPTER 5

If they were frightened by either our presence or the sphere of flame hovering above them, there was little sign of it. They were too busy eating.

They weren't feeding on rubbish. They were feeding on bodies.

Human bodies.

Memories stirred, and a shudder ran through me. I'd seen scenes like this all too often in times of plague and other calamities. The rats had always been there at the end, growing fat on the flesh of the unfortunate.

But in this case, the unfortunate were probably better off, because the flesh the rats were feeding on was that of the red cloaks.

"I guess that answers the question of what happened to the cloaks." Jackson's voice was grim.

"Not entirely," Sam said. "There're probably only twenty or so bodies here. Luke had a much larger force than that."

"The rats wouldn't be back if there were some cloaks still alive," I said. "Rats are many things, but they're not stupid."

"And if there *were* some left alive," Jackson said, "they'd surely be hungry enough to have swarmed both the military and us by now."

"True," Sam said, "but it does make me wonder why Rinaldo—if he is able to control them—would only keep a small force of them alive to attack you two."

"Those cloaks attacked Frederick before they turned on us, remember, and I doubt Rinaldo would have ordered that." I shrugged. "If he *does* control them, maybe his connection is telepathic rather than hive based."

"A possibility with those who, like me, are infected but not hive bound," Sam said. "But the cloaks had no mind to control."

He took a cautious step forward. The nearest rats briefly glanced his way but otherwise didn't move.

"Bold bastards, aren't they?" Jackson said. "I don't know about anyone else, but I'm rather reluctant to walk through a damn sea of them. So if no one minds . . . ?"

He didn't wait for an answer; he simply unleashed the heat that had been building within him. A thick stream of fire shot past Sam, then spread out, becoming a fiery wave that hit the nearest rats, setting both them and the remains of the cloak they were feeding alight. As their high-pitched cries of pain filled the air, the wave rolled on, seeking out the rest of them. But they were already on the move, scurrying away into the darkness beyond both Jackson's fire and the mother's light.

I briefly raised the intensity of the fire to put the burning rats out of their misery, then cindered the bodies of the cloaks. The light breeze stirred the ashes into a gentle flurry, and brought with it the stench of burned flesh.

But it wasn't coming from the dead inside the room. It was coming from somewhere up ahead.

I sent the sphere of light forward. It revealed a low row of skeletal offices and a door at the far end.

An open door.

"Now there's an invitation if I ever saw one," Jackson said. "Anyone care to bet on it being a trap?"

The sphere hit the doorway and went through. There didn't appear to be anything more than rubble and rubbish in the street beyond, though that wasn't to say there wasn't a cast of thousands hiding in the shadows beyond the illuminated area. I released the mother's light and allowed the darkness to close in around us again. If it *was* a trap up ahead, then I needed to conserve as much energy as I could.

Sam led the way forward again, stirring up the remains of the newly cindered. I cupped my hand over my nose and mouth. I knew it was unlikely the ashes could infect me, but I had no desire to draw them into either my lungs or my body.

"We should be almost level with the top of the barrier that sits atop the rubble now," Sam said. "Em, feel anything different?"

"No heat or fire, just the lash of magic. What about you?" I asked. "Sensing any life out there?"

"Not human life."

"What about nonhuman?"

"None of them, either." He shrugged—and it was only then that I realized the heavy darkness was beginning to lift. "If there's anything else waiting out there, we'll have to uncover it the hard way. The senses of a pseudo vampire aren't up to dealing with the spirit kind."

And yet he'd always been able to sense my presence

in a room, even before he'd become aware that I was something more than human. But maybe that stemmed from a connection of hearts and souls than anything else. That connection still seemed to exist, and part of me hungered to believe that somewhere deep down he still cared, even if his actions of late suggested the exact opposite.

But as much as my crazy heart might wish otherwise, he was this lifetime's heartbreak. And given fate had allowed no other outcome in all the many centuries I'd lived, loved, and lost, I couldn't see it having a change of heart this late in the game.

The sting of magic suddenly got stronger, the weight of it so powerful, I stumbled. Sam half twisted around and somehow caught me before I could run into his back.

"Okay?" he asked.

I nodded. "We just hit the barrier."

"I know." His voice was flat and filled with frustration. "I can't move."

I frowned and stepped sideways as he moved back a step. "But you just did."

"Yes, backward, but I can't move any farther forward."

"So much for the hope that this warehouse wasn't protected." Jackson took a cautious step forward, then a second, and a third. "Interesting that the barrier stops you and not me."

"That's because Rinaldo wants us in there." I took several cautious steps forward until I was level with Jackson. The weight of magic lifted so abruptly, I almost stumbled again.

"He what?" Sam's voice was sharp. "Why?"

I swung around in surprise, eyebrows raised. "I thought you read our report."

"I did, but that wasn't in it." His annoyance burned the air. "What does Rinaldo want you to retrieve?"

"Research matter. What that actually means, I have no idea."

"Meaning he has the scientists?"

My confusion deepened. "Yes, and I certainly *did* mention that."

"Well, it wasn't in the damn report."

"Then maybe the agent who took the report simply forgot to add it."

"Rogers never forgets."

"Well, I'm not sure what's going on, but I'm not fucking lying, Sam, whatever you might believe."

"I'm not saying you are—"

I snorted. "Maybe not verbally."

Jackson cleared his throat. "We can argue about it later. Right now, we need to keep moving."

Sam released a frustrated breath. "Indeed. I'll monitor the situation from here. Keep the mics open and the cameras on."

"Why?" I bit back. "It's not like anyone can come running if we get into trouble."

"True, but we nevertheless need to know what's going on in there." Sam's voice was every bit as sharp as mine. "We *will* send people in here once the witches manage to breach the barrier. It'd be nice not to send them in blind."

"But it's perfectly fine to send us in blind." Which wasn't fair, but sometimes annoyance got the better of common sense.

"If I had any choice in the matter, I'd gladly swap positions," he growled. "So cut the crap, Em, and just go. And be careful, both of you."

I opened my mouth to reply, then thought better of it and simply swung around and strode toward the open door. Jackson drew a gun as we neared it. I simply flexed my fingers; sparks spiraled through the darkness.

What do you think? He paused to the left of the door.

My gaze skimmed what I could see of the street. There were shapes out there, shapes that vaguely resembled human bodies. More dead cloaks, no doubt, and the dead could hardly hurt us. And yet, that vague sense of unease was growing. Which hardly made sense given it was unlikely Rinaldo would have set a trap for us; not when he wanted us to retrieve whatever information the scientists had left behind.

I think there's a reason Rinaldo and his pet witch didn't come in here themselves, I replied. *And I believe we might just be about to uncover it.*

Can you see anything more than dead cloaks? Sense anything more?

No. Not even magic. I took a deep, calming breath. *I'll go left; you go right. On three.*

I raised a hand and began the countdown. As my last finger dropped, we moved as one. He headed left and high; I went right and low.

Nothing happened. The street was empty of life, but it was not empty of death. There had to be at least fifty cloaks between this side of the road and the other, all of them in various states of decay. The stench was incredible.

"Rinaldo didn't do this." Jackson's nose wrinkled with distaste. "He might be a strong telepath, but even he wouldn't be capable of such mass destruction. And I can't see any sort of evidence of bullet wounds."

"No." I stopped beside him and surveyed the street. The fiery dome that arched high above us cast a weird, almost surreal light over the entire area. There *was* fire here, but it was some distance away, and the force of it was fading. Whatever fuel had been feeding, it was running low; I doubted it would last much longer.

The remains of the building I'd brought down partially blocked the street to my right, but beyond it I could see a number of run-down two- and three-story buildings. The street itself was a dead end, however, thanks to the high wall of metal and old building material that now blocked it. It was a similar story to our left. Luke had obviously wanted this area isolated from the rest of Brooklyn, which possibly meant this had been the heart of his hive.

Was this where he'd kept the scientists?

De Luca had denied it, but that didn't mean anything—especially given we'd been sent in to retrieve their research material. Frederick had been a part of Luke's plans for a while now, so he'd have at least some idea of what was—and wasn't—going on in the area.

My gaze stopped on the building directly opposite. Even though it was coated in ash and grime, it was in far better shape than any of the other buildings in the area. There was little sign of the decay and destruction that blighted the rest of them. The double-glass entranceway was whole, and open.

We were very obviously meant to go that way. There was even a vague path through the mass of decaying cloaks.

"I'm not liking the feel of this." Though Jackson's voice was soft, it seemed to echo across the silence. Something stirred in response.

Or maybe that was simply my fear, projecting forward.

I flexed my fingers again, sending sparks spinning like fireflies into the night. "Shall we take the obvious path, or go sideways again?"

Jackson hesitated, and then shrugged. "There's only one building that looks in good enough condition to house a laboratory, so I can't see the point in checking the others first."

And with that, he moved forward, into the sea of dead. I followed, body tense, waiting for something— anything—to happen. Nothing did. The stench of rotting flesh increased, until it became a putrid cloak that clogged my pores and overwhelmed my senses. I stepped over arms and legs that had become detached from torsos, and avoided eyes that had rolled out of sockets and seemed to glare at me with an odd sort of life. It was macabre and frightening, and all I wanted to do was get the hell off the road. Jackson increased his pace and, in very short order, we were free of the dead and walking through the glass doors that led into a wide, dark foyer.

I created another sphere of fire and tossed it into the air. Other than a thin layer of dust and soot, the area was in pristine condition. The guard station could have still been in use; there was a coffee cup sitting next to the phone, and a half-unwrapped sandwich sitting on the desk, suggesting the guard had been called away before he'd been able to eat it.

Jackson walked across and picked it up. "No mold." He finished unwrapping it, then sniffed it. "Chicken's off, though."

"So it's possible it could have been there for anywhere between one and three days."

He dropped the sandwich back onto the desk. "It'd have to be three—no one has been in this area since the trench was created."

"Meaning this place had been secure right up until the very end. Wonder what happened to the guard." I spotted the stairs and walked across. The door creaked as I pushed it open, and soot fell across my face and arms. Faint echoes of life reverberated through me, and I shivered. That ash had once been human, but whether it was a cloak or someone else, I couldn't say.

"He's probably either dead or hiding with the scientists." Jackson came up behind me. "They *have* to be here. There's no way they could have gotten out."

"You forget the helicopters that attacked us." I opened the door fully and sent my sphere upward. It revealed nothing more than an everyday concrete stairwell. "Besides, while De Luca might have confirmed Luke had the scientists, he didn't actually say where they were being kept."

"De Luca was a self-important, delusional prick."

"Yeah, but he was a prick who had the foresight to steal the original research notes both scientists had made on this virus, and secure them where they could not be found." Sam's voice was somewhat tinny as it echoed in my ear. "How about less conjecture on the dead, and more details on the current situation?"

I began to climb the stairs. "Why? Aren't the cameras working?"

"Randomly. There seems to be some sort of interference."

"So do you want me to go back and intimately describe the foyer and the dead sandwich?" Jackson's voice was bland.

"No, I do not. Stop being an ass, Miller."

I grinned. "We've found the stairwell and are heading up to the first floor. The building has six floors; not sure if there's a basement."

"Is the building you're in directly opposite the one I'm in?"

"Yes." I reached the entrance to the first floor and carefully opened the door. The light from my sphere fanned out, illuminating several doors immediately opposite.

"I'll bring up the floor plans. They might help."

And they might not. But I refrained from saying that and stepped into the corridor. It stretched to either side of us and had a series of doors running off it. "I'll go left; you go right."

Jackson nodded, his expression somewhat distracted. A heartbeat later, a sphere of light appeared in front of him, though it was larger and more volatile-looking than mine.

He flashed me a rather pleased grin. "I think I'm getting the hang of this. Meet you around the other side."

I headed left, providing a running commentary as I checked each room. Jackson was doing the same. Most of them were empty, without even cobwebs or dust. The lack of webs was decidedly odd if the rooms had been abandoned for some time. Daddy longlegs, at the very least, should have taken up residence by now. At the far end of the long hall, I found a room filled with filing cabinets. I quickly checked them, but all were empty.

I rounded the corner; there were no offices, just a short corridor that led to the other side of the building. I repeated the process there, and the result was the same—nothing.

Jackson cautiously opened the stairwell door and sent his sphere in. "The next level is blocked."

I ducked under his arm and peered up. The flickering light of his fireball gleamed off a mix of concrete and metal.

"I can probably blast it, but I doubt it's worth the effort. Sam, do both sets of stairs have exits onto the second floor?"

"Yes. The building initially belonged to a bio skincare manufacturer, but in more recent years was used by a couple of dope kings. The cops busted their operation about three years ago. According to the information I have, there are smaller labs on the second floor, but the main base of operations was on the third."

"Meaning Luke simply made use of what was already here." I glanced at Jackson. "It might also explain the blockage. It's easier to control one exit than two."

"But hardly necessary since he controlled the entire area."

"Luke wasn't the trusting type." I swung around and led the way back to the other stairwell. The two spheres bobbed along several feet in front of us, their flickering light lending warmth to the cold white walls. "But then, liars and cheats rarely are."

"So why would he trust Frederick, even after he'd infected him?"

I shrugged, pushed the stairwell door open, and directed my sphere upward. Once again, there was no indication that anything untoward waited on the next floor.

So why did that odd sense of unease suddenly ramp up several degrees? What did that innate part of me that sent me dreams of death sense that I could neither see nor hear?

I climbed the steps warily, one hand on the railing and the other clenched against the fire pressing against my fingertips. When we reached the next landing, I paused and carefully scanned the door. There didn't seem to be any alarm or tripwire connected to it, and I couldn't feel any sort of magic. Yet the feeling that something was very off was growing.

I glanced at Jackson. "Can you sense anything in there?"

"No. But just in case . . ." He drew a gun. "Ready?"

I nodded and flexed my fingers. He flung the door open with so much force, it slammed back against the wall and sent concrete dust flying. The crash echoed, a forlorn sound that spoke of emptiness.

Nothing jumped out at us. Nothing moved, not even rats, if there were indeed any here.

I sent the sphere in and flared it brighter. The darkness lifted, revealing a corridor directly opposite that ran the entire length of the building. Four doors led off it—two on this side, two on the other. I reported this to Sam, then glanced at Jackson. "Shall we split again?"

He shook his head. "Not with the bad vibes I'm getting."

I raised my eyebrows. "You are?"

"And you're not?" He snorted. "Intuition aside, we're right in the heart of the enemy's territory. Said enemy might be dead, but I have no doubt he left a surprise or two behind."

"Said surprise," Sam cut in, "might have just activated. The door between the warehouse I'm in and the road beyond just slammed shut."

"Are you picking up any sign of movement?" I asked. "Has the military been attacked?"

"We're still catching interference on the cameras and monitoring equipment, so I can't answer the first question, but the military reports no sign of life as yet."

Meaning whatever Luke planned, it revolved around this place—especially since the slamming door seemed to coincide with our opening this one.

"Well, no matter what the bastard has planned, there's little point in hanging about in this stairwell."

With that, Jackson slipped around the corner, paused briefly, and then strode toward the first door, his now slightly smaller sphere bobbing above him. I followed, keeping to the right side of the building, every sense alert as the thick sense of wrongness increased and my skin crawled.

Jackson stopped at the first door and glanced at me. "Ready?"

I pressed my back against the wall and nodded. The

two spheres hovering between us sent firefly-bright sparks spinning through the shadows.

Jackson sent the door crashing backward again. As the wall shuddered under the impact, I sent my sphere into the room and flared it brighter, potentially blinding anyone who might have been waiting in there.

No sound, no response.

We went in as one. The large room was filled with all sorts of laboratory equipment, some of which was familiar, some not.

"Computer," Jackson said, walking to the left. "Looks brand-new."

I started opening the various drawers and cabinets that lined the walls. "The power was cut ages ago, so there must be a generator around somewhere."

"If there is, it currently isn't on."

"Maybe it ran out of juice. It *has* been three days since Luke died."

The cupboards held little more than chemicals and lab paraphernalia. Other than the lone laptop, there was nothing that could be used to jot down equations—not even a whiteboard. It couldn't have been a lab Professor Baltimore—one of the lead scientists working on a cure for the virus, and whose murder had gotten me involved in the whole mess—had worked in; he'd been an old-fashioned kind of guy who'd preferred to make his initial notes on paper. I doubted being infected would have changed the habits of a lifetime—not when Luke needed him to be one of the saner cloaks. A muddled, empty mind would not have given him the cure he was seeking—if indeed that was what he'd been after. Luke hadn't actually been playing with a full deck mentally, so who actually knew?

Which didn't mean the lab couldn't have belonged to Professor Wilson, the other lead scientist who'd been infected and brought under Luke's control. While Wilson had seemed more up-to-date in his note-taking methods, he'd apparently kept a backup of all his research on USBs, just as Baltimore had. While we were still searching for those backups, the two locker keys we'd recently found in Wilson's garden shed had at least taken us a step closer to finding them. One of those keys had led us to a USB stored in an old-style gym locker. Whatever information it had held was now in PIT's hands, and although we'd retained a copy, we hadn't yet had time to check it out. We were still looking for the locker the second key belonged to.

"Nothing else of note here," Jackson said. "It doesn't actually look as if the lab has been used much."

"Check the rest of them," Sam said. "There has to be something more, if only because Rinaldo wanted you two to retrieve it."

"He might just want the laptop," I said.

Jackson glanced at me. "He could have taken that when he took the scientists."

"That's presuming he *has* the scientists," Sam said. "There's no proof that either of them are even alive."

"Well, Baltimore *did* walk out of the morgue." My tone was dry. "If that's not proof of life, I'm not sure what is."

"Maybe I should have said there's no proof that either of them are *still* alive." Sam paused. "Heads up—something is coming your way."

That heavy sense of wrongness sharpened abruptly. It might simply have been a reaction to his warning, but I doubted it.

"Care to get a little more descriptive than 'something'?" Jackson said.

"I would if I could," Sam said. "Whatever it is, it's moving in a mass and coming at you from two sides."

"Two? How?" I said. "There's only one stairwell."

"It's coming from both the street level and from the roof."

"Leaving us the meat in the sandwich. Lovely." Jackson glanced at me. "Do you want to do the honors, or shall I?"

"You keep searching the labs. Fire still drains your strength too fast."

He grunted and headed down to the next doorway. I ran back to the stairwell and carefully opened the door. The thick stench of decay hit like a slap in the face and made me gag. We'd obviously left the ground-floor door open for the smell to be this bad. But other than that, there was no sound and nothing that would indicate anything else had changed.

"Sam, are you sure they're coming up the stairwell?"

"I didn't mention the stairwell. I said it was coming at you from top and bottom."

"Then how—" I stopped as an odd sound echoed up from the emptiness below. It was little more than the soft bounce of a stone down concrete steps, but it nevertheless sent a chill down my spine. Sam might not have mentioned the stairwell, but there was definitely *something* in here.

I sent the sphere in, making it bright enough to light

the entire stairwell, then walked over to the metal railings and peered down.

And saw faces looking up at me.

The decaying dead had come back to life.

I swore and called fire to my fingertips. Even as I did, the cloaks roared—the sound oddly garbled and barely resembling anything human—then surged up the stairs toward me, moving so fast that bits of flesh and god knows what else sprayed across the concrete walls.

"Em, report." Sam's voice was sharp. "What's going on? What's that sound?"

"The dead are screaming," I said, "so shut up and let me deal with them."

Which probably wasn't the wisest thing to say to the man who was technically my boss—at least for this mission—but hey, what was the worst he could do? Sack me?

I flung several streams of fire at the nearest cloaks. The flames leapt from one rotting carcass to another, until the entire stairwell was lit by a moving mass of burning flesh.

It didn't stop them.

Maybe they *couldn't* stop. Maybe Luke's very last order had been to protect the labs at all costs.

I drew in a breath and called to the mother. Her power tore through me, almost seeming intent on tearing me apart as she erupted from my flesh and arrowed undirected toward the burning cloaks. In an instant, they were ash. I sighed in relief and released her, but she didn't retreat. Rainbows of light pulsed across the darkness, and my heart momentarily beat in time.

And *that* scared the hell out of me.

If I became too in tune, I would become one with her. Everything I was, and everything I could be—all my hopes and dreams and energy—would become a part of her. There was no escape from such a fate, no rebirth.

And while that was the eventual fate of all phoenixes, it was not yet my time to fade into her sweet embrace. I was not yet tired of life, however much I might wish our ill-fated path to love would, just once, end differently.

I backed away from the rainbow flare, and the connection between us snapped, the force strong enough that it sent me staggering backward. I flung a hand against the wall and briefly closed my eyes, battling the lethargy that washed through my limbs, though it stemmed as much from relief as weakness.

One thing was *very* obvious—I'd have to stop relying so much on the mother to get me out of tough situations. Her grip—and the temptation that came with it—was becoming a little too strong.

I pushed away from the wall and sent my sphere of flame spiraling upward. Thankfully, no more rotting, broken faces were revealed.

"One stairwell clear of cloaks," I said. "Are the sensors still catching movement, Sam?"

"At the moment, no. I've called in the military to guard the perimeter of the shielded area, though, just in case they try to escape."

I doubted they were trying to escape, but it was nevertheless a good idea. If the cloaks were all contained within the area—for whatever reason—then it was better to keep it that way.

Even if it wasn't exactly better for *us*.

"Heading back to finish checking the labs, then."

I stepped back into the hallway, then hesitated. While the stench of decay should give ample enough warning that there were cloaks on the move, I wasn't about to risk anything else sneaking up on us. I directed my sphere back to the doorway and fanned the energy out until it covered the entire exit. It didn't contain much heat and certainly wouldn't damage either the door frame or the walls around it, but if anything went through it, I'd feel it.

I found Jackson in the third lab. "Anything?"

He shook his head. "Another laptop, but that's it."

I frowned. "No notes? Because Baltimore preferred to jot his findings down as he was going, and he hated using computers during that stage of the process."

"Not a one." Jackson touched my back and ushered me out the door. "We'll check the final one, then head up to the next floor. Hopefully we'll have more luck there."

"Sensing movement again," Sam said. "Coming solely from the rooftop this time."

"I'm guessing the damn cloaks are the reason Rinaldo and his witch didn't want—"

"No," I said before Jackson had finished. "Frederick was surprised by the cloaks' actions in the Carlton Gardens. He wouldn't have been if he'd already clashed with them."

"Sensors indicate they're almost on you," Sam said.

"Your sensors must be copping interference again," Jackson said, "because there's no sign of them."

"Then something odd is happening, because there's

no interference, and we're reading them as being right on top of you."

I wasn't sure how much odder it could get than the decaying dead finding life, but I sure as hell didn't want to find out.

"I've got the door alarmed, Sam, so they must be waiting in the stairwell."

"That's not what I'm reading." Tension filled Sam's voice. "Be careful when you enter that last lab."

I'm thinking I'm not included in that "you." Jackson pressed his back against the wall and reached for the door handle.

I doubt he wants you dead, Jackson. Too much paperwork involved.

I waited as Jackson pushed the door open. Nothing moved in the darkness beyond, and the air was free from the putrid smell of rotting cloaks. Jackson sent his sphere in, and I flared it brighter. Aside from a couple of metal tables, the place was empty. We nevertheless entered cautiously. The only thing that stirred was dust. The room hadn't been used in a very long time.

"Well, this is a bust. Onward and upward." Jackson spun around and headed back out.

I started to follow him, then paused as I spotted something small and white sitting near the second table's leg.

"Hang on." I walked across and picked the item up. It was a torn bit of lined paper—the same sort of paper that came from the notebooks Baltimore had used. Heart hammering, I quickly unfolded the tiny scrap. *CH3COOH*, it read. Though I had no idea what it meant,

I'd worked long enough with Baltimore to know it was some kind of chemical formula.

"Found something." I read it out. "It might be a clue; it might not."

"We'll check." Sam paused. "Are you sure there's no activity in your vicinity? We're still seeing movement right above you."

"No—" I paused as something hit my shoulder. I frowned and flicked it off. Dust. Why would dust be hitting my shoulder? We hadn't stirred it up that much . . . The thought died.

Above us, Sam had said.

Oh *fuck.*

As I looked up, the ceiling collapsed.

CHAPTER 6

It hit me like a ton of bricks, and I collapsed under its weight. But it wasn't just plasterwork and metal, but also flesh, blood, and decay. The cloaks were all around me—even on top of me—and they used hands and teeth and god only knows what else to tear at my body, until the sharp scent of blood overrode even the stench of their rotting bodies. Pain was a wave that threatened to toss me into unconsciousness, and reflex and self-preservation rather than any conscious thought swept me from flesh to spirit.

The nearest cloaks erupted into flame, but it didn't stop their attack. They continued to slash at me even as my flames ate at their flesh, their actions filled with an odd sort of desperation.

For the first time since I'd first come across them, pity stirred. Most of them would not have invited this fate. Most of them would have done nothing more than cross the path of a madman intent on using the virus to do what he would never have been able to on his own—become a leader. A major player.

"Emberly!" Jackson's desperate shout was both verbal and telepathic, and it cut through my drifting, still-hazy thoughts. "Where are you?"

Here. I'm okay. But I was in fire form and still dazed,

and I had no idea if he'd understand me. I couldn't speak any form of English when in this form, but maybe sending thoughts was different.

"Not sure what language that was," he said, "but at least you're alive and aware enough to reply."

The fire burning the cloaks around me suddenly ramped up several notches. Jackson was feeding the fire I'd created, trying to eradicate the cloaks as quickly as possible. As they screamed and raged and fell apart around me, I started making my way up through the pile of debris and bodies. When I was finally free, I gasped in relief and, for several seconds, moved no farther. I simply hovered above the flames devouring both flesh and rubble with equal ferocity, and sucked in the strength and heat of it. It wasn't enough—nowhere near enough—to completely refuel me, but it at least knocked the edge of weariness away.

I turned around and spotted Jackson standing in the hall—or rather, spotted the very top part of his head. The ceiling's collapse had blocked all but a foot or so of the doorway, which certainly wasn't enough space for a man of Jackson's size to crawl through. And while he could undoubtedly use the force of his flames to blast enough of a gap to get in, he'd feared to do so until he knew where I was and whether I was in human or spirit form.

Our connection, I noted, was definitely getting stronger if I was now sensing such information without his telepathically sending it.

I gave him two fiery thumbs-up to indicate I was okay, then glanced at the ceiling. Three-quarters of it had come down, and not by accident. The metal struts that remained—poking out like fingers across the now-empty space—had been cut. And not recently. The trap had been prepared long before, but why would Luke set it over an empty, unused lab?

I glanced back to Jackson and motioned upward.

"I'll head up the stairs and join you," he immediately said.

I spun several fingers of fire out from my body and quickly wrote, *No, wait here.*

"Damn it, Em, be sensible."

Wait, I repeated in fire. *Trust me.*

"I do. I just don't trust the bastard who used to run this area."

Safer, I signed. *Report to Sam.*

I rose without waiting for his answer. A growl of frustration followed me, but a quick look back revealed he was doing as I asked and talking into the com unit.

The room above looked to have been some sort of storeroom. Metal shelving still lined three of the walls, and what little remained of the floor bore markings that indicated there had been other units as well—they were probably down below, in among the rubble and the dead. Dust sprinkled across my flames, and I glanced up at the ceiling. Only it wasn't there.

It wasn't one ceiling that had come down on top of me, but two. Which really *didn't* make much sense.

I resisted the urge to go through the second hole to see what lay above, and moved to the storeroom's door instead. It was locked, but a quick burst from fiery fingers soon fixed that. The next room was vast and seemingly empty. I flared brighter, fanning the orange-yellow glow of my flames out farther. There were no more gaping holes in either the floor or the ceiling on this level, but a quick check revealed both had been weakened in several spots. There was also some sort of black, almost oily-looking moisture dripping from the ceiling.

Trepidation stirred, though I had no idea why. If it were in any way dangerous or explosive, my flames would have set it off. I turned around and saw, down at the very end, a rather ornate door. I blasted it open with flames and headed in. It was an office—a huge one—that stretched the entire width of the building. A rather expensive-looking teak desk that had to be at least twelve feet long dominated the central area of the room, and there was a no-less-impressive executive chair behind it. Several smaller chairs sat in front of the desk and, to the right, there was a seating area complete with a coffee machine, its size rivaling that of the one Jackson had installed in our office. To the left of the desk there was, rather surprisingly, a sleeping area. Behind that was an exit, somewhat oddly positioned given that the bed made access difficult.

I did a quick check of the entire room, looking for anything out of place, or anything that suggested there might be another trap waiting. I didn't see anything, so I shifted back to human form and walked around the bed to inspect the oddly placed door. It was locked, but a quick spurt of heat took care of it. Behind it was a six-foot corridor and a second door. But this wasn't any old door—it was a heavy-duty metal one, and it rather resembled an air lock.

Answers, that inner part of me whispered again.

Hoping the whisper was right but partly suspecting it was merely delusional, I stepped forward and tried to open the second door. The handle didn't budge and, after a quick search, I discovered why. There was a key-coded lock and scanner behind a cleverly hidden panel on the right—and it was the sort that required not only the right number sequence but also the appropriate fingerprint scan.

If it required Luke's fingerprints, we were well and truly up that proverbial creek.

"Houston, we have a problem."

"I'm on my way up," Jackson said at the same time as Sam asked, "What sort?"

"A big fucking air-lock-armed-with-a-scanner sort of problem. I can try shorting out the control box with fire, but—"

"Don't!" Sam's voice was urgent. "We have no idea how the air lock is protecting or what reaction breaking it might set off."

"Which is exactly what I was about to say before you jumped in. Jackson," I added, "be careful coming up here. The floor above the other labs and near the stairwell has been tampered with, and it might be primed to collapse."

"No prob." He paused. "Is there any more activity on your monitors, Turner? Because the stench in this stairwell seems to be getting worse the nearer we get to the roof."

I hadn't felt him pass through the net I'd placed across the exit on the floor below, so it had obviously faded when the ceiling had collapsed on me.

"There's nothing showing, but these scanners are primed for human life," Sam said. "If it's inhuman—spirit—then we wouldn't pick it up."

Meaning they wouldn't pick *me* up when I was in spirit form—a very handy thing to know. "So what do you want me to do about this air lock?"

"Nothing. We'll deal with it."

"After all the shit we've gone through to uncover the thing, I'm not happy about walking away without knowing what it fucking contains." Frustration filled my voice.

"Unless you can find a secondary entry point into the area, we have no other option."

"And *is* there a secondary entrance?"

"There's nothing indicated on the plans we have."

"What about the old police files?" I asked.

"No mention there, either."

Jackson strode into the office and stopped just behind me. "It's a rather sturdy-looking mother, isn't it?"

"Yep." I placed my fingers against the wall to the right of the scanner. The plaster burned away from my touch, the white dust puffing outward as I pressed deeper into it. I was expecting it hit either a wood or metal frame, but instead I discovered a sheet of thick metal. I grabbed the edge of the plaster and tugged it away. Not just metal, but an entire wall of one. The plasterboard was little more than camouflage.

"Why would he even bother?" Jackson had repeated the process on the other side to reveal more of the metal wall. "It doesn't make any sense when he controlled the entire area."

"I doubt Luke was responsible for this," I said. "It was probably done by the drug cartel using this place before he got here."

Jackson grunted. "I guess we've no choice but to keep searching and hope we find something we *can* get into."

We retreated and made a thorough search of the office. But there were no other exits, hidden or otherwise, and nothing in the way of computers, files, or paperwork of any kind. In fact, there was absolutely nothing other than the unmade bed and a lack of dust to even indicate this place had been used recently.

"How many more floors has this building got?" I asked as we carefully made our way back to the stairwell.

"Two," Sam said, "including the rooftop."

"And the cloaks?"

"If there *are* any more around, they're certainly not moving."

"Which hopefully means the rest of the bastards are dead rather than just smelling like it." Jackson thrust open the stairwell door and looked up. "All clear."

We made our way up to the next level, and with every step the stench increased, until it felt like we were breathing in a cesspit. The sphere of light cast orange shadows across the bare concrete walls, highlighting the long strings of cobwebs and sending all the spiders, except for the daddy longlegs, skittering away. There was nothing else here, nothing that gave any hint as to why that smell was so bad. *Not* that I really wanted a hint. Hell, I'd be more than happy to simply retreat and leave whatever it was alone. But I rather suspected neither PIT nor Rinaldo would appreciate such a move.

The next door was locked. Jackson hit it with fire, melting the mechanism with a little more finesse than he'd used previously. The door swung open, and the stench immediately became a million times worse.

"I really didn't think we'd ever find anything that

smelled worse than the decaying cloaks," he said, slapping a hand over his nose. "But for fuck's sake, this is *vile*."

Which was vastly underdescribing it, in my opinion. I'd never, in all my years of existence, smelled anything that came near the stench coming from this floor. Not even during the years when the Black Death was at its peak and the putrid corpses were tossed into the streets like any other rubbish.

This *wasn't* just the stench of diseased or rotting flesh; it was also thick with the smell of ammonia and shit.

Swallowing heavily and trying not to breathe too deeply, I quickly spun more energy into the sphere and sent its light across the heavy darkness.

What it revealed was as gruesome as the smell.

The entire floor was a vast sea of human remains—not *whole* remains, but bits and pieces. There were decaying heads piled up in mounds and entrails hanging from the metal ceiling struts. Bones were scattered everywhere, many of them bearing teeth marks but all of them clean picked.

"I think we just discovered one of the feeding pits for the cloaks," Jackson said. "Although it could also be a rather awesome horror-movie set."

I took a couple of steps into the room, but stopped when the carpet began to squelch underfoot. I really, *really*, didn't want to know what the black liquid that oozed away from my weight was.

"This wasn't always a feeding pit. Not initially, anyway." I pointed at the nearest bones. "They're human. The ones in the sewers were mostly animals."

"Maybe he simply ran out of animals."

"And maybe these cloaks were placed here to protect whatever might be hiding in the metal room below us, and they simply began to turn on one another when hunger became too great." I waved toward the far side of the room. "I'm betting if we walked across, we'd see a hole that lines up perfectly with the portion of the ceiling that collapsed on me."

"That theory would make more sense if the collapse had happened in Luke's office, not in an empty lab two floors down."

"Maybe he simply wanted to stop anyone long before they got anywhere near his office." I shrugged. Luke was dead, so we were never going to really know what he'd intended here. "Shall we retreat to the roof and check that?"

"What about the rest of that floor?" Sam cut in.

"If you want this stinking cesspit checked, you can fucking do it. There's not enough money on this entire planet to entice me to take another step into this room." Jackson paused. "And anyway, it's not like you're paying us, is it?"

"You're not in jail or otherwise confined," Sam bit back. "Right now, that's payment enough."

Jackson snorted. "*That* would be a more acceptable answer if you weren't also using us to do your dirty work."

"Gentlemen, enough." The inspector's tone was curt. "Emberly, if there's nothing obviously related to the current search in that area, move on to the rooftop."

I stepped back into the stairwell and headed up. The rooftop door had been propped open by a large piece of metal, and the space beyond was littered with more body parts and dark pools of liquid. At least in the open air, the stench wasn't so bad. We did a quick check of the entire area, but there was nothing else here beyond blood-sprayed satellite dishes and silent air-conditioning units.

We reported all this and headed back down, detouring only to collect the three laptops we'd discovered. The cloaks that had littered the street in front of the building were gone; obviously, they were the ones I'd burned in the stairwell. The door leading into the old warehouse remained closed, but as we approached, its surface began to shimmer.

"And that," I said, "is warning enough that we'd better exit via the rubble pile."

Jackson immediately swung around and started heading toward it. "Wonder why the magic is still active? Rinaldo wants information, and he's hardly going to get it by keeping us locked in—especially since the entire area is crawling with PIT and military personnel and not even a gnat could get in here right now."

"Maybe he's not responsible for it. Maybe it was part of Luke's trap."

"Luke was many things, but he wasn't capable of magic," Sam said.

"Are you sure? Because he infected Frederick and the three witches, and maybe *that* connection enabled him to do minor magic."

"I don't think the hive actually worked like that," Sam replied. "If it did, he would have simply infected other scientists and passed the relative information to them from Baltimore and Wilson."

"Who says he hasn't?" Jackson said. "For all we know,

there's a whole hive of scientists still working away in that metal box."

"Given there's been no reports of other scientists being snatched, that's extremely doubtful," Sam said. "I'll meet you out in the lane."

We began climbing the rubble. As I'd feared, it wasn't exactly stable; bits of metal and brick slipped out from under each step and bounced down the steep slope, until it seemed half the pile was racing away from us.

"This thing is going to collapse." Jackson caught my hand. "Run."

We raced up the slope as it grew more and more fluid, until we almost seemed to be running through a river of metal, brick, and plaster. The flaming barrier of magic was pulsing, fading in and out of existence, as if the slide were also affecting it. Its magic burned across my skin as we tore through it, but it held little heat and certainly no threat. We began slipping—sliding—down the other side, and this time the rubble chased us, hitting our legs and backs with scary accuracy.

It sounded like a goddamn express train was bearing down on us.

Sam wasn't waiting for us at the base, and we certainly couldn't stop to look for him. As bigger and bigger bits of concrete began bouncing around us, Jackson tugged me over to the warehouse and all but threw me through the window. The laptop I was holding went flying as I did an awkward half roll and skidded on my back for several feet before coming to a halt hard up against the remains of a wall. I twisted around and saw Jackson in midair. He rolled with a little more elegance than I, and somehow ended up standing. A heartbeat later, the entire wall shuddered as dust and small bits of stone came blooming through the window.

"That was a little *too* close." He walked across and offered me a hand. "You okay?"

I nodded and let him haul me up. "Where are the laptops you had?"

He grinned and tugged his somewhat loose bullet-proof vest forward, revealing the slim sides of the two laptops. "Nice and safe. Yours?"

I waved a hand in the general direction it had flown. "Over there somewhere."

"Actually," Sam said as he appeared out of the gloom, "it hit me square in the chest and knocked the breath out of me. If I didn't know better, I'd swear it was deliberate."

I raised an eyebrow. "How do you know it wasn't?"

"Because you have the worst throwing arm I have ever seen." His tone was dry. "I'll take the rest of those laptops, Miller."

Jackson crossed his arms. "And what about Rinaldo? He threatened to send the cloaks into an infecting rampage if we didn't hand over whatever information we found."

"I doubt there're any cloaks left—"

"He said he had the scientists," I cut in. "And two men is enough to cause chaos. Do you and the inspector really want to risk that?"

"No," the inspector said before Sam could reply. "Hand over the laptops, Miller. We're working on a solution."

"It had better be a good one."

He handed the laptops to Sam, who took them across to the window. A black-clad figure appeared, and fire sprung to my fingers before I realized he was military.

Sam handed the soldier the three units, then said, "Laptops on their way, Inspector."

"Excellent. Remain where you are until otherwise advised."

"Remain where we are?" I echoed, "What the hell for?"

"Because we're undoubtedly being watched even if this *is* a controlled area." The inspector's voice was curt. "Until we know what is on the laptops, it's better if no one is aware we've retrieved them."

"The minute anything leaves Brooklyn, Rinaldo will know about it." Especially if he *did* have a mole in PIT's ranks.

"That is not a problem as the laptops are not leaving," the inspector said. "We have specialists waiting in a nearby building. The hard drives will be cloned, then any pertinent information erased and the laptops returned to you."

Jackson snorted. "And you don't think he'll realize that's happened?"

"No, because you'll be 'escaping' our clutches and finding your own way out of Brooklyn."

"There *isn't* another way," I said. "A bloody great trench surrounds the entire area, remember?"

"That shouldn't be a problem for a being who can become flame or take a winged form," Sam commented.

So they knew about my firebird form. I wondered how, given it wasn't something mentioned that much in all the myths about us. "It's the middle of the goddamn night. I'm not about to risk outing myself by taking on a form that hasn't been seen in centuries around these parts." If it had *ever* been seen around these parts.

"And it's not like I can grow wings or become flame," Jackson said. "So the trench remains a problem."

"I'm sure there's enough rubble and scrap around to form a makeshift bridge," the inspector said. "You have little choice, I'm afraid. Not if you wish to keep Rinaldo onside and endanger no one else."

And *that* was the shitty part of this whole situation. If we didn't do as we were told, people would suffer. I already had the blood of one innocent on my hands; I really didn't want any more.

I sat back down. If we were going to be here for a while, then I might as well be comfortable.

Sam stayed near the window, his arms crossed and his stance relaxed while Jackson prowled around like a caged animal. I closed my eyes and tried to catch some much-needed sleep; I must have succeeded, because when the inspector spoke again, I jumped.

"The laptops have been cleansed and are on their way." She'd barely finished saying that when the black-clad figure appeared at the window again and handed Sam a backpack. "Hardie Street provides the best exit point—the trench is slightly narrower there."

"Have the guards been warned we're coming out?" I asked.

"No. We need it to look like an authentic escape." She paused. "Sensors have been placed on both sides of the trench. The minute you near it, the guards will be notified."

Meaning we'd be chased—and possibly even shot at. Wonderful.

"Sam," the inspector continued, "give them ten minutes, then report back to base."

"Will do."

"Oh, and, Jackson? Stop dumping the phone we gave you whenever you don't want us to know your location. We need to be able to contact you on short notice."

"Noted."

In other words, he'd do what he damn well wanted, same as always. He flashed me a grin, then detached the com unit and undid the vest before dropping both on the ground. I did the same. Once we got out of Brooklyn, they would only attract unwanted attention.

"Hardie Street runs off Francis. Follow it and you'll come to the trench." Sam handed Jackson the backpack. "The military aside, there's no sign of movement in the whole area."

"And will the military stop us?" I asked.

"No."

"What about the witch's shield?"

"It's gone."

Meaning whatever had been used to anchor the spell in position *had* been part of the rubble pile. When it had collapsed, it had either shifted or destroyed the anchor and shorted out the rest of the spell.

"I might just do a quick scout first," Jackson said, handing me the pack. "Not that I don't trust your intel, Turner, but, well, I don't."

His grin flashed as he disappeared out the window.

"I don't know how you work with that bastard." Sam turned his com unit off. "But his distrust at least gives you and me a chance to talk."

"And what do we have to talk about?" I crossed my arms and gave him a flat stare.

"With our history? Plenty." His voice was grim. "But the fact of the matter is we have to work together. I think it would be beneficial to clear the air."

Beneficial. It was such an inoffensive word but one that somehow had annoyance rising. "Again, why? Hasn't everything that needs to be said already been said?"

"Yes. No." He thrust a hand through his short hair, and for the first time since I'd rescued him, I saw a hint of uncertainty. Maybe even a touch of vulnerability.

Don't read too much into it, that internal voice warned. *Remember what he said in Brooklyn, and heed the warning.*

I might often ignore that inner voice when it came to matters of the heart, but not this time.

"Damn it, Em," he continued, "just meet with me once. Let me say what I need to say."

"Why can't you say it here?"

"Because Miller is on his way back, and I'd rather *not* have an audience. This is between the two of us. Not PIT, and certainly not him."

I hesitated. Meeting with Sam would be the stupidest move I could ever make. I knew that, but it didn't stop the desire to say yes. If I heard what he had to say, then perhaps I could gain some sort of—if not resolution, then maybe peace—from the bitterness that still lay between us. And while Sam now understood the reason I'd had to be with Rory even though I'd sworn my love for *him*, his refusal at the time to listen to any sort of explanation remained a festering wound deep inside. Maybe if we sat down and talked about it like the adults we were both supposed to be, we could finally move on from the past.

Not that I actually *could* move on. He was it as far as this lifetime's love was concerned. In all my many lifetimes, fate had never gifted me with a second chance. It never would; heartbreak was our destiny, our curse.

I opened my mouth to agree, but what came out was a very flat, "No."

His expression tightened, but he didn't say anything; he simply nodded and stepped back. The darkness wrapped around him like a blanket and snatched him from sight. It was a vampire trick the virus had gifted him with, and one that had both annoyance and disappointment surging. I guess part of me had been hoping he'd argue the point and try to change my "no" to a "yes."

But maybe his desire to meet had been nothing more than a token gesture on his part—something he felt he had to do to appease whatever emotion I'd briefly glimpsed, and one he'd known would be rejected.

Whatever the reason, I doubted the offer would be repeated. Which was a good thing.

And if I told myself that often enough, I might actually believe it.

I spun around, hauled myself out the window, and strode up the street to meet Jackson.

"Whoa," he said, holding up his hands as if to ward me off. "Don't aim all that fury at me."

"I'm not." I kept on walking.

"Good." He swung in beside me and matched the

length of his steps to mine. "What happened in the brief few moments that I was gone?"

"Nothing."

"And that's what you're angry about?"

I gave him a look. He merely grinned.

"Do tell. Or shall I have to ferret away at your thoughts until I find out?"

"*Nothing* happened, as I said. Now quit it so we can both concentrate on getting the hell out of here."

"The old saying, 'Liar, liar, pants on fire,' is decidedly appropriate right now, given you're spitting flame all about the place."

I glanced down and saw that he was partially right. I wasn't spitting fire, but every footstep unleashed a shower of fiery sparks. I laughed, as he'd no doubt intended, and reined the sparks in. "Did you find our exit?"

He nodded. "I also checked out the trench. It's just beyond leaping length."

Which was no surprise, as that was exactly what Dmitri and Adán had intended when they'd created the thing. "Anything we can use to make a bridge?"

He shrugged. "Maybe. But I'm thinking we shouldn't exit where they want us to."

I frowned. "Why?"

"Because we're supposed to be running from PIT's clutches. It'd be much more believable if we actually stirred up trouble."

"I suspect you have a plan." And given his admitted addiction to the rush of adrenaline, it was probably a dangerous one.

He grinned again. "That I have, my dear. Come along."

We jogged through the darkness until we reached

the start of Hardie Street. Old warehouses and rusting containers lined one side of the road. On the other were a railway line and open space, although the line currently wasn't usable because the trench had taken out a huge portion of it. On the far side of the trench, about a third of the way farther down the street, a temporary guard station had been set up. Lights constantly swept the area, and I could see at least four men. I had no doubt there were more.

"So what's this plan of yours?"

"You blow the guard station up and cause some havoc, while I make my way beyond it and construct some sort of bridge."

I frowned. "I'm not going to hurt—"

"I don't want you to. I just need you to distract them with some noise while I create a believable escape route. Then we retreat to the other side of Brooklyn."

I raised my eyebrows. "Why? Sam said this was the narrowest point."

"It is. But Dmitri and Adán are only a call away, and they can easily build a temporary bridge for us."

"They still have to get past security."

"No, they don't. They can reshape the earth from a distance."

I hesitated, and then nodded. While I wasn't entirely sure the subterfuge was worth the effort, it also went against the grain to be following PIT's orders. Especially when PIT was all take and no give.

"Right." Jackson cracked his knuckles, his anticipation burning the air. "Give me twenty minutes to find what I need, then blast away."

"Right," I echoed.

He quickly climbed the mesh fence and disappeared into the shadows of the containers beyond it. I followed him and kept close to the darkness, hugging the old warehouses until I reached the first line of old containers. They were almost directly opposite the guard post, allowing me to keep an eye on what was happening without the risk of going too near the trench and setting off the sensors.

Five minutes passed, and two more men appeared. One patrol leg accomplished, obviously.

Once the twenty-minute mark had hit, I said, *Ready? Always.*

I smiled and peeked around the corner of the container again. *One of the guards has just entered the temporary shelter. I need you to make a slight noise.*

The clang of metal against metal rang across the night. My smile grew. *That wasn't slight.*

I'm not known for doing things by halves. If you don't know that by now, we're in trouble.

Five of the guards immediately raced toward the sound, their weapons drawn. The sixth remained in the shelter, talking into his phone. I swore softly and targeted one of the cars instead. The explosion was impressive and loud. The five guards dove for cover as bits of metal and fire shot above their heads and, in the distance, sirens began to wail. I blew up a second car, and, a heartbeat later, a Klaxon-like alarm sounded—caused by Jackson moving through the sensors, I suspected. The guards picked themselves up and raced forward. As they disappeared into the darkness, Jackson reappeared.

"That," he said, "was fun. Now, let's get the hell out of here."

He twined his fingers through mine and led me away. Although the trenched-off portion of Brooklyn wasn't overly large, it nevertheless took us close to forty-five minutes to get to the opposite end of it. This was because not only did we have to contend with the military—who undoubtedly would have reported our presence had they spotted us, and wasted our subterfuge efforts—but also because streets had been altered or blocked by either the cloaks or the criminals who had controlled this area before them.

Eventually the strange hush of the place wrapped around us again, and we were alone in the battered remnants of what had once been a thriving community. Jackson paused as we neared the trench again, and he studied the skyline for a minute.

"There." He pointed to a small, double-story house. While it wasn't the only one on the street, it was one of the few that still retained its outer skin. Most of the others were little more than skeletal shells. "We'll wait for the cavalry's arrival there."

I raised my eyebrows. "You've already called Dmitri?"

"Yes." The old gate creaked as he opened it. "And then shut down the phone. Didn't want PIT knowing we were still in the area."

I followed him up steps that bounced and groaned under our weight—an indication that this house wasn't all that far off from becoming as skeletal as the others on this street. "I'm surprised you didn't toss it."

"Oh, I thought about it." He opened the door and waved me in. The house was an old Victorian and, as such, had a central corridor from which all the rooms ran off. Stairs to the first floor were on my right, with a bigger room at the end. Grime and rubbish lay everywhere, and many of the old floorboards had been torn up. The smell of smoke lingered heavily, suggesting that not too long ago, someone had used the boards to fuel a fire.

I headed up. Things were a little better here—the floor was at least in one piece, although many of the walls had been kicked out and either the ceiling had been pulled down or had simply collapsed in two of the three bedrooms. I walked down to the room that overlooked the grasslands and the trench. Lights blazed from guard stations at either end of the street, but this portion of the trench remained in shadows.

I leaned a shoulder against the wall. "How does Dmitri intend to get past the sensors?"

"By building a bridge that spans above both them and the trench." Jackson glanced at his watch. "He'd said he'd be here about midnight, so not long to wait."

I raised an eyebrow, a smile teasing my lips. "So we're just going to stand around and watch the dust stir?"

"Oh, I'd love to do more, trust me on that." His tone was dry. "But this is hardly the ideal time or situation."

"A fire fae admitting there is—occasionally—an inappropriate time for sex? I'm *shocked*."

"So am I." He shook his head, his expression one of mock horror. "Especially as the words are coming out of *my* mouth."

I smiled. "I'm guessing some tender ministrations will be required to remedy the situation once we get out of here."

"Or not so tender." His grin flashed. "Because let's be honest here, the dam is so full, the first release is likely to be hard and fast."

My pulse skipped along happily at the thought. "I think I can handle that."

"Good." He motioned toward the backpack. "Why don't we make use of our time and see what those laptops have on them?"

I swung the pack from my shoulder and opened it up. After handing him two of the computers, I sat down and booted up the third. It immediately asked for a password. Fuck.

"Similar story here." Jackson shut down the computer and started up the last one. "Ha. Better luck this time."

I shoved my computer into the backpack, then scrambled over. The home page was basic and uninspiring, and a quick look through Finder didn't reveal anything suggesting it had been used for anything more than ordering stores and chemicals.

"They really *have* removed everything remotely related to the virus." Jackson slammed the laptop lid down. "And I don't think that was a wise move."

"Maybe they had no other option. Or maybe this particular laptop really *was* just used for ordering." I shrugged. "PIT doesn't want Rinaldo to carry through with his threat any more than we do. I imagine there'll be remnants on the other—"

I stopped as my phone rang three times and then fell silent.

"That'll be Dmitri. Give me the phone."

When I did, he hit the flashlight app, ran the bright light across the window three times, and turned it off.

After shoving the two laptops into the backpack, he scrambled upright, then helped me up. "Let's get the hell out of here."

We rattled back down the stairs and made our way through the wreckage of the ground floor. The rear yard was tiny, the fence little more than a couple of support posts and a few weatherworn fence posts that were barely hanging on. Once we'd slipped through the biggest gap, all that lay between the trench and us was a sea of waist-high grass and weeds. Jackson paused, his gaze narrowed and body tense. A heartbeat later, the ground shuddered ever so slightly and, up ahead, a slender bridge of dirt and stone began to form.

He tugged me forward. The bridge was still forming as we stepped onto it, but it arched gracefully over the trench and never once felt as if it were going to collapse underneath us. Which was rather weird, given it was also *deforming* and, just for a heartbeat, it simply hung in the air, connected at neither end.

Then we were on the other side. The bridge had become nothing but earth again, and Dmitri was striding toward us. Like Jackson, he didn't exactly fit the classic image of a fae—at least as described in literature and common myths. The earth was a solid element, and that very much described the fae who controlled it. Dmitri— like most of them—was about five foot nine and had a very stocky build, with rich brown skin and hair. The only way you could really tell any of them apart was via their facial shape and eyes. Dmitri's features were a little sharp, and his eyes the color of burned earth.

"Ah, it's the lovely Emberly," he said, ignoring Jackson completely as he caught my hand and kissed it. "It's always a pleasure to see you."

I grinned. All fae were outrageous flirts, even if fire

fae were the ones who had the reputation for corrupting the innocent. Not that there was a chance of *that* in my case.

"It's lovely to see you, too, Dmitri. Thanks for coming to our rescue again."

"It was a pleasure, my dear, and an excuse to once more gaze upon your lovely countenance."

I laughed and gently pulled my fingers from his. Most fae didn't need a whole lot of encouragement to start a pursuit, and one fae was more than enough for me.

"If you've quite finished," Jackson said, his voice dry, "we need to get away from this area before the patrols return. Did you bring the scooter?"

"Scooter?" I looked from one man to the other. "You expect me to get on the back of a scooter with you two?"

"While I could think of nothing more pleasurable than having you behind me," Dmitri said, "I'm afraid it is a pleasure that is not for me. I, sadly, have a car."

I smiled. "Maybe some other time."

"I might just hold you to that."

Jackson groaned. "Now you've done it. Don't you know those of dirt and stone are akin to lava—slow moving but relentless?"

Dmitri grinned. "And those of fire are quick to ignite and just as quick to wither away."

My smile grew. "So why do we have a Vespa rather than a car?"

"Because Dmitri cannot be seen with us, and because no one in their right mind would choose it for a getaway," Jackson said. "Therefore, it is unlikely to attract much attention."

"So if you would follow me, I will show you to your new chariot." He paused. "Although I really would rather be following you."

"*That* pleasure," Jackson said, "is all mine."

I shook my head at their banter and followed Dmitri through the long grass. We crossed a small creek bed, then made our way across a major road toward a very familiar and—if the sudden rumblings from the general direction of my stomach were anything to go by— most welcome sign.

"Jackson said you might be hungry," Dmitri said, making me wonder if he'd heard my stomach. It really was that loud. "And it was safer for me to park here. Less obvious."

He led us through the parking area and stopped at a beautifully restored F100.

"Lovely car," I said as he opened the rear door and carefully removed the Vespa.

"Thanks. It took me years to restore it." He placed the Vespa down, then handed Jackson the keys. "I've borrowed it, so please return it in one piece."

Jackson grinned. "Always do."

"Yeah." Dmitri's droll tone suggested otherwise. He blew me a kiss, then nodded at Jackson and climbed back into his car. Seconds later, he was gone, though the pleasant rumble of his car's engine seemed to echo across the darkness for a while.

Jackson wheeled the Vespa closer to the main entrance. "Let's grab something to eat and decide our next step."

I raised an eyebrow. "I thought our next step was already decided? Or have your little swimmers gone into a state of hibernation?"

"I resent any use of the word 'little' when it comes to my working parts." He flicked the scooter's stand down and pressed a hand against my spine, guiding me forward. "However, not even *I* could concentrate on the business of loving with the noise your stomach is making."

"It isn't *that* bad."

"Trust me, it is."

He opened the door and ushered me through. Once we'd received our burgers, fries, and drinks, I said, "Table or booth? Or would you rather leave and find somewhere close to satisfy those other urges?"

"As much as I'd love the latter, I can't ride a Vespa and eat at the same time."

"And here I was thinking you were multitalented." I started unwrapping my burger. "Besides, I have two hands. I'm quite capable of holding several bags of food until we get to whatever hotel we decide on."

"It'd be our luck I'd take a corner too fast and the hot drinks would go everywhere, scalding all sorts of important bits. No thanks." His smile flashed. "Besides, remaining close to the trench might actually be safer than moving away from it right now. Normal people would run, not remain in the danger zone."

"And we're about as far from normal as you could get." I scooped up several fries, munching on them as I added, "I need to get back to Rory by dawn, and it's going to take us a while on that fucking scooter."

"Never fear, I actually do have a car arranged."

"From who?"

"Makani. Who is," he said, before I could ask, "a friend. One of her current lovers runs a car dealership."

"That's rather handy."

"Indeed. I did have to promise her a weekend at some posh spa resort in return for said car, but I decided the sacrifice was worth it."

"Oh yeah." My tone was dry. "A weekend spent in a hot tub with a hot woman will be so tough."

"You have no idea." He glanced at his watch. "We have to meet her in an hour."

"Where?"

"At the yard in—"

He stopped as my phone rang. I pulled it out of my pocket and glanced at the number. "It's an office call being rerouted—do you want me to answer it?"

He hesitated. "No, but I've got a feeling we'd better."

"Your little feelings are becoming as inconvenient as mine." I hit the ANSWER button.

"Emberly?" a gruff and all-too-familiar voice said. "Radcliffe."

Or, to give him his full title, Marcus Radcliffe III. He not only owned a string of secondhand stores that were little more than a front for a roaring trade in black market goods and information, but he also happened to be the man who ran the underground gambling operations for the rat shifters—operations that Rinaldo had recently attacked.

"What can I do for you, Radcliffe?"

"You wanted a meet?" he snapped. "We do it. Right now."

My stomach clenched, and my gaze rose to Jackson's. *He's here. The bastard's here.*

Yes, but it's not like he can do anything—not with all the security cams around this place. Jackson paused. *Actually, that's probably why he's ringing. We did beat him up the last time we met him, remember.*

It was hardly a beating. More a little singeing. I returned my attention to the phone and Radcliffe. "How did you know we were here?"

He chuckled. It was a cold, somewhat smug sound. "Rats are everywhere. There isn't much we don't see or know."

"Which makes it even odder you didn't stop Rinaldo's attacks on your gaming venues before they actually happened."

"*That* is the only reason I'm talking to you now, when all I really want to do is wipe the stain of your existence from this earth."

My smile held very little in the way of humor. "Try it, and I'll return the favor."

"You won't catch me out like that again—"

"Radcliffe," Jackson cut in, "enough with the bluster. If you want to talk, come in and talk. I'll even buy you and your goons a coffee."

"Be there in five minutes," he said.

I hung up and shoved the phone back into my pocket. "Meaning he's close."

Jackson nodded. "He's obviously got a lair somewhere near here and was undoubtedly keeping an eye on events in Brooklyn."

Which was probably the only reason he—or his men—spotted us. "PIT isn't going to be happy if we give him any sort of useful information."

Jackson shrugged. "It's not like we have a whole lot of useful information, at least when it comes to Rinaldo."

That was true enough—and part of the reason we'd asked for a meet with Radcliffe in the first place. I quickly finished my burgers, then gazed out the window, watching for the rat's appearance and wondering if he'd come in a car or walk. It was a question soon answered when three figures appeared out of the gloom and strode toward the main door. Two of them I didn't recognize, but the third was Radcliffe. He was a thickset, muscular man with thin, pockmarked features and an arrogant set to his mouth. His eyes were typically ratlike—small and beady—but he moved like a man who owned the world. Which meant Jackson was probably right—his lair *was* very close to this area.

Radcliffe swept in, paused until he spotted us, and then strode over. One of his men stayed near the door, but the other followed Radcliffe across. If the slight bulge in the pockets of their ill-fitting jackets was anything to go by, they were both armed. Obviously, Radcliffe hadn't yet learned guns weren't a very effective weapon when it came to phoenixes.

Jackson rose and waved Radcliffe toward the booth seat. "Coffee?"

"No." Radcliffe sat with little grace and crossed his arms on the table. Anger oozed out of every pore, and the gleam in his dark eyes very much suggested all he wanted to do was reach out and strangle me. "Tell me what you know about Rinaldo."

I raised an eyebrow and leaned back. His scent was sharp, musky, and slightly tainted with the aroma of dampness—though that seemed to be coming from his clothes rather than his skin, suggesting his lair, at least in this area, was underground. It made me wonder if he or his men had had any altercations with the red cloaks.

"I want a fair exchange of information, or you get nothing."

Radcliffe snorted. "Oh, so *now* you want a fair exchange—"

"If you want to stop Rinaldo from destroying any more of your gaming venues," Jackson said, his voice hard, "it would be in your best interest to help rather than hinder us."

Radcliffe's gaze rose to his. "I'm here. Unless you prove you have something worthwhile, you're getting nothing from me." He paused. "And if you try, in *any* way, to burn me or my men, this entire building will come under attack. And from what I know about you, you wouldn't sleep with the blood of innocents on your hands."

No, because I already had enough on them. But I kept the thought inside and let flames flicker ever so briefly across my fingers. His expression tightened.

"You can try such an attack," I said quietly, "but I really wouldn't recommend it."

Radcliffe studied me for several seconds, eyes narrowed. Judging me, and weighing his options. Eventually he said, "I can't tell you much about Rinaldo. The man is a fucking ghost."

"So you have no idea where his den is?"

"None at all." Frustration touched Radcliffe's voice. "If we *did*, we'd have already wiped him out."

"Rinaldo has a dark witch working for him, so any direct attack on either him or his den is likely to be repelled by magic," Jackson said. "The sindicati think he's also using it to hide his location."

Radcliffe raised an eyebrow. "And you believe this?"

"The witch certainly exists—we've met him."

"If you've met him, why haven't you used him to get to Rinaldo? Better yet, why is the bastard still alive?"

"Because he used magic to hide his form and shield himself from my flames," I said. "Which is something you've apparently been looking into."

"Is that any fucking surprise?" He snorted. "But the fact that Rinaldo holds the leash of a witch does, at least, explain why we cannot find him."

"Which I find really odd," I said. "Even if his location *is* being screened by magic, surely a den of vampires could not go unnoticed in a local community."

"Trust me," Radcliffe growled. "We would have been notified if there'd been the slightest rumor of a new den. As I said, we have eyes everywhere."

"Meaning maybe he hasn't got a den." I glanced at Jackson. "Maybe he's using hired vamps and De Luca's get to do his dirty work."

"The vamps that attacked us weren't vamps for hire," Radcliffe said. "Nor were they from Victoria."

I glanced at him. "How do you know that?"

His smile was all teeth and little humor. "We killed a few of the bastards, that's how."

"And they were carrying IDs?"

He snorted again. "Of course not. We ran a trace on their prints and got zero results."

No great surprise given no one could apparently trace Rinaldo's background, either.

"Have there been any more attacks on your venues?" I asked.

"No, but we did ramp up security after the last one." He paused. "If he *has* got the services of a witch, though, we might have to do more."

I doubted a witch of *any* standing would agree to work with Radcliffe, and those who did almost certainly wouldn't be capable of creating a spell powerful enough to withstand Frederick's magic. But I wasn't about to say that. There was no point in aggravating Radcliffe any more than necessary, especially since he was being cooperative. Surprisingly so.

But it was probably a matter of his need to get rid of Rinaldo being greater than his hatred of me.

"We were told that Rinaldo was in charge of the most recent raid on the gaming venue—is that true?" I asked.

He nodded. "The security cams recorded the whole thing. The bastard was obviously aware of them, and just as obviously didn't care." His gaze narrowed slightly. "Why?"

"Because at the same time as he was attacking your venue, he was also confronting us in Rosen Senior's apartment building."

"Impossible."

"Apparently not." I took out my phone and showed him the photograph I'd taken of Rinaldo in his Professor Heaton persona. "This is him, isn't it?"

Radcliffe leaned forward and studied the picture for a moment. "Yes. But it's impossible to be in two places at the same time unless you can clone yourself. And *that* isn't possible just yet. Not when it comes to humans, anyway."

"Cloning may not be," Jackson said, "but it's more than possible that whoever he'd sent in his place when he attacked your venues was using a glamor to make it *seem* like he was there."

The vampire who'd confronted us definitely *hadn't* been using one. While glamors could change your appearance, they couldn't alter your voice. The Rinaldo who'd confronted us at Rosen's was very definitely the same vampire who'd tried to grab me at the Chase Medical Research Institute—the place where I'd quite happily worked as Baltimore's research assistant before this whole mess had begun.

"I see no point in using a glamor in that sort of situation, but I guess we're dealing with a very old vampire. Who knows how those fuckers think." Radcliffe frowned. "What were you doing at Rosen's place?"

"Looking for Professor Wilson's missing research notes." I took a sip of tea, then added, "Don't suppose you know anything about them, do you?"

His smile flashed. All teeth, no sincerity. "I'm not likely to tell you *that*."

Meaning, I suspected, he was as clueless as the rest of us. I doubted he would have been able to contain his smugness had it been otherwise. "Would it be possible to view the tapes of the attack?"

"No." He paused. "But why would you want to?"

"To compare *that* Rinaldo with the one we know. We might be able to tell from the footage whether there was a glamor in use."

He frowned. "I didn't know glamors were detectable."

They often weren't, but I wasn't about to tell him that. Not if lying got us those tapes. "There're always tells when it comes to magic. You just have to know what to look for."

Radcliffe grunted. "If I give you that tape, what do I get in return?"

"How about the file Rosen was keeping on Rinaldo?" Jackson said.

Whoa, I said. *Is that wise?*

What else have we got? he replied. *We'll remove the page about the inverter, although he probably already knows about that.*

The inverter was a device that made the wearer immune to telepathic intrusion via an inversion process. Rosen's company had been working on it before his death.

Radcliffe was more than likely already aware of the device, given he'd been bleeding Rosen of information for months—if not years—and then selling it via the black market. Although Sam *had* intimated that PIT had put a psychic block on Rosen in order to stop him from babbling about certain projects, so maybe not.

"Rosen had a file on Rinaldo?" Surprise edged Radcliffe's gravelly voice. "I had no idea."

"That's the problem with drugging someone to grab information," I said drily. "They can only supply what you ask for."

The look he cast my way very definitely wasn't friendly. "The tapes for the file."

"Agreed," I said. "When and where?"

He hesitated, seemingly surprised—and almost immediately suspicious—of my ready agreement. "Your office, tomorrow morning."

"We won't be there before ten." I hesitated. "I also want a truce on hostilities."

He laughed, a sharp sound that had heads turning. He ignored the looks and leaned forward. "After what you've done to both me and my men, what makes you think I would *ever* agree to something like that?"

"Because the only way *any* of us is going to stop Rinaldo is by working together."

He snorted. "Good luck getting either the sindicati or the wolves to agree to something like that."

"They already have," Jackson said. "Or at least there's an agreement to exchange information when it comes to Rinaldo."

Which wasn't exactly the truth, but Radcliffe was unlikely to check the story, given rats generally kept their dealings with vampires as brief as possible. While they did sell information and black market items to them, they certainly hadn't developed a more permanent business partnership, as Baker's wolves had. Partly, I think, because the two had a long history of distrust that stemmed from darker times, when vamps had considered weres good hunting material. Humans might always have been a vampire's main diet, but shifters certainly provided more of a challenge for those so inclined. And rats had always been more plentiful than the larger weres.

Radcliffe's gaze swept between the two of us, his expression giving little away. "If I agree to a truce, I want any and all information you might get from either Baker or the vamps."

"If you agree to do the same, sure."

His eyes became little more than black slits, but after a moment, he nodded, the motion short and sharp. He stuck his hand out. "A deal shaken on is a deal that must be honored."

I gripped his hand. His grip was tight—overly so—but I resisted the urge to press more heat into my fingers. "No attacks from *either* of us," I said, "until this is over."

He nodded and released my hand. "Agreed."

I fought the desire to wipe the stain of his touch away on my jeans and simply watched as he rose.

"Tomorrow at ten," he said, and then walked away.

Jackson waited until all three had left, then sat down and reached for his coffee. "That went better than expected."

"Yeah." I drained my tea in one long gulp. "I'm not sure we should trust the bastard, though."

"They'll stick to the terms agreed," Jackson said. "He can't afford not to, particularly in this case."

I glanced at him curiously. "It sounds as if you've had some dealings with him."

"Not Radcliffe specifically, but I've certainly dealt with rats on a few occasions." He shrugged. "As Radcliffe said, there's not much that goes on that the rats don't see or know about."

I frowned. "Is it possible Rinaldo has rats working for him? It might explain why they haven't been able to trace him—and why Radcliffe got no warning about the attacks."

"Radcliffe's lair might be the most powerful in the city, but it's certainly not the only one," Jackson said. "It's more than possible one of the smaller lairs has decided to work with Rinaldo in order to destroy Radcliffe and take his lair's position."

"I didn't know rats were so competitive—I thought they all just basically stuck to their own territories."

"Regular rats tend to. But we're talking rat shifters here, and that comes with all the usual human vices such as greed and desire." Jackson's voice was dry. "And I'm not talking sexual desire."

I raised an eyebrow, a smile teasing my lips. "You're not? That would have to be a first."

"Indeed." He glanced at his watch. "If we leave now, we'll have just enough time to go grab the car. And then, my dear Emberly, we can discuss the notion of desire to our hearts' content."

"I'd rather do than discuss."

He grinned. "An even better idea—shall we go?"

I rose and followed him out the door. After donning one of the helmets attached to the Vespa, I climbed on behind Jackson and lightly held on to his hips as he started the thing and drove off. And although it wasn't a particularly powerful machine, there was still something very pleasant about riding through the dead of night, with the stars bright overhead and the wind cool against my skin.

It took us about twenty minutes to get across to the car yard. Jackson pulled into the parking area and stopped. In the brief moment of silence, a car door slammed, and then a woman appeared. She was tall and slim, with silvery white hair and the most amazing blue eyes I'd ever seen. It wasn't just the color—which was a blue as rich as a summer sky—but rather the sense of otherworldliness that hit the minute my gaze met hers. It was almost as if I were staring at someone who wasn't simply flesh, but something far greater. Something ethereal and powerful.

Air fae, that inner voice whispered.

"Emberly," Jackson said, "meet our savior, the lovely Makani."

She raised a silvery eyebrow, her expression amused. "Have you ever noticed he's so much more generous with his compliments when he's after something?" She held out her hand. "It's a pleasure to meet you, Emberly."

The minute my skin touched hers, the air stirred and, just for a moment, it seemed to be filled with whispers. They weren't ones I could understand.

But *she* could. Her eyes widened fractionally as she ever so gently disentangled her grip from mine.

"What did you see?" I asked.

She hesitated, her expression briefly uncertain. "Trouble and darkness, but also glimmers of hope."

"Air fae," Jackson said, his tone dry, "are rather like witches. They cannot abide speaking in simple, understandable terms."

Makani elbowed him. "Shut up and give me your hand."

He raised an eyebrow but did as she bid. She cocked her head to one side, obviously listening to the voices I now couldn't hear. Eventually, she sighed and released him.

"It would appear your fates have been tied together. And you, my dear friend, have stepped well away from the path fate initially mapped out for you."

"Meaning the death your father saw for me no longer applies?" he asked. If he was at all concerned by this prospect, I wasn't sensing it.

She hesitated again. "I believe not. But we're reaching a time of flux, and you two are going to be right in the middle of it."

"So we've been warned before," I said.

She nodded. "By both Lan and Grace, I believe."

Surprise ran through me. Lan was the old Filipino shaman who'd helped us stop the Aswang—the spider spirit who'd been using her victims as fodder for her young. He'd also given us a rather dire warning—that a time of metaphysical darkness was approaching Melbourne, and it was a darkness that would draw even darker creatures and events. The Aswang and the virus were, apparently, just the beginning of our troubles.

"I'm surprised you know them—I thought air fae tended to be soloists," I said.

"While it is true we generally don't mix with shaman and witches, all of us who read the future—be it through earth or the air—have felt this period of flux coming for a while now." She shrugged. "It has forced us to unite and discuss the matter."

"And have said discussions led to a possible solution to the problem?" Jackson asked. "Or have you all taken the politician's path—lots of rhetoric and little action?"

She elbowed him again, this time hard enough to draw a grunt. "I'll give you lots of rhetoric and little action next time you want to get lusty if you're not damn well careful."

I grinned. The little I'd seen of air fae had made me believe they were all delicate, somewhat fragile beings who often weren't grounded in any way, but it seemed that belief was very wrong—at least when it came to Makani.

"Both Lan and Grace were rather vague on what this flux might entail," I said. "I don't suppose you can clarify it any?"

She was shaking her head even before I'd finished asking the question. "Not even my father can see that, and he has been reading fate for nearly a millennium now."

I blinked. Even for a fae, that was *old*.

"All any of us can do is monitor the situation, and provide support for those on the front line when and where needed."

"Meaning us, I'm gathering."

"Yes." A smile touched her lips. "I also believe, in the very near future, that you will need the services of a good secretary capable of providing mystical support."

"And you're volunteering?" Jackson said. "Most excellent."

"Well, it was either me or Lan, and as much as I admire the shaman, he wouldn't be able to put up with your bullshit for long." She gave him a somewhat severe look, though amusement lurked in the depths of her blue eyes. "There will, however, be no fraternization during work hours."

He groaned. "That is nothing short of torture times two. Fate obviously has it in for me this decade."

Makani raised an eyebrow as she glanced at me. "You already have this rule?"

"It's a very sensible one, given the amorous tendencies of the fae in question," I said. "It'd be hard to get any work done without it."

"Indeed. While those of fire do rank rather high on the overly sexed scale, I rather suspect *this* one stood in line twice."

"Ladies, I *am* standing right next to you both."

"Indeed," Makani repeated, her amusement stronger. She reached into her coat pocket, pulled out a set of keys, and offered them to me. "It's the black SUV at the back of the lot. It's got full insurance, but please try not to make too much of a mess of it."

My fingers brushed hers as I took the keys, and again the whispers swirled. Her eyes went wide.

"What?" I immediately said.

"You need to get back to your partner. *Now.*"

CHAPTER 7

Fear stepped into my heart. I didn't say anything; I didn't even question her. I simply wrapped my fingers around the keys and ran for the back of the lot.

"Open the rear cargo," Jackson said.

I pressed the appropriate button on the remote, then pulled off the backpack containing the laptops and threw it onto the backseat. Jackson dumped the Vespa into the cargo area, then climbed into the passenger seat. I was reversing out of the bay even before he'd closed the door. Makani was still standing where we'd left her, her arms crossed and her expression troubled. She raised a hand as we sped past; I didn't acknowledge it. I didn't dare take my hands off the wheel, given the speed at which we were already moving.

"It'll be okay—"

"Don't," I said, my voice sharp, and then took a deep breath, trying to calm down. "Sorry. I shouldn't be snapping at you."

He reached across the center console and squeezed my leg. "It's okay, Em. We're connected, remember? And wouldn't you feel it if he was dead?"

"Normally, yes. But Rory's still in a weak state, and that could hinder our connection and my ability to call to his ashes."

"So there's a distance restriction when it comes to that sort of thing?"

"Like any signal that has no amplification, it grows weaker the farther you move away from the primary source."

"So you'd never risk going interstate or overseas without him?"

"No. I couldn't anyway—we need to reaffirm our connection on a regular basis."

He grunted. "Fate really has got it in for your lot, hasn't it?"

"Our life isn't bad, Jackson. It can just get complicated."

"To say the least." He shook his head. "I think I'd rather juggle a hundred women than do what you and Rory do century after century."

I glanced at him. "Even you can't juggle a hundred women."

He raised an eyebrow. "Want to bet on it?"

I laughed. "No, I do not."

I swung the SUV onto the freeway ramp and hit the accelerator, reaching for every ounce of speed the Range Rover had. As the big engine kicked into gear, he said, "If Makani *does* come to work with us, she won't want to be just a secretary. She'll want to be a full partner."

He was, I knew, talking to keep my mind off what might be happening with Rory. "I have no problem with that, but I *am* surprised. She's an air fae, and they're even less inclined to remain around cities than your lot."

"I suspect she's been sent here by her father."

I raised an eyebrow and glanced at him. "I didn't think *any* of the fae remained in family groups."

"We don't, but both parents always remain a part of any child's life, no matter how young or old that child is."

Meaning they were a whole lot better than we phoenixes at keeping in contact once their children had flown the nest. "I was under the impression you hadn't talked to your dad for years."

"I haven't, but I'm also much older than Makani. Besides, given how long we live, years are more like months."

"Just how much older are you?"

He grinned. "When you tell me your true age, I'll tell you mine."

"Fair enough." I concentrated on overtaking a long truck for a minute, and then added, "What makes you think her dad sent her here?"

Because I certainly hadn't gained that impression by anything she'd said or done in our brief meeting.

"It was something she said when I first contacted her—that she'd been expecting my call."

I frowned. "She's air fae. That goes with the territory, doesn't it?"

"Yes, but Makani stepped away from reading the wind after the death of a lover some years back."

"Meaning she read the wind wrong?"

"Quite the opposite—he wouldn't listen to her."

Meaning he was an idiot. "Did he know she was fae?"

A smile touched his lips. "*He* was fae, and he was also the one who read the wind wrong, not her. He died; she discovered two weeks later that she was carrying his child."

I swung onto the Hume Freeway ramp, keeping the big vehicle in line as we took the sweeping turn far faster than the sign recommended.

"That would have been hard."

"Yeah." Jackson was silent for a moment, and then added, "Makani stepped away from reading the wind the minute she discovered that."

I frowned. "I would have thought she'd do the opposite to keep her child safe."

"Reading is not without its risks. There have been instances of *fiosaiche* losing all sense of self and becoming little more than air."

Fiosaiche, I knew, was basically the fae term for shaman. If she'd been one, then she was a very gifted reader indeed. "So if she's once again doing so, it's because she's been asked?" When he nodded, I added, "But why would her dad ask her rather than simply do it himself?"

"Because the older air fae get, the more stretched they become, until they are so thin, they appear little more than gossamer. He wouldn't have the strength to counter whatever events this so-called flux is going to throw at us."

"I'm seriously doubting he intends Makani to actually fight."

"No, but she's a fae in the prime of her life, and she'll be able to withstand the exchange of forests for the bleakness of the city far longer than he."

"And her child?"

"Is now in his thirties, and in training to become *fiosaiche* when his grandfather eventually dies."

"So it's a position that's handed down?"

Jackson nodded. "But generally to the male of the line, not the female."

"So she was training because there were no sons?"

"Yes. But to become *fiosaiche* is to forgo children."

"He obviously didn't." Nor did Makani, for that matter.

"Makani was conceived before he stepped into the position. I have no doubt Hava will have done the same now that he is undergoing the training. As for Makani—she also stepped away from training simply because she wanted to spend more time with her son than the position would have allowed."

"Huh." I concentrated on the road for a while, and eventually asked, "Do you have any problems with working with her?"

He shook his head. "She'll be an asset. Not to mention easy on the eyes."

"Remember the no-touching rule."

"Oh, trust me, I'm remembering. The swimmers are aching at the mere thought of it."

I grinned. "They will get relief. Eventually."

"I'll probably explode before then." His expression was gloomy, but amusement teased his lips. "At this rate, I'll have to take matters into my own hands, and that's a very depressing thought."

I chuckled softly. "I'm sure you're more than capable of such an action, even if it *is* a very foreign one for you."

He sniffed, a sound that somehow managed to be disdainful. "The point is I shouldn't *have* to."

My amusement grew, but I resisted the urge to reach across and pat his leg in sympathy; not only would that have been dangerous, given the speed we were going, but also because I knew he really *was* sexually frustrated. I could feel the heat of it running through the back of my thoughts, a river of desire that could so easily sweep me away if I wasn't very careful.

And, right now, with everything going on, we really couldn't afford that happening.

If he heard that particular thought, he didn't reply to it. Maybe the reality of it simply depressed him too much. I drove on into the night. Luckily there didn't seem to be any cops about, but even if there had been, I wouldn't have stopped. The need to get back to Rory, to see what was happening, was beating fast and strong within me, and while I was now close enough to know that he wasn't dead, that didn't mean he wasn't injured or close to that state.

I needed to know. Needed to get there and find out.

As I swung onto the dirt road that led down to the river and our cabin, flashes of red and blue began to cut through the trees—not from flames, but from emergency vehicle lights. My heart began to race a whole lot faster, even though I still had no sense that Rory was dead.

A police car blocked the road near the first cabin, forcing me to stop. I did so and rolled down the window.

"I'm sorry, miss," the officer said, "but there's been a fire, and we're not—"

"We're PIT associates." Jackson leaned past me to give the officer his badge. "And we've been called in to investigate."

The officer frowned as his gaze swept the badge. "I can't see why PIT would even be here, let alone send associates."

"Emberly here was staying in one of the cabins," Jackson said. "What building went up? And have there been any injuries or fatalities?"

"It was the last cabin, and yes, there've been injuries. We're still trying to determine the latter."

I briefly closed my eyes and fought the urge to run into the area and find Rory. If he were dead, I'd know. I had to cling to that, if nothing else.

"We need to get in there, Officer. *Now,*" Jackson added when the officer hesitated.

"Wait here while I check with the inspector." He stepped back and began talking into his two-way. I tapped my fingers against the steering wheel, my gaze on the lights up ahead. Smoke swirled through the night, but I couldn't see any flames, and there was little in the way of heat riding the crisp air.

"Okay," the officer said, handing Jackson's ID back. "You're cleared. But you'll have to leave the SUV here— just pull it off the road a bit more."

I did so, then grabbed my coat and climbed out. The farther I got down the road, the stronger the scent of smoke became. One of our neighbors nodded at me as we strode by, and the cabin nearest ours bore scorch marks. That fact alone suggested our cabin hadn't just caught fire; it had exploded.

I rounded the corner and was met by a scene of utter destruction. There was little left of the cabin but a pile of smoldering wood. Even the old stone chimney hadn't withstood the explosion—there were only a few bricks left at the base to indicate its existence. We were stopped again as we drew near the cabin, but once we'd both shown our IDs, we were motioned over to a somewhat disheveled-looking gentleman whose short gray hair stuck out in all directions and who seemed to be wearing a striped pajama top under his sweater.

"Inspector James Cobden," he said, his voice gruff but not unfriendly. "What's PIT's interest in this case?"

I introduced us both, then added, "I was staying here with a friend—"

"If his name is Rory Jones, he's currently being checked by the ambulance crew," the inspector said. "Can you think of any reason why someone might have wanted to harm either of you?"

Relief swept me, and I didn't bother hiding it. "PIT isn't well liked, even among our fellow officers. Do you mind if I head over to talk to my companion?"

"I'll stay here and answer any questions you might have," Jackson said, even as he gave me a light push toward the ambulance.

I didn't really need the encouragement and walked away before the inspector could answer.

Rory was sitting on the back of the ambulance, his right arm being bandaged by a paramedic and his hair somewhat singed—both of which suggested he'd been unable to draw in the fire and stop it from affecting him for some reason. He was wearing a pair of old jeans and a shirt that hung like a tent on him, but his feet were bare and blackened with soot.

The paramedic glanced up as I approached. I flashed my badge, then sat beside Rory. "You okay?"

"Yeah. Close call, though."

He put his free hand between us, and I placed mine on top. Though there was no telltale spark or heat, he instantly began drawing on my strength. He was weaker—far weaker—than when we'd left him, which basically confirmed that *he'd* been the reason the cabin had exploded. Not that I'd really had much doubt about that; the only other way the cabin could have gone up like that was if the gas bottles had exploded.

"What happened?"

"Break-in of some kind that went wrong." He shrugged, a casual move that was anything but. Tension and anger rode him, but the paramedic's presence was preventing him from saying anything. "It's just lucky I happened to be in the bathroom—it probably saved me from the explosion."

"Who broke in? Any idea?"

He glanced at me, his amber eyes aglitter, but he said only, "No. That's a job for the coroner—if he can find anything left of them in the ashes, that is."

Meaning he'd made *damn* sure nothing was left.

"And the clothes?"

A smile ghosted his lips. "Donation from the guy two doors up. He told me it wasn't right to be walking around buck naked when there were kiddies about."

I raised my eyebrows. "There are kids here? I don't remember seeing any."

"That's because said kiddies are actually teenagers who were very unimpressed by the term."

"I can imagine."

"Right," the paramedic said as he finished bandaging Rory's arm. "The painkiller I gave you should hold for a couple of hours, but you might need something after that. You *should* go to the hospital, in my opinion."

A smile ghosted Rory's lips. "I'm a firefighter. The boys would give me merry hell if I went to the hospital for a burn as minor as this."

"Partial second-degree burns are hardly minor." The paramedic's expression was disapproving. "Sounds like your work mates are a bunch of idiots."

"Their teasing is simply a way of relieving tension," Rory said, his tone a little sharp. "You should know that."

The paramedic grunted and stepped back. "Given you won't take my advice, you're free to go."

Rory released me and rose, somewhat cautiously, to his feet. I stood with him, one hand near his elbow, ready to catch him should he show any sign of toppling. After a minute, his smile flashed, and he pointed with his chin toward the somewhat blackened trunk of an old river gum to the right of the cabin ruins.

Once there, he sat down and released a somewhat shuddering breath. "Well, *that* was a fucking interesting night."

I glanced around to make sure no one was close enough to overhear us. "What actually happened?"

"As I said, I was attacked. But I certainly wasn't in the bathroom at the time." The fury I'd glimpsed before was fully evident now. "The bastards came equipped with magic."

"Fuck—what sort?"

"The sort that restrains our access to fire but *not* our access to the mother." The smile that touched his lips was cold. *Very* cold. "They found *that* out very fast."

Which explained why he was so drained. Reaching for the mother when he was still in the recovery stage of rebirth had been a very dangerous thing to do. I twined my fingers around his again, needing the comfort of his touch. I could have so very easily lost him, because there would have been no calling him back. Not from the mother.

"Any idea who they were?"

"Well, they were very definitely vampires. Other than that, no."

I frowned. "De Luca's get has come after me and Jackson a few times now, but I can't see why they'd drive all the way out here to attack you. Besides, how would they even know you exist?"

"I was at Highpoint when Parella shot De Luca, remember? Maybe one of his crew mentioned it to them."

I wrinkled my nose. "Even if that were true, Parella and his people couldn't possibly have known about the connection between us."

"Maybe it's simply a matter of the den wanting to erase *anyone* connected to you."

"Maybe," I said even as doubt gnawed at me. While it wasn't beyond the realm of possibility that De Luca's get had indeed decided to erase anyone I was close to, I doubted they'd have either the funds or the foresight to go to a witch and purchase a restraining spell. Not now that their creator was dead.

"If they were vampires, they must have driven up here. Did you hear a vehicle of any kind?"

Rory shook his head. "The police suspect they parked it in the scrub farther up the road and walked in."

I frowned. "Suspect? Meaning they haven't found it yet?"

"Not that I've heard, but they're not likely to tell me even if they had." He paused and reached into the pocket of his borrowed jeans. "I did manage to grab a couple of wallets before I cindered the bastards."

I took the two of them, then dropped one onto my knees and opened the other. There were a couple of credit cards bearing the name Harry Jones, and a driver's license that apparently belonged to a Stephen White. I flipped it around so Rory could see the ID picture. "Is that one of the vamps?"

He studied the picture for a moment, then shook his head. "But it's not really surprising they'd be holding stolen IDs. Most vamps who take a commission don't carry anything that could accurately identify them."

"What makes you think the attack was a commission?" I opened the second wallet and discovered another credit card and driver's license bearing different names, although this time both were female.

Rory shook his head again when I showed it to him. "It's just a feeling I got. They weren't moving as a team, but rather separate entities. It was almost as if they were racing each other to get the kill." He hesitated, then half laughed, although it was a sound that held little in the way of amusement. "That haste was probably the only thing that saved me."

"You heard them coming?"

"Not initially. But one of them disengaged the safety as he was coming at me rather than doing it outside. It was only a soft click, but it was so out of place that it was enough to wake me."

I frowned. "If they had guns, why didn't they just shoot the shit out of the cabin? They would have known your position by the sound of your heartbeat."

"Aside from the fact it would have woken the entire neighborhood, you mean?"

I half smiled. "Yes."

He shrugged. "Good question, and one I can't possibly answer given the state of both the cabin and my five attackers." He disentangled his fingers from mine. "If I drain any more of your strength, you're going to be as weak as me."

In any other circumstance, I would have protested. But he was right; the simple fact was my reserves were already riding too low.

"We need to find somewhere else for you to recover in safety."

"If they found this place, they're bound to find any other location we decide on."

"Not necessarily," Jackson said as he walked over and then squatted down in front of us. "Tell me, just how the hell did you, of all people, get burned?"

A smile ghosted Rory's lips. "I forgot about the gas bottles on the side of the cabin when I incinerated the place. Their explosion sent me tumbling, and it tore me from spirit to flesh form."

"But even then, the fire shouldn't have affected you," Jackson said.

"There were witnesses by that stage. I *did* stop the fire burning too deeply, but I could hardly walk out of a firestorm completely untouched—not without raising all sorts of suspicions."

Jackson grunted and glanced at me. "The cops told me there's no unaccounted car in the area. The vamps must have been dropped off."

"Which means they'll probably have a pickup arranged."

He nodded. "I told the cop we'd position ourselves up near the main road and nab anyone who comes down here."

"Did you now?"

He ignored the sarcasm in my voice. "And I also have a solution to the accommodation issue."

"Let me guess," I said. "You've volunteered the home of one of the ladies from your harem."

"Well, no, because I really don't want to put any more of them in any sort of danger. I was thinking more along the lines of Adán."

Adán being the second earth fae who'd helped create the trench around Brooklyn. "Really? Why?"

"Because he not only lives in Thornton, which is only about fifty minutes from here, but his home is something of a fortress."

I wrinkled my nose. "Fifty minutes adds a whole lot to our traveling time when we're in the city."

"But you don't have to come back to me every night, Em," Rory said. "I may still be weak, but as long as I've got fire, I'll be all right for a couple of days."

"I don't know—"

"The real problem," Rory said, cutting me off with a gentle squeeze of my arm, "is that if they found this place, they're more than likely to find others. And I'd hate to put Adán in any sort of danger."

Jackson snorted. "Adán's an earth fae. Trust me, those buggers don't scare easily, and they certainly don't die easily. He'll jump at the opportunity for some action."

I did believe him, because he'd already done just that when we'd called both him and Dmitri to help us in Brooklyn. "Maybe what we need is a little subterfuge."

"Like what?" Jackson asked.

"Well, there're only two ways those vamps could have found this place. Either they were tracking us—"

"We checked the cars regularly. We weren't bugged," Jackson said.

"There's more than one way to track," Rory said. "Winged shifters, for instance."

"PIT were certainly using hawk shifters to tail us," Jackson said. "But I was under the impression they'd stopped."

I snorted. "Just because the inspector *implied* that doesn't mean she actually did it."

I liked the woman, but she was in the middle of a battle she couldn't afford to lose, and there was no doubt in my mind she'd do whatever she deemed necessary to twist the odds in her favor. If that included following two people who were knee-deep in the same shit, then she'd do so.

"And if we *weren't* followed," I continued, "then the only other way they could have found us is if they were told."

Rory frowned. "Did you tell anyone we were here?"

"No."

Jackson held up his hands. "Don't look at me."

"Which means they either had psychic help or PIT did indeed track us here, and the squad does indeed have a mole."

"There's an easy way to get an answer to one of those questions." Jackson pulled out his phone and hit the DIAL button, then held the phone between the three of us so we could all hear.

"Chief Inspector," he said the minute she answered, "I have a rather urgent question for you."

"Indeed? Please proceed."

"Have you set a hawk on our tail?"

She paused. "And if I have?"

"You need to call him off."

"Only if you start carrying your phone so we know your location. It's imperative that we keep track of all operatives right now—"

"Inspector," I cut in, "we're not operatives. We're associates, and your tracking us almost led to the death of a friend."

"Would this friend be Rory Jones, the man nobody witnessed coming out of Brooklyn?"

I hesitated. "The same."

"Care to explain how he got out?"

"No—and that's not important right now," I said. "Are you, or are you not, having us tailed?"

"I am."

"Then you need to call them off. Someone betrayed our position, Inspector."

"There is no leak or mole in my department, Pearson." Her tone was frosty. "If your hideout was blown, then it was not due to anything we did."

"No one knew where we were, Inspector. There were no bugs on our cars, and we dumped Jackson's phone long before we got to our current location."

"The sindicati are not averse to using winged shifters to follow targets," the inspector said.

"Yes, but we would have noticed two birds following us. And undoubtedly your hawk would also have noticed another tag." I hesitated. "Besides, we have a truce with Parella. He wouldn't be following us."

Not by air, at any rate, Jackson said. *Not if the past efforts are anything to go by.*

"If you believe that," the inspector said, "then you are both fools."

Maybe we were. Maybe it *was* the sindicati behind all this, given it was vampires who attacked Rory. But that little voice inside me, the one that dreamed of death and was very rarely wrong, suggested PIT was somehow connected. It wasn't behind the actual attack, of that I had no doubt, but the information about our location had certainly come from the organization. Somehow.

"Inspector," Jackson said, "if you can guarantee, with one hundred percent certainty, that PIT is secure and has no leaks, then I'll keep my phone and even tell you where we'll be staying. But call off the hawks, because the next time we spot one following us, we'll fry it."

"I would advise against doing that. I really don't appreciate my people coming under friendly fire." Her voice was flat. "Where are you staying?"

"I'll tell you that when we decide where to go next. Thanks, Inspector." With that, he hung up. "There's only one way we're going to prove whether PIT has a leak, and that's by exposing it."

"That could get dangerous," Rory said.

"Not if we're sneaky about it."

A smile touched Rory's lips. "I didn't think sneaky was in a fire fae's vocabulary."

"We generally do prefer to be up-front about things, but hey, needs must, and all that." Jackson plucked one of the wallets from my hand. "And I'm thinking these could provide access to sneakiness."

I smiled. "So we book two rooms at a hotel, using the stolen credit cards for the second one, then leave your phone in one and keep watch from the other?"

"It's almost as if you read my mind." His grin flashed. "Then we give the inspector the address, and see what happens."

"And if nothing does, it might at least mean PIT is secure."

"Exactly. But it may take a few days for someone to bite, so we'll have to be careful about coming and going."

"It's also probably best if I visit Rory alone."

"Agreed." Jackson rose. "I'll go see if Cobden is happy to release Rory, then make calls to both Parella and Adán. Then we can head up to the main road to keep an eye on things while we wait for Adán to arrive."

"I really doubt anyone will be back to retrieve the vampires. They must know something has gone wrong by now."

"Oh, I agree, but we've got nothing to lose." Jackson shrugged, then spun around and walked away.

I glanced at Rory. "Are you sure you're going to be okay? You're still on the wire when it comes to strength."

"So are you." He brushed his fingertips down my cheek. "I'll be okay. Just don't get yourself killed when there's such a distance between us, because that might be problematic."

"Trust me, I'm doing my best to avoid getting dead."

"Good." He hesitated. "What happened in Brooklyn?"

I gave him a quick update on everything. Rory frowned. "If he *is* using magic to hide his location, why haven't the witches discovered it? Surely using that much power would have caused some ripples in the earth's energy fields?"

"So I would have thought. But maybe he's not using

much. Maybe the spell is just big enough to conceal Rinaldo's presence and nothing else."

"Which would suggest he hasn't a den of his own. At least not yet." Rory paused. "It could also mean he's using the Coalition to hire people. If *that's* true, then maybe tonight's attack came from him."

The Coalition's full name was the Coalition of Non-humans. It was an independent resource center that provided financial and legal help to both vampires and werewolves, and it was mostly funded by member contributions. The CNH tended to be low-key, not only because of the rise of anti-werewolf and -vampire sentiment in recent years but also because it had a smaller, less-known—but very profitable—side department. This department basically handled nonhuman business activities that were not only more than a little illegal, but which required anonymity—things like kidnapping and killing. It had no official phone number and couldn't be reached via the CNH's switchboard; if you wanted something done, or if you wanted to contact someone you might have dealt with previously, the only way to do so was via snail mail.

Which was what we'd done a few days ago. We'd sent a letter requesting a meet with Lee Rawlings, the Coalition bagman who'd been sent to collect me the first time I'd been kidnapped. We'd been hoping that he'd be able to tell us more about the state of play between the sindicati factions and maybe even Luke, but we'd since uncovered a lot of that information ourselves. It'd still be handy to talk to him, though, if only because he might have some information about Rinaldo. The bastard might be off radar, but surely someone, somewhere, had to know *something* about him.

"It's possible, but I don't see why Rinaldo would go to such lengths," I said. Besides, Radcliffe had said the vamps who'd attacked his venues *weren't* mercenaries. If they'd come from the Coalition, they would have been.

"Remember, you're talking about a very old vampire. In his mind, I'm probably nothing more than an incomplete lesson. Until I *stay* taken out, said lesson would have little impact."

I could totally see Rinaldo thinking that way—especially given what he'd done to Shona and the wolves. "Which means if he does discover your new location, you and Adán will come under attack."

"From the little I've seen of Adán, I wish them luck trying." Rory patted my leg. "Stop worrying, and help me up."

I did so. Thankfully, he was a little more secure on his feet this time, but I still hovered close as we made our way over to where Jackson stood talking to Cobden.

"You're free to go," he said. "Just remain reachable, in case we have any further questions."

"My phone has been destroyed," Rory said, "but you can get hold of me via either Emberly's work number or Jackson's."

Cobden nodded and stepped away. We walked back to the car, then drove it along the old road and pulled into the trees just off the main road.

"Any success with Parella?" I asked Jackson.

"He denies the use of winged shifters to tag us, and he didn't order the hit. He didn't, however, rule out the possibility of that happening in the future if we didn't start relaying more information."

"Hard to relay what we haven't got." And the stuff we *did* have we certainly didn't want in their hands.

"I did say that. He didn't believe we don't have the information."

"And Adán?" I asked.

"Reckons he'll be here by four," Jackson said. "I'll keep an eye on things if you two want to nap."

I didn't argue. I just settled more comfortably into the seat and went straight to sleep. The slamming of a car door jerked me awake. I sat upright too quickly and just about strangled myself on the seat belt as it snapped taut. I swore, released the thing, then scrubbed the sleep from my eyes and peered through the somewhat foggy windshield.

Jackson was greeting another man who would have been an almost identical replica of Dmitri if not for the shape of his face and nose, both of which were broader.

"Rory," I said, "Adán's here."

I climbed out of the car without waiting for a response, crossing my arms and shivering a little as the chilly night air hit like a slap across the face.

A grin split Adán's lips when he spotted me, and his eyes—a warm chocolate color—gleamed with pleasure. And, I suspected, more than a little desire. But then, he *was* fae.

"It's a real pleasure to see you again." He caught my hand, tugged me closer, and kissed both my cheeks. "I do so hope having Rory stay at my place means you will come visit me."

"If you're cooking, I'll be there."

"Excellent." His gaze moved past me. "That's a rather becoming outfit you're wearing there, Rory."

"Oversized and ill-fitting are the next new trend." His tone was dry. "I appreciate your taking me in on short notice like this."

Adán's grin widened. "Although Jackson assures me there shouldn't be any problems, I'm always up for a good fight. You ready?"

Rory nodded, then gave me a wink and followed Adán across to his Land Rover. Once they were gone, I said, "We need to find somewhere to rest, but I doubt there'll be many hotels open at this hour. Not in this area, anyway."

"No." Jackson scrubbed a hand through his hair. For the first time since I'd known him, he actually looked tired. "Why don't we just head back to the office? We need to make arrangements for Rinaldo to pick up the laptops, and we have to be there to meet Radcliffe at ten, anyway."

I frowned. "That's an hour-and-a-half drive—I'm not sure either of us can do it."

"Well, it's either that or we sleep in the SUV."

"Let's do the drive." The Range Rover was a comfortable beast, but nothing could beat a real bed.

It was a long drive back to Melbourne, but our wakefulness was boosted by several coffee stops along the way. The office remained as we'd last left it and was as cold as hell, but I didn't care. I stripped as I headed up the circular staircase, and all but fell onto the mattress. Jackson had stopped downstairs to make the call to Rinaldo, and I have no memory of him joining me in the bed. I was already asleep by that time.

A harsh rapping woke me some hours later. I sat upright, my heart hammering, for an instant confused as to where I was. The sun was shining in through the big window to my right, highlighting the mess that surrounded us—a mess caused by vamps searching both the office and this upper living area.

The rapping echoed again, and I scrubbed a hand across my eyes and glared, somewhat blearily, at the clock. Ten o'clock.

Oh *fuck*.

"Jackson, get up." I scrambled out of the bed. "The rats are here."

"Too early," he mumbled. "Come back to bed."

I tossed his jeans at his face. "It's ten. Is the file still behind the coffee machine?"

"Yes." He swung out of bed and began climbing into his jeans. "You get the door. I'll get the file and remove the appropriate bits."

As we clattered down the stairs, someone leaned on the doorbell and let it ring long and loud. "All right, all right, I'm coming," I shouted back, doing up my shirt as I walked—albeit slowly—over to the door.

I took my time undoing the bolts but left the chain on as I opened the door a fraction and peered out.

"You were the one who set the time," Radcliffe said, clearly amused. "If it was inconvenient, you should have said."

"Sorry, it's been a long night. Hang on." I closed the door again and glanced across at Jackson. He nodded and fired up the coffee machine. I undid the chain and opened the door wider. "Come on in."

Radcliffe stopped several steps in, his gaze sweeping the mess and the remains of the chalky outline of where Rosen's body had been dumped. "I think you need to change your decorator, because this isn't a look that would garner any sort of respect from clients."

He was, it seemed, in a rather jovial mood. Given both he and his goons were wearing expensive-looking suits, it was highly likely he'd come straight from the casino and a rather nice win. Radcliffe might run underground gaming venues, but he certainly didn't spend his cash there—undoubtedly because he knew just how rigged the games were. Rats weren't generous souls, and if the rumors I'd heard were true, his gaming venues were profit-generating machines—which was undoubtedly why Rinaldo wanted to take them over.

I waited until his two goons had entered, then closed the door. "You got the tape?"

He glanced at one of his men, who reached into his pocket and produced it. "You got the file?"

Jackson picked it up from the coffee table and walked across. "There's not a whole lot of information in it, but it does state Rinaldo's first name is Reginald and that he arrived in Melbourne three years ago."

"Wonder how Rosen uncovered that when the rest of us can't get squat against the man." Radcliffe opened the file and flicked through. "Not much, as you said, but more than we'd previously had. The deal proceeds."

"Good." I paused. "How do we make contact if we find anything else?"

Radcliffe produced a card. "It's a messenger service, but any call you make will be treated as a priority."

I accepted the card and tucked it into my shirt pocket. "We expect the same sort of courtesy. You can use the office number."

"Excellent. But I'm not leaving without the tape, as I have no desire for it to land in PIT hands. View it, and tell me what you see."

I glanced at Jackson, who shrugged minutely. *Can't see the harm.*

I tossed it to him. He walked across to the desk, switched on the computer, and then slipped the tape into the attached player. A second later, images began to scroll across the screen. The tape had clearly been edited, because the action started almost immediately. Unsurprisingly, Rinaldo and his men were the poster boys of efficient brutality, and the gaming venue was theirs in a matter of minutes.

"Play it back at half speed." I pulled a chair closer and sat down.

Jackson did so. "If he's using a glamor to hide his form, it's a damn good one."

"What makes you say that?" Radcliffe said.

He was standing behind us, and his nearness was making my spine itch. We might have a truce, but I still wasn't trusting it would hold up against his desire to slip a knife into my back.

"A glamor usually can't withstand any sort of touch. No matter how perfect it is from either a distance or close up, if it brushes against either an object or a person, there is a telltale shimmer." I pointed at the screen. "But if you watch carefully, when Rinaldo snaps the neck of your security guard, there's no such shimmer. This *is* him. It's not someone else using a glamor."

"Which means," Jackson said, "Rinaldo might, in fact, be two people rather than one."

"Turn up the sound," I said.

He did so, and we listened to Rinaldo barking orders and threats. "It's not the same voice. The tone is slightly different."

Jackson nodded. "Yeah, it is."

I swore and leaned back in the chair. "Well, this just makes things all the more difficult."

"Not really," Jackson said. "The only thing that's changed is that we're now hunting two people, not one."

"It does at least explain how he can be in two places at once," Radcliffe said. "And surely there can't be too many identical twin vampires turned in the last few hundred years."

"Rinaldo's a very ancient vampire," I said. "The council isn't likely to have a record of him."

"That may be true of the Australian branch," Radcliffe said, "but I'm betting their European counterparts might be a little more helpful."

I swung around to look at him. "You have contacts over there?"

His smile flashed. "I have contacts everywhere."

I resisted the urge to smite the smug look from his face. "Then contact them; we'll see if PIT can dig up anything."

They may be able to, Jackson said. *Whether they'll actually tell us anything is a totally different thing.*

That could be said about Radcliffe, too. He might be emitting all the right signals when it came to being cooperative, but I doubted it would last if he actually got a worthwhile lead on our vampire. I very much suspected Radcliffe would not, in any way, share his chance of retribution.

"Deal," Radcliffe said. "Talk to you soon."

With that, he collected his tape and strode to the door, one goon in front, the other behind. The latter did not shut the door after him.

"Pricks," I muttered as I pushed up and walked across to lock up again.

Jackson's arms slid around my waist as I slammed the dead bolt home. "I'm thinking we finally have a few moments to ourselves," he murmured, his warm breath teasing my left ear. "Care to spend them relieving a mild ache or two?"

I spun around and draped my arms around his neck. "Mild tension? Does that mean you actually took care of business while I was asleep?"

He laughed. "No, it most certainly does *not*. But stating the obvious—that I'm going to explode if I don't get inside you soon—sounded a little crude."

"Since when has that stopped you?"

"I do occasionally like to surprise people, you know."

"What time did you tell Rinaldo to drop by and pick up the laptops?"

"This afternoon, when we're not here."

"Shame you didn't say ten. It would have given Radcliffe his chance at killing the bastard."

"Rinaldo is hardly likely to come here himself, given he's well aware we have a deal going with the sindicati." He pressed me tighter against his groin. "And can we change the topic? Talking about those two is seriously deflating."

I smiled. If anything *was* deflating, I sure as hell wasn't feeling it. "Well, that can't be allowed to happen. What can I do to fix it?"

"Kiss me."

Even as he said it, his lips came down upon mine. Hard. As kisses went, it was glorious—all passion and need and urgency. It drew me in and swept me away, until I couldn't think of anything more than him and me, and the desire that threatened to burn out of control between us.

Eventually he pulled away, his breathing harsh and unsteady. He didn't say anything; he simply grabbed the ends of my shirt and ripped it open. As buttons went flying, his mouth came down on my right breast, and he began to alternately suck and lick my nipple. As a gasp escaped my lips, I threw my head back against the door and arched my spine to give him greater access. He moved from one breast to the other, continuing to tease, until my body was quivering under the delicious assault of teeth and tongue. I slipped my hands down his muscular stomach and quickly undid his jeans, pushing them down his hips. His cock was thick and hard and oh so ready for action, but Jackson jerked away from my touch, his laugh vibrating against my chest.

"Do *that*, and this all will be over far too soon."

"I thought *that* was the point."

"Oh, it is, but a little foreplay never goes astray. Slip off your jeans."

I did so, kicking them to one side. His jeans swiftly joined mine; then he claimed my nipple again and lightly nipped. A shudder ran through me even as his tongue replaced his teeth, gently soothing. Then his free hand found my clit, and he began to stroke and tease me, bringing me close to the edge, then pulling me back, until my whole body was shuddering with the need for release.

"Oh god, don't," I somehow managed as he pulled his touch away yet again.

"Don't what?" he murmured. "Do this?"

His fingers brushed my clit and slipped inside. A shuddering gasp escaped.

"Or this?" he added, and removed his caress.

I didn't reply. I *couldn't* reply. I just tightened my grip around his neck, wrapped my legs around his waist, and thrust him deep inside. His groan was every bit as deep and needy as mine had been only moments before; then his hands cupped my butt and he began to thrust, his movements so violent, the door rattled in rhythm. I didn't care. All I wanted, all I needed, was him—deep, hard, and fast. Then the dam of pleasure he'd built so masterfully finally broke and, just for an instant, I couldn't breathe, couldn't think, could only feel. And lord, it was *glorious*.

He came a heartbeat later. As the last shudders of pleasure left his body, he leaned his forehead against mine and closed his eyes. Neither of us moved. The only sound was the harsh rasp of our breathing and the light ticking of the wall clock. It really *hadn't* taken all that long, foreplay or not.

"Well," he said, pulling back enough to look me in the eyes, "I think we both needed that."

I brushed sweaty strands of hair away from his forehead and then dropped a kiss on his nose. "So, back to work?"

"Hell *no*."

He shifted his grip on my butt, then swung around and walked toward the stairs. "I have a bed upstairs, and I'm not afraid to use it."

"If you can get me up those stairs without either separation or breaking something, I'll give you two hours."

He raised an eyebrow, amusement touching his lips. "And if I don't?"

"Half an hour."

"Challenge accepted."

And, needless to say, overcome.

Jackson slowed the Range Rover and turned left into Scott Grove. "What number are we looking for again?"

I opened the file sitting on my knee and scanned the somewhat scant information on Janice Green, Rosen Senior's secretary. We were vaguely hoping that she might be able to cast some light on Professor Wilson's habits, which in turn might help us find the lock that matched the second key we'd found in his shed.

"Thirty-eight," I said.

"Keep an eye on the numbers. I'll concentrate on getting this tank through the cars."

"Wonder how many of them belong to residents, and how many belong to students trying to avoid the university's parking fees?"

"Probably most." He paused to squeeze the big SUV between two similar-sized vehicles. It was a tight fit. "I know when I was a uni kid, I'd do anything and everything to avoid paying parking fees—including walking a fair distance to get to the place."

"Somehow that doesn't surprise me." I checked the street numbers and added, "Have you heard anything about Rosen's replacement?"

We certainly hadn't heard anything from the company itself, and were currently working on the presumption they still wanted us to find Professor Wilson's missing research notes. But that didn't mean Jackson hadn't heard other rumors about the company. He had more contacts than I had years behind me.

"I seriously doubt *that*," he said with a half laugh, replying to my thought rather than my actual question. "And I haven't got a contact who'd actually know anything about Rosen Pharmaceuticals."

"Then how did you find out all this stuff about Janice? Via your police contact?"

"No, taxation. There's no better source for basic information."

That was true given just how much information the Taxation Department wanted from people these days. "Janice's place is on the right—the one with the high picket fence."

He drove past and pulled into a driveway two houses down. I twisted around. Thirty-eight was a small, white-painted weatherboard home with a weatherworn tile roof and a small green carport on one side. There were two cars in the driveway—one a Hyundai, the other a small Honda.

I looked at Jackson's notes again. "Janice drives the Honda."

"Wonder who the other one belongs to. Because if I remember right, she isn't married and had no lovers."

"It might be a friend rather than a lover."

He glanced at me, amusement evident. "At lunch-time? On a workday?"

"People have been known to go home for lunch."

"They've also been known to go home for a bit of afternoon delight."

"Did she seem like the type for a little lunchtime rendezvous to you?"

"Well, no, but never judge a book by its cover and all that."

I snorted and glanced back at the house—just in time to see the front door open and Amanda Wilson—the professor's less-than-loving wife, and a woman who'd been bleeding him of information for the sindi-cati from the very first time they'd slept together—step out. "Duck," I said, and slid down behind the headrest.

"I'd really prefer just to grab the bitch."

"Do that, and we might just lose our one chance of uncovering who her controller is."

Jackson grunted and lifted up enough to look at the side mirror. "She's in the car."

"You follow her. I'll go inside and see if Janice sur-vived the encounter with our black widow."

He frowned at me. "Do you really think it's a wise move to split up?"

"Given Amanda's history, yeah, I do."

"But she has a history of seducing men for informa-tion, not women—"

"Which doesn't mean anything if her mind has been seized." I watched the Hyundai reverse out of the driveway. "Wish we had a damn tracker."

"We do. It's in the little bag of tricks I threw onto the backseat."

I gave him the look—the one that said, *Don't be daft.* "I meant on the car."

"Something that can still be achieved if you get your lovely ass out of the car so I can go stalk our quarry. I'll call once I know anything."

"Ditto." I stripped off my sweater and wrapped it around my head to conceal my hair. Amanda was far enough away now that she'd probably think the sweater was a scarf of some sort, which was infinitely better than her spotting the blaze of coppery red that was my hair.

I climbed out and waited until Jackson had reversed out of the driveway, then ran across the road to Janice's. The Honda's hood was still warm, suggesting she hadn't been home all that long.

The front door was locked, but a quick spurt of fire soon fixed that. I pushed it open with my fingertips. "Janice? It's Emberly Pearson—I'm with Hellfire Investigations. We need to ask you a couple of questions."

There was no answer. Aside from the soft ticking of an unseen clock, the house was silent. I frowned and took a wary step inside. "Janice?"

Still nothing. There were four doorways along the somewhat narrow hallway, but only one of those was open. Instinct was annoyingly silent when it came to suggesting which one to investigate first.

I took another step forward, then stopped. Heat teased my senses, but its flame was little more than a soft caress. It was coming from the room to my right, from what was most likely a bedroom, given most houses of this age tended to have their bathrooms either in the middle of the house or off the kitchen at the rear.

I moved toward it, only to stop as I realized the air smelled . . . odd. I took a deeper breath.

Fuck, *gas.*

I bolted into the room that held that flickering heat source. Janice lay in among the tangled blankets; her eyes were closed and her face slack. On the bedside tables there were at least half a dozen lit candles.

I waved a hand to snuff them out, then quickly felt Janice's neck for a pulse. Not only was it there, but it was strong and steady. Relief surged, but we weren't out of the woods just yet.

I spun and ran for the kitchen, opening the doors to check each room as I went past. There were at least another dozen lit candles split between the various rooms. I erased every tiny flame, then slid into the combined kitchen and living area, found the oven, and quickly turned off all the jets. The stink of gas in this area was particularly strong, and it wouldn't have taken all that much longer for the buildup to reach the other rooms. Amanda had obviously intended to be well away from the place before it blew. I opened the back door and as many windows as I could, then went back into the bedroom.

"Janice, wake up." I sat on the edge of the bed and roughly shook her shoulder.

She didn't open her eyes, just waved a hand at me somewhat airily. "Need sleep. Go away."

"Who was the woman who just left? What is her name?"

"Felicity." Her slow smile basically confirmed what the state of the bed suggested. "It was the oh-so-lovely Felicity."

"And she's your lover?"

"Yes." Her smile grew. "So lovely."

And *she* seemed to be answering my questions alto-gether too readily—especially given she probably had no idea who I was. There should have at least been some sort of reaction to my presence in her bedroom—something other than this happy compliancy, anyway.

"Does Felicity have a last name?"

I couldn't smell any alcohol on her breath, so I gently opened one eyelid. Her pupils were heavily dilated, sug-gesting she'd been drugged. But why, when Amanda was a powerful telepath who'd made a fortune stealing secrets from the minds of her lovers during intercourse?

And while it was obvious Amanda had intended to blow the house apart—taking Janice and any evidence she might hold with it—it was also possible that what-ever drug she'd given the older woman to make her talk might be lethal. I dragged out my phone, called an ambulance, and then repeated my question.

"Hocking," Janice said, after a moment. "Felicity Hocking."

"And how long have you and Felicity been lovers?"

"A few weeks." She shrugged and finally opened her eyes. The faintest hint of alarm crossed her expression. "Who are you? Do I know you?"

If Amanda had been her lover for a few weeks, it meant she'd been so *before* the sindicati had kidnapped us both and her mind had been taken over.

"I'm Emberly Pearson—I'm one of the private inves-tigators your boss employed to investigate the theft of research notes."

"He's dead." She closed her eyes again. "Can't be sad about that."

Which wasn't a surprising comment. Rosen Senior certainly hadn't endeared himself to me in the brief time I'd known him, and I couldn't help but think he'd have been a difficult man to work with.

"Don't go to sleep, Janice. You need to stay with me."

"I need to sleep. Go away."

"Felicity has drugged you with god only knows what. You sleep, you might die."

"She wouldn't do that. She cares for me."

"Trust me, the woman you know as Felicity only cares about herself." And she not only *could* kill, but had, and multiple times. "Do you know where she lives? Have you ever been to her place?"

"No, but she has an apartment in Docklands."

The Docklands area was currently very trendy—and therefore very expensive—so it wouldn't be surprising if Amanda *did* live there. But there was a hell of a lot of apartment buildings in that area, so we needed a little more information than that to track her down. "She never gave you an address?"

"No."

Again, that wasn't really surprising, but it *was* frustrating. "Did you at least get her phone number?"

"Yes." She waved her hand airily, almost smacking me in the face. "But you can't have it. She has a jealous husband who doesn't understand her."

I snorted. Amanda had certainly had plenty of husbands over the years, but most of the poor buggers were well and truly dead.

"I saw him the other day," Janice continued. "I don't think I was supposed to. Cold-looking fellow."

Instinct stirred. "Can you describe him?"

"Tall, gray haired, regal sort of nose." She sniffed. "Drove a big black SUV. I took a picture."

I blinked. "Of him? Or the car?" Because while that description might be on the vague side, it could easily fit Rinaldo. If it *was* him, we might have just gotten our first break.

"Both."

"Can I look at it?"

"Will you leave me alone?"

"I told you, I can't. You need an ambulance."

"I need sleep."

She was drifting off again. I let her go for a moment and rose. Looking around the bedroom didn't reveal a handbag, so I walked down to the kitchen and found it sitting on the dining table, along with an empty wine bottle and two glasses.

I opened the bag, then rummaged through until I found her cell. It wasn't locked, so I went straight into her contacts list and looked for Felicity's name. Unsurprisingly, it had been erased. I hit the ALBUM button, not expecting to find much, but the very first picture that came up was Rinaldo himself. His face was cool and controlled, but there was something in the way he was standing, watching Amanda approach, that made me want to reach into the photo and wrench her out of harm's way. Amanda was as far from innocent as you could get, but that look very much suggested he was using her in *every* way possible. And I couldn't imagine Rinaldo would be either a gentle *or* generous lover.

I zoomed in on the rear of the SUV and almost cheered—the number plate was crisp and clear. We finally had something that might help us track the bastard down.

I shoved her phone into my back pocket and returned to the bedroom. Janice was asleep, so I shook her roughly. Her response was sleepy and somewhat colorful.

I grinned and glanced at my watch. I probably had another five minutes or so before the ambulance arrived, so I decided to use that time to see what other information I could uncover.

"Janice, what can you tell me about the inverter device the company was developing?"

"I've already answered that question," she said, her voice holding a hint of annoyance.

Not to me, she hadn't. And if that was one of the questions Amanda had been asking, then it meant Rinaldo hadn't yet gotten his hands on the device. "I know, but tell me again anyway."

She yawned hugely. "We had prototypes up and running, but some official government department came in a few weeks ago and secured the whole project. It was all very dramatic."

A few weeks ago meant it had happened before Rosen had been murdered. Which meant—hopefully—that they were government officials rather than sindicati goons or rats in disguise. As the wail of an approaching siren got louder, I said, "What can you tell me about the project Professor Wilson was working on?"

She shrugged. "Nothing. It was all very hush-hush."

"And Wilson himself? Do you know much about him?"

"Not really. Rosen called him into the office a couple of times, but I can't tell you why."

She couldn't really tell me much about anything, it seemed, and it made me wonder why Amanda—and therefore Rinaldo—had made the attempt to kill her. Unless, of course, he was simply making sure no one else could pull any information out of her.

The sound of the approaching siren was so close now, the ambulance could only be a street or so away. I pulled Janice's cell from my pocket, then dug out my phone to grab the inspector's number and called her.

"Chief Inspector Henrietta Richmond speaking." Her tone was cool and somewhat reserved—no doubt because I was calling her from an unknown number. And undoubtedly it was already being traced. "How may I assist you?"

"Inspector, it's Emberly. Amanda Wilson just made an attempt on Janice Green's life after apparently pumping her for information over the last couple of weeks."

There was a slight pause. "Interesting. I take it Janice is still alive?"

"Yes, but she's been drugged with who knows what. I've called an ambulance."

"Yes, I can hear it. What happened to Amanda?"

"Jackson's following her. We're hoping she might lead us to Rinaldo's location."

"We weren't aware Amanda was working for him."

"Nor were we." Though we had suspected it. "Janice apparently saw them together. She has a pic of them beside an SUV, and the number plate is crystal clear."

I read it out to her.

"I'll get it traced immediately," the inspector said. "Stay with the secretary. I'll get someone over to check out her house. If they attempted to erase her, she must know something. Keep me informed on her condition."

"Will do, Inspector." I hesitated. "Were you aware

that some government officials took the inverters and all the information relating to them from Rosen Pharmaceuticals a few weeks ago?"

"Yes, I am."

"So they were actual government officers, and not fakes?" I persisted.

"Yes." Amusement touched her tone. "You are not one for giving up until you get what you want, are you?"

"It depends on what it is I want," I replied. "Did you discover what that chemical formula was?"

"It's vinegar, apparently. We're searching the buildings under the Skipping Girl Vinegar sign, as that's the most obvious place to start."

Luke was unlikely to have done anything obvious, but I guess the search had to start somewhere. "What about the original premises on Burnley Street?"

"Those buildings were demolished, but we've nevertheless sent the military to the area, as well as several other, smaller factories that are actively producing vinegar."

"I doubt they'll find anything at such a place," I said.

"I agree, but they must still be checked."

The wail of the siren stopped, and the silence was almost eerie. I walked down to the front door. Two men climbed out of the ambulance and were walking toward me, the first of them holding a medical kit.

"The patient is inside." I stepped to one side to let them both in.

But as I did, I realized the second man was wearing jeans and sneakers rather than the usual black or blue pants and black boots. Government funding might be tight right now, but I doubted the use of casual clothing as part of their everyday uniform had been approved.

"The first bedroom?" he said, his gaze cold and altogether too watchful.

Tension crawled through me, but I forced a smile. "Yes. I think she's taken something."

"Emberly?" the inspector said. "Everything okay? You didn't answer my question."

I didn't even *hear* her question. I forced a smile, then said, "No, sorry, it's not."

"We'll get people there ASAP. Leave the line open."

"Fine. See you soon." I shoved the phone into my back pocket, but, as ordered, didn't hang up.

"She conscious? Talking?" the first ambulance officer continued.

"No." I stepped back again, giving him plenty of room to pass. The second man didn't follow him; instead, he stopped and placed a hand on the door frame, effectively stopping me from leaving. And though I didn't feel the wash of any sort of power, the charm at my neck sprang to life, its heat a warning that magic was being aimed my way.

"You related to the victim?" he asked, the faintest hint of a smile touching his thin lips.

Overconfidence had been the downfall of many a thug.

"No, I'm not."

I threw a ball of fire sideways to catch his gaze, then took a step forward and kicked him hard in the nuts. As he gasped and doubled over, I swung a fist at his chin and smashed him sideways. He hit the wall hard enough to dent it, then collapsed in a heap on the floor.

Though I heard no footsteps, the warm rush of air past the back of my neck was warning enough that the other thug was closing in. I swung round but wasn't quite fast enough. The blow hit me low in the stomach and sent me tumbling backward. I landed on my spine and slid backward for a yard or so, gathering splinters from the porch's old boards. I swore and struggled to my feet, fire flickering across my fingertips, ready to defend or attack. Something hit my arm, and I glanced down to see a silvery dart sticking out of it.

Fuck.

I wrenched it out and reached for my fires, then heard a shout from the street and swung around to see two women watching me.

"You all right?" one asked.

No, I wasn't, because they were there and that meant I dared not take on fire form and reveal what I truly was.

"Fine," I muttered, and ran for the gate.

The thug didn't chase me.

He didn't need to.

I was out before I got anywhere near the front gate.

CHAPTER 8

The rise to consciousness was abrupt. One minute I was out; the next I was awake. It was the sort of abruptness that wasn't natural, but rather the result of some sort of stimulant. I could feel it coursing through my body, making my heart race.

But worse than that was the sudden awareness that I wasn't alone—that there were two others in the place with me. Both were male, and if their voices were any guide, they were very familiar.

One of them was Rinaldo's witch. The other was Theodore Hunt, the werewolf hit man who'd sworn to kill me because I'd apparently ruined his reputation by stopping him from committing murder. Not once, but twice.

Fire rose unbidden, but rather than erupting from my skin, it continued to rage within me and seemed to hold little in the way of heat. Something—someone— had managed to restrict my most powerful weapon.

It wasn't difficult to guess who.

I forced my eyes open.

Something dangled in front of my gaze. I blinked, trying to focus, and saw what looked like multicolored strings entwined together.

It was Grace's charm, loosely wrapped around a decidedly bony-looking finger rather than my neck.

That was the reason my flames were restricted—with the charm no longer around my neck, its protective barrier had been deactivated, and Frederick's spell had finally been able to curtail my flames. But was my access to the mother similarly stopped? And dare I even reach for her after what had happened last time?

"This," Frederick said, his voice conversational, "is a rather brilliant bit of spell casting. Who made it for you?"

"A witch."

It came out croaky. I swallowed heavily, but it didn't ease the dryness in my throat. I wondered how long I'd been out; wondered what in hell they'd given me.

"Obviously," he said. "But who? She's someone I'd be interested in speaking to."

"I doubt speaking is what you'd be doing. Not after what happened to those three witches you helped infect."

"Infect, yes, but you, my dear, killed them." He leaned closer, his pale features looming out of the darkness in an almost ghostlike manner. Or maybe it just seemed that way, thanks to his gaunt, almost skeletal features. "Tell me who it is."

"How about you go fuck yourself."

I reached for the mother. Energy surged at my call, but it was a distant thing—a heat I could feel but not yet use. Frederick's spell had placed a barrier between us, but it was one that restricted my access rather than completely forbade it. And *that* suggested his power *was* the darker kind—the kind that came from blood sacrifice and personal energy rather than from the earth and the energy of the world itself. He undoubtedly knew about both, but he'd have little experience with the mother and no true understanding of her.

Which was both good and bad. It meant I should be able to access her given time, but time was something I might not have a whole lot of.

Frederick sighed. "Theodore? Please show Ms. Pearson the error of her ways."

Heat surged at his words, but once again it did little more than flare across my skin. "Touch me," I said, "and I'll fucking kill you."

Hunt chuckled. It was a cold and oddly demented sound. But then, he and sanity had never particularly been bosom buddies.

The darkness near my feet shifted—became something that was big and powerful, and whose eyes promised death. With almost loving care, he gripped the littlest toe on my left foot. Knowing what was coming, I began to struggle, but I was tied down far too well, both physically *and* magically. All I could do was send heat surging down to my foot and hope it was enough. My skin began to glow so fiercely, it cast an orange light across the shadows and lent Hunt's gaze a bloody glow.

It didn't help.

Either Hunt didn't feel the heat or he simply didn't care, because he gripped my toe tighter and simply forced it backward.

Pain ripped through me, and I screamed.

Hunt sucked in a deep breath, then sighed, the sound almost orgasmic. *Bastard*, I thought dazedly. *Sick, dead bastard.*

Fingers gripped my chin and forced my head sideways. Frederick's skeletal features came into view. "Tell me the name of the witch who gave you that charm, or would you rather Hunt break another toe?"

Hunt's fingers moved to my next toe; they were trembling slightly, but whether that was anticipation or desire I had no idea—and no real wish to find out.

I reached again for the mother; this time, the wash of her heat was stronger, and the invisible wall between us seemed to shudder. Time. I just needed goddamn time!

And that meant I had to keep them talking—keep them from doing whatever it was they intended doing. "Like he isn't going to anyway."

"Oh, trust me, he intends a *whole* lot more than merely breaking toes." He lightly patted my arm, as if to comfort me.

It was only then that I realized I was naked. Fuck, fuck, *fuck* . . .

I closed my eyes and tried to control the wash of panic. I could get through this. I could survive it.

And it wasn't like it hadn't happened before. No one, man or woman, could live through as many decades as I had without being violated in some way. Not even those of us who weren't human.

"The name, Emberly," Frederick said.

"Call Hunt off and you might have a deal."

"You are in no position to make any sort of deal, I'm afraid." He slid his bony fingers down my arm and then across to my stomach, letting them rest just above my pubic bone. "You are, however, in a perfect position to fuck. And while that is something Hunt wants so very much, I rather suspect you do not."

I couldn't help glancing down at Hunt. His eyes glowed in anticipation.

"Answering all your questions isn't going to stop him doing that," I said, "and we both know it."

"Perhaps not. But the only way you will know for sure is to answer the question."

I closed my eyes. The mother's heat was close, so damn close. I could almost touch her now, and the fact that I couldn't had tears of rage and frustration stinging my eyes. I took a deep, shuddering breath and released it slowly. Patience. I just had to have patience.

"Why do you want her name? What do you and your psycho boss want from her?"

"My psycho boss wants nothing from her," Frederick said. "In fact, he would be rather peeved by my actions."

I blinked. "You're not here on his orders?"

"No." Frederick drew in a deep breath and smiled benignly. "I do so love the smell of fear and rampant need. The latter is Hunt's, of course, not yours."

He was as sick as Hunt. And just as dead. Or would be, when I broke through to the mother.

"I wouldn't think going against someone like Rinaldo would be the best idea," I said.

"You're right, it's not." He produced a knife and flicked the blade open. "But what he doesn't know won't hurt him. The name, Emberly. Otherwise, this knife will taste the sweetness of your flesh."

I hesitated. The knife's point replaced his fingers

against my pubic bone. Sweat broke out across my brow and dribbled down the side of my face. Or maybe that was tears. "Ronda Peterson. Her name is Ronda Peterson."

"Indeed?" Frederick glanced at Hunt. "Do we believe her, Theodore?"

"With the drug in her system, she can't lie." His reply was little more than a low, husky growl. "It has to be the truth."

I bit back a harsh laugh. If they believed *that*, then they truly knew little about phoenixes. No drug designed to work on a human would ever be able to withstand the sheer amount of heat currently boiling through my system.

"Indeed," Frederick repeated. "What did you and Miller find in Brooklyn?"

"Rotting dead people," I replied. "What sort of sick spell was that?"

"It was neither my magic protecting that area nor my spell cast on those cloaks."

"Then why were they rotting?"

"That, it would appear, was an unfortunate side effect of the virus."

I blinked. "It rots you?"

"Not everyone. Did you never wonder why some infected were branded, and some were not? It was easier to identify which type of 'infected' we were dealing with."

"Meaning those who were branded were the ones who would putrefy?"

"Yes. It is also what sends them mad."

Meaning Sam—and Jackson, if he *was* still infected—

should be safe. Unfortunately, it also meant that Frederick was. Not that *that* would really matter. Not once I got free.

"What else did you discover?" he said.

"Nothing much."

The tip of the knife pierced my skin, and blood began to flow. "I'm not believing that," Frederick said.

"If you were Luke's second, you should know what was in that area."

"Oh, I know there were labs somewhere in Brooklyn, but he would never reveal their location."

"So much for your earlier boast that he completely trusted you," I said.

Frederick smiled benignly. "Boasts and lies all have one purpose—to make people like you do as we wish. And if that doesn't work . . ."

The knife sliced deeper into my skin, and pain flared brighter. I really was going to enjoy hurting this bastard . . .

"Did you teach Luke to use magic?" My voice was still surprisingly without inflection. Which was a good thing—Hunt was already enjoying himself far too much for my liking.

"That, I believe, was an unfortunate side effect of the infection. He could not control me, but he did have some access to my thoughts and memories. Did you find the labs, Emberly?"

"I don't fucking know. We found an air lock that's accessible through a hidden entrance in his office, but whether that's the labs or merely a large safe is anyone's guess."

There was little point in lying about what we'd

found—if Rinaldo did have a mole in PIT, he was probably aware of what went down there.

It also meant all this was pretty pointless. Unless, of course, Frederick was simply confirming information they already had.

"And did you manage to gain access?"

"No. It was code locked and had a hand scanner attached."

"Meaning it will take some time to break in." His expression was irritated. "Which means more unfortunate delays."

"For whom? And where are the scientists?"

I didn't really expect an answer, and I didn't get it. Instead, he withdrew the knife's tip from my skin. "You, my dear, are far too dangerous to keep around. Rinaldo might think he has you by the short and curlies—" He paused, amusement touching his thin lips as he wiggled the knife back and forth across my pubic hair. Tension rolled through me as I waited for the flick of pain that came with flesh being pierced, but it didn't happen—not this time, at any rate. "I, however, do not believe that to be wise."

"He hasn't finished with me, Frederick. I wouldn't—"

"Oh, he's going to be incredibly annoyed by my actions," he cut in. "But he and I have been business partners for a very long time. One might even say decades. He will, in the end, respect my actions."

Decades? That wasn't possible—not without him either being nonhuman or a thrall. But even if he *had* sworn blood service—thereby becoming Rinaldo's human servant and gaining a very extended lifespan in exchange—he wouldn't have the free will to do something like this. Unless, of course, being a dark witch gave him some sort of immunity.

Hunt's hand came down on top of Frederick's and stopped the knife's movement. Relief washed through me, though it was tempered not only by the knowledge that Hunt's ministrations would be far worse, but also by the feel of his fat fingers splayed across my belly.

"Enough," he growled. "She is mine to take apart, remember."

"Indeed." Frederick's gaze came back to mine. "Which also means I can hardly be held accountable for your death—especially given there are no witnesses to your kidnapping."

No witnesses? "What about those women?"

"Those women only saw two ambulance officers who are now no longer with us." He smirked. "Dead men can tell no tales, after all. Of course, the same can be said of dead women. Perhaps it would be better if I simply rid the world—"

"We have a deal," Hunt cut in. "One sworn on blood and magic."

If Hunt believed Frederick would keep any deal that didn't suit him, then he was a bigger fool than I presumed.

Of course, he was also a fool who had the upper hand right at this moment. But only for as long as I was restrained from the mother's power.

"We do indeed," Frederick said, altogether too cheerfully. If *that* didn't warn Hunt the deal wasn't worth the blood it was sworn on, nothing would. "Which means, dear Emberly, I must now leave you to Theodore's tender ministrations."

Hunt removed his hand, and Frederick raised the blade. He licked its tip, and then sighed almost wistfully. "In many respects, it is such a shame to waste your blood—there is such power in it. But a deal is a deal. Good-bye, Emberly."

With that, he turned and disappeared into the darkness. A second later a door closed, and footsteps retreated down what sounded like a metal walkway.

Leaving me alone with Hunt.

I closed my eyes, reaching for strength and the fires that burned deep within. All that did was make my skin glow; there was no heat in my fire. No threat. Frederick had designed his spell very well indeed.

Hunt chuckled again, but it was the accompanying sound that sent fear and desperation rushing through me.

He was stripping off.

I twisted and heaved, fighting the cables that bound my arms and legs, trying to find some give, trying to free myself. My wrists and ankles became raw and slick with blood, but it did little good. I swore and raged and reached harder for the mother. Her fires twisted and spun, a whirlpool of heat that was close—so damn close—that I could feel the wash of it. But while the threads of magic holding her from my grasp were beginning to unravel against the constant pressure, they hadn't yet collapsed.

"I have dreamed of this." The thick scent of his desire was suffocating, and his eyes were glazed and unfocused—drunk on desire and the sight of my helplessness. "For endless nights."

"I *will* kill you," I spat back. "Be it in this time or another."

He smiled benignly, hoisted himself up on the table, and knelt inside my splayed legs. His cock was thick and hard, and stood out from his body like a lance waiting to be used.

His hands came down both sides of my shoulders, and heat and hate were all I could smell, all I could see.

"I'm going to fuck you senseless, and then I'm going to tear you apart piece by tiny piece and scatter you to the four winds. Try coming back from that, phoenix."

With that, he thrust inside of me. It hurt—god, how it hurt—but I bit back my scream and my instinctive need to fight both the bonds and the man that pinned me. That had already proven useless—just as useless as my fire for as long as the witch's spell was online. I needed to reach the mother. Needed to concentrate on shattering the magic that separated us rather than on what was happening to my body.

But as much as I tried, I couldn't entirely ignore Hunt's invasion. When he was fully sheathed within me, he shifted his weight, then stopped. I didn't react. I just kept my eyes closed and kept reaching for the mother. The magic was so thin, it was little more than gossamer. I could feel her heat and her rage now, but neither would do me much good if the gossamer held on.

Hunt wrapped a hand around my jaw and squeezed hard. "Look at me."

"Never."

His grip tightened. Tears slid down my cheeks.

"Don't think I won't break your jaw. Look at me."

I did. There was little point in doing anything else, and I certainly didn't want a broken jaw in addition to a broken toe.

Hunt's expression was gloating. He didn't release me; he simply began to thrust again. "Call me master."

"Master," I said tonelessly.

His movements became more intense. "Again."

"Master."

His breaths were becoming shorter, sharper, and his eyes more glazed. "Again. Again. Louder."

"Master," I intoned dutifully. "You are my master."

He made a strangled sound, his body stiffening against mine. But even as he came, the wall finally shattered. The mother swept through me and into Hunt, searing both his seed and his cock in one swift action.

And then she paused, as if waiting for reaction to set in. It did—his eyes bulged, and his groan of ecstasy became a scream of sheer and utter agony.

A heartbeat later, the mother snatched the rest of him from existence. There was nothing left; nothing except the lingering echo of his agony.

The cables binding me were treated with similar contempt; then the mother's energy wrapped around me, warm arms that offered comfort and a place of safety. Part of me wanted to linger, to grow strong in her grip, to give in and let go.

But that part of me had little hope against the greater sum that wanted revenge.

I had a witch to catch and no time to waste.

I hauled myself off the metal table, standing on one foot as I studied the room. If the machinery parts still scattered about were anything to go by, this place had once been some sort of pump room. I couldn't spot any spell stones on either those bits and pieces or the floor,

but the rainbow flare of the mother's light made something glitter in a small, recessed section of the grimy
wall to my right. I directed her energy at it, and, with
very little fanfare, the entire wall disappeared. Dust
ballooned, catching in my throat and making me
cough. I didn't care, because the minute that wall collapsed, my fires returned. I was torn from flesh to
flame in an instant, a process made even headier by the
mother's presence. Her song continued to spin around
me, sweet and beguiling, but it was a temptation that
stood little chance against the darker tune in my heart.
I dismissed her and flamed under the doorway.

I wasn't entirely surprised to discover I was once
again in a sewer tunnel. I flowed down the metal steps
to the tunnel's floor, sending spiders and rats scattering
as I raced after the footsteps I could no longer hear.

In very little time, I came to a junction, and it was
one that felt oddly familiar. I paused, the brightness of
my flames sending yellow-white light spinning across
the grimy bricks and highlighting not only the gated
entrance to one of the offshoot tunnels, but also the
shattered remains of a metal barrel.

This was the junction where two of the kidnapped
witches had eaten their friend, and where I'd been
attacked—and almost killed—by hellhounds.

The place was silent now, and though the tunnel
that had held the hounds was once again barred, I had
no sense that anyone—or anything—was in there.

Instinct tugged me left, into the tunnel opposite the
one Jackson and I had used . . . The thought stalled.

Jackson.

What if Amanda had been nothing more than a

ruse? What if she'd been used to split us? The best way to conquer was to divide—history and experience told me that—and Rinaldo obviously knew enough about my character to guess that I wouldn't leave without at least checking that Janice was safe.

Even if Frederick *was* being honest and his actions were his alone rather than Rinaldo's orders, Amanda's presence at the house could still have been some sort of trap—especially given neither of us had reported back to him as specifically ordered.

But to contact Jackson and make sure he was okay, I'd have to change form, because only another phoenix could understand me when I was in this one. And as much as I hated to admit it, my need to grab Frederick was stronger than my fear for Jackson.

I moved on, into the smaller tunnel, the same one the red cloaks had come from as the hellhounds had attacked in the junction. I could once again hear footsteps, but they were distant and oddly seemed to be moving toward me rather than away.

Had Frederick forgotten something? Or had Rinaldo caught wind of his little scheme and ordered him back?

I flamed around another corner, only to run right into someone. As my flames surrounded him, energy surged, a response that was protective and familiar.

It wasn't Frederick. It was Jackson.

"Em," he yelled, both aloud and in my head. "It's me! Tone down the heat!"

I did so and immediately changed form. "What the fuck are you doing here?"

"What the fuck do you think I'm doing here?" He grabbed me, pulled me close, and wrapped his arms around me. Tightly. His whole body shook, and I doubted it was a reaction to almost being crisped. It actually felt a whole lot like rage. "I'm here to rescue you."

"I'm okay—"

"Don't give me that shit. I know what happened."

I pulled away from him, my gaze searching his. Not only was there rage, but also horror and a very deep sense of defilement.

Oh fuck . . . He'd *felt* it.

Everything that had happened to me in that old pump house had echoed through him.

"I'm sorry, Jackson. I should have thought—"

"Don't," he growled, "because you have nothing to apologize for."

"But—"

He placed a finger gently against my lips, stopping me. "Are you okay?"

"I'm cut, and my damn toe is broken—"

"I don't just mean physically."

I knew that. "I'll be fine."

Eventually. It wasn't like it was the first time it had happened, and while that didn't really ease the trauma of *this* event, I not only knew how I'd probably react but also how to cope with the flashbacks, nightmares, and anger if they *did* occur.

But I doubted Jackson had *ever* experienced something like that, even if it was just an echo rather than a real event.

I raised my hand and gently cupped his cheek and chin. "The real question is, how are you?"

"I haven't really stopped to think about it. I just wanted to get here, get to you, and stop it happening."

He took a deep breath and released it slowly. "At the very least, there will be anger. But we can get through it together."

I hoped so. Hoped that he'd talk about it rather than let it fester in the deeper recesses of his mind, gathering guilt and blame, until it poisoned our relationship and he ended up hating me.

"So how did you find me?"

"Tracked your phone. Or rather, PIT did. I know you wanted that number kept private, but—"

This time, I put my finger against *his* lips. "It's okay, Jackson. It wasn't my phone, and I would have done the same thing anyway."

"Good." He released me, stepped back, then stripped off his coat and held it out so I could slip my arms into it. "It also means that three PIT officers are no more than a few minutes behind me."

Which wasn't really surprising—not with Rinaldo's right-hand man having been involved. "I don't suppose you came across Frederick on your way here, did you?"

"As a matter of fact, we did. He's currently unconscious and being hauled none too gently back to the scene of his crime."

I frowned. "Why is PIT bringing him back here rather than taking him to PIT headquarters?"

"Because the man in charge just happens to be Sam, and he was decidedly determined to make sure you were okay."

Under normal circumstances, news like that might have made my heart do a little jig, but I was all out of that sort of happiness right now.

"Then ring him and tell him I'm okay." As much as

I wanted to question Frederick myself, it was probably better if I didn't. I wasn't entirely sure my control could withstand the desire to make the bastard pay.

"No need," Sam said as he appeared around the corner. The flashlight's beam swept me, no doubt taking in my near nakedness, the bloody bruises around my ankles and wrists, and the dried blood trails down my legs—the only indication that I'd suffered wounds elsewhere. Something hardened in his eyes, and the air around him grew dark—almost explosive. He and I might no longer be an item, but if that darkness was anything to go by, Frederick was going to pay for his actions.

Big-time.

He stopped to the right of both Jackson and me, his expression giving little away, but the darkness still fierce and bright and very, *very* scary. "Where's Hunt?"

"So dead he's not even dust."

"Good. Where did the assault happen?"

Though his tone was so matter-of-fact it edged toward curtness, I couldn't help but notice his hands were clenched. Couldn't help but sense he wanted revenge every bit as badly as either Jackson or I.

And maybe he would have reacted the same way had I simply been a fellow PIT officer or even a member of the public, but I suspected the fact we'd once loved each other had a whole lot to do with whatever he was now planning.

"It happened in what I think is an old pump room." I paused. "Why?"

"Because, if you're up to it, Frederick is going to receive a little of his own medicine." The smile that touched his lips was an ugly thing to behold. "It's more than deserved, don't you think?"

"*That* is something of an understatement," Jackson commented, even as I said, "I'm up to it."

More lights began to pierce the gloom, accompanied by the sound of footsteps as well as something being dragged. I couldn't help hoping that something was Frederick.

"Lead the way," Sam said.

I wrapped the ends of Jackson's coat tighter around my bruised body, then spun and hobbled forward. Jackson muttered something under his breath, then swept me up into his arms. "You direct. I'll do the walking."

"Just follow this tunnel until we hit the junction." I glanced across at Sam. Though his expression was remote, something in the set of his mouth spoke of annoyance. "Have the searches of the various vinegar factories turned up anything?"

"Vinegar factories?" Jackson said.

"That's what the chemical formula you found in Brooklyn was," Sam said, his tone clipped. He stepped over the rotting carcass of what looked like a cat, then added, "And no, it hasn't yet. It's possible it was nothing more than a red herring."

Maybe it was, but something within me doubted it. "It might have been the only clue they could leave without being obvious."

"The scientists are infected," Sam said. "I doubt they would have even considered such a thing."

"I think the scientists are more likely to be like you than regular red cloaks." I paused, remembering what Frederick said about the decaying cloaks we'd discovered in Brooklyn. "Were you aware that the cloaks with the brand on their cheeks had a variation of the virus that rotted them out?"

Sam's smile was grim. "Yes. And we're not entirely sure that it's a variation rather than a path that all of those who are infected will travel."

"If that was going to happen, there'd at least be signs by now."

"You can't be sure of that. No one can."

"Luke was." I might not have asked him that question, but I nevertheless believed the truth of my answer. "And I'm pretty sure if you ask Frederick about the virus, he'll confirm it."

"There are bigger questions to be asked before we get to something like *that*," Sam said.

Like, where were the scientists? And where the hell was Rinaldo? "I think Frederick is a thrall. He implied as much when he was questioning me."

Sam's gaze shot to mine. "What was he questioning you about?"

"He wanted the name of a witch. I wasn't inclined to supply it."

"Why would he want that sort of information from you?" Jackson said.

"He was impressed by her skill and creativity. Take the tunnel on our immediate right," I added as we hit the junction once again.

"Why is this place familiar?" Jackson said.

"It's where the hellhounds attacked me."

"I won't even ask," Sam said. "I gather the creativity Frederick was talking about was the twined rope charm he was clutching when we nabbed him?"

"Yes. Don't suppose you have it with you, do you?"

He pulled a plastic bag from his pocket but didn't immediately offer it to me. "What is it designed to protect you against?"

"Any magic or spell created to stop me from accessing my fire form."

"Magic can do that?"

"It can if you know the right magic. Few do." My gaze narrowed. "Why? Are you thinking about pursuing such a spell?"

"There's no need to, now that you're working with us rather than against."

He held out the plastic bag; after a moment's hesitation, I accepted it. "Don't you have to hand it in or something?"

"I'll log it, but it's better off with you rather than sitting in an evidence locker." He paused. "I would, however, like to talk to the witch who created it. PIT could certainly use some means of protection against spells."

My eyebrows rose. "Has that actually been a problem?"

"Only minor to date, but yes."

"I'm surprised PIT hasn't got witches on the books," Jackson commented. "It would seem a rather logical step if you ask me."

"We do have witch consultants," Sam said. "But I don't think they're powerful enough to create something like that charm."

Given Grace was powerful enough to work through— and understand—the earth mother, that wasn't really surprising. I doubted there were many witches in Melbourne capable of such a feat—not now that three of them had died in these damn tunnels.

"Getting back to the problem currently being dragged along behind us," I said, "what's the point of bringing Frederick back to the scene of his crime when, as a thrall, he would never betray his master?"

"He may not be willing to tell us anything, but he could certainly be forced to."

"Rinaldo will stop him. We both know that." I spotted the metal stairs that led up to the half-wrecked pump room and silently directed Jackson toward it.

"Rinaldo can only stop him if he is aware of the situation. He won't be."

"And how do you intend to stop that?"

"I can't. Adam, however, can. He's one of the men dragging Frederick here, and he should be able to prevent Frederick from linking with Rinaldo."

Adam was Sam's partner, and a vampire to boot. I'd met him only a couple of times, but he seemed pretty decent. He'd certainly been a whole lot less frosty toward me than Sam had been in the early days of the investigation.

"But Rinaldo's an extremely powerful telepath—one capable of entirely taking over mind *and* body," I said. "Will Adam have the telepathic strength to counter that? Because I rather suspect Rinaldo will kill Frederick rather than risk him telling us anything."

"I doubt Rinaldo will waste such a valuable resource—"

"Don't doubt," Jackson said as he clattered up the metal steps. "He would discard anything and anyone, no matter how valuable, if it suited him."

"Perhaps." Sam's tone suggested he didn't agree.

Jackson kicked the door open, then strode into the

old pump room. It was as I'd left it, only the dust had had a chance to settle. "How do you want to play this, Turner?"

"Once we get Frederick securely tied to the table, we'll all retreat back to the sewers except for Emberly and Adam."

Jackson frowned. "What about the possibility of him using magic?"

"He's a dark witch and, from what I understand, they not only need some sort of blood sacrifice to create their spells, but also their Athame," Sam said.

"I wouldn't be sure about that," I said. "If Frederick's a thrall, he could be far older than he looks. Older witches often don't need ceremonial devices. They just need the power of their thoughts and their soul to create a spell, especially if it's only a simple one such as forcing his will on another."

"I know someone who'd be able to tell us." Jackson carefully placed me on my feet near the table; then, as the sound of footsteps coming up the metal stairs began to echo, he got out his phone and made a call.

"Grace, sorry about the late hour, but I have a rather urgent question for you." He paused for a moment, listening, and then added, "Yeah, we did find the dark witch. But we need to question him, and we want to know if he can use magic against us using just his thoughts and will."

He paused again, listening. His expression suggested the answer wasn't one he wanted. "Right. Thanks, Grace."

He hung up and shoved his phone back into his pocket. "Em's right. He'll more than likely be able to perform at least minor magic against us. However, she said if we use some form of hallucinogenic drug, it should impair his mind enough to stop that."

"No matter what either of you think of PIT," Sam said, his voice dry, "we generally don't carry any sort of drugs around with us."

Adam and one other PIT officer came into the room, dragging the still-unconscious Frederick between them. Once they'd lifted him onto the table, they began tying him up with what looked like plastic cables. PIT might not carry drugs around with them, but it seemed they *did* come equipped with black cable ties.

"Frederick woke me with some sort of stimulant," I said, looking around. "It's possible there's some sort of medical bag in the room—especially given he used an ambulance to transport me."

"It's over in the corner," Jackson said. "And so are your clothes and purse, by the look of it."

He retrieved all three items, shaking off the brick dust from my clothes and purse before handing them to me. Then he dumped the medical bag on top of Frederick's stomach and opened it up. "There's all sorts of stuff in here. Anyone know anything about drugs?"

"Adam?" Sam said.

"Adam's a medic?" I couldn't keep the surprise from my voice.

"No, I'm not," he said, his expression amused. He was a tall, thin man with blondish hair and cool gray eyes. He looked nonthreatening, even for a vampire, and for that reason alone I suspected he was very much the opposite. "But I can contact base, and someone who is."

"Instant communication is one of the benefits of having a telepathic partner," Sam said.

Adam began inspecting the contents of the bag, studying each item and presumably relaying the information back to whomever he was in contact with. I used the time to pull on my jeans. Surprisingly, Janice's phone was still in my back pocket. I pulled it out, ended the call, and then quickly added a password. Having a second phone could come in handy.

I didn't bother putting on my shoes—I doubted my broken toe would be too pleased with the sudden pressure—nor did I bother with my sweater or bra, instead shoving both into my handbag. I wasn't about to strip off to put either on, even if half the men in the room *had* seen me naked, be it in the present or the past. Which left my T-shirt, and I used that to belt Jackson's coat tighter.

After a few more minutes, Adam handed Sam a small vial and a needle. "According to Billy, this should do the trick."

"Excellent." Sam filled the syringe, then roughly jabbed it into Frederick's arm. Once he'd dumped both the vial and the syringe back into the bag, he glanced at me and said, "We'll retreat. Adam will remain here with you, but Frederick shouldn't sense him."

I nodded. Jackson gripped my shoulder briefly, and warmth leapt from his skin to mine. Warmth and concern. I smiled and silently said, *I'm okay, Jackson. Really.*

He didn't say anything, just gave me a somewhat disbelieving look, then followed Sam and the other PIT officers out the door. As it clanged shut, I glanced at Adam and said, "So how do we play this?"

"This is your game. I'm just here to stop any sort of connection happening."

Sparks danced across my fingertips in anticipation. "How close is he to consciousness?"

"Close enough."

"Good." I hobbled forward, raised a hand, and slapped Frederick across the cheek. The blow was hard enough to snap his head sideways, but there was no immediate response. I slapped him again. His eyes popped open, and he swore. But the words were slow and somewhat slurred.

Then his gaze narrowed, and I rather suspected he was reaching for some sort of magic. I didn't wait to see if the drug we'd administered had worked; I simply slapped him for a third time. I might not know a whole lot about magic, but I knew spells needed the caster's undivided attention. If rattling his teeth disrupted that, I was more than happy to keep doing it.

"Frederick, you have one chance, and one chance only, to tell me what I want to know, or I'm going to burn you piece by tiny piece, until you're screaming for the salvation of death."

Frederick's smile was cool and altogether too calm. "You can hurt me as much as you like, but I will never tell you anything. I can't."

"I'm not so sure about that," I said. "I'm thinking your inability to give me answers might rely on your master's restrictions rather than on any sort of mental strength on your part."

"Perhaps that is so, but it still means I can't give you anything."

"A statement that is true only if you can actually reach Rinaldo—and I rather think you can't right now."

He was silent for a minute, his expression slackening, suggesting he was attempting to reach Rinaldo telepathically; then it came to life again filled with a mix of fury and fear.

"What have you done to me?" His body jerked as he tried to leap at me, but he was too well tied to move even the smallest amount. So he settled for raising his head and spitting.

I sizzled the globule long before it got anywhere near me. "It's not much fun being on the other side of things, is it?"

"I'll get you for this, bitch."

Sweat was beginning to dot his forehead. I wondered if it was fear, or the drug taking hold. If it *was* the drug, then maybe I needed to speed things along. Keeping him confused as well as fearful was probably my best means of assault right now.

I dropped my right hand and streamed fire from my fingertips, and then shaped them into humanoid forms that slowly grew, until the table was surrounded by fiery beings that glared at him balefully.

"What the fuck?" he said, his voice high. "Who are they?"

"The thing about attacking a spirit," I said conversationally, "is the fact we are rarely ever alone. And we do tend to get pissed off if you hurt one of us."

He pushed up against the cable ties again. "I can't tell you anything."

"I don't believe you."

I pulled a slither of fire from the flame form nearest

his hips and let it press down on his groin. He screamed, even though I hadn't yet started to burn.

"Where are the scientists, Frederick?"

"I *don't* know. For fuck's sake, you've got to believe me. You've got to stop him."

"Him" being my fiery alter ego, I gathered. "Like you stopped Hunt from raping me?"

His gaze snapped to mine; this time, the panic was sharper. "I can't give you what I don't know."

"So the claim that you and Rinaldo had the scientists was yet another boast?" Just as Jackson had believed.

"Yes, for god's sake, yes. I honestly don't know where they are."

"I really don't think honesty and you are all that familiar," I said. "But perhaps the loss of a small piece of your anatomy will encourage you to become so."

I pressed the fiery hand deeper. A pulse began to beat heavily in my head, a warning that I was once again pushing my limits. I once again ignored it. "Tell me where the scientists are, Frederick."

His jeans began to smolder, the material peeling away from my fiery touch. The stench of burning hair soon stained the air, but I didn't press any further. Not yet.

"I don't know, you have to believe me, I *don't*."

His words tumbled out over one another, his gaze wide, desperate. Yet there was something in the deeper recesses of his eyes, something that spoke of cunning. He thought he could fool me. Thought I wouldn't carry through with my threat.

I burned his cock.

He screamed. It was a god-awful sound, but I had no intention of showing him any sort of compassion or mercy. He didn't deserve it, and not just because he'd left me to Hunt's tender mercies, but because of what he'd helped do to those witches and undoubtedly to countless others. The virus might have made them Luke's to control, but it had been Frederick's magic that had helped make their capture possible.

"Tell me," I said, lifting the flames from his flesh again. His cock was red and already beginning to blister. Part of me hoped he would lose function. Part of me hoped he would continue to stall and I could finish what I started. "Or face life as a eunuch."

He was panting and sweating now, his expression one of pain and desperation. "I haven't got that information. *Please*, you must believe me."

This time, I raised the hands of all my fiery creations. The beating in my head got stronger. I gripped the table to keep upright and said, my voice harsh, "I'm afraid I don't. You're Rinaldo's thrall, and he's trusted you for generations to hide his presence and keep his schemes running undetected beneath a veil of magic. You cannot do either without knowing location details."

I pressed the raised hands down. As his entire body began to smolder, he screamed, "All right, all right, just stop it—stop them."

I drew the fire back into my body, but it didn't ease the ache in my head. Only food, green tea, and fire could do that now, and not necessarily in that order.

"Tell me where the scientists are," I said yet again.

"I don't fucking *know*. We never have." He shook his

head, as if trying to clear it. "That's part of the damn reason we sent you and the fae into Brooklyn."

"You think they're still there?" I asked, surprised.

"Yes. They *have* to be—there's no other place in Melbourne they could be."

"We didn't find them there."

"You found a damn air lock—one that's more than likely protecting the labs. Where else could they be?"

Where else indeed? And if that *was* the case, what was the connection to the vinegar formula written in dust?

Or was it, I thought, my heart racing a little bit faster, not a clue but rather a code?

The code to the air lock's scanner, perhaps?

Had we had the answer all along and just been overthinking it?

"Luke kept cloaks in other locations," I said. "So why do you expect me to believe he wouldn't keep the scientists off-site, in an ultrasafe location?"

"Because there *was* no place safer than Brooklyn. It was his castle and the home of most of his troops."

"So where will we find Rinaldo's castle?"

The sudden switch had him blinking; then he swore at me and fought against his restraints again. The scent of blood began to taint the air, and though I doubted the aroma would tempt Adam, part of me couldn't help but hope for a sudden loss of control.

"Even if I tell you, it won't do you any good," Frederick said. His pupils were becoming more dilated, his words more slurred. The hallucinogen had taken a firm hold of him now, but he obviously needed just a little more pushing—and maybe not the pain-filled kind.

"Tell me," I said, even as I became flame and shaped my fire into a vague resemblance of Rinaldo. As Frederick's gaze widened, I shifted back, added, "Tell them," in a deeper tone, then took on Rinaldo's fiery figure again.

Frederick's harsh rasping filled the air. For an instant, I didn't think he was going to fall for the ploy, but then he said, "Risley Street, Richmond. He has a warehouse there."

I doused my flames again and said, "What number?"

"Fourteen. Please, stop them."

I glanced past him. "Anything else we need to know?"

Adam stepped forward and placed his hands on either side of Frederick's head. After a moment, Frederick closed his eyes, and his breathing deepened. He was asleep.

"That's quite an impressive trick," I said. "Sam wasn't kidding when he said you'd be able to stop this bastard from communicating with his boss."

"Stopping it wasn't without problems." He ran a hand through his pale hair, and it was only then that I noticed the pallor of his skin. "And Rinaldo will undoubtedly sense *something* has happened."

"Can he reach Frederick's thoughts even though he's now asleep?"

"Yes. But I've mangled his memories and removed any evidence of him being forced to give Rinaldo's location." He paused and glanced at the door. "Sam, we need to move if we want any hope of catching Rinaldo."

The door opened, and the three men entered. Sam's gaze met mine, and he gave me a brief nod. "Well done."

I smiled and wondered if he *actually* meant well done on not killing the bastard.

"Contact base," Sam continued. "We need a full-scale operation in place, stat—"

"Don't," I said hurriedly. "It's too much of a risk."

"PIT does *not* have a mole," Sam said, his tone curt.

"Rinaldo implied that he did," I snapped back, "and I don't want to risk losing the bastard just because you and your boss are pigheadedly determined not to even *consider* the possibility."

Adam coughed and seemed to be struggling to keep his expression flat. Sam simply glared at me as the shadows stirred around him. If it was meant to intimidate, it wasn't successful. I'd all but flatlined when it came to *any* emotion but anger and determination right now.

"I very much suspect the three of us will not be enough to take the—"

"It's not three," Jackson said, "but five. If you think we're not going to be part of an operation to bring this bastard down, you've got rocks in your head."

"Remember, too," I said, "that you can't stop me from leaving this room right now and heading over there by myself."

The darkness that was the virus sharpened significantly, but after a glance at Adam, he waved a hand and said, "Fine. Come with us. But you follow orders, understood?"

I nodded. "What about Frederick?"

"He won't wake until I order him to," Adam said. "And even if Rinaldo overrides that order, Frederick can't escape because he's strapped down."

"He'll be able to use magic once the drug wears off."

"Undoubtedly," Adam said. "But I don't think he'll get the chance. Rinaldo won't risk his thrall talking."

I hope he's right, Jackson said. *And I seriously hope that the rats are feasting on his flesh* before *death happens.*

Jackson could, it seemed, do revenge even better than me.

He bent, picked up my shoes and then me, and said, "The stage is yours, Turner."

Sam didn't say anything. He simply spun and led the way out of the pump room.

And I crossed my fingers and hoped like hell that we were quick enough to catch the bastard.

CHAPTER 9

Risley Street was narrow and lined with warehouses on one side and a parking lot on the other. At the far end, there was a small park surrounding a high-rise building—community housing, I knew, having seen the ugly design in other inner-city areas.

Jackson and I climbed over the fence protecting the vacant lot opposite the park, then ran for the nearest building. I was once again wearing my shoes, but I'd burned a hole in the left one to take the pressure off my injured digit and, in case that wasn't enough, was keeping it fire rather than flesh. If anyone happened to be looking our way, they'd catch little more than a flicker of light no bigger than a match flame. It was better *that* than being left in the car because I couldn't damn well walk properly.

We pressed against the sidewall of a graffiti-covered building and peered down the narrow lane that divided the Risley Street buildings from those of the street behind it.

No cars, Jackson said. *And no lights evident in any of the buildings.*

I hope Frederick wasn't feeding us a lie.

I doubt he was capable of even thinking up a lie, Jackson said. *There's another fence to climb—barbed wire on top.*

I hated barbed wire. No matter how careful I was, the damn stuff always snagged either me or my clothes. *Anything we can use to throw over it?*

Nothing I can immediately see.

Well, fuck. I took a deep breath and released it slowly. I could no doubt melt the damn wire, but that might just give Rinaldo a warning that we were coming. *Go. I'll follow.*

He disappeared around the corner; a heartbeat later, there was a slight rattle as he climbed the fence. I scanned the area for any unwanted interest in what we were doing, and then followed him. The barbed wire snagged his jacket and ripped one side open as I jumped down on the other side.

Sorry about that. I tucked the torn bit under the T-shirt I was now wearing.

He shrugged. *It's only a jacket.*

Yeah, but it's a nice one.

His grin flashed. *So buy me a replacement. Or compensate me in some other way.*

Now that's *the Jackson I know and love.*

Seriousness can only last so long. He paused. *Which isn't to say I'm not still furious over what happened—*

To both of us, I cut in softly. *And we'll talk, but not now.*

He didn't say anything to that, and I had to wonder if talking was something he was actually willing to do.

We moved on, keeping close to the grimy, graffiti-strewn redbrick wall. Rinaldo's warehouse began at the end of it. Beyond it lay a more modern-looking building; then the lane swept around the corner and joined Risley Street.

We stopped for a second time. Jackson peered around

the corner. *Two entrances, ground level and first floor, just as Google Street View promised. No cars in the parking space and bars on all the windows.* He glanced at his watch. *Better tell Sam we're ready.*

I pressed the com earpiece Sam had given me and softly said, "In position."

"Right," came his reply. "Everyone head in. And be careful."

I didn't reply; I just followed Jackson around the corner, then took the metal steps up to the first floor, keeping as close to the wall of the next building as practical. I paused on one side of the first barred window and carefully peered inside. The room beyond was pitch-black. If Rinaldo was in there, he was one with the darkness.

And if he *was* there, then he was more than likely aware of my presence. He was, after all, a vampire, and my racing heart probably sounded like a damn alarm to him.

I took a deep breath, then ducked past the window and paused again beside the door. Why anyone would bar the windows and then put an unprotected, double-glass door between them was anyone's guess, but at least it gave me a somewhat easier way in.

Ready when you are, Jackson said.

I flexed my fingers. Sparks flew, tiny fireflies that spoke of tiredness more than tension. *Go.*

Even as I said that, there was a crash from the front of the building—Sam and Adam were heading in.

I called fire to my fingertips, then pressed them against the lock. It instantly began to glow and, in very little time, was little more than liquid. I pushed the door open but didn't immediately step inside. Instead, I threw a ball of fire into the darkness and flared it out.

What my flames revealed was a bedroom, and it was a goddamn mess. There were clothes everywhere— both over the floor and on the bed. Either Rinaldo was extremely messy, or someone had gotten here before us.

There was an en suite to my right, but it, too, was in shambles, with drawers pulled out of the cabinet and razors, soaps, and aftershave bottles strewn all over the crisp white floor tiles; some of the bottles were broken, perfuming the air with their pungent scents.

I sent my sphere of light into the hallway and carefully followed. The one additional room on the floor was another bedroom and en suite. It, too, looked as if it had been hit by a cyclone. I headed back to the door, then stopped and swung around, my gaze scanning the clothes again. Was it my imagination, or were those clothes identical to the ones scattered all over the other bedroom?

I went back in to check. It wasn't my imagination.

"Anything?" Sam said.

"Negative," Jackson said.

"Also negative," came Adam's comment.

"Emberly?" Sam said, his voice a little sharper.

"Nothing but a goddamn mess and two identical sets of clothing." I thumped the wall in frustration. It seemed luck had once again turned a blind eye.

"How the fuck could he possibly have known we were on the way?" Jackson said, sounding every bit as angry as I was. "With Frederick out of the picture and PIT not informed of the operation, there's no way he should have gotten any sort of warning."

"Unless it was the mere fact of being unable to contact his thrall that set off alarms," Adam said. "If the state of this place is anything to go by, we didn't miss him by much."

"It doesn't matter whether we missed him by a minute or an hour," Jackson growled. "We still fucking *missed* him."

"Enough," Sam said, his tone curt. "Em, what do you mean by two sets of identical clothing?"

"Just that. There're two bedrooms, and each one holds the exact same clothes—same cut, same style, same colors." I paused. "After talking to the rats, we've come to the conclusion that Rinaldo might actually be two people."

"Indeed? And when were you planning to inform *us* of this conclusion?"

"The minute I thought about it," I snapped back. "Between Rory almost getting killed and then me getting kidnapped, informing PIT of *anything* kinda took a backseat."

"What makes you believe there're two people using the Rinaldo alias?" His voice held a less accusatory note now—which was a good thing, because anything else would have tempted me to burn his ass. "What have you seen that we haven't?"

"The rats let us view the tape showing Rinaldo's hit on his gaming venue." I picked up a T-shirt and sniffed it. I was no wolf, and my olfactory senses weren't all that much sharper than an ordinary human's, but I could nevertheless smell the scent of sweat and cool mint on the T-shirt—a rather odd combination. "At the same time as he was doing that, he was confronting us at Rosen's apartment building."

I swung around, walked into the other bedroom, and picked up the identical T-shirt. The scent on this one was woody—spicy. So while the two men might look and dress exactly the same, it seemed they preferred very different colognes.

"Are you sure one of them wasn't using some form of mask or a glamor?"

"Positive. And there're two of everything up here in the bedrooms."

"At least that explains a few inconsistencies," Adam said. "Though it doesn't make finding him any easier."

"What else did the rats say?" Sam said. "And how did you convince them to even talk to you in the first place?"

"Radcliffe wants Rinaldo far more than he wants me." I headed out of the bedroom. "And he didn't say much else, other than that he believes Rinaldo hasn't yet set up a den."

"His use of this place would certainly suggest that," Adam said. "Although he *is* using interstate vampires who don't appear to have a record anywhere."

Sam grunted. "We'll take over operations from here. Jackson, Em, go home and get some rest."

Annoyance surged, but it wasn't mine. *Don't bite back*, I warned. *This is PIT's operation, not ours. Besides, I could really use the sleep right now.*

And, I'm thinking, fire.

Yes.

Then we head to the blacksmith's first so we can fuel up, then find a hotel and see if PIT really does have a mole.

Excellent plan. I clattered down the stairs and joined the three men in the combined living room, kitchen, and what appeared to be an office area. It also resembled something a cyclone had left behind.

Sam was picking through the paperwork and files on the desk, but he glanced up as I entered the room. "Thanks for your help—both of you."

That almost sounded genuine, Jackson said, mental tones wry. *Maybe he's going soft in his old age.*

Unlikely. Out loud I added, "You know that formula we found in Brooklyn? The one written in the dust?"

He raised an eyebrow. "The same one that's currently got us investigating every building in Melbourne with even the slightest connection to vinegar? Yeah, I do."

"What if it's not a location, but rather the number code for that air lock we found?"

He blinked. Clearly, he hadn't considered that option, either. "That is certainly possible."

"It won't solve the thumbprint problem, but it might at least be one part of the puzzle."

"The thumbprint isn't actually a problem—Luke's fingerprints are a matter of police record, and the recent developments in fake skin mean we can reproduce a good enough copy to use on the scanner."

"You *will* let us know what you find in there," Jackson said. "Otherwise, my ass is going to be parked outside that damn door until you do."

The hint of a smile touched Sam's lips. He really *had* begun to thaw out—and I had to wonder how much of that was because he'd given in to his body's need to ingest blood.

A lot, I suspected.

"I can't promise anything, but if you happen to receive a thumbs-up on your phone, you'll know we've discovered the scientists." He paused. "Which might just be a good enough reason to keep your damn phone on you."

"Maybe," Jackson said.

He touched a hand to my back and lightly guided me toward the broken front door. I nodded a good-bye at both Sam and Adam, but I could feel the weight of Sam's gaze following me as we left the building.

But he was a puzzle I had no energy to concentrate on.

Jackson ushered me into the car, then ran around to the driver's side and jumped in. In very little time we were cruising toward the city.

For the first time in ages, he actually parked at the front of our office. He obviously caught my surprise, because he half shrugged and said, "With PIT tagging us, it's pretty pointless parking anywhere else and walking."

"But what about using the blacksmith's?" Jackson had an ongoing agreement with the owner for twenty-four-hour, no-questions-asked access, even though Jackson tended to go there only at night—not because he was a night owl, but because he didn't want anyone knowing it was the source of his fire. As an elemental fae, he had to regularly commune with his element or risk fading, and even death.

I opened the door and climbed out. The evening was crisp and clear, the stars bright in the sky. Most of Stanley Street was retail businesses these days, and, as a result, the only lights visible were the streetlights.

"I've actually invested in another means of getting

into the blacksmith's," he said, his eyes gleaming brightly in the darkness.

I raised an eyebrow. "Meaning what?"

"I broke into their roof."

I laughed. "You *didn't*."

He ushered me through the front gate, then jumped ahead to open the front door. The cleaning fairy *hadn't* paid us a visit since we'd last been here, and paperwork and files were still scattered everywhere.

"It was a simple matter of installing a trapdoor in our roof," he said, "and then adjusting one of the sky-lights in theirs."

"And of course the bad guys watching aren't likely to spot us leaping from one roof to another."

"Well, no, not if we keep low. Our old Victorian has a pediment, remember, and that should stop anyone spotting us."

"You've thought of everything."

He placed his phone on the nearest desk—a desk that no longer held the backpack containing the laptops. Rinaldo's people had indeed come to retrieve them.

"Yes, I have," Jackson said. "I even have a rope long enough to reach their floor."

"Handy." I followed him up the stairs and tossed my bag toward the bed.

"Very. It's certainly better than jumping down." He walked toward what he laughingly called the bathroom— a tiled area tucked into one corner of the vast room that had a shower, bath, and basin sitting in it. With no screen or curtain, it was in full view of the rest of the room, so too damn bad if you wanted privacy while bathing. But at least he *did* have a separate toilet—there were some things in life and relationships that were better left un-shared.

A trapdoor had been built to the right of this area, midway between it and the bathroom area. He pressed a button on the wall; the trapdoor slowly opened, and a metal ladder began to unfold.

He climbed up, opened another door in the roof, and then motioned me up. In very little time, we were jumping across to the blacksmith's and sliding down a rope into the building.

Though the flames in the old-fashioned brick fur-nace had been banked for the night, the heat of the em-bers still called to me.

"Ladies first," Jackson said, propping himself up on one of the old wooden workbenches.

I stopped beside the furnace and brought the coals back to life, until the roar of the flames was all I could hear and the heat of it washed over my skin. I threw my hands and head back and called it to me, though I didn't immediately feed, instead allowing the flames to play around my body for several minutes. I was enjoying the fierceness of them, the rush of heat, energy, and plea-sure that came with them. Then I sighed and somewhat regretfully drew them in, refueling the inner fires.

My skin still glowing with heat, I broke the connec-tion and stepped away. Jackson's eyes gleamed, but it had nothing to do with fire and everything to do with desire. But he said only, "Why don't you go back and eat? I could be a while."

I didn't argue; I just shimmied back up the rope and made my way back to our building. The first thing I did was to make a somewhat belated call to Rory.

"You okay?" I asked.

"Yeah," he said, his voice sounding sleepy. I'd obviously woken him. "I'm well fed and well protected, although our earth fae is seriously hoping for an attack. I'm beginning to think all fae are mad."

I grinned. "Make that all sex mad, and you might be right."

"True. How are things with you? For a while there, I was getting some very troubling vibes."

"That's because some nasty shit went down, but I'm here, I'm alive, and the inflictor of said nasty shit is not."

He hesitated. "Anything we need to talk about?"

"Hunt is no longer a problem," I replied, unable to keep the satisfaction from my voice—and it was infinitely better than hurt or anger. Either emotion would only have alarmed him, and he didn't need that sort of worry when he was still recovering from rebirth.

"Ah." He paused. "Did he hurt you too badly?"

"Nothing I haven't handled before."

He was silent for a longer stretch this time, telling me he'd guessed what had happened. "I hope his ending was slow and painful."

"It was."

"Good. Anything else I need to know?"

"Frederick has been captured and is in PIT custody."

"I'm surprised he's not dead."

"I think they're hoping he'll lead them to Rinaldo."

"A false hope, I rather suspect."

"Me, too." I paused. "Do you need me back there soon?"

"No. Not for a day or so. The fire's enough until then."

Which meant he really *was* getting stronger. Relief spun through me.

"I'll see you in a couple of days, then."

"Take care."

"Always do."

He snorted and hung up. I shoved my phone back into my bag, then set about making something decent to eat. It was nearly two hours before Jackson finally reappeared. By then, I'd not only eaten my way through a box of donuts but also had "potluck" risotto ready on the stove.

"That smells divine." He leaned past me to scoop up one of the sausage pieces I'd mixed in. "Tastes pretty good, too."

"I thought it was about time we refueled our bodies with something *other* than hamburgers and fries." I grabbed two large bowls and divided the contents between them. "There's also some buttered toast if you want it."

"We had bread?"

I grinned. "It had a green spot or two, but I cut them off."

"The odd green spot has never harmed this cast-iron stomach."

"I figured that."

I picked up my bowl and some toast and followed him across to the sofa. For the next ten minutes or so, there was no talking, just consuming.

"That is exactly what I needed. Thanks." He rose and held out a hand. "You finished?"

I nodded and gave him my bowl. "Have you any suggestion as to which hotel we should use to book the two rooms and do our PIT mole test?"

He shook his head. "Just Google something with ground-floor access."

He washed the dishes while I did just that. "There's a Best Western not too far from the airport that has ground-floor accommodation."

"Ring up and book a room with the ID we snatched from the vamps Rory crisped," he said. "Then I'll book another in my name."

I rose, grabbed my purse to fish out the appropriate wallet, then rang up the hotel and booked a deluxe room under the name of Margaret Jones—the name on the stolen credit card.

Jackson made his call, and then we packed fresh clothes and toiletries into a bag because who knew how long we were likely to be at the hotel. On the way out, Jackson grabbed a wireless motion-sensor alarm from his "odd bods" storage unit—the same unit that held the imagining radar device he'd used at Rosen Senior's apartment.

It didn't take us all that long to drive across to Attwood. The hotel was also a conference center, which meant there was plenty of parking. We walked down to reception and requested adjoining rooms, then grabbed our bags and headed into the room Jackson had booked.

The ground-floor room was clean and rather spacious, fitted out with a king-sized bed, a TV sitting on a storage unit, a small desk, and a couple of chairs. The bonus, however, was the glass sliding door that led out to a patio area—very handy if we wanted to be sneaky about our comings and goings.

Jackson handed me his bag and began setting up the motion-sensor alarm. I continued on through the adjoining door; the second room was the mirror image of his. I dumped both bags onto the bed, then headed into the bathroom for a shower—a long and very hot shower that eventually managed to erase Hunt's scent from my skin.

I wished it could do the same for my memories.

By the time I'd finished, Jackson was already in bed and asleep. I climbed in beside him, snuggled up to his back, and very quickly joined him in slumber.

I was woken hours later by his body twitching and shuddering. I blinked sleep from my eyes and then, as a cyclone of hurt and horror swirled through my mind—emotions that were *his* rather than mine—realized abruptly that he was dreaming about the assault.

I cursed softly and half reached out to wake him, then paused. I wasn't entirely sure he'd talk to me about the dreams, let alone the assault, so maybe it was better if I used the link rather than make any attempt to discuss what he'd experienced because of it.

I closed my eyes and reached to him mentally, sending wave after wave of soothing thoughts. As his movements finally began to calm down, I added the belief—the need—to express his feelings, to give them voice and, as a consequence, give the experience less power to hurt him in the future. I had no idea if it would help, but I also had nothing to lose by trying. He might have only felt echoes of what had been happening to me, but that didn't make his sense of defilement any less real.

It took me a while to drift back to sleep, and I wasn't

entirely sure my dreams were any less traumatic than Jackson's, because I woke up feeling less than refreshed.

A knock at the door in the other room jerked me awake. I sat upright, sparks instinctively flying from my fingertips. A murmur of voices followed; then the smell of bacon and toast hit my nostrils, and my stomach rumbled in response. I threw off the sheets, dragged some fresh clothes from my bag, and got dressed.

"Morning, sunshine," Jackson said as he came back into the room. "It would appear we didn't have any uninvited guests last night."

"I gathered that, given the alarm didn't go off." I tucked one leg under me as I sat down at the small table. "How did you sleep last night?"

He shrugged. "Had a few dreams but nothing too bad."

Right. "Jackson, we need to talk—"

"As a certain redhead keeps insisting, I'm okay." He placed the tray on the table between us, then pulled the covers off the plates, revealing not only bacon and toast, but eggs and beans as well.

"I don't think that's exactly true—"

"Fae don't do emotions—"

"Fae don't do *love*," I cut in. "But you have the full quota of everything else."

He grinned. "That I do."

I picked up the napkin and tossed it at him. "I'm trying to be serious here."

"Then I seriously don't want to talk about it."

I hesitated, but there was little point in going on about it. It'd only annoy him, and possibly make him even more reluctant to talk. "I'm here when you do."

"Good." He took one of the plates and a couple of slices of toast. "So what is our plan of attack today?"

"Well, I never did get to search Janice's place, so maybe we should go back there. She *must* know something. Otherwise, why would Amanda have tried to get rid of her?"

"Maybe she was simply cleaning up after herself—getting rid of anyone who could pin a connection between her and Rosen Pharmaceuticals."

"Maybe." I slapped a couple of pieces of bacon between two slices of toast and took a bite. "Janice had a photo of Amanda and Rinaldo on her phone—and that photo just happened to show the car's number plate."

Jackson's eyebrows rose. "Interesting that you didn't give *that* piece of information to PIT."

"I actually did. But there's no reason we can't also pursue it." I took another bite of my sandwich. "Especially given the inspector didn't tell me *not* to."

"I'm gathering you still have that photo?"

"Yeah, I do." I rummaged around in my handbag until I found Janice's phone, then brought up the pic and handed the phone to Jackson. "I'm guessing your police source will be able to trace it for us."

"No need to use her," he said. "Not when I have a contact at VicRoads."

Which was the other name for the Roads Corporation of Victoria. "Is this another one of your stable ladies?"

"No, it's a male friend. I do have them, you know." He glanced at his watch. "I'll send him a text, as personal calls are somewhat frowned upon during working hours these days, apparently."

"Huh." I waited until he'd sent the text, then said, "It

might also be worth talking to Janice again. I did question her, but she'd been drugged, and while she was answering all my questions truthfully, I'm not entirely sure the drug wasn't also messing with her mind. She might remember more with a clearer head."

"Given who she was sleeping with, it's more likely that Amanda, not the drug, was messing with her memories." Jackson sat back in the chair and scrubbed a hand through his damp hair. He'd obviously been up long enough to shower before breakfast had arrived. "Let's try her house first. It's a long shot, but if Amanda *was* using her to steal information, it's possible she was bringing files home."

"It certainly wouldn't be the first time in history someone had been used by his or her lover to gather information."

He raised an eyebrow, amusement once again touching the corners of his eyes. "And is that personal experience speaking?"

"Maybe." A grin twitched my lips. "And maybe not."

"I'm beginning to think it'd be easier to get blood from a stone than information about your past from you." He drained his coffee, then rose. "Shall we go?"

"Just let me do my teeth first."

"Good idea. Grotty green teeth on a redhead would not be a great look."

I snorted, tossed a bit of crust at him, and then headed into the bathroom. Twenty minutes later, we were on our way.

Janice's street was once again jammed with cars. As Jackson squeezed the SUV past several of them, a cab pulled into Janice's driveway. A few seconds later, she got out and strode toward the front door.

"Why the hell is she out of the hospital so soon?" I said.

"Maybe she wasn't actually released." Jackson pulled up behind a Ford. "Maybe she simply signed herself out."

"Surely PIT would have stopped that. They know she was targeted."

"Maybe that's the exact reason *why* she's been let loose. Maybe they're hoping Amanda will come a-calling again."

"In which case, there'd be an agent somewhere." I glanced around. "And I'm not seeing one."

"PIT employs shifters. You probably wouldn't." He unclipped his seat belt. "We might as well go talk to her."

"I guess so." I climbed out of the car, waited for another vehicle to squeeze past ours, and then walked across to the other pavement. "What happened yesterday, when you were following Amanda?" I asked Jackson.

"We ended up at an apartment complex in Docklands. According to the security guard I questioned, she lives on the eighth floor." He paused. "Interestingly, she was registered under the name of Felicity Hocking."

Which was the name Janice had given me earlier. "Did you go question her?"

His smile held little in the way of amusement. "No. It was about that time I got the feeling you were in big trouble. But by the time I got back here, you were gone and PIT were here." He paused. "It might be wise to contact Baker and let him know Hunt no longer exists."

The cab reversed out of the driveway and drove past us. I gave it a cursory glance, then did something of a double take and stopped.

"What?" Jackson said immediately.

"I've seen that driver before—and not in a cab." I frowned, trying to remember where, but the memory was decidedly elusive.

Jackson grabbed his phone and took a quick snap of the disappearing cab. "Maybe PIT can run a plate check and see if it's legit."

"The cab's legit. It's the driver that might not be." I continued on, hurrying toward Janice's. "And it might be that I'm wrong. Janice did get home safely, after all."

But even as I said that, part of me knew the future was whispering of death.

We were three steps away from the drive when the entire house blew up.

CHAPTER 10

The blast was so intense it sent us both tumbling. I ended up halfway under a nearby SUV and drew my body into a tight ball as bits of wood, metal, and god knows what else speared all around me. The SUV took the brunt of the debris, but the twinges of pain in my spine told me I hadn't escaped unscathed.

Heat quickly followed, and with it came the roar of flames—although I would have thought that after the power of such a blast there'd be little left to burn.

I twisted around, looking for Jackson, and spotted him half kneeling behind the driver's side rear wheel.

"I'm okay," he said, "but I'm guessing Janice won't be."

I looked over at the house. Though the air was thick with dust and smoke, it didn't do much to hide the devastation. The house was one huge pile of debris. Only one exterior rear wall remained upright, and flames were already beginning to consume that. Metal carport supports were embedded in one neighbor's wall and holes were punched into his roof, and Janice's little Honda was now sitting in the same neighbor's yard, on its back and on fire. The house on the other side had enough blast damage to expose the front interior wall, and the fence between the two properties was on fire.

I climbed out from under the SUV, then pulled off my jacket and shook it free of rubbish. "Amanda—or someone else in Rinaldo's employ—obviously came back to finish what she'd started."

"Yeah." Jackson stopped beside me, his expression glum. There were scratches on his face, a chunk taken out of his chin, and his jeans were torn and somewhat bloody. But all in all, there wasn't much damage, considering how close we'd been.

"I'll ring PIT," he said. "You want to douse those flames and see if you can spot anything in the mess?"

"I'm not sure the police or even PIT will appreciate us contaminating a crime scene." And there wasn't much left to find—not without carefully sifting through that pile of remnants, anyway.

"I'm not really caring what they think right now." His voice held an angry edge. "Not when they could have kept Janice safe and didn't."

"That's a bit harsh, Jackson. They do have bigger problems right now." Not to mention a lack of staff to cope with it all. As priorities went, it wasn't really surprising Janice had been low on the list.

"Except Janice may have been the key they needed," he said. "Rinaldo obviously feared she could tell us *something*, given he came back for a second shot at her."

Which was true enough. I glanced around at the sound of approaching footsteps and spotted a number of people hurrying down the street toward us. There was no reaction or movement from whoever owned the houses on either side of Janice's. They were going to get one hell of a surprise when they returned from wherever they were.

"Go," Jackson said. "I'll stop those people from coming too close."

As he strode toward them, I headed for the broken front gate and lifted my right hand, as if warding off the heat of the fire consuming the little car. The flames flared briefly, as if in protest to my drawing the heat from them, then quickly faded until only the pungent smell of burned rubber remained. I turned my attention to the fire biting through both the remnants of the rear wall and the dividing fence. Its heat swirled around me, through me, and I briefly closed my eyes, enjoying the sensation before I drew it in and snuffed out the flames.

But that enjoyment had come at the cost of a life. Rinaldo, I thought grimly, was going to pay for all these deaths. One way or another, no matter how long I had to fruitlessly search for the bastard, I was going to make sure of that.

The fires had now disappeared, but I had no idea if any other threat remained. I stopped several feet away from the area where the front door had once been and surveyed the huge pile of rubbish—all that remained of the house and the person who'd lived here.

I couldn't go into that. I wouldn't. I'd seen death in many disguises, but if there was anything left of Janice beyond a splash of blood or the shredded remnants of flesh, then I didn't want to be the one to find it.

I spun around and walked across to Janice's Honda instead. Aside from the melted tires and the dents and scrapes that were a result of being tossed through the fence, the car had actually come through relatively intact—at least when compared to the house.

I knelt down and peered in through the driver's side

window. Heat still radiated from the front portion of the car, but there was no scent of leaking fuel; hopefully, the thing wouldn't blow up in my face.

There didn't seem to be much more than the usual assortment of rubbish and clothing that accumulated inside cars over time, but I nevertheless tugged my sleeve over my hand and—after a bit of a tussle—wrenched the door open.

"You're worried about leaving fingerprints?"

The unexpected comment made me jump. I swung around and slapped Jackson's arm. "Don't sneak up on me like that!"

"Sorry." He sounded—and looked—anything but. "The question stands, however."

"The handle was hot, and we're being watched." I looked pointedly at the gathering crowd. He might have managed to keep them at a distance, but some of them had cameras, and there would no doubt be videos posted on YouTube sooner rather than later.

"The handle wasn't glowing with heat, so no one would have given two thoughts about your opening it with bare hands."

"I'd still rather be safe than sorry, thanks."

I ducked down, then crawled inside the car. There wasn't a whole lot of space, but that was more because it was a small car than because it was upside down. I opened the glove compartment, and papers, tissues, and the car's service book all fell out. I gathered the papers and handed them to Jackson, then checked the storage bin in the center console. Small change, phone chargers, and candy wrappers joined the rest of the rubbish on the floor—or rather, the roof. I swept a hand under the driver's seat but couldn't find anything, repeated the process for the passenger's seat, then twisted around and began sifting through the mess that had come from the backseat. It appeared that Janice shared our love for McDonald's—most of the rubbish consisted of their coffee cups and the occasional hot apple pie wrapper.

"Anything interesting in all that paperwork?" I asked Jackson. I ran my hands around the sides of the seats, just in case something had been jammed between them and the console.

"Nothing more than service receipts and registration papers going back a couple of years." He paused as the wail of sirens began to get louder. "We don't have much longer."

"No." Something pricked my finger. I swore and wrenched it free. Whatever it was had drawn blood, even if it *was* little more than a fine droplet.

"You okay?" Jackson squatted in front of the door.

"Yeah, something just stabbed my finger." I sucked the blood from it and peered a little closer, but couldn't immediately see anything sharp.

"Approach it from under the seat," Jackson suggested.

"I did that before and didn't find anything." I teased a bit of flame to a fingertip and pushed the seat cushion with my other hand, creating more of a gap. Something small and metallic gleamed back at me.

"It's a pin of some sort."

I carefully reached down and pried it free. It was one of those pin-on plastic name-tag things companies gave short-term visitors. This one read just that—VISITOR—

along with a company name: HOLDRIGHT INDUSTRIES. The name, for some reason, rang a bell.

I handed the name tag to Jackson, then crawled out of the car. "Never heard of the company," he said, helping me up.

"I have, but I can't tell you where or why." I glanced around as a police car pulled up. "And the fun begins."

"At least we now have PIT badges to speed up the process." He pocketed the name tag. "Do you want to put Google to use while I go talk to the cops?"

I nodded and dragged out my phone. Holdright Industries, I soon discovered, made industrial shelving and racking. I didn't really know the difference between the two, but obviously there was one.

But the real question was, why would Rosen's secretary have that badge in her car? Even if Rosen's company *did* use either the shelving or the racking, it was unlikely Janice had gone out there personally to arrange quotes. She would have simply sent a purchase order to their office supplies department.

Which meant we probably needed to contact Rosen Pharmaceuticals and talk to someone who might give us some insight—either on Holdright Industries or as to why Janice might have had the badge.

A police officer approached. I shoved my phone away and resigned myself to answering his questions. Jackson had no doubt already made a statement, but I couldn't complain about cops being thorough. The fire brigade and the ambulance soon appeared, with the ambulance paramedics giving Jackson and me a quick check-over before declaring us both okay.

It was a good half hour before we managed to get away; by that time, I seriously needed a caffeine hit.

"I noticed our favorite café has a franchise not far away on Plenty Road." His tone was amused. "We can grab something to go from there. Any luck on the Googling front?"

"I learned Holdright Industries makes industrial shelving."

"It didn't jog any memories loose?"

"Not a one. I guess our best option now is to go talk to Rosen Pharmaceuticals—but *not* before I have tea in hand."

"I wouldn't even dare suggest otherwise."

"Wise man."

He grinned and, in very short order, we not only had our hot beverages in hand, but also a large fries to share as we drove across to Power Street, where Rosen's company was located. It was a rather plain-looking four-story building with a café on one side of the ground floor and a lawyer's office on the other. The entrance to the building sat between the two.

There was no parking allowed on the street immediately outside the building, so Jackson turned onto Lynch Street and found a spot there. I drained the last bit of tea from the cup, then jumped out of the car and followed him across the busy road.

The building's glass doors swished open as we approached, revealing a small, somewhat dark foyer. There was a bank of elevators to our immediate left, and I spotted two armed security guards, one near the elevators and the other near what I presumed was a rear entrance, possibly the loading dock. A reception desk was in the middle of the foyer, with a small seating area to the right.

A rather handsome middle-aged blonde glanced up from her computer as we approached the desk, and gave us a polite smile. "Welcome to Rosen Pharmaceuticals. How may I help you?"

"We need to talk to whoever handles the purchase of storage and shelving units." Jackson pulled out his PIT badge and showed it to her.

"That badge," she said, "says 'associate.' I do not believe it has power of investigation—"

"And you would be wrong," Jackson said, his tone as polite as hers. "However, if you wish to check our authority, you can give PIT a call—the person you'll need to talk to is Chief Inspector Richmond."

"I'll have to discuss this with someone in management. Please take a seat—I shouldn't be long."

"A woman immune to your charms," I murmured as we walked over to the waiting area. "I didn't think that was possible."

"Neither did I. What's more interesting, however, is that they've seriously ramped up security." He motioned toward the two security officers. "That's the first time they've had armed guards in the foyer."

"It's not really a surprising step, given research was stolen and Wilson, Rosen, and now Janice were murdered."

"True—although they surely wouldn't know about Janice's murder yet." He sat down and crossed his legs, his expression contemplative as he studied the blonde. "I might have to come back when all this is over. I do so like a challenge."

"Seriously, haven't you got enough women to deal with already?"

"Oh, I'm not talking about anything serious. A simple flirtation lasting no more than a night or so will do."

"I don't think I'll ever understand the sexual drive of a dark fae."

"There's nothing to understand," he said easily. "We simply live for sex."

The woman in question replaced the receiver and gave us another of those polite smiles. "Brad Jenson will be down to assist you shortly."

"Thank you," Jackson said, his tone warm. There was little response from the blonde.

I grinned and leaned back in my chair. About five minutes later, a chime sounded as an elevator arrived; then a tall, thin man with receding brown hair strode toward us.

"Brad Jenson," he said. "How may I help you both?"

As he propped himself on the sofa beside me, I caught a whiff of garlic and tuna—lunch, obviously.

"Are you in charge of ordering storage and shelving items?" I asked.

He nodded. "Rosen Pharmaceuticals is a large company, and we have a range of suppliers—why?"

"Is one of the companies you deal with Holdright Industries?"

"No—they specialize in the manufacture of warehouse storage rather than stuff suitable for our needs."

I frowned. "So there'd be no work-related reason why Janice Green would have a visitor tag from them in her car?"

His expression became somewhat perturbed. "Janice Green is our founder's secretary, so certainly not."

I glanced at Jackson. *Maybe she knew someone who worked there?*

Possibly. He paused. *We might have to go through her phone and do a check of all the numbers.*

Tedious. And it was extremely doubtful we'd find anything, given Amanda had deleted at least one number—her alias's—from Janice's phone.

Amanda—and Rinaldo—will make a mistake sooner or later, Jackson said.

I hoped he was right, but I wasn't counting on it.

"Is Janice in some sort of trouble?" Brad asked, his gaze darting between the two of us.

Jackson glanced at me, and I blew out a breath. "How well did you know her?"

"Only casually, via work functions and the like." He paused. "'Did'? Has something happened to her?"

"I'm afraid she was murdered this morning." *And,* I silently sent to Jackson, *why is it always the woman who has to give the bad news?*

In this case, because you're prettier than me, meaning he's less likely to take it badly.

I'm sure there's logic in that statement somewhere.

Brad scraped a hand through what little hair he had. "Shit. How did it happen?"

"I'm afraid I can't say anything more right now," I said. "But you can't think of a reason why she might have visited Holdright?"

"Not officially, no."

"And unofficially?"

"I didn't know her that well, so I couldn't say."

I grimaced and stood up. "Thank you for your help, Mr. Jenson."

Jackson handed him a business card. "If you do think of anything, please contact us."

He glanced at the card and frowned. "I thought you were PIT officers?"

"We're temporary ones—we've been seconded onto the current investigation."

"Ah." He pocketed the card. "I hope you catch her killer."

"Thanks." I gave him a smile, then headed out. "Well, that was a waste of time."

"It wasn't, because we've at least ruled out the possibility she was there on official business."

"Which still leaves us down a rabbit hole with no exit in sight," I said.

"True." He paused while we dashed across the road. "Do you need to go see Rory?"

"Not until tomorrow. Why?"

"Because I think we have two courses of action right now—we continue the fruitless search for a lock to fit that second key we found at Wilson's place, or we go back to the office and share the odious duty of going through Janice's phone and checking all the numbers." He unlocked the car, and we both climbed in. "Of course, it might be a whole lot easier if your memory would come to the party with the information of where you'd seen that name before."

"Undoubtedly, but until that happens, there is a third choice."

He raised his eyebrows. "That being?"

"A choice piece of work called Amanda. You did find her apartment, did you not?"

"I did indeed, and I think that's a very fine suggestion." He gave the satnav an address in Docklands, then pulled out into the traffic. "And I seriously hope the bitch is home—taking out another of Rinaldo's soldiers can only work in our favor."

"With Frederick's disappearance, he more than likely has her under some sort of protection."

"Only if he believes we know her location, and why would he think that when we've lost her every damn time we've spotted her?"

I didn't think he'd be that careless after his close shave at the warehouse. He'd have known the information about his location could only have come from Frederick. Still, even if Amanda *wasn't* at the apartment, we could search it. While it was likely Rinaldo already had any information she'd gathered, it was also possible he hadn't had the opportunity to collect whatever she'd gotten from Janice more recently.

If she'd gotten anything and wasn't just covering her tracks.

Jackson found a parking spot on Bourke Street, and we walked through to Amanda's building, which fronted the Victoria Harbour Promenade. The building itself was a glass and concrete structure with large balconies that overlooked not only the harbor, but also the Bolte Bridge and the Melbourne Star Observation Wheel. The first two levels seemed to consist of nothing more than restaurants and pool and gym facilities for the residents—none of which the apartment building Rory and I shared had. Maybe we should move . . . I killed that thought almost immediately. Moving would mean pulling apart the fire room we'd created in the third bedroom and restoring it to its original condition, and that just sounded like too much hard work.

We walked into the foyer and approached the reception desk. Jackson flashed his badge again, but the guard waved his hand. "Remember you from yesterday. What can I do for you now?"

"I'm afraid we need to get into Felicity Hocking's apartment."

He frowned. "Don't you need a warrant for that?"

"Not if we think she's in danger," Jackson replied easily. "Her lover was murdered yesterday. We have every reason to believe she may also be in danger."

"I'm not sure—"

"Listen, Mike," I said, glancing at his nameplate. "We'll sign in, and we'll give you the name of our boss so you can confirm we are who we say we are, but we seriously need to get into that apartment."

He hesitated, then said, "I'll call the supervisor down. He has the master keys, in case of emergencies."

In other words, he was passing the decision-making buck. Couldn't blame him for that. "Tell him to hurry."

He nodded and made the call. Three minutes later, a well-built, dark-skinned man strode into the foyer, followed by two others—one male, the other female. Both projected a "Don't mess with me" vibe, and all three were armed.

"You're the PIT officers?" the first man said. According to his badge, his name was Gale. Whether that was a first name, last name, or some sort of warning was anyone's guess.

Jackson offered up his badge again. "We're associate officers, seconded to investigate the murder of one Janice Green—Felicity Hocking's lover."

"And you need to get into her apartment—"

"Because we feel she may be in danger," I repeated. "It *is* rather urgent, so if we could move this along, we'd appreciate it."

The supervisor grunted. "Give Mike your boss's contact details—I hope you don't mind, but we *are* going to check your credentials. And if you're carrying any weapons, leave them at the desk."

"We're associates—sadly, they won't give us guns."

Because there's a real need for either of us to have guns, Jackson said, his mental tone wry.

I gave him "the look." His grin grew. Once I handed the guard the information, he did the required check, then handed me the phone.

"What is this about, Emberly?" the inspector said.

"We're at Felicity Hocking's apartment, just about to check on her."

"Felicity Hocking aka Amanda Wilson?"

"Yes."

"Excellent work. Do you need backup?"

"Is there anyone available to help if we did?"

"Given the number of times you've both been attacked *and* left without your main weapons, as well as the quality of the information you've been retrieving, we'd find them."

Which was nice to know. "I think we're all right for now."

"Keep in contact."

She hung up, and I handed the phone back to the security guard. "They check out," he said.

Gale nodded, dismissed his two people, then said, "Follow me, please."

We headed up to the eighth floor and walked along the wide corridor until we reached a door situated near the building's corners. The views, I thought, would be outstanding.

He knocked on the door and said, "Ms. Hocking? Security here. We need to talk to you."

There was no answer. After a second try, he swiped his card through the reader to the right of the door and opened it. "I'll remain here," he said, and stepped to one side.

The longish corridor that confronted us led to what I presumed was the living area. The hallway itself was rather bland—cool gray walls, white ceiling, and little in the way of embellishment. Maybe that was the whole point, because the view from the windows in the living area was certainly spectacular if the bit I could see was anything to go by.

"You take the door on the right. I'll take the one on the left," Jackson said.

I nodded and headed down the hall. The plush gray carpet swallowed any sound our footsteps made, and the place was eerily quiet. There was little in the way of scents in the air, which suggested Amanda didn't spend a whole lot of time here.

I carefully opened the door. Like the corridor, the room—a bedroom—was a soft gray with white accents. The wall to my right was lined with built-in wardrobes, and there was an en suite to my left. A bed and a couple of bedside tables were the only furniture in the room.

Amanda lay fully clothed on the bed.

Not in it. *On* it.

And if she was breathing, I wasn't seeing it.

Jackson, in here, I said telepathically, to avoid alerting Gale I'd found her.

I walked over and felt for a pulse. It was so slow, it could have been a vampire's. I lifted an eyelid. Her pupils reacted to the light, but she didn't stir.

She dead? Jackson came into the room and stopped beside me.

No. Unconscious.

It's more likely she's been placed into a hibernated state until Rinaldo has another mission for her.

He could have at least allowed her to undress and be comfortable.

I don't think the comfort of others is all that high on Rinaldo's list of priorities. Jackson's tone was wry. *We should probably use the time to search her apartment. I doubt she'll cooperate when she wakes.*

She can't, not if Rinaldo has control of her mind. I hesitated, my gaze sweeping her length. Though there'd been no movement, no sign that she was, in any way, stirring, a sense of foreboding was beginning to pulse through me.

"I think we'd better—"

I didn't get to finish the sentence, but that sense of foreboding sharpened abruptly. I spun around to see Gale standing at the door, his weapon out and aimed at the two of us.

He was going to shoot.

Amanda was awake, all right, and controlling him.

I swore, knocked Jackson out of the way, then flung a line of fire toward the gun and ripped it from the guard's grip. It discharged as I did so, the bullet digging into the wall above the bed rather than into either of us. Quicker than a rattlesnake, Amanda was up and running. She didn't get far—Jackson flung out one leg, caught hers, and brought her to a crashing halt face-first onto the carpet.

The security guard immediately threw himself at Jackson. As the two men fought—with Jackson trying to stop the guard rather than hurt him—I flung myself at Amanda, landing on her back just as she was trying to scramble upright. She went down with a grunt and swore violently at me. I grabbed a fistful of hair, yanked her head back, then wrapped a ribbon of flame around her throat, blistering her skin rather than totally severing her neck, as part of me longed to. And it wasn't even the *vicious* part of me.

"Release him now," I growled, "or I *will* burn off your face."

She hissed, and then said, "Was the death of Shona and the two werewolves assigned to protect her demonstration not enough for you, Ms. Pearson?"

I blinked. Though the voice was Amanda's, the pronunciation definitely *wasn't*.

"I'm going to fucking kill you for doing that, Rinaldo."

"You were warned, were you not? You failed to live up to our agreement—"

"It was hardly a fucking agreement," I bit back. "And it doesn't change the fact you are a dead man walking."

"Technically, all vampires *are*." His amusement ran

through Amanda's tone. "And it doesn't change the fact you were warned to contact me nightly and you did not. Those deaths are on your conscience, not mine."

He was right; they were. But better three lives than the hundreds—thousands—that might die if Rinaldo ever got his hands on all the virus information. I didn't know why he wanted it, and I didn't care; I just knew I would do whatever it took to stop him from getting it.

Even if more people had to die.

"We've had nothing to damn well report at the time," I said. "So it was pretty useless ringing."

"That is hardly true, given your recent excursion into Brooklyn."

"Which netted you the laptops—and if you didn't get them, I don't know who did, because I didn't fucking tell anyone else about them."

The sound of fighting ended abruptly. Jackson came up behind me, shaking his right hand. *That bastard has a jaw of steel.*

Keep an eye on him, just in case knocking him out isn't enough.

Rinaldo was, after all, a strong enough telepath to control someone right down to their body functions and breathing . . . The thought stalled.

Was he strong enough to do that from a distance? Or was he, perhaps, somewhere close?

Good thought. Keep him talking while I check the rest of the apartment.

Jackson snagged the keycard from the guard, spun some fire around him to keep him secure, then stepped over the two of us and went looking.

"There was very little on the laptops, as I'm sure you're well aware," Rinaldo said.

"That's not my fucking fault."

"No, because we both know PIT was responsible for *that* little inconvenience."

Meaning he *did* have someone inside PIT. How else could he have known PIT cleaned them out of anything useful before we got them back? "I did warn you that we wouldn't get out of Brooklyn with anything of value. But whatever they erased could probably be retrieved with a clever enough tech guy."

"*That* is the only reason I am not currently following through with my threat to flood the streets with the infected."

Which was an odd statement if he *did* truly have someone in PIT. Or did his source simply not know about the state of the cloaks, and that they were all dead or dying? Rinaldo actually *couldn't* follow through with his threat—and not just because the majority of the cloaks were dead and he didn't appear to have the scientists.

"And how do you intend to do that, given Frederick is dead?" It was a guess on my part, but a safe enough one. As Adam had noted, it was unlikely Rinaldo would risk his thrall giving us too much information, no matter how useful Frederick might have been over the years. "He was your access point in controlling the cloaks, wasn't he?"

"It would appear you gained entirely too much information from that man. I should have killed him the minute I noticed his absence."

Meaning he *was* dead, and that the rats *would* be feasting off his flesh if PIT hadn't gotten around to retrieving him—and I really hoped that was the case. And that desire *did* come from the vicious part of me.

"If you keep killing off your lieutenants willy-nilly, it will eventually put a crimp in your style."

"Not when there are so many more able-bodied witches in this world—some of whom, apparently, have the means and the power to create a spell capable of restricting the magic of others." He paused. "That is something Frederick wasn't capable of."

"Actually, he was, because his last spell *did* succeed in fully curtailing my fire."

No one else in the apartment, Jackson said. *I'll go check the remaining apartments on this floor.*

Watch your back.

You watch yours.

"And yet," Rinaldo said, "here you are, still annoyingly alive."

"Which is just as well, considering I can hardly get the information you want if I'm dead."

"True. I have, however, reconsidered my position. It seems Frederick was correct in his summation of you."

And with that, Amanda went limp in my grip. I spun around and withdrew the ropes of fire containing the guard—and none too soon.

He made an odd shuddering sound and then somewhat groggily looked around. "What the fuck just happened?"

"You tried to shoot us."

His gaze jumped to mine. "No—"

"Yes." I pressed two fingers against Amanda's neck. No pulse—which wasn't really surprising. We'd already gained information from his thrall; he wouldn't take a similar risk with Amanda, even if her mind and body *were* his to control. "The woman you know as Felicity Hocking we know as Amanda Wilson. She's not only a wanted killer but also an extremely strong telepath. She took your mind over."

He scrubbed a hand across his jaw. "Well, fuck."

"Yeah." I rose but didn't give him back his weapon, just in case. "I'm afraid I'll have to call this mess in. PIT will need to talk to you."

He nodded, his gaze on Amanda's body. "She dead?"

"Yes."

"Did you do it?"

"No." And I wasn't about to go into a detailed explanation of what had happened. Instead, I got my old phone out of my bag, brought up Rinaldo's picture, and showed it to him. "Do you recognize this man?"

He frowned and took the phone for a closer look. "He doesn't live here, but his face is familiar, so it could be I've seen him around."

Which didn't really help much. I shoved that phone into my pocket, then got out Janice's and used it to call the inspector.

"We can trace your location via this phone," she said by way of hello. "Using different phones to contact me really doesn't make all that much difference."

"Maybe it just makes me feel safer," I bit back. "Amanda's dead, Inspector, at Rinaldo's hands. It seems he's now intent on killing rather than using me."

"Suggesting he doesn't fully understand what you are."

"Or that he simply doesn't care." I glanced at Gale. "We have a security guard on location who thinks he's seen Rinaldo in the building. Might be worth getting someone here to interview him more fully."

"I'll send one of our telepaths. In the meantime, get his people to secure the apartment."

"Will do, Inspector." But not before we did a more thorough check. I put the phone away, then returned my gaze to Gale and said, "You up to guarding this place until PIT can get more people here?"

He nodded and climbed to his feet. "We'll lock the floor down for everyone except residents."

"Thanks."

He went out as Jackson came back in. "Anything?"

Jackson shook his head. "There're seven other apartments on this floor, but he wasn't in any of them."

"I showed Gale his picture—he's seen him, even if he can't place him."

"Then that's something PIT can check. You called them?"

I nodded. "They're sending people over."

"Which means we need to run a check of this place ASAP, then get the hell out. I do not want to take part in another Q and A session."

We began a thorough search but didn't turn up anything—not even anything that suggested Amanda spent a whole lot of time here. Beyond clothes, there was little in the way of food or even the usual bits and pieces that came with living in one place for any length of time.

"Well, I guess it was a somewhat forlorn hope," Jackson said.

I dumped the gun on Amanda's bed, then headed

for the front door. "True, but it's nevertheless frustrating that we keep hitting walls."

Gale looked around as we approached; there was a decent-sized bruise forming on the right side of his jaw. "Finished?"

"Yes." Jackson gave him back the keycard. "Keep this place locked until PIT gets here. And sorry about the bruise."

"What about my gun? Will that be needed as evidence, because I'll have to report it if so."

"That's not my call. The weapon is inside, however."

He nodded and we retreated. The two security officers who'd been downstairs were now stationed near the elevators; neither of them said anything as we called the elevator and walked inside.

"So, back to the office?" I said as the doors closed.

"I guess so. It's not like we have many other options right now."

No, we didn't—not unless we wanted to conduct the proverbial needle-in-a-haystack search, and wander around Melbourne looking for the locker that matched the second of Wilson's keys.

Once we were back in the office, I'd made us both a drink, then bumped the contact list from Janice's phone across to his. "I'll take A to M, and you can take the rest."

"Righto."

He sat down, booted up his computer, and began checking the numbers online. I did the same thing. Janice, unfortunately, had a lot of people in her contacts list.

"This," I said, after twenty minutes, "is as tedious as I thought it would be. I need another tea."

"Is that a hint for me to get off my rump and get you one?"

I smiled. "Yes. How far along are you?"

"Just hit X."

I raised an eyebrow. "Someone has a surname starting with X?"

"Xavier, though I have no idea whether it's a first or last name. The number doesn't seem to be listed on Google."

"Must be a private number." I scrolled to the next screen—the H section.

"Probably. I'll call it and see what happens." He pushed up. "You want a donut with that cuppa?"

"There's none left—I demolished them last night when I was making the risotto."

"Gluttony at its finest."

"Totally. I do believe there're chocolate chip—" I paused and sat upright as a name practically jumped out at me. "What the hell is Janice doing with James Hamberly's number in her phone?"

Jackson frowned. "Who?"

"James Hamberly—he was Denny Rosen Junior's sometime lover and one of the victims of the Aswang."

"Ah, him." Jackson propped his butt on my desk rather than heading down to the coffee machine. "I was under the distinct impression Senior hated Hamberly, so why would Janice have his number on her phone?"

"Maybe she called Hamberly for him. Rosen must have talked to him at some point—why else would Junior say that Hamberly couldn't be bribed?"

"And yet, despite that, Senior considered him a leech,"

Jackson said. "That strikes me as a little odd now that I think about it."

"Doesn't it just." I pressed the number and listened as the call went through.

"Holdright Industries," a male voice said. "How may I help you?"

I was so totally caught off guard that I didn't immediately answer.

"Hello?" the voice said again.

"Ah, sorry. I'd like to speak to James Hamberly, please."

"Oh, James is no longer with us. I can, however, put you through to his replacement, Mark Terral."

"No, it's a personal matter. Thanks."

"As Alice was wont to say, curiouser and curiouser," Jackson said. "And that's undoubtedly the reason why Holdright Industries rings a memory bell—if Hamberly worked there, he probably had their name tags or other paraphernalia at his house."

"He might also," I said slowly, "have a range of industrial shelving or racking, both at his office *and* at home."

"Indeed. And given that name tag you found, our first port of call would have to be his office." Jackson walked across to his desk and snagged his jacket off the back of the chair. "You got the key?"

"There's no indication Wilson had anything to do with Hamberly." Even so, I grabbed my bag to check.

"Doesn't mean there isn't some sort of link. We might not have uncovered it yet, that's all."

"Possible." Though I personally doubted it. I found the second locker key sitting in a side pocket. "Still there. I'm glad Frederick was so intent on torturing me for information that he failed to check what I might be carrying."

Jackson motioned me toward the door. "Wonder if PIT has rescued him yet."

"They'd only be collecting his body if they do. Rinaldo did kill him."

"I'm betting no one will be sad about that."

"I'm betting you're wrong. I think Sam and PIT had plans for our dark sorcerer."

"I know Sam did, but it didn't actually involve anything official."

I glanced at him. "And what, exactly, are you implying by *that*?"

Amusement crinkled the corners of his eyes. "You know exactly what I'm implying. But if you want it spelled out . . . he was extremely angry when he discovered what had happened to you."

"Yeah, he was so damn angry, he allowed you to come running ahead of the three of them."

"He couldn't have stopped me." Jackson started the SUV and set the satnav for our destination. "And I did get a head start on them while they were dealing with Frederick."

"He's a vampire—or at least a pseudo one," I replied. "If he wanted to catch up, he would have."

"He did. He wasn't far behind when you ran into me, remember." He cast me a curious look. "Why don't you want to believe that some part of the man still cares for you?"

I sighed. "Because it would just lead to heartbreak, and I've really had my fair share of that this lifetime."

"But it could also lead to happiness, and that's what you've been searching for all these centuries, isn't it?"

A smile ghosted my lips. "It's not going to happen."

"You're sure of that?"

"Yes."

"I still think you could at least talk to the man—he obviously has something he wants to say."

I crossed my arms—a move I was well aware spoke of a need to protect myself. "And *I* think that you should keep your nose out of this particular aspect of my life."

"Impossible."

"Then how about you concentrate on driving?"

"I am one of those rare males who can actually concentrate on two things at once."

I snorted. "Then think about the fact that if something does happen between me and Sam, the sexual part of our relationship is finished."

"As I've already said, *that* is already a foregone conclusion."

Or so he'd dreamed. When I'd combined our spirits and saved his life, I'd apparently not only created the link that allowed us to now communicate telepathically, but I had also leaked some of my ability—or curse, depending on how you viewed it—for prophetic dreams.

I shifted slightly to look at him more fully. "Have you had any more dreams?"

"No. And don't change the subject."

I blew out a somewhat frustrated breath. "If I agree to talk to Sam when all this shit is over, will you drop the subject as of now?"

"Yes."

"Good. Done," I said.

"I expected a follow-through report."

"And I expect *that* won't be at all interesting."

The navigation system politely informed us we'd missed a turn. So much for his being able to concentrate on two things at once.

Holdright Industries was in one of the new industrial estates in Cranbourne. Jackson pulled into one of the parking spots at the front, and we both climbed out. The building was unremarkable—a typical metal-roofed concrete warehouse with a two-story office section stuck onto the front. The reception area was on the small side but comfortably furnished.

A middle-aged woman looked up from the reception desk and smiled. Unlike the woman at Rosen Pharmaceuticals, this one was actually genuine. "Welcome to Holdright Industries. How may I help you both this afternoon?"

I showed her my badge. "We need to talk to someone in charge."

"Sure. If you don't mind waiting a couple of minutes, I'll ask Frank to come down here."

She made the call while we waited, and a few minutes later a balding man in his fifties came down and offered his hand. "Frank Newton," he said. "How can I assist you both?"

"This may seem a somewhat strange request," I said, "but we need to get into James Hamberly's office and inspect whatever storage units he has there."

He frowned. "You know James Hamberly is dead, don't you?"

"Yes, we do. We still need to check out his office, I'm afraid."

"Sure, but can I ask why?"

"We're not really in a position to say," Jackson said, "but it involves the theft of some research matter."

Frank's eyebrows rose. "And you think James was involved? Because he was a decent man, and I refuse to believe that's possible."

Many an otherwise decent man had gotten involved in shady dealings, but I bit the comment back and simply said, "At the moment, we're only checking possible leads. It may turn out that this is just another red herring."

Frank grunted and turned around. "This way, then."

He led us through a door to the rear of the reception room and up a set of stairs. There was a long corridor lined with a series of glassed offices; James Hamberly's was the last one on the right.

Frank knocked, then entered without waiting for a response. Mark Terral—a sallow-skinned, brown-haired man—looked at us over the top of his glasses. "Is there a problem, Frank?"

"These two PIT officers need to check out the storage units Hamberly was using."

"That's those three over there by the wall and the up-right near the door. The ones behind me are new." He paused, his gaze scanning us. "What's Hamberly done?"

"Possibly nothing." I started checking the units, looking for a number that matched the key. "We just have the tedious task of checking all possibilities, however remote."

"Does this have anything to do with his murder?" he asked.

"Not his murder, no," Jackson said. "Does the name Janice Green mean anything to you?"

Both men shook their heads. None of the locks matched the number of my key, so I moved across to the upright.

"Why?" Frank asked.

"Because she was murdered yesterday, and there was a Holdright Industries badge in her car. She also had Hamberly's number in her cell."

"We deal with a lot of people," Frank began doubtfully.

Jackson held up his hand, stopping him. "I know. As we've said, we're merely chasing down all possibilities."

"No match with these units," I said. "Do you mind if I double-check the remaining ones, just in case?"

Mark waved a hand in invitation. "Where did she work? I might not know her name, but I'll probably know the company."

"Rosen Industries," Jackson said.

"Not a company we supply to." Mark hesitated. "I think we did do a quote for them at one stage, though. Hang on, and I'll grab the file from the archive."

The archive turned out to be a box sitting on the top of the upright cabinet. Mark fished through it until he found what he was looking for—a file in a suspension folder bearing the name of Rosen. He handed it to Jackson who opened it up and did a quick scan. "Just quotes, as you said, and several years old at that." He handed back the file, then glanced at me. "Anything?"

I checked the desk drawer, just in case. Unsurprisingly, it also wasn't a match. "No."

"Sorry we couldn't be of more help," Frank said.

I shrugged. "It was always a long shot, but thanks for your cooperation."

Frank nodded and took us back downstairs. Once

we were in the car again, I said, "Now what? Hamberly's place?"

"I don't think we have any other choice. I'm right out of options as to where else to look."

"That makes two of us." I sighed and scrubbed a hand through my hair. It'd been a hell of a day, and my energy levels were beginning to flag. Not because I needed fire, but simply because I was tired. Even a phoenix needed a decent night's sleep occasionally.

"We can leave Hamberly's until tomorrow if you'd prefer," Jackson said, obviously catching those thoughts.

I wrinkled my nose. "I'd rather just get it over with. That way we've a clear run for new options tomorrow."

Jackson snorted. "Because we're so overrun with options right now."

"Hey, we just might be after a decent night's sleep."

"And tomorrow the wish fairy will serve us Rinaldo's head on a platter."

I grinned. "Or the rats will."

"*That* is even more unlikely." He paused as he reversed out of the parking spot. "You want to punch Hamberly's address into the GPS?"

As I did, he added, "If the rats uncover Rinaldo's whereabouts, I very much doubt they'll inform us, no matter what they might have agreed to."

"And I think they will, if only because Radcliffe knows how dangerous I can be and will want that firepower as backup."

"He's too egotistical. He wants Rinaldo's scalp all to himself."

"He may have an ego the size of a planet, but he's already lost a number of men in Rinaldo's attacks—"

"The very reason *why* he won't want our help. He'll want to save face and prove he can handle any situation."

"I guess time will tell which of us is right."

His grin flashed. "We can always place a small wager on the matter."

I raised an eyebrow. "What kind of wager? Or is that a *really* stupid question?"

"It can be anything you want."

"Fine. Dinner at a fancy restaurant of my choice."

"Done. And if I win—" He paused, as if considering his options. The wicked grin that touched his lips had all sorts of possibilities racing through my mind.

"Yes?" I said when he didn't immediately go on.

"You do my ironing for a week."

"What?" I all but spluttered. "Are you crazy?" "Have you seen the state of my wardrobe?"

"Yes, but me, ironing?"

"You're disappointed it's not something sexual. Go on, admit it."

"I'm shocked more than disappointed." I grinned. "It seems you still have a few surprises up your sleeve."

"It'd quickly get boring if I didn't."

I was pretty sure that being involved with Jackson, on any level, would *never* get boring.

"And I, my dear Emberly, would say exactly the same thing about you."

"I was very boring before I met you. It was supposed to be Rory's turn to raise merry hell this century."

"Once all this shit with Rinaldo and the research is over, PIT will go back to ignoring us, and things will get back to normal." He paused. "Or as normal as things ever get when you're running a PI agency."

Somehow, I really doubted "normal" was something that would ever be applied to our lives again. Not if what both Lan and Grace had said was true.

Hamberly lived in one of those beautiful old Melbourne streets with wide footpaths and huge plane trees that arched over the road, creating a living green tunnel to drive through.

His house was hidden behind a six-foot green metal fence, but it was nowhere near as tidy as the other houses on the street. Weed and bushes scrambled wildly over the fence, and it wasn't a result of his being dead. It had been like this the last time I'd come here.

As we walked over to his gate, I rather warily eyed the bushes that all but hid his neighbor's yard. The elderly woman who owned the place had jumped out at me with questions—and scared me half to death—when a prophetic dream had sent me here after the Aswang, but far too late to save Hamberly. Thankfully, the old girl appeared to be elsewhere today.

We opened the gate and walked up to the front door. This time it was locked, and yellow and black police tape was barring our entry.

Jackson took the lock picks out of his pocket and in very little time, the door was open. He stepped through the tape, his footsteps echoing as he moved into the front room—Hamberly's bedroom. I followed him in. That odd, almost chemical smell that had been here last time was gone; the air held only a slightly acidy taint that spoke of the fire that had almost wiped out the kitchen.

Jackson walked across to the mahogany wardrobe. "Nice, but not lockable."

"No." I glanced around the room, but other than fingerprint dust, nothing seemed to have changed. "I wonder why this place is still under police wraps? We know what killed Hamberly, *and* we've dealt with it."

"Yeah, but the wheels of officialdom tend to move very slowly, so his body might not have been released by the coroner as yet." He opened the wardrobe doors and rummaged around. "No files or any other paperwork."

Though I doubted Hamberly would have kept anything important in his bedside tables, I nevertheless checked them. As expected, there was nothing more than socks and undies. I headed out. The letters I'd seen in my dream were still sitting on the small table in the hall, and one of them caught my eye.

"*That's* why Holdright Industries seemed so familiar." I picked one up and showed it to Jackson. "Hamberly had mail from them."

Jackson frowned. "Why would they be sending him mail when he worked there?"

"I can find out." I ripped the envelope open and quickly scanned the letter. "It's nothing more sinister than a superannuation update."

"Huh." Jackson moved past me and went into the next room. "There're a couple of cabinets in here."

"On my way." I dropped the letter onto the table and stepped away, only to stop suddenly when the return address on the other letter caught my eye—Rosen Industries.

I quickly opened it; inside were a letter and a check for two thousand dollars. "Holy fuck."

Jackson's head appeared around the corner. "What?"

"Rosen Senior was sending money to Hamberly." I scanned the letter's content, but all it said was *For ser-*

vices rendered, July, with Rosen's signature at the bottom. "A couple of grand a month, if this is any indication."

"Wonder if the company was paying him or if it was coming out of his own pocket."

I glanced at the envelope again and realized that it hadn't actually been posted. Was that why Janice had been at Holdright Industries? Had she been delivering the money for her boss? "If I had to guess, I'd say personal payment. Otherwise, he'd be using company checks, not personal ones, wouldn't he?"

"Well, if it *was* a bribe to keep Hamberly away from Junior, he wasn't honoring it."

"But it does at least explain why Rosen thought he was a leech." Even if the bastard had lied to us about not having much contact with Hamberly.

I dropped the envelope back onto the desk, then walked into the next room. This was a combination office and spare bedroom and, because it was closer to the kitchen and the fire that had threatened to wipe the place out, it had the faintest sprinkle of soot over everything. There were two cabinets to one side of the desk, but neither had our key's number.

"Wonder if he had a shed." I moved out of the bedroom and headed toward the kitchen. I didn't bother checking the living area, as I knew from the last time I was here there were no cabinets in there and the only paperwork was old newspapers and magazines.

"I'll go look." Jackson pressed a hand against my hip, lightly pushing me to one side so he could get past. As he went out into the rear yard, I started searching the kitchen drawers and cabinets. The bottom drawer near the end of the counter turned out to be filled to the brim with all sorts of bills and other bits. Though I doubted anything useful would be found, I nevertheless pulled the drawer out, dumped it on top of the counter, and began sifting through the papers.

Jackson came back just as I'd finished. "Anything?" I asked.

He shook his head. "There're a small shed and several drawers containing tax and super paperwork, but nothing even remotely interesting."

I frowned and shoved the drawer back home. "There's *got* to be something here. That money can't have been a bribe to keep Hamberly away from his son—Rosen was well aware the relationship was ongoing when we asked him about it. There *has* to be another reason behind Rosen giving Hamberly that sort of money."

"Something like hiding important information, perhaps?"

"Maybe." I shrugged. "Hamberly's certainly the last person anyone would have thought to ask about hidden research information. Senior didn't exactly hide his thoughts about his son's relationship with the man, did he?"

"No." Jackson leaned a hip against the counter. "Maybe Hamberly has storage facilities elsewhere."

"I didn't find any indication of it in the pile of bills, and there surely would have been." I drummed my fingers on the counter, my gaze scanning the scorch marks up the wall and across the ceiling . . . My thoughts stalled.

Old places like this were very popular with renovators because the steep roofline meant it was very easy to build a loft into them. Hamberly's place didn't appear to have one, but that didn't mean he wasn't using the space or storing stuff up there. I pushed away from the bench and headed into the laundry. The access hole was an unusually large one; I jumped up, grabbed the hanging cord, and pulled it down. A set of metal steps similar to the ones Jackson had installed in our office folded down from the roof.

"It appears unusually bright up there," Jackson noted.

I climbed to the top of the sturdy ladder and looked around. "There are a couple of skylights in the rear portion of the roofline."

And that wasn't all. While there might have been no evidence of a loft from the front of the house, the entire area under the roof had been extensively converted. It was bright and white, with two distinct, paneled spaces consisting of a room immediately to my left and an office area to my right. The latter had a large desk and five filing units—two four-drawer and three of the shorter two-drawer ones—and a comfortable-looking sofa. Hamberly obviously hadn't gotten any of those up that ladder, so there had to be a secondary access point somewhere else.

"Anything else of interest?" Jackson asked.

"You could say that."

I climbed into the loft and waited until he did the same.

"Whoa," he said. "Hamberly was certainly intent on keeping *something* secret."

"And from the look of it, neither PIT nor the cops have been up here to investigate. That strikes me as odd."

"Not really. Not given Hamberly was the victim of the Aswang and involved with Junior rather than Senior—at least as far as anyone was aware." He waved a hand to the left. "I'll tackle the room."

His footsteps echoed on the wooden flooring, smothering the sound of mine as I walked across to the desk. There were several folders sitting in an in-tray, each one bearing someone's name. I picked up the top one and flipped it open. The images that greeted me had my eyebrows rising, if only because they were of Hamberly and someone who *wasn't* Rosen Junior in sexually explicit positions. The man might not have looked like much, but he certainly had an imagination, if these photos were anything to go by.

I checked out the rest of the folders; while each one contained a different man with Hamberly, many were not only sexually explicit, but also veered heavily into BDSM, piss play, and even some erotic asphyxiation.

"Hamberly's been photographing his conquests," I said. "Some of these images are . . . interesting, to say the least."

"I don't think I want to know," Jackson said. "But this is where he's processing them—it's a fully kitted-out photo lab."

"Well, he certainly wouldn't be getting these images printed down at the local office supply place, let me tell you."

A door creaked. "There's also a small photography studio set up behind the lab. The setup looks professional."

I put the folders back and walked over to the first of the taller cabinets. It wasn't locked, but the number was so familiar, I stared at it for several seconds before it actually registered.

It seemed I was wrong, and Jackson had been right.

Wilson *did* have something to do with Hamberly, because I'd just found the lock that matched the second damn key.

CHAPTER 11

I grabbed the key from my bag and shoved it into the lock, just to be doubly sure. It turned. "Houston, we have found the cabinet."

"*What?*"

"The missing cabinet—the one that matches our second key—is sitting here right next to Hamberly's desk."

Jackson hurried back, his expression one of disbelief. "Why the fuck would Professor Wilson have a key to Hamberly's filing cabinets?"

"I have no idea." I started going through the files and discovered—rather unsurprisingly given what I'd already seen—an extensive catalogue of explicit photographs.

"He can't have been involved in whatever scheme Hamberly was running," Jackson said. "The government would have run background checks on everyone involved in the virus research, and something like this—which rather looks like some sort of blackmailing scheme if Rosen's check is anything to go by—should have had alarm bells ringing."

"You'd think so." I paused to open the next drawer. More photos, but this time, they were simply nudes rather than sexually explicit images. "Maybe Hamberly was running a photography studio, and the blackmail portion of it was just a profitable sideline . . . Most of these look rather professional."

"To what aim, though?" He picked up a folder and skimmed through it. "Surely there can't be much of a market for naked middle-aged men?"

"We'd probably be surprised." I closed the drawer and moved across to one of the smaller units. It had the same key number, as did the one next to it. I guess it was easier than wrestling with a multitude of different keys, although it still didn't answer the question of why Wilson had a copy of the key in his possession.

I pulled out the top drawer and discovered invoices and receipts rather than photos. I plucked one folder out, dumped it on the table, and started going through it.

Jackson opened another drawer and flicked through the files. "Ah, here we go." He pulled a folder free and opened it up. "Rosen Junior in all his glory—and in some compromising positions with several older men."

"Is one of them Hamberly?"

"Yes. They weren't taken in the studio up here, but rather in the bedroom below." He turned one of the photos around. "Shot from above, too, so I suspect Junior wasn't aware of what Hamberly was up to."

"Or he didn't damn well care," I said. "He didn't have a very high opinion of his father, remember."

"But he *did* have a good opinion of Hamberly, and I doubt that would have been the case if he was aware Hamberly was blackmailing his father."

"It would certainly explain the check, and why Janice was handing it over rather than Rosen. He wouldn't have risked going anywhere near his blackmailer. He wouldn't want anyone wondering why he was so regularly meeting someone he supposedly hated, and to start investigating."

"True," Jackson said.

I opened another folder, and the signature on the first invoice immediately caught my eye, simply because it *didn't* match the signature on all the other invoices I'd seen so far.

"Can you decipher that?" I offered the invoice to Jackson.

He glanced at it, and his eyebrows rose. "No, but I don't have to because I've seen it before. That's Professor Wilson's signature."

I flicked through the rest of the invoices. "He's signed most of these, so he was definitely involved in at least the official portion of Hamberly's business, if not the unofficial."

"Yep." Jackson handed me back the invoice. "I guess the unanswerable question—at least until someone finds the professor—is how the hell the two of them knew each other. They didn't exactly move in the same sort of circles."

"No, but maybe they were school friends or something." I put the folder back and picked up another. "Or maybe the professor had a secret salacity for men and that's how the two met. He certainly had the money to help set up this sort of operation. From the little I knew of Hamberly, he didn't."

"But surely if the professor was bisexual, Amanda would have picked up on it . . ."

"Not necessarily. Plenty of men the professor's age

prefer to hide their true sexuality under the banner of 'normality.' And Amanda was fucking him for specific information. If the professor had been closeted for years, she probably wouldn't have even noticed."

Jackson grunted. "If the two of them were partners, then there's a small chance Wilson might have kept some information here. And that means we'll have to go through every damn drawer and file."

"I don't like our chances of finding anything." I nevertheless dragged the chair across to make myself comfortable for the long task ahead.

As tasks went, this was even more tedious than going through every number on Janice's phone.

Dusk came and went, and my stomach was beginning to send out serious "Feed me or else" signals by the time I reached the final cabinet. I pulled out the first folder, then paused as I caught sight of something sitting at the very back of the drawer. I pulled the files forward, then reached in and grabbed it. It was a small cash tin. I shook it lightly, and something rattled inside— and it didn't sound like change.

I sent a sharp blast of heat at the padlock, melting it in an instant, then pulled it free and opened the tin's lid.

Inside were more than a dozen USB drives.

My heart began beating a little faster, even though I knew it was totally possible these drives held nothing more than explicit photographs.

I rose, turned on Hamberly's computer, and tapped my fingers on the desk as I waited for the thing to boot up.

"You found something?" Jackson slammed the third drawer closed and opened his final one.

"I'll tell you in a minute."

Thankfully, Hamberly didn't have his laptop password protected, so I shoved in a USB and opened it up. Inside was a series of Word files—most of them at least five years old. I picked one at random and double-clicked it. What it revealed were research notes. Not the ones we were looking for, but research notes nonetheless.

"Looks like I was wrong again, and you were right," I said. "I think we might have just found the missing notes. And if we *have*, that means Wilson wasn't only involved in this little blackmail scheme; he was also storing the backup copies of his research here."

"You're fucking kidding me."

"No."

I ejected that USB and inserted another one. More Word files, more research notes. Jackson came up behind me, watching as I continued searching through each of the USBs. We didn't hit anything useful until the eighth one, and while it wasn't about the virus, it certainly *was* about the telepathy inversion device.

I glanced at Jackson. "Was Wilson working on that before he was given the virus project?"

"I have no idea. Try the next one."

I did, but it was back to older notes. The tenth one, however, very much reminded me of the earlier notes I'd taken for Baltimore, Wilson's counterpart over at the Chase Medical Research Institute. The remaining USBs were more up-to-date; we'd definitely found our pot of research gold.

"The question that now has to be answered," Jackson said grimly, "is what the fuck do we do with them?"

I frowned. "We give them to PIT—"

"The minute we do that, all bets are off with the sindicati, and we don't really need to be dealing with their shit when Rinaldo is still on the loose."

"But we can't leave them here—given the amount of time we've been in this place, anyone following us is going to suspect we may have found something." I waved a hand around the room. "This space isn't exactly hard to find."

"No, but it won't matter if we hide them out in the open. I doubt Rinaldo or even Paretti will suspect USBs placed in the various folders hold anything more than backup naked pictures."

"Probably not, but it's still a hell of a risk."

"But less of a risk than taking them with us and getting stopped again."

I hesitated, then nodded. He was right; they probably were a whole lot safer here than they were with us right now. Especially given the possible leak at PIT.

We proceeded to randomly scatter the USBs through the various folders and also placed a couple in the chemical storage unit inside the photo lab. All we had to do now was try to remember all the different locations.

"That's something PIT can worry about," Jackson said as we finally headed out of the house. "After all, we're only associates."

"And hopefully not even that once all this shit is over," I said. "But I'm thinking, given what Lan—"

"Ms. Pearson," an aristocratic and familiar voice said from the shadows of the gate.

I squeaked in fright and jumped several feet sideways, fire automatically leaping to my fingertips—a reaction I was going to have to watch as I really didn't want to out myself as something other than human.

"Sorry, I did not mean to frighten you," Parella continued, amusement clearly evident as he stared at us down the long length of his nose.

Jackson stopped beside me. "Why the fuck are *you* here?"

"We *did* have an agreement, remember—one that you are not living up to," Parella said. "I thought a little chat might be in order before I ordered a resumption of hostilities."

"I wouldn't recommend doing that," Jackson said rather philosophically, "because we're both over being attacked, and are just as likely to kill first, ask questions later, right now."

"So I gathered from that little spark display." Parella shed the rest of the shadows from his body. If he was in any way perturbed by the thought of being crisped, it wasn't showing. "What else did you find in Brooklyn? Or what remains of it after you burned more than half of it down?"

"Other than rotting red cloaks, I'm gathering?" I asked.

He raised a silvery eyebrow. "Why would the cloaks be rotting?"

I shrugged. "The jury is out on whether it's a natural progression of the virus or the result of Luke's death."

"So the rumors are true—you *did* kill him."

"And his tame witch." I paused. "Said witch was also Rinaldo's thrall. It seems you and your bosses were more than a little wrong about the threat he represents."

"We are beginning to see that."

"Then why aren't you taking the fucker out?" Jackson said.

"We might be able to if he's now without both his sor-

cerer and the spells that have been keeping him hidden,"
Parella said. "What is the situation with the research
notes? Did you find them in Brooklyn?"

"No. We found Luke's office and a rather stout-looking
air lock."

"Has PIT accessed that air lock?"

I shrugged. "Your guess is as good as ours. It isn't like
they'd tell us, and we can't exactly ask anyone else, given
Luke is ash and the cloaks haven't a brain between them."

He raised an eyebrow. I suspected amusement, though
it wasn't actually showing in his expression. Maybe it
was such a foreign emotion, his face was incapable of
making the appropriate movements.

"What was in the backpack the rats said you carried
out of Brooklyn?"

"Laptops with nothing more dangerous than office
supply orders." I shrugged. "We gave them to Rinaldo
to get him off our backs."

"And why would you do that without informing us,
the rats, or the wolves?"

"Because Rinaldo's tame witch was infected, and
Rinaldo was using him as a conduit to control the cloaks.
He threatened to infect the city if we even thought about
mentioning them to anyone else."

"Which, I hate to admit, is a perfectly good reason to
not set up any sort of trap." He paused. "Why are you
here?"

"We're here because Janice Green had Hamberly's
name on her phone, and considering the hatred Rosen
had of the man, we figured it might be worth searching
his house."

Parella frowned. "But Wilson had no connection to

Hamberly, so why would you think the notes would be found here?"

"We didn't," Jackson said easily. "We're just covering all our bases."

"I'm still not seeing the connection—"

"James Hamberly had some very explicit photos of Rosen's son with a number of men," I said, "and he was blackmailing Rosen to the tune of a couple grand a month."

"Given it was possible he went after *more* than cash," Jackson continued, "we searched the place from top to bottom. Unfortunately, the only thing we discovered was that Hamberly and his many photo subjects are into some serious kink."

"But you're more than welcome to go discover that for yourself." I stepped to one side and waved a hand toward the house.

"Thanks, but I'll take your word on that particular matter. Hand over your purse."

I did so without comment. He found Wilson's key and held it up. "What is this?"

"The other key we found at Wilson's. We're still searching for a damn match. You already have the information we found with the first key."

He replaced the key and then handed back the purse. I slipped it back over my shoulder, glad he didn't bother checking my phone, which held all the photographs of the notes we'd found at Junior's—notes he *didn't* have.

"I'm gathering you and your sindicati cronies haven't found the research notes De Luca's hidden somewhere?"

"No, we have not." He paused. "Nor does anyone in his den appear to know."

"You know the den is working with Rinaldo, don't you?"

"No, we did not." He contemplated me for a moment. "I don't suppose you would consider working with us when the current search is over? You are very good at uncovering information few others seem able to."

"It's amazing how well the fear of fire will loosen lips," I said. "But you and I working together? One of us would be dead within hours, and it would not, I'm afraid, be me."

I'd been wrong before—his face was capable of cracking a smile, but man, it was a scary thing to behold. "Shame. We could have had an interesting partnership."

"Getting back to the business at hand," Jackson said, his voice holding an edge that expressed amusement rather than annoyance. "I gather you're still having us tailed."

"No need to when the rats are playing that particular game. They certainly don't miss much of what is going on in this city."

"Except when it comes to Rinaldo," I said. "Did you know he has a source in PIT itself? And that he might actually be two people rather than one?"

"The rats told us the latter. And I suspect it's not so much a source at PIT as someone he's able to read from some distance."

Which is probably why the inversion devices were taken from Rosen Pharmaceuticals, Jackson said. *Despite their denials of a leak, maybe they suspect one of their people is unwittingly passing on information.*

Possible. To Parella, I added, "How did you know we were here if you're not tailing us? The rats again?"

"Yes. The fact you were in the house so long had them suspecting something might have been found."

"But why would they then contact you?"

"We have an agreement in place regarding any virus research they might acquire. Because you're a major part of the current search for said research, we're also regularly informed of your whereabouts."

"So why didn't *they* come here and confront us? Why did you?"

The rather scary smile flashed again. "I always make a point of seeing those I suspect might be playing me for a fool, as I believe in giving everyone a chance before I step in and kill them."

How very civilized of him. Jackson's mental tones were dry. *But I'm betting there're hundreds—if not thousands— of corpses rotting in the ground who'd dispute that statement.*

"So this," I said, trying to stop my lips twitching in amusement, "is our first—and only—warning?"

"Yes. Give me information as you find it, or we will come after you whenever we suspect you have something. And if innocents get hurt in the process"—he shrugged—"so be it."

"Warning heeded," Jackson said. "Just don't expect goddamn miracles, because we've done nothing but chase dead ends these last few days."

"And," I added, giving Parella my sweetest smile, "you'd better make damn sure that anyone you send after me is *very* aware of the consequences that come with attacking me. As we've already said, we're seriously sick of being targets, and we *will* burn first and ask questions later from here on in."

"I suspect PIT will not approve of such action," Parella said, amusement cracking his features again. "But to echo your words, warning heeded. Have a good night."

He gave us a polite nod and disappeared into the shadows. I eyed the faint heat of his body until he disappeared into a car, then said, "Shall we go back to the hotel and wait for fate to throw us another surprise?"

"Sounds like a plan." Jackson touched a hand to my spine, lightly guiding me across the road to our SUV. "Do you want to grab something to eat on the way there, or just order room service?"

"The latter." I paused. "I also think we need to ring Baker and update him on events. He needs to know he's looking for two people, not just one."

Jackson nodded as he pulled out of the parking spot. "Might as well do that now; otherwise, we might just get a polite confrontation from them."

I pulled my phone out of my purse and did just that, then shoved the phone away and yawned hugely. "Sorry. Didn't get much sleep last night."

Jackson glanced at me as he pulled out of the parking spot. "Dreams? Or ugly memories resurfacing?"

"Again, the latter." I didn't bother telling him they were his memories as much as mine. I doubted he'd believe me.

"So much for saying you're okay."

"Nightmares are a natural part of any traumatic event, Jackson. It's often the brain's way of trying to make sense of what happened." I paused. "As I've said,

I've learned how to cope, but I'll go to a therapist if it becomes evident I need to. But you've got to promise me to do the same."

"But I wasn't—"

"You *were*," I cut in. "And it would have felt even more invasive for you because you had no warning. At least I knew what was going to happen and could fortify myself mentally against it."

He didn't immediately say anything. "And physically?"

I felt like reaching out and shaking him. "I'm sore, as you can imagine. But that, too, will heal with time and patience."

He nodded, and we drove on in silence. Once we were back at the hotel, we ordered our meal; then I took a long shower, needing to wash the dust and grime of the day away. And wished I could so easily do the same to the lingering physical reminders of both Frederick's and Hunt's attacks. But as I'd said to Jackson, that would eventually come.

Once we'd eaten, Jackson set up the sensor alarm again; then we climbed into bed, where he took me into his arms, kissed me tenderly, and held me as we both drifted into sleep.

We were woken rather abruptly a few hours later by the sharp ringing of a phone. Jackson swore and flung out an arm, groping for the damn thing.

"Hello?" he said as he squinted at the clock on the bedside table. "Shit, it's four in the morning. You'd better have a damn good excuse for calling, Turner."

My heart began to beat that little bit faster. If Sam was ringing, then something had happened. Something bad. I nudged Jackson with an elbow. "Put it on speaker."

He did so.

"I know the fucking time," Sam said, "but I figured you'd like to know someone accessed our computers to run a trace on your phone."

"How long ago?"

"About an hour."

"So why the fuck didn't you ring us sooner than this?"

"Because it was only *just* discovered via a system security check," Sam snapped. "You're lucky to get any warning at all, because the checks were only implemented last night."

Meaning PIT *did* have a mole, just as we'd suspected. "Do you know who it was?"

"Yes, and she has already been apprehended. I just thought—" He cut the rest of the sentence off as the perimeter alarm in the other room went off. "What the fuck is that?"

"Notice that we have company. Talk to you later, Turner." Jackson hung up, then flung himself out of bed and grabbed his jeans. "I'll take the front door."

I nodded, threw on a sweater, and ran for the adjoining door. But just as I got there, the damn thing was thrown open, smacking me in the face and sending me flying backward. I hit the floor hard, momentarily seeing stars as blood gushed both down my face and the back of my throat. I thrust out a hand, shooting fire at whoever was coming through that door, and then created a barrier between us.

I didn't hear any screams, meaning my lance had missed its target. Nor did I hear the gunshot; I just saw something silver shoot through the flames and spear into the wall inches above my head.

I threw myself sideways and just in time, because two more bullets smacked into the floor where I'd been lying. Whoever was behind the gun wasn't mucking about. I became fire, scrambled upright, and moved to the door. The shooter was using the wall as a shield, but I could feel the heat of his body beyond it. I waited. A heartbeat later, he reappeared around the corner. Recognition stirred, but I shoved it aside and wrapped a fiery hand around his, wrenching the gun from his grip before he could fire again.

He wasn't stupid; he turned and ran. I flipped the gun, retained flesh on the hand holding it, and then fired. The bullet ripped through his thigh, and he came to a stumbling, crashing halt, a strangled sound wrenched from his throat as he wrapped his hands around his leg. Blood pulsed over his fingers and spurted onto the floor; I'd obviously hit an artery, meaning he'd bleed out in very quick time if he didn't get help soon. But he wasn't getting it from me, not until the room was secure and I knew Jackson was safe.

I became full flesh again and peered around the doorway. Jackson was battling two men, one of whom was on fire but weirdly not screaming. A third was taking aim at Jackson's head. I raised the gun and fired. It wasn't a particularly good shot and didn't go anywhere near the guy I was aiming at, but it at least drew his attention away from Jackson and focused it on me.

I flung myself back into the room; the bullet aimed at my head gouged into the door frame, sending splinters flying. I took a deep breath, then rolled forward and flung fire at the felon. He swore and threw himself sideways, but my flames followed him, pinning his arm to his body before quickly wrapping him in a co-coon of flame. He screamed, even though they were cindering his clothes rather than his flesh. I threw him roughly against the wall and silenced him.

I switched my focus to the man Jackson had set alight, catching his flames and dragging him away and down before pinning him to the floor. It gave Jackson the chance to concentrate on the other one and, in very little time, all four were under control.

"You okay?" Jackson's gaze was sharp as it swept me.

"Yeah." I carefully wiped a hand under my nose. Becoming fire had at least stopped the bleeding, but my face hurt like hell. "I am, however, seriously pissed off."

"That makes two of us." Jackson stepped over the body of the man he'd knocked out, then bent and grabbed a fistful of the second man's shirt, hauling him roughly upright. "You will talk, or I will ensure that it's your body that burns rather than just your clothes."

The man shook his head violently from side to side, and then raised a hand, urgently pointing at his throat.

I frowned and stepped forward. "You can't speak?"

He nodded and opened his mouth. No sound came out.

"Mute." Jackson dropped him back to the carpet none too gently. "Don't attack us, don't even twitch, or I will follow through with the threat."

He walked across to the felon bleeding out and, with a lance of fire, cauterized the wound. "Your turn. Speak or I will reopen that wound—and we both know that even a vampire can die if he loses enough blood."

The vampire licked his lips. "What do you want to know?"

"What do you think I want to know? Who the fuck sent you here?"

"Rinaldo. He wanted you both out of the picture."

We might have guessed as much, but it was nice to get confirmation—and nice to know there wasn't someone else after us. At least not right now, anyway. "And did he order the use of guns?"

The vamp nodded. "He said you were too dangerous; that we needed to catch you both by surprise and that guns were our best shot."

Jackson cast a grim look my way. "Like we actually needed something else to be on the lookout for."

"Which is why we need to catch the bastard—or bastards—first." I glanced down at the vampire. "Are you from De Luca's den?"

He frowned. "No. And I wouldn't want to be, either."

"Why?"

"The council has issued an erasure edict. If any of them had any sense, they'd be heading interstate rather than hanging about here."

Those in De Luca's get didn't appear to be the brightest bulbs on the block, and I doubted any of them would be running, if only because they seemed to believe Rinaldo would be capable of protecting them.

"So are you one of Rinaldo's den?" I asked.

He shook his head. "Subcontractor."

"Who will in future," Jackson said, "*not* consider any offered action against us."

"Too fucking right. There's not enough damn money in the world that could make me accept another commission like this."

"Say that with a little more sincerity, and I might just

believe you." Jackson's tone was dry. "How did Rinaldo get in contact with you? Because he couldn't have gone through the Coalition—not enough time has passed between his decision to hunt us and your attack."

"I've worked with him before—"

"*That's* why you looked familiar," I cut in. "You're one of the vamps who attacked Radcliffe's gaming venue."

He stirred uneasily. Obviously he thought his actions there had gone unnoticed in all the mayhem. "All four of us were, but that wasn't our first job for him."

"I suggest it be your last. Not just because we'll kill you if we spot you again, but because Radcliffe very much intends revenge on all those involved."

"It was a commission—business—nothing more, nothing less. He of all people should understand that."

"He's also a rat. They're very territorial, and Rinaldo—with your help—is trying to take over their territory." Jackson patted the vamp's arm, as if to comfort him. "If I were you, I'd take some of your own advice and get the hell out of this city until the dust clears."

"Except he can't," Sam said behind us, "because his ass will be locked up tight until he's tried for attempted murder."

I swung around, not bothering to hide my surprise. "What the hell are you doing here?"

"What the fuck do you think I'm doing here?" He waved a hand. "You were under attack because Lidia accessed our computers—"

"Lidia," I cut in. "Who's she?"

"The inspector's second. We won't know for sure, but given her state of confusion when we found her, it's pretty obvious she was under Rinaldo's control at the time. For how long *that* has been the case—and what operations have been compromised—are now the questions we need to answer."

"You'd better warn whoever is minding her that Rinaldo has a thing for killing his pawns rather than letting them speak."

"We are well aware of that." He paused. "Adam and several other PIT officers are on the way to take care of these four."

"Huh," Jackson said. "It appears PIT values us far more than we figured. Of course, if you lot had actually taken our suspicions seriously a whole lot earlier, then we might not have gotten to this point."

"We're not fools," Sam bit back. "And we are rigorous with our personnel checks—"

"But not rigorous enough, obviously." I paused. "How, exactly, was she able to hack in and run the trace?"

"She didn't. As I said, she's the inspector's second, with full access to the system. She just wasn't told we'd installed the new security program." He glanced around as Adam and another man entered. "You want to get this scum back to headquarters?"

Adam nodded, and he and the other man immediately hauled the mute vampire to his feet and marched him out.

Sam returned his gaze to us. "What were you doing at Rosen Pharmaceuticals this afternoon?"

I raised an eyebrow. "I thought you were no longer following us."

"We're not, but we are keeping a watch on both Rosen Pharmaceuticals and Chase Medical Research Institute. Your arrival there was noted."

I guess we should have expected that. I told him why we'd gone there, and then added, "As it turns out, the number she had was for one James Hamberly, who worked at Holdright."

"Hamberly? The Aswang victim?"

"And the man who was apparently blackmailing Rosen for several thousand a month in exchange for not releasing some seriously compromising photos of Junior with several other men."

Sam snorted. "Considering the relationship between father and son, I'm surprised Senior didn't tell Hamberly to jump off the nearest bridge."

"Except that Senior saw the fact that his son was gay as something of a personal affront," Jackson said. "And he would have seen the release of those photos as a smudge on his own reputation."

A phone rang in the other room. "That's mine," I said, and headed in there. I had no idea who'd be ringing at this hour, but the mere fact someone *was* had trepidation skating up my spine. While the office phone *had* been diverted to the number, it was doubtful any of our clients would be ringing at four in the morning. Aside from Rory, the only other person who had the number was Scott Baker. A call from either could only mean something had happened. Something bad.

Thankfully, it wasn't Rory ringing to tell me there'd been another attempt on his life. Nor was it one of our clients.

It was Baker. He didn't say hello, and he didn't apologize for ringing so late.

He simply said, "We've found Rinaldo."

CHAPTER 12

Just for a moment, surprise held me speechless. They'd tracked him down and hadn't yet attacked him? That alone spoke volumes—both about their determination to get him *and* their respect for him.

Or, at least, respect for his abilities to manipulate and control people.

"How did you manage *that*?"

"The rats did, not me. They want you in on the action, but only if you agree *not* to inform PIT."

I blinked. "Why? The only thing that really matters—"

"Is the fact he killed *our* people," Baker cut in harshly. "And for that he must pay. A simple yes or no is all we need, Emberly."

Awareness itched at my back. I spun around and discovered Sam watching me from the doorway.

"Is there a problem?" he said.

I shook my head, then told Baker, "If that's the way you want it, sure."

He gave me the address. "Be there at sunrise."

I glanced at my watch. We had an hour, no more. "Will do."

I hung up and threw the phone back into my purse. "Did you want something?"

Sam eyed me somewhat suspiciously. "I'm heading

off with Adam. The inspector wants you and Jackson to come into headquarters—tomorrow, if possible."

I frowned. "Why?"

"Probably to read you the riot act for misusing those badges she foolishly gave you."

Though his voice was flat, a hint of amusement touched the corners of his eyes. It warmed that stupid part deep inside of me, but I was getting rather good at ignoring that part these days.

"Hey, it wasn't like we wanted the damn things, but you can hardly blame us for using them to our advantage." I paused. "You're not going to drug us again, are you?"

"I doubt it." He eyed me uncertainly for a moment. "Do we need to?"

"No, you most definitely do *not*. What we know, you know." And I resisted the urge to cross my fingers behind my back when I said that.

Though his expression hadn't altered, it was very evident he didn't believe me. "She wants you there at nine."

"We'll try, but we do have an agency to run—"

"Is that what the phone call was about?"

"It's none of you damn business, but yes, it was."

"At this hour?" His voice was skeptical.

"Adultery has no time restrictions, Sam. You of all people should be aware of that. It's what you accused me of, after all."

Which wasn't at *all* fair, given he had every right to do so. Maybe if I'd explained what I was, and what that meant for him and me, things might have been different for us . . . but I couldn't change what I'd done. Not this time, with this man.

But the next rebirth, I was going to do as Rory suggested, and be honest. Hopefully, the next man destined to capture my heart would be more accepting.

And maybe, just maybe, I could live one lifetime happily in love.

Sam didn't bite back, as much as I expected him to. His expression simply shut down, and that cloak of darkness swirled around him again. He didn't fade into the night, but he sure as hell electrified it.

"And you might want to give us an address," I continued, "because we were blindfolded and thrown into the back of a van last time we were there, remember?"

He gave me the address, then, with a nod, turned and walked out.

Jackson walked into the room, an eyebrow raised. "I take it from his expression that the two of you had words?"

"Yes. No." I waved a hand in frustration. "That man just gets stranger and stranger. Maybe the virus has addled his brain."

"Maybe you should stop bringing up the past and concentrate on the future."

"Didn't I tell you to butt out of that part of my life?"

"And I told you that was impossible." His grin was decidedly unrepentant. "Who was on the phone?"

"Baker." I paused and motioned to the other room. "Are you sure they're gone?"

"Yep. Heard a van and a car start up. Why?"

"Because we have to get to Keilor Park stat." I grabbed my jeans and pulled them on. "They've found Rinaldo."

"And you didn't tell Sam that? Your ass is grass when he finds out."

I snorted. "Baker didn't give me an option—either we do this his way, or we miss out on the action."

"And *that* is something I have no intention of doing." Jackson finished getting dressed. "I take it the rats are involved in this showdown?"

"Yes. It was at their request that Baker rang us—no doubt in an effort to stave off any possible reprisals if this all goes ass up."

"Or because he wants our firepower as backup just to ensure the bastards don't get away again." Jackson grunted and grabbed the keys. "Let's hope PIT isn't tailing us."

"There's nothing we can do about it if it is." I followed him out the door. "Oh, and Sam informed me that the chief inspector wants to see us at nine tomorrow."

"Does she now?" He climbed into the car, then said, "If we survive the upcoming encounter, I might just consider it. Or I might not. Depends on what she wants."

"Apparently to castigate us over our usage of the badges."

"Hey, she's more than welcome to have them back." He motioned to the GPS. "You want to type in where we have to go?"

I did so. "What do we have in the way of weapons?"

He gave me the raised eyebrows "Did you really just say that?" sort of look. "Fire isn't enough for you these days?"

"When we don't know who or what we're dealing with beyond Rinaldo, no, it's not," I said. "He won't be alone. Not after that near miss at the warehouse. Hell, for all we know, the rats suddenly locating him is nothing more than a setup."

Besides, that instinctive part of me was suggesting I'd have to reserve every scrap of fire I had if I wanted to get us through this—not something I was about to ignore.

"I'm sure Radcliffe and Baker will be more than aware of that prospect," Jackson said.

I hoped so, because otherwise, it could get ugly.

It didn't take us long to reach Keilor Park. Jackson turned off the headlights as we cruised into Lambeck Drive and headed for the café about midway down. Baker stepped out of the shadows as we pulled into one of the parking spots in front of the place.

I climbed out of the SUV and closed the door as softly as I could. "Where's Radcliffe?" I asked him.

"At the location, keeping an eye on things. Between my men and the rats, we've got the building surrounded."

I frowned. "Frederick's a vampire—he's going to sense the heartbeats."

"We're well aware of that, and we are, currently, out of sensing distance," Baker said.

"And you're sure this isn't a trap?" Jackson moved around to the rear of the SUV and retrieved a number of guns from the trunk. He handed me one and kept the other two, plus a knife, for himself.

"No, we're not," Baker said, "but he's definitely inside."

"Meaning just one of the twins is inside?"

"That is something we're unsure of. We think both are in there, but we haven't sighted the second brother."

"I guess that *would* be hard to confirm since they appear to be in the habit of wearing identical clothes," Jackson said. "What do you want us to do?"

"We're going in through the front door. Radcliffe is looking after the rear and the sewers. We want you to handle the roof access."

I raised my eyebrows. "How many stories does this place have?"

"Three in the office section. The warehouse is an unknown at this stage, but there's no roof exit there from what we can see."

"So we're nothing more than backup?" Jackson said. "Because I'm seriously *not* happy about that. You're not the only one who lost someone, Baker, and I have no intention of being sidelined on this."

"You're not. There's no way in hell Rinaldo would trap himself inside any building without having an escape route ready," Baker said. "Something *you* learned the hard way at the previous warehouse."

"Not the same thing—he was gone before we got there," Jackson bit back. "And you've no guarantee the same thing hasn't happened here."

"Yeah, we have, because we've been watching all the exits for several hours now—not just the building's exits but all sewer outlets and the roof. One of the Rinaldos went in. No one has come out."

"Then don't expect me to sit on that roof and wait for one of them to head my way," Jackson said, "because it's not going to happen."

"Nor do I want that. The plan is to attack from all possible angles. Hopefully, we'll trap the bastard somewhere in the middle of us all." He glanced at his watch. "You have eighteen minutes to get in place."

"And how do you expect us to get onto the roof without Rinaldo or anyone else spotting us?" Jackson said.

"You won't, but that's the whole point. While they're readying for an attack from above, we'll hit them from the sides." He pulled a roughly drawn map out of his pocket and placed it on the hood of the SUV. "This is our target building here. On the corner of Lambert and this street, there are several large trees that reach past roof height. It should be easy enough to shimmy up them and drop onto the roof."

"Do I look like the type that shimmies up trees to you?" I asked mildly.

"I don't know about trees, but Radcliffe's told me you do a rather mean fire shimmy." His grin flashed. "And he's had firsthand experience, apparently."

That he did.

"We do have people watching the roof," Baker continued, "just in case the bastards attempt an escape before you get up there."

"Nothing personal, Baker," Jackson said, "but I really hope the bastard does head our way. I want to watch his face as I pound every ounce of life from his body."

Baker raised his eyebrows. "I had no idea fae could be so damn brutal."

Jackson's grin flashed, but it was a dangerous thing. "That's because most people are sensible enough not to get on our bad side. We are called dark fae for a reason, you know."

"I guess so." Baker folded up his map and shoved it back into his pocket. "Zero hour is six on the dot. Time now is five forty-five."

We adjusted our watches to match his and then all headed down the street, keeping on the opposite sidewalk to our target building in an effort to stop any vamp guards from sensing our heartbeats.

But vamps were blessed with night sight that was very familiar to infrared, so even if they couldn't hear the pulse of life through our bodies, they'd most certainly see us, darkness or not, if they happened to be looking our way.

And I was damn sure that after Rinaldo's previous close call, he wouldn't be foolish enough to camp somewhere without guards.

Tension crawled through me. I flexed my fingers, but I couldn't quite ignore the growing certainty that this was a trap—and one that was going to go to hell in a handbasket all too soon.

Baker crossed the road and disappeared into the shadows of the building next to our target. Jackson and I continued on, crossing over a grassy divide before slipping into the parking lot of the building on the other side of the road. There were several cars and a van parked there; we used the van as cover.

I pressed back against the van, then carefully peered around its side. Our target building was T-shaped, with the three-story office portion being the top piece to the warehouse's stem. The office section was a long, three-story, concrete and glass building. There were no lights shining in any of the windows and no sign of anyone either around the perimeter or on the roof. I couldn't even see the rats or the wolves.

I really don't like the feel of this, Jackson.

No. He paused. *But if Rinaldo is inside—and Baker saw him go in—then fuck the trap. This might be our one and only chance to grab the bastards, and I'm not going to step away from it.*

Neither was I, even if that precognitive part of me was beginning to whisper all sorts of dire consequences if we didn't.

Of course, *that* could have been fueled by fear; by the knowledge that Rinaldo was never going to go down without causing as much mayhem and carnage as possible. He had the vamps in there to do it, but my real concern was, what else—and whom else—did he have?

My gaze drifted to the empty building behind us. Intuition stirred, but it gave me squat as to why. There was no sign of movement, no sense of heat coming from within. The place was empty, and yet . . .

I frowned and glanced at my watch. Three minutes to go. I returned my attention back to our target building. *I wonder why they chose six o'clock as an attack time. Hanging about here is only increasing the chances of discovery.*

Jackson pointed skyward. Faint drifts of pink and gold were beginning to touch the black. *I suspect it has something to do with the sunrise. Vamps are sluggish in the brief time between night and sunset or sunrise.*

I snorted. *Says who? Certainly no vampire I've ever come across has exhibited said sluggishness during those times.*

It's a common belief.

Just like the belief that all fae are small and winged?

His grin flashed. *Humans have always gotten fairies and fae mixed up.*

I've never seen a fairy, not in all the long years I've been alive.

Sure you have. They're those small yellow flowering weeds that form a white parachute-like seedpod.

I lightly slapped his arm. *Idiot.*

He glanced down at his watch, and his amusement fled. *Time to go.*

I hope the rats and the wolves don't waste too much time attacking. I slipped around the corner of the van and ran toward the nearest climbable tree. *And I seriously hope we're not being hung out to dry here.*

Baker wouldn't. He wants revenge too badly.

I agree, but Radcliffe is also involved, and he certainly would.

We're less a threat to him than Rinaldo. He needs to take that bastard down and regain the respect of his mischief.

A smile touched my lips. *I always found that to be a rather incongruous name for a group of rats.*

We reached the tree. I lifted one leg so Jackson could boost me up, then grabbed the nearest branch and climbed onto it. The old eucalyptus had obviously been here even before the area had become an industrial estate, and the thick branches were very easy to climb. I reached the one that stretched out over the building's rooftop and made my way down its length. In very little time, I was on the roof, my fingers lightly brushing the concrete as I steadied myself. Jackson joined me a few seconds later.

Where the fuck is the attack from the— He cut the question off as a gigantic whoosh of debris and heat came from the front of the building. *About time. Let's find the exit.*

We padded through the sea of cooling towers, antennas, and other paraphernalia, eventually finding a stairwell entrance toward the rear of the building, to the right of the edge of where the warehouse met the office portion.

Jackson tested the handle. Unsurprisingly, it was locked, but a quick burst of fire soon fixed that. He opened the door carefully; darkness greeted us, but not silence. All hell had broken loose somewhere down below.

He opened the door wider and peered inside. No fist or gunshot greeted him, so he moved farther into the stairwell. I followed but paused at the edge of the railing and peered down into the darkness. The ongoing noise of the battle below was all-encompassing, but I nevertheless had the vague suspicion someone was headed our way.

Jackson got out one of his guns and flicked the safety off. I did the same. My fire might be my best weapon, but that earlier intuition about reserving my fire was getting stronger.

And I really, *really* didn't want to know the reason behind it. I might just run if I did.

We edged carefully down the stairs, keeping our backs to the wall and our guns trained on the stairs below. The sensation that we weren't alone was growing, but I couldn't hear any breathing or steps.

Could be vamps, Jackson said.

Possibly. But even if they'd wrapped the shadows around their bodies, that wouldn't explain why I couldn't hear their steps.

If Rinaldo has been hiring from the Coalition, it's possible he's gotten a few ex-military types, Jackson said. *Could explain the lack of noise.*

We reached the next landing and the door to the third floor. I glanced down, the hairs at the back of my neck rising. Whoever—whatever—was down there, that instinctive part of me did not like it.

Do you want to check this level while I keep an eye on the stairwell?

He hesitated. *I'm not entirely sure it's a good idea to split up.*

It's not like we have any other option. We can't risk who-ever's below getting past us.

His frustration slipped through me, but I was right and he knew it. *Shout if you need help.*

As long as you remember to do the same.

Always. He opened the door and silently slipped through.

I caught the edge of the door to stop it from closing again. Jackson made no sound as he disappeared down the hall, but I could tell his location by the whereabouts of his body heat.

I wished I could do the same with whoever was creeping up from below. They were still weirdly quiet, and I was getting very little in the way of heat. Which meant that either they didn't have any—and even vampires had detectable body heat, even if it was lower than that of a human—or there was some kind of magic involved.

If it was the latter, it might just be Rinaldo. Who else would bother?

I flexed my free hand; heat burned at my fingertips, but it wasn't showing. Not yet, anyway. From down the far end of the hallway came an odd scrape of sound, almost like a body hitting the ground.

Unease flicked through me. *Jackson?*

He didn't respond. The unease sharpened. *Damn it, Jackson, don't play games. Answer me!*

Still no response.

Fuck.

I thrust a hand through my hair, then glanced down the stairs again as the sense of something approaching also sharpened. I took a deep breath, then released the heat burning at my fingertips and flung it up the stairs, creating a thick, fiery barrier only the foolish would attempt to get through. It also had a secondary benefit—if someone *were* foolish enough, I'd know about it.

I cast another look down the stairs, but even though my fire had burned away the shadows, it still didn't reveal the threat I was sensing.

I spun and raced down the hallway, my gaze sweeping each office as I passed, but there was nothing more than basic furniture and dust. This floor obviously hadn't been used in a while.

Behind me, the stairwell door shut with a soft clang, the sound echoing ominously across the shadows. I reached the end of the building, but there was no Jackson, and no sign of where he might have gone.

Fear swirled through me, but I clamped down on it. If he were dead, I'd know about it. I'd feel the emptiness in that part of my brain that could hear his thoughts and emotions. That part might be silent, but it wasn't severed. He was alive but unconscious.

But who the fuck had attacked him, and where the hell had they gone?

Though dawn was rapidly gaining accession over the night outside, darkness still reigned supreme inside. I cast a small ball of fire into the air, then glanced back down the hall. The door was still closed, and no one had made an attempt to get through my flames. And yet . . . and yet, something had changed. The air felt *different*.

Alive.

I frowned, studying the doorway for a second longer before pulling my gaze back to my immediate surroundings. And that was when I spotted it—blood.

My gut twisted as I strode over and bent down. It was fresh. *Jackson's,* that inner voice whispered. I closed my eyes and tried to remain calm. *He's hurt, not dead. Hold on to that and just find him.*

As I rose, I spotted another droplet of blood, then another. The minuscule trail led me directly to a blank wall.

Or was it?

I ran my hand along the plaster and felt a slight indent. I pressed it, and the wall to my right slid aside, revealing a dark square space and cables that ran down into a deeper darkness. A dumbwaiter, I presumed. I leaned forward a little, but as I did, that sense of wrongness sharpened abruptly.

I threw myself sideways, hitting the carpet with a grunt but somehow managing to keep hold of my gun. I raised it, my finger on the trigger. But there was nothing there.

Was there?

I narrowed my gaze, and saw it—the faintest shimmer of air.

Someone was there all right. They were just using a glamor—and not the type that altered their form, but rather one that hid it completely.

I pulled the trigger. The shot rang out like the boom

of a cannon, but whoever was behind the glamor was quicker than a rattlesnake.

A body hit the ground to my left, the sound almost but not quite smothered. I fired again. This time there was a grunt as the bullet hit home.

I scrambled to my feet, only to be knocked down again as my unseen assailant threw himself at me. As we went down in a tangle of arms and legs, he reached for the gun, trying to tear it from my grip. I swore and became flame, and he screamed as his body went up in a whoosh of fire. I clenched a fist, made it flesh again, and smashed it into his jaw as hard as I could. As he went limp, I threw him from me, then recalled my flames and fully regained human form.

Only to realize there'd been two of them.

Something smashed against the back of my head and sent me flying. I hit the wall hard and felt the black tide of unconsciousness descending. I fought it with every scrap of energy and determination I had in me, and punched upward with my free hand. I didn't hit anything, but it didn't matter because I wasn't actually trying to. Multiple fingers of flame leapt from my clenched fingers and fanned out, seeking, searching, for my attacker. There was a soft curse and the faintest sound of footfalls, but there was no escape from my net. It caught him, wrapped around him, and then flung him—hard—against the nearest wall.

He didn't move. I released the flames and let their energy filter back into me as I forced myself into a sitting position. Bile rose up my throat, and again the tide of black threatened. I sucked in air, drawing it deep into my lungs, into my body, trying to calm the churning in my gut and the weakness washing through my body. It was a weakness that could affect my ability to raise fire as a weapon and was undoubtedly why intuition had been warning me to conserve it.

After several minutes, the tide receded. I pushed upright; the effort made my head pound, and warmth began to trickle down the back of my neck. I tucked the gun into the back of my jeans, then carefully felt the back of my head; not only was there a lump the size of a tennis ball but also a cut at least an inch long.

I briefly became flame to cauterize the wound, but the effort had my senses swimming. Concussion, I suspected.

I walked across to my first attacker—whose position I knew only thanks to the smell of burned flesh—and carefully knelt beside him. Glamors might be capable of hiding your form, but they didn't actually stop anyone from feeling you. There was a slight tingle as I pressed my hands through the glamor's barrier, but it quickly faded as I began searching for whatever artifact the spell had been placed on. I found it around his neck; a pendant on a simple chain, from the feel of it. I yanked on the chain to break it, and then flung both it and the pendant away from him. The air around his body shimmered as the spell faded, revealing a big red-haired man in his late forties. He wasn't a vamp—his skin was too tanned—and he wasn't a wolf. He was human—a hulking great human.

He needed to be if they'd shoved Jackson into the dumbwaiter. Jackson was neither small *nor* light.

I pushed up and went into the nearest office, rummaging around until I found some wrapping tape. Then

I rolled the hulk onto his stomach, hauled his arms behind his back, and wrapped the tape thickly around his wrists and hands. I repeated the process with his feet.

With that one safe, I walked down to the other one, pausing on the way there to stomp on the small plaster pendant. It shattered with a small puff of smoke. I reached inside the glamor hiding my second attacker and felt around until I found the pendant, discovering that this one was a female, not a male.

This time, I undid the chain rather than break it, and I didn't toss it away. Instead, I placed it on my hand and, after a minute, felt my skin tingle as the magic within it reactivated and my hand, arm—and no doubt the rest of me—disappeared. As I'd suspected, these glamors were activated by skin contact and had *not* been specifically designed for either of my attackers. I slipped the pendant around my neck and let it sit next to the charm Grace had given us. Once I'd repeated the tying-up process, I rose and went back to the dumbwaiter.

The thing was on the move.

I stepped back and waited. It rose with tortuous slowness. Sweat trickled down my back, my head was still pounding, and all I wanted to do was find a nice dark corner to curl up in.

But not until Jackson was safe and the two Rinaldos were dead.

The top of the dumbwaiter came into view. Fire boiled through me, wanting release, wanting to lash out and hurt someone.

But there was no one in the dumbwaiter to hurt.

There was just a note. I released the breath I hadn't been aware I was holding and carefully stepped forward. Grace's charm flared to life almost instantly, and I stopped. Obviously, the magic was meant to ensnare me the minute I picked up the note, so that was the one thing I couldn't do.

I rose on my tiptoes in an effort to see what was written on it, but from this distance, it was little more than elegant-looking black scrawls. Rinaldo's writing, I guessed. He—or at least the one we'd met—seemed the elegant type.

I quickly looked around and spotted one of those sticks used to open and close vents sitting in the room I'd gotten the tape from. I retrieved it, then carefully stretched out and tried to snag the note and drag it closer. The burn of the charm at my neck got stronger; then it snapped away, and the note fluttered free from the dumbwaiter. I dropped the stick and picked up the note.

If you want to see him alive, it said, *come to the factory across the road. The one that holds the van you hid behind. And don't inform the rats or the wolves.*

Intuition had been right. It was my senses that had let me down.

A wild mix of fury and fear rushed through me, and the note became cinders in an instant. As its sooty remains drifted to the floor, I spun and walked back to the staircase. It was a trap; I knew that. But I had Grace's charm, I had the glamor, and I had my rage.

It would have to be enough.

I thrust a hand to open the door, then stopped. Whoever I'd sensed coming up the stairwell earlier was now waiting just beyond the door.

I took a deep breath, then raised a hand, caught my

barrier's flames, and smeared them across the entire stairwell.

That was when the screams began. Horrible, pain-filled screams.

Good, that hard part of me thought. I thrust the door open and was greeted by a human torch. I grabbed my gun and shot at what looked like a kneecap. As the man went down, I snatched the fire back into my body, then spun and ran up the stairs.

The sound of fighting was still rising from below, suggesting Rinaldo had one hell of an army down there—maybe even the entirety of De Luca's den. After all, with the council's kill order now hanging over their collective heads, they had nothing to lose and every-thing to gain by fighting for Rinaldo.

I pushed out onto the rooftop. The sky was a wild mix of red, orange, gold, and purple, and it seemed to echo the state of my mind. I flexed my fingers as I strode across the roof but paused near the edge, my gaze scanning the building on the other side of the street. The front door was now open.

It was an invitation I wasn't about to accept.

I glanced up at the tree, took a deep breath that didn't do a whole lot to ease the pounding in my head, and leapt. I caught the branch with one hand, steadied myself with the other, and then clambered up. It didn't take me long to get down to the ground.

I took a circular route to the other building. I had no idea who might be watching, but I had no doubt some-one was. I just had to hope that whoever it was wasn't all that familiar with magic and glamors.

The building belonged to some sort of printing

press, and it was another of those two-story concrete and glass constructions that could be found everywhere in industrial estates like this. There was a driveway between this building and the next, and that was where I headed. I still wasn't getting any sense of heat coming from within the building, but as I walked down to the loading bay area, the awareness of it slipped across my senses. I slowed my steps, trying to keep as quiet as possible. While I was pretty confident no one could see through the glamor, I had no idea who or what was up ahead—although if they were vampires, they'd sense my heartbeat, glamor or not.

I stepped into the loading bay. There were two of them here—one at the top of the steps near the door, the other at the bottom of the ramp.

If I didn't want Rinaldo to know I was coming in from the side entrance, I had to take both out at the same time. And that meant using fire.

Trouble was, I wasn't entirely sure how much more fire I had in me. As intuition had warned, the pounding in my head was sapping all my strength. But it wasn't like I had any other option. If I only attacked one, the other would have the chance to warn Rinaldo.

Besides, time was running out. For Jackson, and for me.

Not wanting to think too hard about *that* bit of information, I picked up a pebble and flung it against the opposite wall. As the two men spun around, I flicked out two ribbons of fire, wrapped one around each, and threw them headfirst into the walls. I didn't bother checking them. The blood beginning to stain the concrete spoke volumes about their life expectancy. I ran up the steps and carefully opened the door. The room beyond was small and dark—some sort of office or receiving area.

I crept forward. There was a window next to the door, and I peered through it from one side. With dawn in full bloom outside, the shadows were lifting inside. The room beyond was vast and filled with printing presses and various other bits of machinery. I couldn't see anyone, and there was no indication of a heat source anywhere in the room. Beyond the presses were several doors; one was open and led into a bathroom. The other was closed.

I carefully opened the door and walked out, keeping my back to the external wall in an effort to protect myself. I still wasn't sensing anyone, but then, I hadn't sensed the red-haired hulk and his companion until it was almost too late, either.

I should have drained the heat from them. It would have bolstered my strength and shored up my reserves, but it was too late for regrets now.

It didn't take me long to reach the closed door, but I didn't reach for the handle. Instead, I pressed a hand against the wood, then closed my eyes and called to whatever heat was inside—something every phoenix could do but rarely attempted, as it drained our strength even as it fed us. Which was why we generally touched people when we fed from them—it was easier and far less dangerous. Doing this now, when I was in an already depleted state, was doubly so.

There *was* heat inside.

It filtered quickly through my fingertips and fed the inner flames, but my head began to pound even more viciously and my form flickered, briefly becoming fire—a sure sign I was reaching my body's limits.

Two soft thuds came from inside. I quickly shut down the feed but didn't immediately move, waiting instead for the flickering between shapes to ease.

Once it had, I grabbed the handle and opened the door. The room beyond was an open office area; one guard lay to the right of the door, and another across the exit on the far side of the room. I knelt down beside the nearest guard—a vampire, and one I'd seen before. He was one of the vamps who'd attacked Sam and me in the cemetery.

Obviously, no lesson had been learned or warning heeded. Not then, not later.

I placed a hand on his and drew every scrap of heat and life he had left in him into my body. His skin went cold, and then his body began to draw in on itself, until there was nothing left but flesh on bone and life had departed.

It helped. Only fractionally, but I suspected even the smallest of fractions would matter. I repeated the process with the second guard—another of De Luca's get—then placed my hand on the door. There was no sense of heat coming from the next room.

I went through. It appeared to be some sort of conference area. I stepped toward the next door, only to halt as a somewhat tinny but all-too-familiar voice said, "I suggest you stop all the fucking about and come to me immediately if you wish your partner to remain alive."

Fire swirled around me, a halo of flame that had nowhere and no one to immediately attack. I glanced around the room and saw the speaker sitting in the far corner.

"I know you're in the building, Emberly. I can feel the pulse of your life in the room below."

Meaning *he* was above. I looked up. The ceiling was one of those suspended grid systems that were easy to get into. The concrete above it wouldn't be, unless I could find a way to circumvent it.

The bathroom . . .

I spun around and walked out.

"Hurry up, dear Emberly; otherwise, your partner will pay the price."

I didn't respond, as much as I wanted to. I strode into the bathroom, punched a hole into the wall behind the nearest toilet, and found the waste pipe. Places like this usually had their bathroom facilities situated in the same location on every floor to make connections for waste and water easier. This place was no different.

If Rinaldo wanted me, he was going to get me. The real me, in all my fiery glory.

I blasted a hole into the plastic pipe, then shifted shape and surged upward. The facilities above provided as little resistance to my heat as the ones below, and in very little time I was out the door and in the main room.

Men flung themselves at me, not seeming to care that I was fire. Their bodies went up the instant they touched me. Two, three, and then more, hit me, momentarily forcing me down under the sheer force of their numbers. But as their bodies became ash, that force lifted and I surged forward again.

Rinaldo was standing alone in the middle of a large

stone circle. Witch stones—not ordinary ones. To one side of him, surrounded by at least a dozen vampires, knelt Jackson. His hands were tied, and around his neck was a silvery pendant not unlike the one I'd stolen. I had no doubt it was restraining his fire, just as I had no doubt that *all* the pendants had come from the small woman kneeling beside him. Even from where I was I could feel the wash of her power—but both she and that power were under Rinaldo's control if her slack features and the emptiness in her eyes were anything to go by.

Rinaldo himself looked calm, but fury radiated from his body, its force so fierce, the air around him seemed to boil. I shot a lance of fire his way, even though the stones around him told me it was pointless. It bounced harmlessly away; I sent another one at one of the stones, but lessons had obviously been learned, because it, too, bounced away. As a last resort, I tried to call to his body heat. That, too, proved useless. The wall of magic surrounding him had been very well designed.

He smiled. It was not a pleasant thing to behold. "Retain your real form, Emberly, or the witch dies."

If Rinaldo thought my flesh form rather than this was real, then perhaps he didn't know as much about phoenixes as he thought. It at least gave me some hope. My gaze met Jackson's as I shifted shape.

You okay? He didn't look it. His skin was gray, and sweat was trickling down the side of his face.

Some gorilla broke my leg, and the witch's charm is restricting my fire. But other than that, just ducky.

"Step into my circle, Emberly."

Said the spider to the fly. I flexed my fingers, then

walked forward. *Do you know what the circle around him is?*

It's not only fire restriction, but it'll restrict your access to the mother.

Meaning the witch was familiar with the mother—and that *she* was probably the reason Frederick's spell had been as well designed as it was. But I'd beaten him, and I could beat this witch—if I had the energy, not to mention the time.

"I was going to kill you swiftly," Rinaldo continued, "but I'm afraid that option disappeared after what you did to my brother."

"I haven't fucking touched your brother—" I paused. Did he mean in the stairwell—the one I'd set alight and then shot?

"I can feel his agony, Emberly. It burns through my body and my brain, and begs me to return it in kind." Rinaldo waved a hand. "I cannot help but comply."

Meaning I'd had him. I'd had the bastard screaming at my feet, and in my anxiety to get to Jackson, I'd let him live. *Fuck.*

I would have done the same, Jackson said.

That's not overly comforting right now. I stopped a few paces outside the stone circle. *Will your broken leg prevent you taking out the guards?*

It prevents me from moving, but if I can access my fire, I can take the guards out no problem. He paused. *But the minute I attempt it, the witch is dead.*

I'm about to fix that problem. To Rinaldo, I said, "Release your grip on the witch before I step into your circle."

He raised an eyebrow. "If you hope that she might help you with her magic, you will be disappointed.

Among the charms she created for me was one that restricts any access she has to magic."

"Release her and you can have me. Don't, and I'll kill your guards, free Jackson, and leave you surrounded in a ring of fire your witch won't be able to tame and you won't get through." To Jackson, I added, *Don't react. Not in any way.*

With that, I called to the mother. She answered swiftly, and with such force that my entire body trembled. I licked my lips and flicked an invisible sliver toward Jackson—even as I let her energy dance across my fingertips to ensure Rinaldo's attention remained on me.

"And then," I added, "I'll go find your bastard brother and finish what I started. I'm sure he couldn't have crawled too far from where I left him."

The pendant disappeared in a puff of smoke even as Rinaldo's face twisted and he took an involuntary step forward. Then he stopped and took a deep breath. But there was madness in his eyes now—madness and pain. It was both his *and* his brother's, I suspected.

"I will very much enjoy tearing you apart piece by tiny piece." As he spoke, the witch took a shuddering breath, then glanced around wildly. "Where am I? What's happening?"

"You were under the thrall of a vampire," I said, keeping my gaze on said vampire, "and have just been released. Stay calm, and don't move, or his guards will kill you."

"Oh my god."

"It's okay," Jackson murmured. "Everything will be okay."

"No, it won't," Rinaldo said, then motioned me forward with his fingers—fingers equipped with nails that were unusually long and razor sharp. He really *was* going to tear me apart. "Come along, Emberly. I haven't all day."

I kept a grip of the mother and took those final few steps. The magic hit me like a club, ripping apart my hold on the mother and sending my senses reeling. I felt rather than heard his approach and threw myself sideways. I hit the ground hard but rolled to my feet, only to be knocked backward by a blow to the side of my face. I swore, fighting tears and pain, but somehow twisted around and lashed out with a booted foot. It connected with flesh but was met with a laugh.

"Is that the best you can do without your fire, Emberly? I'm disappointed."

I blinked, watching him fade in and out of existence— and wasn't sure if it was him or me. He ran at me again. I dodged, but at the last moment he dropped and swept my feet out from underneath me. I somehow twisted as I was going down, landing on hands and knees and scrambling away. He didn't pursue me. He simply waited.

I stood up. He came at me again; again I dodged. The blow aimed at my face tore down my side, shredding my shirt and slashing into my skin.

Distantly, I became aware of fighting, of shouting, and knew Jackson was battling the guards. But he was heavily outnumbered, even with his fire, and was no immediate help to me.

"I can smell your blood," Rinaldo said softly, "and its scent is sweet. Perhaps I should taste it before I kill you."

"Confidence always comes before a fall, Rinaldo," I said, "and your fall is going to be spectacular."

"We both know that is a threat you cannot back up." He charged me. I spun away, but he caught my arm, then kicked my legs out from under me. My back hit the ground, and something hard dug into my back. The gun. *I still had the fucking gun.*

But before I could reach for it, he was on me, his weight pinning me. I tried to buck him off, but he was too heavy. I tried hitting him, punching him, clawing him, but he merely smiled and caught my arms, holding them away from him.

"Checkmate, I believe," he said, and then bent down to feed from me.

I screamed in horror, screamed in pain, but I couldn't move, couldn't do anything, as he drained the life from me.

Emberly! Jackson's urgent cry bit through my panic. *Use me.*

What?

Use our connection. Draw my fire.

The stones will stop it.

The witch said they won't. Try!

Or die. He didn't actually say that last bit, but it was in his thoughts nevertheless. I drew in a shuddering breath, feeling my strength slipping away even as I did so. It was now or never.

And I had no idea how to do it.

Imagine our connection as a tunnel. Reach down through it.

I closed my eyes, did as he suggested, then reached, as I'd remotely reached for the life of the vampires earlier. There was a brief moment of blackness and disorientation; then I felt it—felt his fire and his life, his fury and his fear. But I didn't reach for it—instead, I reached *through* him to the mother, and called to her.

She came. I grabbed her energy with two metaphysical fists and then projected outward, through me and into Rinaldo. The force of it was so strong, it tore him from my neck and threw him across the room. He didn't immediately move, but he lived, even if his entire body was smoking.

I pushed myself onto my hands and knees, sucked in air as my head swam and blood rushed down my neck, then forced myself onto my feet and drew the gun.

"Die, you bastard," I said, and pulled the trigger. And kept pulling, until the clip was empty and there was nothing left of his head. Then the gun slipped from my fingers, and I dropped to my knees.

Someone dropped beside me; then warm fingers grabbed mine. "Feed from me, phoenix. There is still one brother left."

The witch, some part of me whispered. I licked my lip, and tried to ignore the siren call of her body's heat. "It would be dangerous for me to even attempt that. I might kill you."

"I'd be dead if not for you," she said. "But even so, I trust that you will not. It is not within you to kill another that way."

If only you knew.

"Do it," she said. "Now."

Em, please, Jackson said.

I closed my eyes, closed my fingers around hers, and fed. It flowed through me, a molten river that chased the ice from my veins and the weakness from my limbs. It would have been easy, so easy, to keep to the connection, to drain her completely, but her words seemed to echo through her brain; I forced my grip to open, and I released her hand.

Her whole body slumped. "Go," was all she said.

Hit the bastard for me before you cinder him, Jackson said.

I became fire and swirled out of the building and back to the rooftop. I shifted shape again, then opened the door and ran down the stairs.

But Rinaldo's twin wasn't there.

I swore, ran down the rest of the stairs, and thrust the door open. A dozen men immediately swung around; I held up my hands, my gaze searching for, and then finding, Baker.

"Did you retrieve Rinaldo from the stairwell?"

"No, we did not," Radcliffe said, stepping up beside Baker. "You were supposed to handle anyone attempting to escape via the stairwell."

I swore again and thrust a hand through my hair. "Don't give me any of your shit, Radcliffe, because I'm really *not* in the mood. I've killed one of the twins; the other has burns over most of his body and a smashed kneecap. How about you putting some rats to good use, and hunt him down. He can't have gotten far."

But even as Radcliffe snapped his fingers and the rats disappeared, intuition whispered of chances missed.

The second brother had escaped us.

CHAPTER 13

"You want anything from the café?" I asked Rory, sticking my head around the door into his bedroom.

We'd both moved back home a week earlier, and though he still wasn't able to return to work, I suspected it wouldn't be much longer before he did. His skin glowed with renewed health and vitality, and he was getting through a full day now without having to nap.

"A coffee and a bagel would be good." He glanced at his watch. "Aren't you up a little early for a Saturday?"

"Tell that to my stomach. It's the one grumbling so loud, I had no choice but to get up." I might have outwardly recovered from the injuries I'd received during our semi-successful attempt to neutralize Rinaldo, but my body continued to demand calories and fire, suggesting it might take a while yet before I was fully back to normal. Especially since I dared not draw too much from Rory until *he* was back to full strength. "Besides, I've got that damn meeting with the inspector this morning."

"You? Jackson's not invited?"

"I'm sure he wants to be there, but he's got strict orders to remain in bed and give his leg a full chance to heal."

Rory snorted. "Yeah, like that's going to happen."

"It will. I called in someone to make sure he did."

"If it's a female someone, you know how *that's* going to end."

"Makani is wise to his ways. Trust me, until he's more mobile, he won't get anywhere with her."

"Makani? Why don't I know this wonder woman?"

"She's the air fae who gave us the SUV to use."

"I think she and I need to meet."

I snorted. "You must be feeling a whole lot better if you're thinking about future seduction possibilities."

"Oh, I am." His grin flashed. "Do you know what the inspector wants?"

"Probably to berate me for incorrect use of the badges and for letting the other brother escape."

"That was hardly your fault. You weren't to know who he was."

"I should have checked, Rory. I had him, and I let him go."

"He couldn't have crawled out of that stairwell without help. Not in the state he was in."

"I know. It doesn't alter the fact that he *did* escape." And while it was somewhat comforting to know that, with the severity of his wounds and the fact we'd decimated his forces, he'd be incapable of any sort of revenge for a while yet, that didn't mean it *wouldn't* come.

We weren't out of the woods yet. Not by a long shot.

I pushed away from the door. "Just the coffee and croissant?"

"Bagel, not croissant."

"Oh, right." I grabbed my purse from the coffee table and slung it over my shoulder as I headed downstairs. Though it was still only early morning, the light shining through the foyer's glass was bright enough for me to spot the figure waiting for me near the exit.

Sam.

I stopped abruptly. "What are you doing here?"

He peeled away from the wall he'd been leaning against, but didn't move toward me. "We need to talk."

"I'm due in at your office this morning. We can talk then."

A smile touched his lips, and though it was little more than a ghost of the ones that I'd seen so often in the past, it nevertheless affected me as strongly as ever.

"No, we can't, because that's business and this is about us."

I thrust my hands deeper into my coat pocket. "There is no 'us,' Sam. We were over a long time ago."

"I know." He waved a hand toward Portside, the café just up the road and the place I'd been heading for the bagels. "Shall we take this discussion to a more comfortable location?"

"There's no *point*."

"I know, but humor me all the same. I have something that needs to be said."

"What if I don't want to hear it?"

"I'll keep pestering you until you do. Ultimately, it would be simpler and easier to just listen now."

"Fine," I muttered, and stalked past him. The morning air was crisp, but I was too aware of the man at my back to feel it.

I selected a table away from the other patrons and sat down. He slid out the chair opposite.

"What do you want to say?" My voice was flat—almost harsh.

He didn't immediately answer; instead, he smiled at the waitress as she appeared at our table, and he ordered a coffee. I ordered drinks and bagels for both Rory and myself.

"You have until that order gets back," I said. "Then I'm leaving."

"Fine." He laced his fingers together and leaned forward. "What I attempted to say in Brooklyn—and what you obviously took the wrong way—is that I can't have *any* relationship until I know, one way or another, what is going to happen to me with this virus in my blood."

I blinked. "You were having a relationship with Rochelle, weren't you?"

"And you're well aware that she was similarly infected." His smile was tight. "I may not be a saint, but I'm certainly not a monk—although I'll probably have to become one now that she's dead."

"So why are you telling me all this? We're over, Sam."

"Possibly—"

"Possibly?" Annoyance surged, and I thrust forward, my grip on the table suddenly fierce. "It's a fact of every phoenix's love life that the person they love will ultimately hurt or destroy them. We never get a happy ending; do you get that? *Never.* So as much as you might now want otherwise—for whatever fucking reason—it's not going to happen. It *can't* happen." I paused, took a deep breath, and then leaned back. And oddly felt better for unleashing all that.

He frowned. "What do you mean, 'never'?"

"It means, in all the centuries I've been alive, in all the centuries Rory's been alive, we've never found lasting love. Something always happens to shatter it."

"Something like me finding out about you and Rory?"

"Yeah." I scrubbed a hand across my eyes. "And I probably should have told you about him, but your attitude to supernaturals and past history stopped me. Rebirth after being murdered is never a fun thing, let me tell you."

His face paled. "No matter how angry I might have been, I would have never—"

"I know, but past loves *have*." I sighed. "None of which alters the fact that you and I cannot—will not—happen in this lifetime."

He studied me silently for a moment, and then sat back. "I'm sorry for what I said that day, Red. I'm sorry for the way I reacted. And I know I can't change any of that, nor can I alter fate itself. But I'd really at least like to be friends with you."

A somewhat bitter smile twisted my lips. "What, go out for dinners and the like, and act like there was nothing more serious than that in our past?"

"Yes."

"Do you really think that's wise?"

"Probably not. But as I said, I'm not a monk and I need—" He paused. "I need something to hold on to outside work. Something that keeps me distracted from the virus, and keeps me grounded."

"I'm not your ground, Sam. I can't be."

"You *have* to be. I can't infect you, Red. I can't kill you—not with the virus, anyway."

I eyed him for a minute. "The inspector told you about my burning the virus from Jackson's body, didn't she?"

"Yes. And that one fact gives me hope that a cure will eventually be found."

"We don't even know if I actually succeeded in destroying the virus in his system."

"No, but he'd be exhibiting signs by now if he were infected, and he's not."

So the inspector had said, but I wasn't going to get my hopes up. Not until the blood tests came back and we knew for sure.

I scrubbed a hand across my eyes. "This is madness, Sam."

"Does that mean you'll consider it?"

The waitress approached with our drinks and my bagels. I pushed up, grabbed some money, and paid for both.

"Em?" Sam said softly.

My gaze met his. I saw the desperation there, and the ever-threatening darkness that was the virus. I'd saved this man's life twice now, but it was still very much under threat.

I didn't want to get involved with him, because I knew it could only ever end badly. That was just the way it worked for us phoenixes. But by the same token, I didn't want to see him hurt. Didn't want to see him lose this battle.

"I'll think about it," I said.

And knew, even as I walked away, that the decision was already made.

I just had to hope my heart was strong enough to take the mess I was about to get us into.

Don't miss the first Outcast Novel
by Keri Arthur,

CITY OF LIGHT

Available now

It was the whispering of the ghosts that woke me.

I stretched the kinks out of my bones, then glanced at the old metal clock on the far wall to confirm what I instinctively knew. It was barely six p.m., so night hadn't fallen yet. The ghosts were well used to my seminocturnal patterns, so something had to be wrong for them to wake me early.

I swung my legs off the bed and sat up. The tiled floor chilled my feet and the air was cool, though slightly stale. Which probably meant one of the three remaining purifiers had gone offline again. It was a frustrating problem that had started happening more often of late, thanks to the fact that parts for the decades-old machines just weren't made anymore. And while there *was* one place where I probably could scavenge the bits I needed to repair them, it was also something of a last resort. Chaos was not a place you entered willingly. Not if you valued life and limb.

But if one of the purifiers *had* gone down again, then I either had to risk going there or close off yet another level. I might be able to survive short-term on foul air, but I still needed to breathe.

Gentle tendrils of energy trailed across my skin, a caress filled with the need to follow. But it was a touch that held no fear. Whatever disturbed the ghosts was not aimed at our bunker deep underground.

I slipped on my old combat clothes and boots, then grabbed my jacket and rose, shoving my arms into the sleeves as I walked across to the door at the far end of the bunk room. A red warning light flashed as I neared it.

"Name, rank," a gruff metallic voice said. Over the years I'd named it Hank, simply because it reminded me somewhat of the cranky custodian who'd run the base exchange. He still haunted the lower floors, although he tended to avoid both me and the children.

"Tiger C5, déchet, lure rank."

I pressed my thumb against the blood-work slot. A small needle shot out and took the required sample, but the door remained securely closed. Even though I'd adjusted the power ratios and cut several levels out of the security net, it still took an interminably long time for the system down here to react. But then, with only one hydrogen-fueled generator and the banks of solar batteries powering the system during the day, *everything* was slow. And I couldn't risk firing up a second generator when I needed at least two running at night to cope with the main defense systems. I had only three generators in total and—with parts so scarce in the world above—I had to be careful. That meant conserving the system where I could and doing continual maintenance.

The scanner finally kicked into gear. After checking my irises, the door beeped and swung open. The corridor beyond was cold and dark, the metal walls dripping with condensation. Ghosts swirled, their little bodies wisps of fog that drifted along in blackness.

The sounds of my footfalls echoed across the stillness, hinting at the vastness of this underground military bunker. And yet this was the smallest of the three bases humans had used during the race war—a war that might have lasted only five years but had forever altered the very fabric of our world.

The shifters—with their greater strength, speed, and the capacity to heal almost any wound—should have wiped the stain of humanity from Earth. But humans had not wasted the many years leading up to the war, and the bioengineering labs, which had initially produced nothing more than body-part replacements for the sick and dying, had gone into full—and secret—production. These labs had created not only an enzyme that gave humans the same capacity to heal as the shifters, but also the designed humanoid. Or déchet, as we'd become known.

It said a lot about humanity's opinion of us that we were given a nickname that meant "waste product."

Most of us hadn't come from human stock, but were rather a mix of shifter and vampire, which gave us most of their strengths and few of their weaknesses. We'd been humanity's supersoldiers—designed to fight and to die without thought or feeling—and we'd almost turned the tide of the war.

Almost.

But not all of us had been trained strictly as soldiers, just as not all of us were unfeeling. There were a few who'd been created with more specific skills in mind—

chameleons able to alter their flesh at will, and who'd been tasked with either seduction and intelligence gathering or assassination.

I was one such creation.

Of course, while humans might have designed us to be frontline soldiers in their battle with the shifters, they'd never entirely trusted us not to turn against them—even if they'd made that all but impossible through a mix of chemical and medical interventions. Which meant there'd been areas in this base that, as a déchet, I'd been banned from entering.

But as the sole survivor of the destruction that had hit this base at the war's end 103 years ago, I'd made it my business to fully explore every available inch. The shifters had, in an effort to ensure the base could never be used again, blocked off all known access points into the base by pouring tons of concrete into them. While this had taken out sublevels one to three, it still left me with six others—and those six were huge. Which was hardly surprising since this had once been the home to not only a thousand-strong complement of déchet, but to all those who had been responsible for our creation and training.

I passed through several more security points—points that, like the one at the bunkhouse, were fixed and unalterable—and eventually made my way into the tight, circular stairwell that led to the surface level. These stairs had been one of two routes designed as emergency escapes for the humans in charge of the various sections of the Humanoid Development Project, so its presence had been unknown to all but a few, and it had been designed to withstand anything the shifters could throw at the base. As it turned out, it had also withstood the concrete.

It had taken me close to a year to find this tunnel, and a couple more to find the second one, but they gave me much-needed access points to the outside world. It might be a world I ventured into only once or twice a month—generally when food or equipment supplies were low or when the need for company that was flesh-and-blood rather than ghostly became too strong to ignore—but that didn't assuage the need to know what was going on above me on a regular basis. Being able to venture out, to watch from shadows and distance, was all that had kept me sane in the long century since the war. That and the ghosts.

I reached the surface level and pried open the hidden escape panel. Sunlight poured in through the dome over the building's remains, shielding it from the elements and further decay. This level had once contained the day-to-day operational center of the HDP, and the battered remnants had become part of a museum dedicated to the history of a war no one wanted to see repeated. Of course, it was also a museum created by the shifters, so it emphasized both the foolishness and waste of war and also the evils of gene manipulation and bioengineering. The body-part industry and all the benefits it had once provided were now little more than bylines in history.

And though fewer and fewer were visiting the museum these days, one of the most popular exhibits still seemed to be the old tower that held all the remaining solar panels. They might be an antiquated and curiously inadequate technology to those alive today, yet the panels continued to power not only the systems that had been preserved on this floor for demonstration purposes, but all of mine.

The ghosts surrounded me as I walked across the foyer, their ethereal bodies seeming to glow in the fading streams of sunlight bathing the vast open area. As ever, it was little Cat who kept closest, while Bear surged forward, leading the way.

Both he and Cat had always considered me something of a big sister, even though we déchet shouldn't have even understood the concept. Our closeness was primarily due to the amount of time I'd spent in the nursery unit in the years leading up to the war. Even during the war, those lures not out on assignment or in a recovery period were put to use in the nurseries; our task had been to teach and to protect the next generation of fighters.

Because despite what the shifters had believed, there'd been only a finite supply of us. Our creators had discovered early on that while the use of accelerant increased the speed of *physical* growth, it did not enhance mental growth. Déchet might have been designed to be nothing more than superhuman soldiers able to match the strength and speed of shifters, but sending your rifle fodder out with the body of an adult and the mind of a child really defeated the purpose of their creation. So while they'd halved our development time, they hadn't been able to erase it completely.

I came to the tower and unlocked the thick metal doors that led to the rooftop stairwell, then unlatched the silver mesh behind them. There was enough shifter in my blood that my skin tingled as I touched it, but it wasn't as deadly to me as it would have been to a full-blood. I slipped through the mesh and ran up the old concrete stairs, breathing air that was thick with disuse and age. Visitors wanting to see the ancient solar technology did so from the special observation platform that had been built to one side of the tower rather than accessing the panels through the tower itself, simply because the old tower was considered too dangerous. For the last couple of years there'd been talk of tearing it down before it actually fell, but, so far, nothing had actually happened. I hoped it never did. I wasn't entirely sure what I would do if it was knocked down and I was left with only the decaying generators to power my underground systems.

We reached the metal exit plate at the top of the stairs. It was also silver, but it was so scarred with heat and blast damage that it no longer looked it. I drew back the bolts and pushed the plate open.

The children flung themselves into the glorious sunset, and that alone told me there was nothing dangerous nearby. But there was no shaking the years of training, even though the need for such measures had long since passed. I drew in a deep breath and sorted through the various scents, looking for anything unusual or out of place. There was nothing. As I climbed out of the stairwell, a slight breeze tugged at my short hair, and I looked up to see the dome's panels had fissured yet again. It was an odd fact that this section of dome failed regularly. It was almost as if the old tower wanted to feel the wind and the rain on its fading bones. It just might get that wish tonight, because the heaviness of the clouds so tinted by the sun's last dance of the day suggested it wasn't going to be a good night to be out on the streets.

Not that there was *ever* a good night to be out on them.

I zipped up my jacket and walked through the banks of solar panels to the old metal railing that lined the rooftop. The walls of Central City rose before me, and, beyond them, a sea of glass and metal that shone brightly under the strengthening glow of the UV light towers perched on top of the massive metal D-shaped curtain wall. There were also floodlights on the rooftops of the many high-rises, all of them aimed at the streets in an effort to erase any shadows created by either the buildings or the wall itself.

Lying between Central and the bunker's dome was the main rail line, which transported workers in glowing, caterpillar-like pods to the various production zones that provided the city with the necessities of life. But with dusk coming on, there was little movement in the yards, and the city's drawbridge had already risen, securing Central against the coming of night.

The inhabitants of Chaos—which was the long-accepted name given to the ramshackle collection of buildings that clung to the curved sides of Central's curtain wall—had no such protection. It was an interconnected mess of metal storage units, old wood, and plastic that was ten stories high and barely five wide. The upper reaches bristled with antennas and wind turbines that glimmered in the wash of light from Central's UV towers, but the lower reaches of Chaos already lay encased in darkness. Lights gleamed in various spots, but they did little to lift the gathering shadows.

And it was in these shadows that the vampires reigned supreme.

The shifters might have claimed victory in the war, but in truth, the only real winners had been the vampires. While they'd never been a part of the war—or of society in general—their numbers had certainly grown on the back of the war's high death toll. They were creatures untouched by the basic needs of the living. Water, power, sanitation—the very things humanity considered so vital—had no impact on the way vampires lived their lives, because their lives consisted of nothing more than hunting their next meal. And though they preferred to dine on the living, they were not averse to digging up the dead.

Before the war, most cities had relied solely on the UV towers to stop the vampires. But the cities of old had been built on a network of underground service tunnels, which gave the vampires access and protection. With most of these cities lying in ash and ruin after the war, the shifters had taken the chance to rebuild "vampire-proof" cities for both victor and vanquished to live in. So not only were there massive curtain walls and UV towers around every major city, but services now ran aboveground, in special conduits that had been "beautified" to disguise what they were.

Chaos, unprotected by either lights or walls, and still sitting on many of the old service tunnels, was regularly hit by the vampires—but neither the inhabitants of Chaos nor those in charge of Central seemed to care.

Of course, vampires were no longer the only evil to roam the night or the shadows. When the shifters had unleashed the bombs that had finally ended the war, they'd torn apart the very fabric of the world, creating drifting doorways between this world and the next.

These rifts were filled with a magic that not only twisted the essence of the landscape, but also killed anyone unfortunate enough to be caught in their path. That in itself would not have been so bad if the Others had not gained access into our world through many of these rifts. These hellish creatures—creatures the humans and shifters had named demons, monsters, and death spirits, although in truth no one really knew if they were from hell or merely another time or dimension— had all found a new and easy hunting ground in the shadows of our world.

But at least one good thing had come from their arrival—it had finally forced shifters and humans to set aside all differences and act as one against a greater foe.

And yet humanity's fear of vampires had not been usurped by this newer evil. Even *I* feared the vampires, and I had their blood running through my veins. It didn't make me safe from them. Nothing would.

Ghostly fingers ran down my arm and tugged at my fingertips. I followed Cat as she drifted toward the left edge of the building, my gaze scanning the old park opposite. The shadows growing beneath the trees were vacant of life, and nothing moved. Nothing more than the wind-stirred leaves, anyway. I frowned, moving my gaze further afield, studying the street and the battered remnants of what once had been government offices, trying to uncover what was causing the little ones so much consternation.

Then I heard it.

The faint crying of a child.

A *young* child, not an older one, if the tone of her voice was anything to go by.

She was in the trees. At dusk, with the vampires about to come out. An easy meal if I wasn't very quick.

I spun and ran for the stairs. The ghosts gathered around me, their energy skittering across my skin, fueling the need to hurry. I paused long enough to slam down the hatch and shove the bolts home, then scrambled down the steps three at a time, my pace threatening to send me tumbling at any moment.

At the bottom I again stopped long enough to lock up behind me. I might have an instinctive need to save that child—a need no doubt born of my inability to save the 105 déchet children who'd been in my care the day the shifters had gassed this base and killed everyone within it—but I wouldn't risk either discovery or the security of our home to do so.

The ghosts swirled around me, urging me to hurry, to run. I did, but down to the weapons stash I'd created in the escape tunnel rather than to the front door. I fastened several automatics to the thigh clips on my pants, then strapped two of the slender machine rifles—which I'd adapted to fire small sharpened stakes rather than bullets—across my back. Once I'd grabbed a bag of flares and threw several ammo loops over my shoulders, I was ready to go. But I knew even as I headed for the main doors that no amount of weaponry would be enough if the vampires caught the sound of either the child's heartbeat or mine.

The dome's security system reacted far faster than mine, the doors swishing open almost instantly. The pass-codes might change daily, but I'd been around a long time and I knew the system inside out. Not only had the motion and heat sensors installed throughout the museum been programmed to ignore my lower body temperature, but I'd installed an override code for the outer defenses that didn't register on the daily activity log. I might be flesh and blood most of the time, but as far as the systems that protected this place were concerned, I was as much a ghost as the children who surrounded me.

Once the laser curtain protecting the front of the dome had withdrawn, I headed for the trees. Cat and Bear came with me, their ethereal forms lost to the gathering darkness. The others remained behind to guard the door. It would take a brave—and determined—soul to get past them. The dead might not be the threat that the vampires were, but the astute didn't mess with them, either. They might be energy rather than flesh, but they *could* both interact with and manipulate the world around them if they so desired.

Of course, the smaller the ghost, the less strength they had. My little ones might be able to repel invaders, but they could not hold back a determined attack for very long. I just had to hope that it didn't come to that tonight.

City Road was empty of any form of life and the air fresh and cool, untainted by the scent of humanity, vampire, or death. No one—living or dead—was near.

So where was the child? And why in hell was she alone in a park?

I ran into the trees, breathing deeply as I did so, trying to find the scent of the child I'd heard but gaining little in the way of direction.

Thankfully, Cat seemed to have no such trouble. Her energy pulled me deeper into the park as the stamp of night grew stronger. Tension wound through my limbs. The vampires would be rising. We had to hurry.

Bear spun around me, his whisperings full of alarm. Like most of us created in the long lead-up to the war, there was no human DNA within his body. In fact, despite his name, he was more vampire than bear shifter and, in death, had become very attuned to them.

They were rising.

Sound cracked the silence. A whimper, nothing more.

I switched direction, leapt over a bed of old roses, then ran up a sharp incline. Like the crying I'd heard earlier, the whimper died on the breeze and wasn't repeated. If it hadn't been for Cat leading the way so surely, I might have been left running around this huge park aimlessly. While my tiger-shifter blood at least ensured I had some basic tracking skills, basic wouldn't cut it right now. Cat, while not trained to track, was almost pure tabby. Her hunting skills were both instinctive and sharp.

The urgency in her energy got stronger, as did Bear's whisperings of trouble.

The vampires had the scent. They were coming.

I reached for more speed. My feet were flying over the yellowed grass, and the gnarled, twisted tree trunks were little more than a blur. I crested the hill and ran down the other side, not checking my speed, my balance tiger sure on the steep and slippery slope.

I still couldn't see anything or anyone in the shadows, but the desperation in little Cat's energy assured me we were getting close.

But so, too, were the vampires.

Their scent began to stain the breeze, a mix of decay

and unwashed flesh that made me wish my olfactory senses weren't so keen.

Where was the damn child?

I reached for a rifle, unlocked the safety, and held it loose by my side as I ran. Bear whisked around me again, whispering reassurances, his energy filled with excitement as he raced off into the trees. Seconds later I heard his whimper, strong at first but fading as he ran away from us. If the vampires took the bait, it would give us time to find our quarry. If not, I would be neck deep in them and fighting for life.

I broke through the trees and into a small clearing. Cat's energy slapped across my skin, a warning that we were near our target. I leapt high over the remnants of another garden bed, and saw her. Or rather, saw the bright strands of gold hair dancing to the tune of the breeze. She was hiding in the shattered remains of a fallen tree. Beside that tree lay a man. I couldn't immediately tell if he lived. The scent of death didn't ride his flesh, but he didn't seem to be breathing, either. Though I could see no wounds, the rich tang of blood permeated the air—and if I could smell it, the vampires surely would. Bear's diversion probably wouldn't last much longer.

I dropped beside the stranger and rolled him over. Thick, ugly gashes tore up his chest and stomach, and his left arm was bent back unnaturally. I pressed two fingers against his neck. His pulse was there—light, erratic, but there.

Yet it was the three uniform scars that ran from his right temple to just behind his ear that caught my attention. They were the markings of a ranger—a formidable class of shifter soldier who'd once been used to hunt down and destroy the déchet divisions, and who now formed the backbone of the fight against the Others. While it was unlikely this ranger would know what I was by sight or scent—especially given that lures had been genetically designed *not* to have any of the telltale déchet signatures—he still wasn't the sort of man I wanted anywhere near either me or my sanctuary.

Especially *not* when there were nearly three platoons— or, to be more precise, ninety-three—of fully trained adult déchet haunting the lower levels. The children might have few memories of the hideous way the shifters had killed everyone at the base, but the same could not be said of the adults.

I shifted my focus to the log and the strands of golden hair blowing on the breeze.

"Child, you need to come with me." I said it as gently as I could, but the only response was a tightening of fear in the air. But it was fear of *me* rather than the situation or even the night.

Cat spun around me, her energy flowing through my body, briefly heightening my sense of the night. The vampires would be here soon.

The urgent need to be gone rose, but I pushed it down. Dragging the child from the log would only make her scream, and that in turn would make the situation a whole lot worse. Noise was our enemy right now. The vampires weren't the only dangers night brought on— many of the Others tended to hunt by sight and sound.

"The vampires are coming, little one," I continued, even though I was talking to scarcely more than a strand of hair. "Neither of us are safe here."

"Jonas will protect me. He promised." Though her

words were stilted, there was nothing in the way of fear or uncertainty in them. Which was odd.

"Jonas is injured and can't help anyone right now." *Not even himself.* I hesitated, then added, "We need to get out of here before the vampires arrive."

She didn't respond for a moment. Then a dirt-covered cherub face popped up from the hollow of the tree. She scanned me, then stated flatly, "I won't leave without Jonas. I *won't*."

"Jonas is unconscious, but I'm sure he'd want me to get you to safety rather than worrying about him."

She continued to study me, her blue eyes wide and oddly luminous. I had a strange feeling that the child understood all too clearly just what I was saying—and her next words confirmed that. "I won't leave him here to die. I won't let you leave him for the vampires. You have to save him."

"Child—"

"No," she said, her lip trembling. "He saved me. And he'll save you. You can't leave him here to die."

I frowned. He'd save me? A ranger? Even if he didn't realize what I was, it was an unlikely scenario, given rangers had been notorious for forsaking the wounded. And if he *did* realize . . . I thrust the thought away with a shudder and simply said, "His wounds are fairly serious—"

"Promise me you'll help him!"

Cat spun around me, her whisperings filled with urgency. If we didn't get moving soon, we'd be dead. Given I had no wish to die, I had to either snatch the child and race her—screaming—to our sanctuary, or do as she wished. The first would attract all manner of trouble other than the vampires, but to help a ranger . . .

I took a deep breath and released it slowly. I might have been trained to seduce rather than destroy, but that didn't alter the fact that shifters had eradicated everything and everyone I knew or cared about. It went against every instinct I had to save this one.

And yet the instinct—need—to save this child was stronger still.

"Okay, I'll help him."

She eyed me for a moment, a little girl whose gaze seemed far too knowing. "You promise?"

"Yes."

Cat whisked through me. The image of the vampires flowing through the trees rose like a deadly black wave. We had five minutes, if that.

"Who's that?"

The child's blue gaze wasn't on me, but rather on the energy that was Cat as she hovered near my shoulder. I raised an eyebrow. "You can see Cat?"

"Cat? What sort of name is that?"

"It's short for Catherine," I said. Which it wasn't, but I had no idea where this child was from or how much she might have been taught about the war and déchet. Those who'd created us hadn't afforded us real names—couldn't humanize the military fodder in any way, after all. So they used the breed of shifter we'd been designed from, and whatever number we were of that breed. Cat was number 247 in production terms. And while it was unlikely our names would be a giveaway, I wasn't about to take a chance. Not when there were still shifters alive today who'd survived the war. "Mine's Tig."

She didn't ask me what it was short for. Her gaze

went from Cat to me, then back to Cat. "She's not real. You are."

"She might not have flesh, but she's as real as you and me."

The little girl frowned and stood. She was wearing a smock that was grimy and blood-splattered, and there were half-healed slashes all over her arms and legs. Anger rose within me, then swirled away. I needed to make sure we were safe before I could allow any reaction to those cuts.

Because those cuts were too sharp, too straight, to have been caused by anything other than a blade.

"How can she have no body and be real?"

There was still no fear in her voice, and no apparent realization just how close to disaster we truly were. I wondered briefly if she was human. She didn't smell like it, but then, she didn't exactly smell like a shifter, either.

"Because not everything that is real has human flesh."

I clipped the rifle onto a loop on my belt and squatted beside the ranger as Cat's energy hit again. Images slashed through my mind—dark beings running through the trees, their hunger surging across the night. We needed to go. *Now.*

I gripped the man under his shoulder and heaved him over mine. "Do you have a name?"

She hesitated, and then said, almost shyly, "Penny."

"We need to go, Penny." I thrust upward, my legs shaking under the stranger's sudden weight. Holding him steady with one hand, I unclipped the rifle and rested my finger against the trigger. "Run with Cat. She'll take you into a safe place. Wait for me there."

The little girl's lips trembled a little. "And Jonas?"

"Jonas and I will be right behind you."

She nodded, then scrambled over the tree trunk and ran after the energy that was Cat as she retreated through the trees. I followed, Jonas's body a deadweight that allowed no real speed or mobility.

Bear reappeared, his whisperings full of warning. I ran up the hill as the night around me began to move, to flow, with evil.

They were close.

So close.

But there was something else out there in the night. It was a power—an energy—that felt dark. Watchful. At one with the vampires and yet separate from them.

And instinct suggested I needed to fear that darkness far more than the vampires who swept toward us.

I cursed softly and pushed the thought away. One threat at a time. I needed to survive the vampires before I worried about some other, nebulous threat. "Bear, I need your help here."

His energy immediately flowed across mine, allowing me to see everything he saw, everything he felt. While this level of connection wasn't as deep as some we could achieve, *any* bond between the living and the dead could be deadly. All magic had a cost, an old witch had once warned me. While my ability to link with the ghosts wasn't so much magic as a mix of psychic abilities and my own close call with death, it still taxed both my strength *and* theirs. And it could certainly drain me to the point of death if I kept the connection too long.

But for certain situations it was worth the risk—and this was definitely one of those situations.

There was at *least* a score of vampires out there,

which meant this wasn't the usual hunting party. If I'd been alone, if I hadn't promised to keep Jonas safe, I would have shadowed and run. The vampires might sense me in *this* form, but if I became one with the night—became little more than dark matter, as they could—then it was harder for them to pick me out from their own. I knew *that* from my time in the war, when the vamps had overrun a village I'd been assigned to.

But I *had* promised, and that left me with little choice. Using the images Bear fed me as a guide, I raised the rifle and fired over my shoulder, keeping the bursts short to conserve ammunition. The needle-sharp projectiles bit through the night and burrowed into flesh. Three vampires went down and were quickly smothered by darkness as other vampires fell on them and fed. The scent of blood flooded the night, mingling with the screams of the dying.

I crashed through yet another garden bed, my feet sinking into the soft soil. A deeper patch of darkness leapt for my throat, and the pungent aroma of the dead hit. I flipped the rifle and battered him out of the way with the butt, then switched it into my other hand and fired to the right, then the left. Two more vamps down.

I leapt over a fallen branch. Jonas's weight shifted, making the landing awkward and losing us precious speed. Sweat broke out across my brow but I ignored it, grabbing the ranger's leg to steady him as I ran on.

"Bear," I said, my voice little more than a pant of air. "Light."

Ethereal fingers tugged at the bag of flares by my side and lifted one. Energy surged across the night and light exploded, a white ball of fire surrounded by a halo of red.

It was bright enough to force them back, but they didn't go far. They knew, as I did, that the flare would give me only a minute, at most.

And they knew, like I did, that a little ghost probably wouldn't have the energy to light a second flare so soon after the first.

I ran on as hard as I could. The dome's lights beckoned through the trees, forlorn stars of brightness that still seemed too far away.

The flare guarding our back began to sputter, and the black mass surged closer. I fired left and right. The nearest vampires swarmed their fallen comrades, while those at the back flowed over the top of them, hoping to be the ones to taste fresher, sweeter flesh.

Thirteen vampires left, if I was lucky. It might as well have been a hundred for all the hope I'd have if they dragged me down.

Sweat stung my eyes and dribbled down my spine, and my leg muscles were burning. But the end of the park was now in sight. The old tower's searchlights suddenly came on, hanging free from both the tower and the dome, supported by ghostly forms. Their sunshinelike light swept City Road and provided a haven of safety if I could get to it.

Fifty yards to go.

Just fifty yards.

Then the flare went out and the vampires hit us.

Do you love fiction with a supernatural twist?

Want the chance to hear news about your favourite
authors (and the chance to win free books)?

Keri Arthur
Kristen Callihan
P.C. Cast
Christine Feehan
Jacquelyn Frank
Larissa Ione
Darynda Jones
Sherrilyn Kenyon
Jayne Ann Krentz and Jayne Castle
Lucy March
Martin Millar
Tim O'Rourke
Lindsey Piper
Christopher Rice
J.R. Ward
Laura Wright

Then visit the Piatkus website and blog
www.piatkus.co.uk | www.piatkusbooks.net

And follow us on Facebook and Twitter
www.facebook.com/piatkusfiction | www.twitter.com/piatkusbooks

piatkus